Thoma

UNDER THE
GREENWOOD TREE

OUR EXPLOITS AT WEST POLEY
AND
HUMOROUS STORIES

———————

Edited by
JAMES GIBSON

EVERYMAN
J. M. DENT · LONDON
CHARLES E. TUTTLE
VERMONT

Consultant editor for the Everyman Thomas Hardy Series
Norman Page

Selection, introduction and other critical apparatus
© J. M. Dent 1996

This edition first published by Everyman Paperbacks in 1996

J. M. Dent
Orion Publishing Group
Orion House
5 Upper St Martin's Lane
London WC2H 9EA
and
Charles E. Tuttle Co. Inc.
28 South Main Street
Rutland, Vermont 05701, USA

Typeset in Sabon by CentraCet Limited, Cambridge
Printed in Great Britain by
The Guernsey Press Co. Ltd, Guernsey, C. I.

British Library Cataloguing-in-Publication Data
is available upon request

ISBN 0 460 87575 2

CONTENTS

NOTE ON THE AUTHOR AND EDITOR

THOMAS HARDY was born in Higher Bockhampton, near Dorchester, in 1840, the first of four children. His father was a stonemason and builder. At sixteen he trained as an architect and in 1862 went to work in London. He wrote poetry but failed to get it or his first novel, *The Poor Man and the Lady* (1868), published before returning to Bockhampton in 1867.

In 1870 he worked on the restoration of the church at St Juliot in Cornwall where he met Emma Gifford. They married in 1874. Having financed his novel *Desperate Remedies* (1871) he then lost money on it. *Under the Greenwood Tree* (1872) and *A Pair of Blue Eyes* (1873) followed. *Far from the Madding Crowd*, his first real success, was published in 1874. He published *The Hand of Ethelberta* (1876), *The Return of the Native* (1878) and *The Trumpet-Major* (1880). Moving to London 1878–81, he fell seriously ill between 1880–81. *A Laodicean* (1881) and *Two on a Tower* (1882) were followed by *The Mayor of Casterbridge* (1886) and *The Woodlanders* (1887). In 1883 he settled in Dorchester and moved into the house he had designed, Max Gate, in 1885. His first collection of short stories, *Wessex Tales*, appeared in 1888; three further collections were published between 1891 and 1913. *Tess of the d'Urbervilles* (1891) brought him fame, although its advanced moral stance caused an outcry. After further controversy on the publication of *Jude the Obscure* (1896), he returned to poetry, and only *The Well-Beloved*, written in 1892, appeared later, in 1898.

Wessex Poems, his first book of verse, was published in 1898, and followed by seven further volumes. In 1904–8, *The Dynasts*, an epic drama, was published. Hardy was awarded the Order of Merit in 1910. His wife's death in 1912 inspired some of his greatest poems. He married Florence Dugdale in 1914, and died in 1928.

JAMES GIBSON was Head of English at Dulwich College and Principal Lecturer in English at Christ Church College, Canterbury. He was educated at Queens' College, Cambridge and Birbeck College, London, where he obtained his Ph.D. He founded and edited the *Thomas Hardy Journal* and is an Honorary Vice-President of the Hardy Society and former Chairman. Among the many Hardy's works he has edited are *The Complete Poems of Thomas Hardy* and the Variorum edition of that work. In 1994 he was presented with a *Festschrift* by leading Hardy scholars.

CHRONOLOGY OF HARDY'S LIFE

CHRONOLOGY OF HIS TIMES

Year	Literary Context	Historical Events
1840		Great Irish famine Penny Post is introduced
1842		Chartist riots
1846		Repeal of Corn Laws; Irish Potato Famine
1847	Charlotte Brontë, *Jane Eyre* Emily Brontë, *Wuthering Heights*	Railway reaches Dorchester
1848	Dickens, *Dombey & Son* Thackeray, *Vanity Fair* Pre-Raphaelite Brotherhood active	
1849	Ruskin, *Seven Lamps of Architecture*	
1850	Death of Wordsworth Tennyson becomes Poet Laureate	
1851		The Great Exhibition in London
1853	Arnold, *Poems*	1853–6 The Crimean War
1855	Browning, *Men and Women* Elizabeth Gaskell, *North and South*	
1858	George Eliot, *Scenes of Clerical Life*	
1859	Darwin, *The Origin of Species*	
1860	Collins, *The Woman in White*	
1861	Palgrave's anthology, *The Golden Treasury* *Hymns Ancient and Modern*	American Civil War

Year	Age	Life
1860s		Throughout this decade Hardy steadily loses his religious faith
1865	25	A short fictional piece called 'How I Built Myself a House' is published
1867	27	Returns to Dorset; begins his first novel, *The Poor Man and the Lady*
1868	28	Romantic affair with his cousin, Tryphena Sparks. *The Poor Man and the Lady* is rejected by publishers
1869	29	Works in Weymouth for an architect
1870	30	Meets and falls in love with Emma Lavinia Gifford while at St Juliot in Cornwall planning the restoration of the church
1871	31	*Desperate Remedies*, published anonymously, is a commercial failure
1872	32	Has minor success with *Under the Greenwood Tree*
1873	33	*A Pair of Blue Eyes*, Hardy's first novel to appear as a serial. Becomes a full-time novelist
1874	34	*Far from the Madding Crowd*, his first real success. Marries Emma Gifford. For next nine years they move from one lodging to another
1878	38	*The Return of the Native*. Becomes member of London's Savile Club
1879	39	His short story, 'The Distracted Preacher', is published
1880	40	*The Trumpet-Major*. Is taken ill for several months
1881	41	*A Laodicean*
1882	42	*Two on a Tower*. Visits Paris
1885	45	Moves into Max Gate, house on outskirts of Dorchester. Lives there for the rest of his life
1886	46	*The Mayor of Casterbridge*. Sees Impressionist paintings in London

Year	Literary Context	Historical Events
1863	Death of Thackeray Mill, *Utilitarianism*	
1864	Newman, *Apologia pro Vita Sua*	
1865	Death of Elizabeth Gaskell	
1866	Swinburne, *Poems and Ballads*	
1867	Ibsen, *Peer Gynt*	Second Reform Bill
1868		Gladstone becomes Prime Minister
1869	Mill, *The Subjection of Women*	
1870	Death of Dickens	Franco-Prussian War Education Act brings education for all
1871	Darwin, *The Descent of Man*	Trade Unions legalized
1874		Disraeli becomes Prime Minister The modern bicycle arrives
1876	James's novels begin to be published	
1878		Edison invents the incandescent electric lamp
1879	James Murray becomes editor of what was later to become *The Oxford English Dictionary* Ibsen, *A Doll's House*	
1880	Death of George Eliot Zola, *Nana*	
1881	Revised Version of New Testament	Married Women's Property Act
1882	Deaths of Darwin, D. G. Rossetti and Trollope	Daimler's petrol engine
1885	Birth of D. H. Lawrence	Salisbury becomes Prime Minister
1886	Death of William Barnes, friend of Hardy, poet, philologist, polymath	

Year	Age	Life
1887	47	*The Woodlanders*. Visits France and Italy
1888	48	*Wessex Tales*, his first collection of short stories, and an essay on 'The Profitable Reading of Fiction'
1890	50	An essay, 'Candour in English Fiction'
1891	51	*Tess of the d'Urbervilles*; *A Group of Noble Dames* (short stories); an essay, 'The Science of Fiction'
1892	52	Death of Hardy's father
1893	53	On visit to Ireland meets Florence Henniker, for whom he developed a great affection
1894	54	*Life's Little Ironies* (short stories)
1895	55	*Jude the Obscure*
1895–6		First collected edition of novels, entitled 'Wessex Novels'
1896	56	Ceases novel-writing and returns to poetry
1897	57	*The Well-Beloved*, much revised after publication as a serial in 1892
1898	58	*Wessex Poems* (51 poems): Hardy's first book of verse, including his own illustrations
1901	61	*Poems of the Past and the Present* (99 poems)
1902	62	Macmillan become his main publishers
1904	64	*The Dynasts*, Part I. Death of his mother, Jemima
1905	65	Receives honorary doctorate from Aberdeen University, the first of several
1906	66	*The Dynasts*, Part II. About now meets Florence Dugdale
1908	68	*The Dynasts*, Part III. Edits a selection of Barnes's verse

Year	Literary Context	Historical Events
1887	Strindberg, *The Father*	
1888	Death of Arnold; birth of T. S. Eliot	
	About now the works of Kipling and Yeats begin to be published	
1889	Deaths of Browning, G. M. Hopkins and Wilkie Collins	
1890	Death of Newman	First underground railway in London
1891	Shaw, *Quintessence of Ibsenism*	
1892	Death of Tennyson	Gladstone Prime Minister
1893	Pinero, *The Second Mrs Tanqueray*	Independent Labour Party set up
1894	Deaths of Stevenson and Pater	Rosebery becomes Prime Minister
1895	Conrad's first novel, *Almayer's Folly*	Freud's first work on psychoanalysis
	Wilde, *The Importance of Being Earnest*	Marconi's 'wireless' telegraphy
1896	Housman, *A Shropshire Lad*	
1898	Wells, *The War of the Worlds*	The Curies discover radium
1899		The Boer War begins
1900	Deaths of Ruskin and Wilde	
1901		Death of Queen Victoria, who is succeeded by Edward VII
1902	Zola dies; Hardy laments his death	Balfour becomes Prime Minister
1903		Wright brothers make first flight in aeroplane with engine
1904	Chekhov, *The Cherry Orchard*	
1906		Liberals win election
1907	Kipling is awarded Nobel Prize	
1908		Asquith becomes Prime Minister

Year	Age	Life
1909	69	*Time's Laughingstocks* (94 poems)
1910	70	Awarded the Order of Merit
1911	71	Ceases spending 'the season' in London
1912	72	Death of his wife, Emma. The Wessex Edition of his works is published by Macmillan
1913	73	*A Changed Man and Other Tales*. Revisits Cornwall and the scenes of his courtship of Emma
1914	74	*Satires of Circumstance* (107 poems). Marries Florence Dugdale
1915	75	Death of his sister, Mary
1916	76	*Selected Poems of Thomas Hardy* edited by Hardy himself
1917	77	*Moments of Vision* (159 poems). Begins to write his autobiography with intention that Florence should publish it under her own name after his death
1919–20	79	A de luxe edition of his work, the Mellstock Edition, is published
1920 onwards	80	Max Gate becomes a place of pilgrimage for hundreds of admirers
1922	82	*Late Lyrics and Earlier* (151 poems)
1923	83	*The Queen of Cornwall* (a poetic play)
1924	84	Hardy's adaptation of *Tess* performed in Dorchester
1925	85	*Human Shows* (152 poems)

Year	Literary Context	Historical Events
1909	Deaths of Swinburne and Meredith	
1910		Death of Edward VII, who is succeeded by George V
1911	Bennett, *Clayhanger* Brooke, *Poems*	
1912		Sinking of *Titanic*
1913	Lawrence, *Sons and Lovers*	First Morris Oxford car
1914	Pound editor of the first anthology of imagist poetry Frost, *North of Boston*	The First World War begins
1915	Virginia Woolf, *The Voyage Out*	
1916	Death of James Lawrence's *The Rainbow* seized by police	Lloyd George becomes Prime Minister
1917		The Russian Revolution
1918	Sassoon, *Counter-Attack* Hopkins, *Poems*	The war ends Women over thirty given the vote
1919		Treaty of Versailles First woman MP
1920	Edward Thomas, *Collected Poems* Owen, *Poems*	First meeting of League of Nations
1922	Eliot, *The Waste Land* Joyce, *Ulysses*	Mussolini comes to power in Italy Women are given equality in divorce proceedings
1924	Forster, *A Passage to India*	Ramsay MacDonald forms first Labour Government Stalin becomes Soviet Dictator
1926	T. E. Lawrence, *Seven Pillars of Wisdom*	The General Strike
1927		Lindbergh makes first crossing of the Atlantic by air

Year	Age	Life
1928	87	Hardy dies on 11 January; part buried in Westminster Abbey, part at the family church at Stinsford. *Winter Words* (105 poems) is published posthumously. *The Early Life of Thomas Hardy*, his disguised autobiography, is published
1930		*The Later Years of Thomas Hardy*, the second volume of the autobiography, is published. *Collected Poems* (918 poems) followed by *Complete Poems* (947 poems) in 1976
1937		Death of Hardy's second wife, Florence

INTRODUCTION

Hardy has now been dead long enough for us to appreciate the sheer range of his genius – novelist, short-story writer, poet and epic-dramatist. *The Lighter Hardy* collects together the shortest and one of the earliest of his novels, *Under the Greenwood Tree*, a long short story written for children, *Our Exploits at West Poley*, and four comic short stories which deserve to be better known than they are. In one sense this may be seen as the lighter side of Hardy, but it would be wrong to regard it as only that. Hardy was intrigued, like Shakespeare, by the relationship of comedy and tragedy, a relationship he had observed in his own life. He was once described as having 'humour in his mouth and tragedy in his eyes'. Writing to J. B. Priestley on 8 August 1926 he speaks about 'the tragedy that always underlies Comedy if you only scratch it deeply enough'. In his greatest novels he uses comedy at tragic moments, a device which by contrast heightens the tragic note. We laugh, but are made poignantly aware of the tragedy that lies behind the humour. Thus, in *Tess of the d'Urbervilles*, Dairyman Crick tells what seems to be an amusing story of Jack Dollop who has made his girlfriend pregnant, and is being chased by her mother, but to one of the listeners, Tess, the story is so close to her own seduction by Alec d'Urberville that it is a story with tragic undertones.

To understand why Hardy was deeply sensitive to these contrasting interpretations of life, it is necessary to know something about his own life. The humble country cottage in which he was born at Higher Bockhampton on 2 June 1840 stood at the end of a lonely lane some three miles from Dorchester, the county-town of Dorset. His father was a stone-mason and small local builder, his mother had known poverty as a child and had worked as a servant before her marriage, just six months before Hardy was born. She was a serious, earnest and hard-working woman who was largely responsible for Hardy's own assiduous observance of the work ethic which was such an important part of Victorian life. Although occasionally he seems to query the value of education, hard work and success, as when Clym in *The Return of the Native* asks his mother (so anxious that her son should succeed in life), 'Mother, what is doing well?', Hardy himself never stopped working and clearly enjoyed his success as an author and the material benefits which that success brought him.

The Hardys were a close-knit family, and his mother was a possessive parent determined to keep a tight hold on her four children and help them to do well in life. Hardy was the oldest and the only one to marry, and Jemima was not at all happy when he did. In the 1840s and 50s Hardy grew up in the cottage with his paternal grandmother, Mary Hardy, his mother, father and his brother and sisters. The smallness of the cottage meant that they were bound to be close to each other. In the absence of any social diversions, and at a time when mobility was much restricted – the railway did not reach Dorchester until Hardy was seven – the family had to make its own amusements. For Hardy, who was an avid reader and encouraged to be so by his mother, there were books and music (he played the violin) and, above all, the constant telling of anecdotes and tales both true and fictitious, tales which ranged from the darkness of superstition, cruelty and violence, to the lightness of broad-humoured jokes and comedy. As they sat together around the fire they heard many stories from the grandmother about her past which took them back as far as the French Revolution and the Napoleonic Wars. It seems probable that Mary Hardy's view of life was essentially a tragic and serious one which would have been shaped by memories of the hardships of her own childhood. In Hardy's autobiography (hereafter called *The Life)*, we are told that she had spent her first thirteen years at Fawley in Berkshire as an orphan, and that her memories of that period were 'so poignant that she never cared to return to the place'.

Inspired by her experiences, Hardy wrote several poems about his grandmother. In 'Domicilium' (written when Hardy was eighteen) he remembers her talking about her early days at the cottage, built by Hardy's great-grandfather for his son and Mary to move into in 1801 shortly after their marriage. He describes her talking to him in 1851 about life as it had been fifty years before, and of the changes which had taken place while she was living there. Compared with the speed of change in the twentieth century, the changes Mary mentions seem small, but her own awareness of the passing of time and of change was an influence on Hardy whose own tragic view of life was very much the result of his sensitivity to what in *The Life* he calls the 'ongoingness of time'.

This melancholy sense of the transience of all things was present in spite of a reasonably happy childhood in a stable family with a strong sense of togetherness. Like Heraclitus, he soon recognised that 'Nothing is permanent but change.' A country boy is much more conscious of the seasons and of nature's inescapable onward rhythms, and Hardy's astonishing ability to observe and remember – he described himself in his poem 'Afterwards' as a 'man who used to notice such things' – made lifelong impressions on him. Wordsworth might not have talked about 'Nature's Holy Plan' if he had lived as close to nature as did Hardy who, as a child, would have been painfully aware that 'Nature's law was mutual butchery.' Every year the Hardy household had a pig which, like thousands of others, was slaughtered to provide food for the winter, and his description of the pig-killing in *Jude* depicts the horror he felt about this. Hardy knew even better than Tennyson that nature could be 'red in tooth and claw' and his reading of Darwin's *The Origin of Species*, soon after it was published in 1859, confirmed much that he already knew about the life of country things he saw around him every day.

There was yet another influence on him which would have predisposed him to see life seriously. Many of the agricultural workers, whom Hardy called the 'work-folk', lived in conditions of considerable hardship. Infant mortality was high and although we laugh at Thomas Leaf there is nothing laughable about the fact that he is the only one of his mother's twelve children who survived. Hardy mentions his father's attending a coroner's inquest on a farm boy who had died, and that the total contents of his stomach was one swede. He remembered all his life how, as a young boy, he had picked up a dead bird, 'as light as a feather, all skin and bone, practically starved' (*The Life*). Hardy himself at the age of sixteen was present at the public execution of a woman and he was never to forget the experience.

Jemima Hardy's ambitions for her son were such that she paid for him to be at school until he was sixteen, and then somehow found the money to apprentice him to an architect. Much of his architectural work was concerned with church restoration and here again he was surrounded by relics of the past, by memorial notices, and gravestones and tombs. He worked as an architect in London between 1862 and 1868, where one of his jobs was to supervise the removal of the dead from a cemetery, which was in the way of railway development, to another cemetery where their presence would not inconvenience the railway company. It was a macabre experience, especially when one coffin was found to contain one skeleton but two skulls.

It would not have been surprising if, as a result of all these experiences, Hardy's outlook on life had been gloomy and pessimistic and he is often described as such by those with a superficial knowledge of his work. But he is almost always saved from being so by a quality which is present in all great writers, the ability to appreciate life's ambivalences and complexities and to see that laughter and tears are close to each other. Expecting him to be gloomy because so much of his work is concerned with serious issues, his critics fail to recognise a strong humorous strain in much of his writing. He says of himself in *The Life*: 'Hardy had a born sense of humour, even a too keen sense occasionally.' His humour is often the dry kind of the Dorset countryman. When a society lady at a London party asked him what Tess meant to him, he looked at Sir Frederick Macmillan to whom he was talking and said: 'I don't know what she meant to you, Sir Frederick, but she's been a very good milch-cow to me.' The astonished lady almost certainly failed to realise that Hardy was having a private joke, with no intention of talking to a stranger about something which meant so much to him. Many of the anecdotes and stories which the Hardy family discussed round the fire at the cottage were based on strange and often very funny incidents in the past. Some of these found their way into *The Life*, and they contributed something to Hardy's fiction and particularly to the short stories.

Thus, we see that Hardy's upbringing and surroundings made him very conscious of the suffering of 'all God's creatures' and of the ultimate seriousness of things, of the passing of time, of change, and of the presence of death. However, this awareness was made bearable by his sense of humour, and was made even more bearable by the catharsis which his writing provided and by an ability to see that there was beauty and joy in life. In one of his most enjoyable poems, 'Great Things', which might almost be a companion-piece to *Under the Greenwood Tree*, he celebrates some of the 'great things' in life – cyder, dancing and love. The first verse mentions the inn at which Dick and Fancy stop for tea on their way to Budmouth:

> Sweet cyder is a great thing,
>   A great thing to me,
> Spinning down to Weymouth town
>   By Ridgeway thirstily,
> And maid and mistress summoning
>   Who tend the hostelry:
> O cyder is a great thing,
>   A great thing to me.

From an early age Hardy had wanted to be a writer, and above all he wanted to be a poet. However, there was no possibility of earning a living, as he had to do, by writing poetry so he turned to novel writing. Partly because it was a satirical attack on the upper class, his first completed novel, *The Poor Man and the Lady*, had failed to find a publisher, and Hardy was advised by a publisher's reader to try his hand at the kind of detective, sensation novel which Wilkie Collins had made so popular. Hardy dutifully complied and wrote a story about a murder which is often taken more seriously than it should be because readers fail to realise that Hardy himself is not taking it seriously. *Desperate Remedies* was published in 1871. It was a failure, and Hardy even lost the money which he had put up in order to have it published. The reviews were not good but some of them did commend Hardy's ability to portray country people and the rural scene. As a young ambitious writer he listened earnestly to the advice being given him and began writing what was to become *Under the Greenwood Tree*. This was finished in the summer of 1871 and sent to Macmillan, the most prestigious publisher of that time. Alexander Macmillan liked the book but did not mention an immediate acceptance and Hardy, either through a misunderstanding or impatience, sent it to Tinsley, the publisher of *Desperate Remedies*. He published it but took advantage of Hardy's ignorance of publishing procedures by paying him a miserable £30 for the copyright. It was published in two volumes in June 1872. The reviews were mostly favourable, although there was some patronising of this unknown writer from Dorset. No one would have guessed from its reception that the book would still be widely read more than a century later.

Under the Greenwood Tree

Under the Greenwood Tree is the only Hardy novel in which the individuals of the so-called 'rustic chorus' become the main characters throughout the book. In his later novels they are minor characters, there to provide humour, comment in their often wise and fatalistic way on the actions of the main characters, and sometimes by their actions contribute to the plot itself. In *Under the Greenwood Tree* they are major characters, and the lives, loves and interests of the Dewy family provide the solid centre to the story and have a life and substance about them which may result from the strong autobiographical element which is a feature of this novel.

Hardy often draws heavily upon people and places he knows as an initial stimulus to his creative imagination, and nowhere is he nearer home than in *Under the Greenwood Tree*. Mellstock is clearly recognisable as the parish of Stinsford with its two hamlets of Higher and Lower Bockhampton. The 'long low cottage with a hipped roof of thatch, having dormer windows breaking up into the eaves, a chimney standing in the middle of the ridge and another at each end', is Hardy's own home, the very cottage in which he is writing the story. Mellstock Church is Stinsford church as it was in his father's and grandfather's time, with the gallery where they played their music. The schoolmistress's house is the school in Lower Bockhampton which was Hardy's first school. Recognisable among the characters are William, Hardy's grandfather who had such a love of music, Reuben who has many of the characteristics of Hardy's father, and Mrs Dewy who has a certain likeness to his mother. The picture of Reuben is of a simple but kindly man, friendly, generous, long-suffering and fair almost to a fault. On his death in 1892 Hardy compared him to Hamlet's friend, Horatio, and the likeness of Reuben to his father is inescapable. We can only guess whether his mother grumbled at his father as much as Mrs Dewy grumbles about Reuben, but we do know that she was critical of her husband for his easy-going ways. But Hardy also portrays her as a good and hospitable housewife and a loving and caring mother. There is genuine affection here for both characters.

The portrayal of the other members of the choir, Robert Penny, Elias Spinks, Joseph Bowman and Thomas Leaf, is amusing and each is given some recognisable eccentricity which serves to distinguish him. They may seem foolish when confronted with someone so different from them as the Vicar, but there is a certain dignity, kindness, common-sense and friendliness about them which deserves our sympathy, though it is a pity that Leaf is more of a caricature than the rest and to some extent destroys the homogeneity of the characterisation. In her essay 'The novels of Thomas Hardy' Virginia Woolf describes Hardy in these early novels as 'feeling his way to a method', and he made a number of mistakes on the way.

No mistakes are made with the two main characters, Dick and Fancy. Dick is present throughout the book, he is the hero, the character with whom most of us would identify. His falling in love with Fancy enables Hardy to laugh sympathetically at first love and to take a 'what fools these mortals be' attitude to Dick's behaviour as he desperately tries to win his Fancy. The satire about love expressed in Reuben's comment, 'Ay, that's a part of the zickness. Distance belongs to it, slyness belongs to it, queerest things on earth belongs to it!' (Part II, Chapter 3) echoes Shakespeare's satire on love in *As You Like It*, and Hardy who had experienced the joys and pains of being in love himself may well be looking back at his own experience.

Dick is simple, genuine, honest and in every way likeable but we know that he will be no match for Fancy, who is an altogether more subtle and complex piece of characterisation. Her introduction into the story is cleverly done over a number of chapters. Shoemaker Mr Penny talks about the attractiveness of her shoes and her good looks are commented upon. Then we see her, a vision in white with her 'marvellously rich hair, in a wild disorder' (Part I, Chapter 5) standing at the window of the schoolhouse, thanking the carol singers and having such an effect on Dick that it seems a case of love at first sight. His father shrewdly remarks a little later that 'she'll wind en round her finger, and twist the pore young feller about like the figure of 8' (Part I, Chapter 5). At the Christmas party at the tranter's house, Dick falls even more in love and Hardy describes her as having 'a certain coquettishness' (Part I, Chapter 7). With this goes vanity – 'such lots of people will be looking at me there, you know.' (Part IV, Chapter 1) – and a love of clothes that seems to be greater than her love for Dick. With Dick she has an air of superiority and an ability to get her own way, and her self-confidence is shown in her 'I think I can manage any vicar's view about me if he's under forty' (Part II, Chapter 7). Her reluctance to declare her love for Dick as they drive out of Budmouth hints at the reservations she has about allying herself with someone who is of a lower social status than herself. Shiner is, of course, no real contender for her hand but Maybold's interest in her is suggested early on in the story and his expression of love for her is well-motivated, even if his class-consciousness makes him come out with such expressions as 'you have enough in you for any society, after a few months of travel with me' (Part IV, Chapter 6). There is something of Mr Collins in Jane Austen's *Pride and Prejudice* here. That Fancy, already engaged to Dick, then agrees to marry Maybold is prompted by the worst of motives, her own snobbery, and reveals the weakness in her character.

Hardy was fascinated and very sensitive about class distinctions, some of which had affected his own life, and his interest in them manifests itself again and again in his writing. The educated and Reverend Maybold thinks he is a class above the educated school-teacher, Fancy, who is convinced that she is a class above Dick and his family. Fancy's near betrayal of Dick and the final words of the book bring a serious note to what would otherwise have been a completely happy ending. Other indications of the later, more serious Hardy can be seen in the reference to 'some small bird that was being killed by an owl in the adjoining wood' (Part IV, Chapter 2) and the remark which ends the chapter in which Dick returns Fancy's handkerchief: 'He wished that before he called he had realised more fully than he did the pleasure of being about to call' (Part I, Chapter 9).

Dick and Fancy are not only enjoyable pieces of characterisation, they play an important part in the structure of the novel, being part of both the main themes of the book: the dismissal of the church choir instrumentalists and the nature of love between men and women. The latter subject was to become the dominating theme of almost all of Hardy's later novels. He once said that love between men and women was the only subject to write about, and his treatment of that love shows an astonishing development from the comparative lightness and laughter of *Under the Greenwood Tree* through to the sombreness and pain of *Jude the Obscure*. The Hardy of fifty-five saw life very differently from the Hardy of thirty-two, but then by the 1890s he had an assured market for his literary wares, while in the early 1870s he was struggling just to get published and was obviously more anxious to give the Victorian readers what they wanted than he was to be later. He knew that a light-hearted story with a 'happy' ending had a good chance of selling. The love theme is explored in a narrative device that he had already used in *Desperate Remedies* – the lovely heroine is wooed by two or three men and the reader's interest is aroused by the hope that Mr Right will win her. Fancy is wanted by three men and we all hope that Dick will be successful, and he is. Hardy was not so obliging in his later novels because, as he said more than once, he was not aware that life always had a happy ending. Although *Under the Greenwood Tree* lacks the penetrating psychological portrayal of characters which we find in later novels, it is a gentle, satirical look at first love and the very different approaches of the characters to it.

There is evidence to show that what might be regarded as the minor theme of the story – the ousting of the choir instrumentalists and their replacement by an organ played by Fancy – was at first intended by Hardy to be the major theme. One of the subjects of conversation and reminiscence among the Hardy family must have been just such happenings in Stinsford Church when he was a very young child. Hardy's own intense interest in and love of music comes from his paternal relatives. His grandfather, father and uncle, with their viols and violins, had been the backbone of the Stinsford choir for many years. Here is a passage from *The Life* (p. 262):

> August 14 (1892). Mother described today the three Hardys as they used to appear passing over the brow of the hill to Stinsford Church on a Sunday morning, three or four years before my birth. They were always hurrying, being rather late, their fiddles and violon-cello in green-baize bags under their left arms. They wore top hats, stick-up shirt-collars, dark blue coats with great collars and gilt buttons, deep cuffs and black silk 'stocks' or neckerchiefs.

In 1843 the Vicar of Stinsford decided to replace them with an organ and what had been an important community activity came to an end. Hardy, always so aware of change in the community, and looking around for a subject for his second book saw in these events a good story and the possibility of immortalising what was to him an intriguing part of his family's history. For Hardy immortality was being remembered by the living, and with *Under the Greenwood Tree* still such a popular book the Stinsford choir with its Hardy instrumentalists has surely been immortalised. The lightness of Hardy's touch should not blind us to the fact that we learn a great deal about the instrumentalists and their playing, and even what they play. The singing of the carols on Christmas Eve is almost certainly a faithful record of many such occasions attended by the Hardy family, a moving recording of history as it was:

> Then passed forth into the quiet night an ancient and time-worn hymn, embodying a quaint Christianity in words orally transmitted from father to son through several generations down to the present characters, who sang them out right earnestly. (Part I, Chapter 4)

The sense of community and of tradition, and the reference here to the oral transmission which was such an important part of life for so many centuries, provide *Under the Greenwood Tree* with a solid background against which the events of the story can be enacted. They make the novel a unique Wessex period piece.

In writing his preface to the 1912 Wessex edition of the novel forty years later, Hardy comments:

> In rereading the narrative after a long interval there occurs the inevitable reflection that the realities out of which it was spun were material for another kind of study of this little group of church musicians than is found in the chapters here penned so lightly, even so farcically and flippantly at times. But circumstances would have rendered any aim at a deeper, more essential, more transcendent handling unadvisable at the date of writing ...

But it would not have been easy to write a serious novel around the theme of the extinction of those instrumentalists. Evidence suggests that the standards of many of them were very low and it was easier for a clergyman to deal with a single organist than with a mixed group of local instrument-playing worthies. Of course it was sad that they were being superceded, but Hardy – no pessimist but a fact-facing realist – would have accepted the inevitable while regretting the passing of something which had provided so much cultural pleasure. It would have been a pity if *Under the Greenwood Tree* had been anything other than what it is – a thoroughly enjoyable short novel and the best possible introduction to Hardy's novels. Although so different in tone and mood from what was to come later, it is inescapably Hardy's work and it provides a fascinating light overture to the great novels which will follow. Here can be seen nearly all of the themes which were to be treated more seriously in his later novels – love between men and women and the rivalry this creates, class distinction and the difficulties this produces in sexual alliances, changes in the community, the impact of the new on the old and of the 'outsider' on what has been a closed community, and the close relationship between human-beings and the natural world. In Hardy's beginning was his end.

Our Exploits at West Poley

Our Exploits at West Poley has a strange history. It was Hardy's only attempt to write a short story for the young and resulted from an invitation in 1883 from a popular American magazine called the *Youth's Companion* to write something for them. For some unknown reason it was not published by that magazine in 1884 as planned but first appeared in another American magazine, called *The Household*, in six monthly instalments between November 1892 and April 1893. There is some irony in the fact that *The Household* was a little-known magazine 'Devoted to the Interests of the American Housewife'. Hardy, who was very businesslike in all his dealings with publishers, seems, unusually, to have lost track of it or forgotten it, and not until the 1950s was it rediscovered and published as a short book.

Hardy believed that 'a story *must be worth the telling*', and the story he created for *Our Exploits* is a good one with plenty of action that holds the attention. The idea of a source of water which, as a childhood prank, is diverted and thus causes distress to one village and joy to another is one rich in possibilities as we see also in Pagnol's film *Manon des Sources*. The idea is cleverly developed and holds the attention throughout with particularly strong moments when the two main characters are in danger of being drowned, and when Steve almost blows himself up. A good plot requires strong characterisation and

Hardy's tale is made richer by the contrast between the two main characters, Leonard, the narrator, and Steve. Leonard, the younger of the two, is impressionable, prudent and cautious; Steve lacks 'intellectual power', but is strong and courageous enough to explore and get things done.

In the late twentieth century there has been a reaction against stories with a moral, but until this century almost all literature was intended to instruct, and Hardy's stories were seldom written in order solely to entertain. This didactic motive is felt strongly in *Our Exploits* because the story was written for the young. Hardy is saying that tampering with nature can have dangerous consequences: an irresponsible prank may have disastrous results. Bathsheba's levity, in *Far From the Madding Crowd*, in sending the Valentine card to Boldwood and the tragedy to which it led, is an example of this. The moral nature of *Our Exploits* is emphasised, some may think a little awkwardly, by the introduction of 'the Man who had Failed'. To him is given almost the final word, and it is essentially Hardyan, 'Quiet perseverance in clearly defined courses is, as a rule, better than erratic exploits that may do much harm.'

The Four Short Stories

Hardy's short stories have been unduly overshadowed by the greatness of his novels. Of the fifty or so that he wrote between 1865 and 1900, in response to a rapidly growing demand because of the growth in literacy, at least a dozen are among the best which have been written in English. They were collected into four volumes, and the four stories chosen for this book all come from *Life's Little Ironies*, first published in 1894. In 1891, while he was working on *Tess of the d'Urbervilles*, Hardy wrote a group of what he later called 'Colloquial Sketches' for *Harper's New Monthly Magazine*. These nine sketches appeared in four monthly instalments with the title 'Wessex Folk', changed in *Life's Little Ironies* to *A Few Crusted Characters*. Hardy called them 'Colloquial Sketches' because they are all narrated by the occupants of a carrier-van – the omnibus of that time – on their journey from Casterbridge (Dorchester) to Longpuddle (Piddletrenthide), and they are all shorter than his typical short story. One of the occupants of the van is John Lackland who thirty-five years previously had emigrated but has now returned with the idea of possibly settling down in his native village. Asking his companions in the van about the people he had known in his youth, they respond with stories about them. But so many changes have taken place in Puddletown, so many of Lackland's friends are dead, that he has to face the truth that 'Time had not condescended to wait his pleasure, nor local life his greeting.' His roots with the past have been broken by his long absence and he is no longer a member of the community which gave his birthplace a meaning for him. Hardy is saying, as he often does, that it is the people who surround a place with emotional significance, not the place itself.

'Tony Kytes, the Arch-Deceiver', is an enjoyable romp, based upon a humorous situation which builds up cleverly to a climax when the wagon overturns and Tony is exposed as an 'Arch-Deceiver'. Hardy had dealt with a similar man and three women relationship in *The Woodlanders*, but Fitzpiers' philanderings are serious and tragic, here Tony's philanderings are farcical. The story is, however, given a certain sense of reality by the use of carefully observed detail, as in the reference in the opening lines to the scar left on his face by smallpox, and by the narrator's 'When he reached the foot of the very hill we shall be going over in ten minutes . . .' The three women are carefully differentiated in character and Hardy, as always, makes us aware of the sexuality of love by his reference to the bawdy folk-song, 'The Tailor's Breeches' and by Mr Jolliver's asking his daughter to refuse Tony, '. . . if yer virtue is left to 'ee and you run no risk'.

The three other short stories, 'Andrey Satchel and the Parson and Clerk', 'Old Andrey's Experience as a Musician' and 'Absent-Mindedness in a Parish Choir', also reveal Hardy's delightful sense of humour, but we are aware, even while we are laughing, of the gap between the work-folk and the squire and the parson, and we meet again Hardy's sensitivity about class. His work-folk may drink too much and have to marry because a baby is imminent, but there is something good and genuine about them which is plainly missing from the parson, whose main worship is hunting, and from the squire, wittily described as 'a wickedish man . . . though now for once he happened to be on the Lord's side'. The squire reveals his priorities with his 'not if the Angels of Heaven come down . . . shall one of you villainous players ever sound a note in this church again; for the insult to me, and my family, and my visitor, and the pa'son, and God Almighty . . .' The power of the squire in the lives of these poor rustics is made manifest in his threat to move Andrey out of his cottage for such an inadequate reason, a threat which might well have been carried out if it had not been for the kindness of the squire's wife.

It is music and the telling of stories which help to make the lives of these rustic characters bearable, and they particularly like a story which gives them a good laugh. In telling his story of 'Andrey Satchel and the Parson and Clerk', the master-thatcher says to John Lackland that the story 'may cheer 'ee up a little'. There is much in his stories to cheer us up a little even if Hardy was never to forget that 'Comedy is simply a funny way of being serious.'

JAMES GIBSON

The Country of *Under the Greenwood Tree*

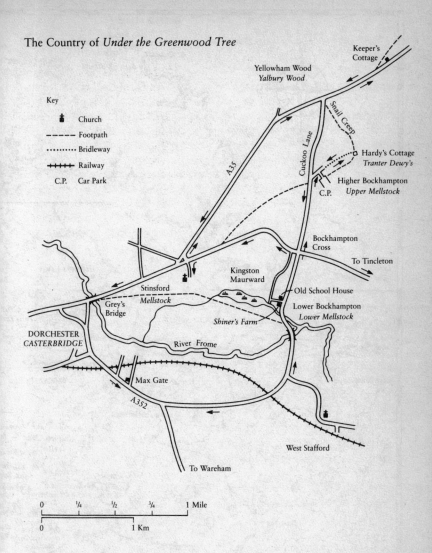

Key

- 🕇 Church
- – – – Footpath
- ·········· Bridleway
- +++++ Railway
- C.P. Car Park

Keeper's Cottage

Yellowham Wood
Yalbury Wood

Snail Creep

Cuckoo Lane

Hardy's Cottage
Tranter Dewy's

A35

Higher Bockhampton
Upper Mellstock

C.P.

Bockhampton Cross

To Tincleton

Kingston Maurward

Old School House

Stinsford
Mellstock

Lower Bockhampton
Lower Mellstock

Grey's Bridge

Shiner's Farm

DORCHESTER
CASTERBRIDGE

River Frome

Max Gate

A352

West Stafford

To Wareham

| 0 | ¼ | ½ | ¾ | 1 Mile |
| 0 | | 1 Km | | |

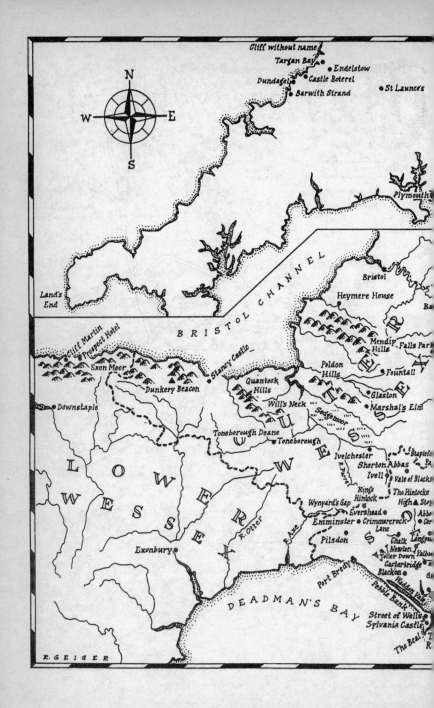

UNDER THE
GREENWOOD TREE

PREFACE

This story of the Mellstock Quire* and its old established west-gallery* musicians, with some supplementary descriptions of similar officials in *Two on a Tower, A Few Crusted Characters*, and other places, is intended to be a fairly true picture, at first hand, of the personages, ways, and customs which were common among such orchestral bodies in the villages of fifty or sixty years ago.

One is inclined to regret the displacement of these ecclesiastical bandsmen by an isolated organist (often at first a barrel-organist) or harmonium player; and despite certain advantages in point of control and accomplishment which were, no doubt, secured by installing the single artist, the change has tended to stultify the professed aims of the clergy, its direct result being to curtail and extinguish the interest of parishioners in church doings. Under the old plan, from half a dozen to ten full-grown players, in addition to the numerous more or less grown-up singers, were officially occupied with the Sunday routine, and concerned in trying their best to make it an artistic outcome of the combined musical taste of the congregation. With a musical executive limited, as it mostly is limited now, to the parson's wife or daughter and the school-children, or to the school-teacher and the children, an important union of interests has disappeared.

The zest of these bygone instrumentalists must have been keen and staying, to take them, as it did, on foot every Sunday after a toilsome week through all weathers to the church, which often lay at a distance from their homes. They usually received so little in payment for their performances that their efforts were really a labour of love. In the parish I had in my mind when writing the present tale, the gratuities received yearly by the musicians at Christmas were somewhat as follows: From the manor-house ten shillings and a supper; from the vicar ten shillings;* from the farmers five shillings each; from each cottage-household one shilling; amounting altogether to not more than ten shillings a head annually – just enough, as an old executant told me, to pay for their fiddle-strings, repairs, rosin, and music-paper (which they mostly ruled themselves). Their music in those days was all in their own manuscript, copied in the evenings after work, and their music-books were home-bound.

It was customary to inscribe a few jigs, reels, hornpipes, and ballads in the same book, by beginning it at the other end, the insertions being continued from front and back till sacred and secular met together in the middle, often with bizarre effect, the words of some of the songs exhibiting that ancient and broad humour* which our grandfathers, and possibly grandmothers, took delight in, and is in these days unquotable.

The aforesaid fiddle-strings, rosin, and music-paper were supplied by a pedlar, who travelled exclusively in such wares from parish to parish, coming to each village about every six months. Tales are told of the consternation once caused among the church fiddlers when, on the occasion of their producing a new Christmas anthem, he did not come to time, owing to being snowed up on the downs, and the straits they were in through having to make shift with whipcord and twine for strings. He was generally a musician himself, and sometimes a composer in a small way, bringing his own new tunes, and tempting each choir to adopt them for a consideration. Some of these compositions which now lie before me, with their repetitions of lines, half-lines, and half-words, their fugues and their intermediate symphonies, are good singing still, though they would hardly be admitted into such hymn-books as are popular in the churches of fashionable society at the present time.

August 1896

Under the Greenwood Tree was first brought out in the summer of 1872 in two volumes. The name of the story was originally intended to be, more appropriately, *The Mellstock Quire*, and this has been appended as a sub-title since the early editions, it having been thought unadvisable to displace for it the title by which the book first became known.

In rereading the narrative after a long interval there occurs the inevitable reflection that the realities out of which it was spun were material for another kind of study of this little group of church musicians than is found in the chapters here penned so lightly, even so farcically and flippantly at times. But circumstances would have rendered any aim at a deeper, more essential, more transcendent handling unadvisable at the date of writing; and the exhibition of the Mellstock Quire in the following pages must remain the only extant one, except for the few glimpses of that perished band which I have given in verse elsewhere.

T.H.
April 1912

CONTENTS

Part IV: AUTUMN

Part V: CONCLUSION

PART I
WINTER

MELLSTOCK LANE

To dwellers in a wood almost every species of tree has its voice as well as its feature. At the passing of the breeze the fir-trees sob and moan no less distinctly than they rock; the holly whistles as it battles with itself; the ash hisses amid its quiverings; the beech rustles while its flat boughs rise and fall. And winter, which modifies the note of such trees as shed their leaves, does not destroy its individuality.

On a cold and starry Christmas Eve within living memory* a man was passing up a lane towards Mellstock Cross in the darkness of a plantation that whispered thus distinctively to his intelligence. All the evidences of his nature were those afforded by the spirit of his footsteps, which succeeded each other lightly and quickly, and by the liveliness of his voice as he sang in a rural cadence:

> With the rose and the lily
> And the daffodowndilly,*
> The lads and lasses a-sheep-shearing go.*

The lonely lane he was following connected one of the hamlets of Mellstock parish with Upper Mellstock and Lewgate, and to his eyes, casually glancing upward, the silver and black-stemmed birches with their characteristic tufts, the pale grey boughs of beech, the dark-creviced elm, all appeared now as black and flat outlines upon the sky, wherein the white stars twinkled so vehemently that their flickering seemed like the flapping of wings. Within the woody pass, at a level anything lower than the horizon, all was dark as the grave. The copse-wood forming the sides of the bower interlaced its branches so densely, even at this season of the year, that the draught from the north-east flew along the channel with scarcely an interruption from lateral breezes.

After passing the plantation and reaching Mellstock Cross the white surface of the lane revealed itself between the dark hedgerows like a ribbon jagged at the edges; the irregularity being caused by temporary accumulations of leaves extending from the ditch on either side.

The song (many times interrupted by flitting thoughts which took the place of several bars, and resumed at a point it would have reached had its continuity been unbroken) now received a more palpable check, in the shape of 'Ho-i-i-i-i-i!' from the crossing lane to Lower Mellstock, on the right of the singer who had just emerged from the trees.

'Ho-i-i-i-i-i!' he answered, stopping and looking round, though with no idea of seeing anything more than imagination pictured.

'Is that thee, young Dick Dewy?' came from the darkness.

'Ay, sure, Michael Mail.'

'Then why not stop for fellow-craters* – going to thy own father's house too, as we be, and knowen us so well?'

Dick Dewy faced about and continued his tune in an under-whistle, implying that the business of his mouth could not be checked at a moment's notice by the placid emotion of friendship.

Having come more into the open he could now be seen rising against the sky, his profile appearing on the light background like the portrait of a gentleman in black cardboard. It assumed the form of a low-crowned hat, an ordinary-shaped nose, an ordinary chin, an ordinary neck, and ordinary shoulders. What he consisted of further down was invisible from lack of sky low enough to picture him on.

Shuffling, halting, irregular footsteps of various kinds were now heard coming up the hill, and presently there emerged from the shade severally* five men of different ages and gaits, all of them working villagers of the parish of Mellstock. They, too, had lost their rotundity with the daylight, and advanced against the sky in flat outlines, which suggested some processional design on Greek or Etruscan pottery. They represented the chief portion of Mellstock parish choir.

The first was a bowed and bent man, who carried a fiddle under his arm, and walked as if engaged in studying some subject connected with the surface of the road. He was Michael Mail, the man who had hallooed to Dick.

The next was Mr Robert Penny, boot- and shoemaker; a little man who, though rather round shouldered, walked as if that fact had not come to his own knowledge, moving on with his back very hollow and his face fixed on the north-east quarter of the heavens before him, so that his lower waistcoat-buttons came first, and then the remainder of his figure. His features were invisible; yet when he occasionally looked round, two faint moons of light gleamed for an instant from the precincts of his eyes, denoting that he wore spectacles of a circular form.

The third was Elias Spinks, who walked perpendicularly and dramatically. The fourth outline was Joseph Bowman's, who had now no distinctive appearance beyond that of a human being. Finally came a weak lath-like* form, trotting and stumbling along with one shoulder forward and his head inclined to the left, his arms dangling nervelessly in the wind as if they were empty sleeves. This was Thomas Leaf.

'Where be the boys?' said Dick to this somewhat indifferently matched assembly.

The eldest of the group, Michael Mail, cleared his throat from a great depth.

'We told them to keep back at home for a time, thinken they wouldn't be wanted yet awhile; and we could choose the tuens,* and so on.'

'Father and grandfather William have expected ye a little sooner. I have just been for a run round by Ewelease* Stile and Hollow Hill to warm my feet.'

'To be sure father did! To be sure 'a did expect us – to taste the little barrel beyond compare that he's going to tap.'

''Od rabbit it all!* Never heard a word of it!' said Mr Penny, gleams of delight appearing upon his spectacle-glasses, Dick meanwhile singing parenthetically –

'The lads and the lasses a-sheep-shearing go.'

'Neighbours, there's time enough to drink a sight of* drink now afore bedtime?' said Mail.

'True, true – time enough to get as drunk as lords!' replied Bowman cheerfully.

This opinion being taken as convincing they all advanced between the varying hedges and the trees dotting them here and there, kicking their toes occasionally among the crumpled leaves. Soon appeared glimmering indications of the few cottages forming the small hamlet of Upper Mellstock for which they were bound, whilst the faint sound of church-bells ringing a Christmas peal could be heard floating over upon the breeze from the direction of Longpuddle and Weatherbury parishes on the other side of the hills. A little wicket* admitted them to the garden, and they proceeded up the path to Dick's house.

2
THE TRANTER'S

It was a long low cottage* with a hipped roof* of thatch, having dormer windows* breaking up into the eaves, a chimney standing in the middle of the ridge and another at each end. The window-shutters were not yet closed, and the fire- and candle-light within radiated forth upon the thick bushes of box and laurestinus growing in clumps outside, and upon the bare boughs of several codlin-trees* hanging about in various distorted shapes, the result of early training as espaliers* combined with careless climbing into their boughs in later years. The walls of the dwelling were for the most part covered with creepers, though these were rather beaten back from the doorway – a feature which was worn and scratched by much passing in and out, giving it by day the appearance of an old keyhole. Light streamed through the cracks and joints of outbuildings a little way from the cottage, a sight which nourished a fancy that the purpose of the erection must be rather to veil bright attractions than to shelter unsightly necessaries. The noise of a beetle* and wedges and the splintering of wood was periodically heard from this direction; and at some little distance further a steady regular munching and the occasional scurr* of a rope betokened a stable, and horses feeding within it.

The choir stamped severally on the door-stone to shake from their boots any fragment of earth or leaf adhering thereto, then entered the house and looked around to survey the condition of things. Through the open doorway of a small inner room on the right hand, of a character between pantry and cellar, was Dick Dewy's father Reuben, by vocation a 'tranter', or irregular carrier. He was a stout florid man about forty years of age, who surveyed people up and down when first making their acquaintance, and generally smiled at the horizon or other distant object during conversations with friends, walking about with a steady sway, and turning out his toes very considerably. Being now occupied in bending over a hogshead* that stood in the pantry ready horsed* for the process of broaching,* he did not take the trouble to turn or raise his eyes at the entry of his visitors, well knowing by their footsteps that they were the expected old comrades.

The main room, on the left, was decked with bunches of holly and other evergreens, and from the middle of the beam bisecting the ceiling hung the mistletoe, of a size out of all proportion to the room, and extending so low that it became necessary for a full-grown person to walk round it in passing, or run the risk of entangling his hair. This apartment contained Mrs Dewy the tranter's wife, and the four remaining children, Susan, Jim, Bessy, and Charley, graduating uniformly though at wide stages from the age of sixteen to that of four years – the eldest of the series being separated from Dick the firstborn by a nearly equal interval.

Some circumstance had apparently caused much grief to Charley just previous to the entry of the choir, and he had absently taken down a small looking-glass, holding it before his face to learn how the human countenance appeared when engaged in crying, which survey led him to pause at the various points in each wail that were more than ordinarily striking, for a thorough appreciation of the general effect. Bessy was leaning against a chair, and glancing under the plaits* about the waist of the plaid frock she wore, to notice the original unfaded pattern of the material as there preserved, her face bearing an expression of regret that the brightness had passed away from the visible portions. Mrs Dewy sat in a brown settle* by the side of the glowing wood fire – so glowing that with a heedful compression of the lips she would now and then rise and put her hand upon the hams and flitches of bacon lining the chimney, to reassure herself that they were not being broiled instead of smoked – a misfortune that had been known to happen now and then at Christmas-time.

'Hullo, my sonnies, here you be, then!' said Reuben Dewy at length, standing up and blowing forth a vehement gust of breath. 'How the blood do puff up in anybody's head, to be sure, a-stooping like that! I was just going out to gate to hark for ye.' He then carefully began to wind a strip of brown paper round a brass tap he held in his hand. 'This in the cask here is a drop o' the right sort' (tapping the cask); ''tis a real drop o' cordial from the best picked apples – Sansoms, Stubbards, Five-corners, and suchlike – you d'mind the sort, Michael?' (Michael nodded.) 'And there's a sprinkling of they that grow down by the orchard-rails – streaked ones – rail apples we d'call 'em, as 'tis by the rails they grow, and not knowing the right name. The water-cider* from 'em is as good as most people's best cider is.'

'Ay, and of the same make too,' said Bowman. ' "It rained when we wrung it out, and the water got into it," folk will say. But 'tis on'y an excuse. Watered cider is too common among us.'

'Yes, yes; too common it is!' said Spinks with an inward sigh, whilst his eyes seemed to be looking at the world in an abstract form rather than at the scene before him. 'Such poor liquor do make a man's throat feel very melancholy – and is a disgrace to the name of stimmilent.*'

'Come in, come in, and draw up to the fire; never mind your shoes,' said Mrs Dewy, seeing that all except Dick had paused to wipe them upon the door-mat. 'I am glad that you've stepped up-along at last; and, Susan, you run down to Grammer* Kaytes's and see if you can borrow some larger candles than these fourteens.* Tommy Leaf, don't ye be afeard! Come and sit here in the settle.'

This was addressed to the young man before mentioned, consisting chiefly of a human skeleton and a smock-frock,* who was very awkward in his movements, apparently on account of having grown so very fast that before he had had time to get used to his height he was higher.

'Hee – hee – ay!' replied Leaf, letting his mouth continue to smile for some time after his mind had done smiling, so that his teeth remained in view as the most conspicuous members of his body.

'Here, Mr Penny,' resumed Mrs Dewy, 'you sit in this chair. And how's your daughter, Mrs Brownjohn?'

'Well, I suppose I must say pretty fair.' He adjusted his spectacles a quarter of an inch to the right. 'But she'll be worse before she's better, 'a b'lieve.'

'Indeed – poor soul! And how many will that make in all, four or five?'

'Five; they've buried three. Yes, five; and she not much more than a maid yet. She do know the multiplication table onmistakable well. However, 'twas to be, and none can gainsay it.'

Mrs Dewy resigned Mr Penny. 'Wonder where your grandfather James is?' she inquired of one of the children. 'He said he'd drop in tonight.'

'Out in fuel-house with grandfather William,' said Jimmy.

'Now let's see what we can do,' was heard spoken about this time by the tranter in a private voice to the barrel, beside which he had again established himself, and was stooping to cut away the cork.

'Reuben, don't make such a mess o' tapping that barrel as is mostly made in this house,' Mrs Dewy cried from the fireplace. I'd tap a hundred without wasting more than you do in one. Such a squizzling and squirting job as 'tis in your hands! There, he always was such a clumsy man indoors.'

'Ay, ay; I know you'd tap a hundred beautiful, Ann – I know you would; two hundred, perhaps. But I can't promise. This is a' old cask, and the wood's rotted away about the tap-hole. The husbird* of a feller Sam Lawson – that ever I should call'n, such, now he's dead and gone, poor heart! – took me in completely upon the feat of buying this cask. "Reub," says he – 'a always used to call me plain Reub, poor old heart! – "Reub," he said says he, "that there cask, Reub, is as good as new; yes, good as new. 'Tis a wine-hogshead; the best port-wine in the commonwealth have been in that there cask; and you shall have en for ten shillens,* Reub," – 'a said says he – "he's worth twenty, ay, five-and-twenty, if he's worth one; and an iron hoop or two put round en among the wood ones will make en worth thirty shillens of any man's money, if—"'

'I think I should have used the eyes that Providence gave me to use afore I paid any ten shillens for a jimcrack* wine-barrel; a saint is sinner enough not to be cheated. But 'tis like all your family was, so easy to be deceived.'

'That's as true as gospel* of this member,' said Reuben.

'Mrs Dewy began a smile at the answer, then altering her lips and refolding them so that it was not a smile, commenced smoothing little Bessy's hair; the tranter having meanwhile suddenly become oblivious to conversation, occupying himself in a deliberate cutting and arrangement of some more brown paper for the broaching operation.

'Ah, who can believe sellers!' said old Michael Mail in a

carefully-cautious voice, by way of tiding-over this critical point of affairs.

'No one at all,' said Joseph Bowman, in the tone of a man fully agreeing with everybody.

'Ay,' said Mail, in the tone of a man who did not agree with everybody as a rule, though he did now; 'I knowed a' auction-eering feller once – a very friendly feller 'a was too. And so one hot day as I was walking down the front street o' Casterbridge, jist below the King's Arms,* I passed a' open winder and see him inside, stuck upon his perch, a-selling off. I jist nodded to en in a friendly way as I passed, and went my way, and thought no more about it. Well, next day, as I was oilen my boots by fuel-house door, if a letter didn't come wi' a bill charging me with a feather-bed, bolster, and pillers, that I had bid for at Mr Taylor's sale. The slim-faced martel* had knocked 'em down to me because I nodded to en in my friendly way; and I had to pay for 'em too. Now, I hold that that was coming it very close,* Reuben?'

''Twas close, there's no denying,' said the general voice.

'Too close, 'twas,' said Reuben in the rear of the rest. 'And as to Sam Lawson – poor heart! now he's dead and gone too! – I'll warrant, that if so be I've spent one hour in making hoops for that barrel, I've spent fifty, first and last. That's one of my hoops' – touching it with his elbow – 'that's one of mine, and that, and that, and all these.'

'Ah, Sam was a man,' said Mr Penny, contemplatively.

'Sam was!' said Bowman.

'Especially for a drap o' drink,' said the tranter.

'Good, but not religious-good,' suggested Mr Penny.

The tranter nodded. Having at last made the tap and hole quite ready, 'Now then, Suze, bring a mug,' he said. 'Here's luck to us, my sonnies!'

The tap went in, and the cider immediately squirted out in a horizontal shower over Reuben's hands, knees, and leggings, and into the eyes and neck of Charley, who, having temporarily put off his grief under pressure of more interesting proceedings, was squatting down and blinking near his father.

'There 'tis again!' said Mrs Dewy.

'Devil take the hole, the cask, and Sam Lawson too, that good cider should be wasted like this!' exclaimed the tranter. 'Your thumb! Lend me your thumb, Michael! Ram it in here, Michael! I must I get a bigger tap, my sonnies.'

'Idd it cold inthide te hole?' inquired Charley of Michael, as he continued in a stooping posture with his thumb in the cork-hole.

'What wonderful odds and ends that chiel has in his head to be sure!' Mrs Dewy admiringly exclaimed from the distance. 'I lay a wager that he thinks more about how 'tis inside that barrel than in all the other parts of the world put together.'

All persons present put on a speaking countenance of admiration for the cleverness alluded to, in the midst of which Reuben returned. The operation was then satisfactorily performed; when Michael arose and stretched his head to the extremest fraction of height that his body would allow of, to restraighten his back and shoulders – thrusting out his arms and twisting his features to a mass of wrinkles to emphasize the relief acquired. A quart or two of the beverage was then brought to table, at which all the new arrivals reseated themselves with wide-spread knees, their eyes meditatively seeking out any speck or knot in the board upon which the gaze might precipitate itself.

'Whatever is father a-biding out in fuel-house so long for?' said the tranter. 'Never such a man as father for two things – cleaving up old dead apple-tree wood and playing the bass-viol.* 'A'd pass his life between the two, that 'a would.' He stepped to the door and opened it.

'Father!'

'Ay!' rang thinly from round the corner.

'Here's the barrel tapped, and we all a-waiting!'

A series of dull thuds, that had been heard without for some time past, now ceased; and after the light of a lantern had passed the window and made wheeling rays upon the ceiling inside the eldest of the Dewy family appeared.

3

THE ASSEMBLED QUIRE

William Dewy – otherwise grandfather William – was now about seventy; yet an ardent vitality still preserved a warm and roughened bloom upon his face, which reminded gardeners of the sunny side of a ripe ribstone-pippin;* though a narrow strip of forehead, that was protected from the weather by lying above the line of his hat-brim, seemed to belong to some town man, so gentlemanly was its whiteness. His was a humorous and kindly nature, not unmixed with a frequent melancholy; and he had a firm religious faith. But to his neighbours he had no character in particular. If they saw him pass by their windows when they had been bottling off old mead,* or when they had just been called long-headed* men who might do anything in the world if they chose, they thought concerning him, 'Ah, there's that good-hearted man – open as a child!' If they saw him just after losing a shilling or half-a-crown,* or accidentally letting fall a piece of crockery, they thought, 'There's that poor weak-minded man Dewy again! Ah, he's never done much in the world either!' If he passed when fortune neither smiled nor frowned on them, they merely thought him old William Dewy.

'Ah, so's – here you be! Ah, Michael and Joseph and John – and you too, Leaf! A merry Christmas all! We shall have a rare leg-wood* fire directly, Reub, to reckon by the toughness of the Job I had in cleaving 'em.' As he spoke he threw down an armful of logs which fell in the chimney-corner with a rumble, and looked at them with something of the admiring enmity that he would have bestowed on living people who had been very obstinate in holding their own. 'Come in, grandfather James.'

Old James (grandfather on the maternal side) had simply called as a visitor. He lived in a cottage by himself, and many people considered him a miser; some, rather slovenly in his habits. He now came forward from behind grandfather William, and his stooping figure formed a well-illuminated picture as he passed towards the fireplace. Being by trade a mason, he wore a long linen apron reaching almost to his toes, corduroy breeches and gaiters, which, together with his boots, graduated in tints of whitish-brown by constant friction against lime and stone. He also wore a very stiff fustian* coat, having folds at the elbows and shoulders as unvarying in their arrangement as those in a pair of bellows: the ridges and the projecting parts of the coat collectively exhibiting a shade different from that of the hollows, which were lined with small ditch-like accumulations of stone and mortar-dust. The extremely large side-pockets, sheltered beneath wide flaps, bulged out convexly whether empty or full;

and as he was often engaged to work at buildings far away – his breakfasts and dinners being eaten in a strange chimney-corner, by a garden wall, on a heap of stones, or walking along the road – he carried in these pockets a small tin canister of butter, a small canister of sugar, a small canister of tea, a paper of salt, and a paper of pepper; the bread, cheese, and meat, forming the substance of his meals, hanging up behind him in his basket among the hammers and chisels. If a passer-by looked hard at him when he was drawing forth any of these, 'My buttery,'* he said, with a pinched smile.

'Better try over number seventy-eight before we start, I suppose?' said William, pointing to a heap of old Christmas-carol books on a side table.

'Wi' all my heart,' said the choir generally.

'Number seventy-eight was always a teaser – always. I can mind him ever since I was growing up a hard boy-chap.'*

'But he's a good tune,* and worth a mint o' practice,' said Michael.

'He is; though I've been mad enough wi' that tune at times to seize en and tear en all to linnit.* Ay, he's a splendid carrel* – there's no denying that.'

'The first line is well enough,' said Mr Spinks; 'but when you come to "O, thou man", you make a mess o't.'

'We'll have another go into en, and see what we can make of the martel. Half-an-hour's hammering at en will conquer the toughness of en; I'll warn it.'

''Od rabbit it all!' said Mr Penny, interrupting with a flash of his spectacles, and at the same time clawing at something in the depths of a large side-pocket. 'If so be I hadn't been as scatter-brained and thirtingill* as a chiel I should have called at the schoolhouse wi' a boot as I cam up along. Whatever is coming to me I really can't estimate at all!'

'The brain has its weaknesses,' murmured Mr Spinks, waving his head ominously. Mr Spinks was considered to be a scholar, having once kept a night-school, and always spoke up to that level.

'Well, I must call with en the first thing tomorrow. And I'll empt my pocket o' this last* too, if you don't mind, Mrs Dewy.' He drew forth a last, and placed it on a table at his elbow. The eyes of three or four followed it.

'Well,' said the shoemaker, seeming to perceive that the

interest the object had excited was greater than he had anticipated, and warranted the last's being taken up again and
exhibited, 'now, whose foot do ye suppose this last was made
for? It was made for Geoffrey Day's father, over at Yalbury
Wood. Ah, many's the pair o' boots he've had off the last! Well,
when 'a died, I used the last for Geoffrey, and have ever since,
though a little doctoring was wanted to make it do. Yes, a very
queer natured last it is now, 'a b'lieve,' he continued, turning it
over caressingly. 'Now, you notice that there' (pointing to a
lump of leather bradded* to the toe), 'that's a very bad bunion
that he've had ever since 'a was a boy. Now, this remarkable
large piece' (pointing to a patch nailed to the side), 'shows a'
accident he received by the tread of a horse, that squashed his
foot a'most to a pomace.* The horse-shoe came full-butt* on
this point, you see. And so I've just been over to Geoffrey's, to
know if he wanted his bunion altered or made bigger in the new
pair I'm making.'

During the latter part of this speech Mr Penny's left hand
wandered towards the cider-cup as if the hand had no connection with the person speaking; and bringing his sentence to an
abrupt close all but the extreme margin of the bootmaker's face
was eclipsed by the circular brim of the vessel.

'However, I was going to say,' continued Penny, putting down
the cup, 'I ought to have called at the school' – here he went
groping again in the depths of his pocket – 'to leave this without
fail, though I suppose the first thing tomorrow will do.'

He now drew forth and placed upon the table a boot – small,
light, and prettily shaped – upon the heel of which he had been
operating.

'The new schoolmistress's!'

'Ay, no less, Miss Fancy Day; as neat a little figure of fun as
ever I see, and just husband-high.'*

'Never Geoffrey's daughter Fancy?' said Bowman, as all
glances present converged like wheelspokes upon the boot in the
centre of them.

'Yes, sure,' resumed Mr Penny, regarding the boot as if that
alone were his auditor; ''tis she that's come here schoolmistress.
You knowed his daughter was in training?'

'Strange, isn't it, for her to be here Christmas-night, Master
Penny?'

'Yes; but here she is, 'a b'lieve.'

'I know how she comes here – so I do!' chirruped one of the children.

'Why?' Dick inquired with subtle interest.

'Pa'son Maybold was afraid he couldn't manage us all tomorrow at the dinner, and he talked o' getting her jist to come over and help him hand about the plates, and see we didn't make pigs of ourselves; and that's what she's come for!'

'And that's the boot, then,' continued its mender imaginatively, 'that she'll walk to church in tomorrow morning. I don't care to mend boots I don't make; but there's no knowing what it may lead to, and her father always comes to me.'

There, between the cider-mug and the candle, stood this interesting receptacle of the little unknown's foot; and a very pretty boot it was. A character, in fact – the flexible bend at the instep, the rounded localities of the small nestling toes, scratches from careless scampers now forgotten – all, as repeated in the tell-tale leather, evidencing a nature and a bias.* Dick surveyed it with a delicate feeling that he had no right to do so without having first asked the owner of the foot's permission.

'Now, neighbours, though no common eye can see it,' the shoemaker went on, 'a man in the trade can see the likeness between this boot and that last, although that is so deformed as hardly to recall one of God's creatures, and this is one of as pretty a pair as you'd get for ten-and-sixpence* in Casterbridge. To you, nothing; but 'tis father's voot and daughter's voot to me, as plain as houses.'

I don't doubt there's a likeness, Master Penny – mild likeness – a fantastical* likeness,' said Spinks. 'But I han't got imagination enough to see it, perhaps.'

Mr Penny adjusted his spectacles.

'Now, I'll tell ye what happened to me once on this very point. You used to know Johnson the dairyman, William?'

'Ay, sure; I did.'

'Well, 'twasn't opposite his house, but a little lower down – by his paddock, in front o' Parkmaze Pool. I was a-bearing across towards Bloom's End, and lo and behold, there was a man just brought out o' the Pool, dead; he had un'rayed* for a dip, but not being able to pitch it* just there had gone in flop over his head. Men looked at en; women looked at en; children looked at en; nobody knowed en. He was covered wi' a sheet; but I catched sight of his voot, just showing out as they carried en along. "I don't care what name that man went by," I said, in my way, "but he's John Woodward's brother; I can swear to the family voot." At that very moment up comes John Woodward, weeping and teaving,* "I've lost my brother! I've lost my brother!" '

'Only to think of that!' said Mrs Dewy.

''Tis well enough to know this foot and that foot,' said Mr Spinks. ''Tis long-headed, in fact, as far as feet do go. I know little, 'tis true – I say no more; but show *me* a man's foot, and I'll tell you that man's heart.'

'You must be a cleverer feller, then, than mankind in jineral,' said the tranter.

'Well, that's nothing for me to speak of,' returned Mr Spinks. 'A man lives and learns. Maybe I've read a leaf or two in my time. I don't wish to say anything large, mind you; but nevertheless, maybe I have.'

'Yes, I know,' said Michael soothingly, 'and all the parish knows, that ye've read sommat of everything a'most, and have been a great filler of young folks' brains. Learning's a worthy thing, and ye've got it, Master Spinks.'

'I make no boast, though I may have read and thought a little; and I know – it may be from much perusing, but I make no boast – that by the time a man's head is finished 'tis almost time for him to creep underground. I am over forty-five.'

Mr Spinks emitted a look to signify that if his head was not finished, nobody's head ever could be.

'Talk of knowing people by their feet!' said Reuben. 'Rot me,* my sonnies, then, if I can tell what a man is from all his members put together, oftentimes.'

'But still, look is a good deal,' observed grandfather William absently, moving and balancing his head till the tip of grandfather James's nose was exactly in a right line with William's eye and the mouth of a miniature cavern he was discerning in the fire. 'By the way,' he continued in a fresher voice, and looking up, 'that young creature, the schoolmis'ess, must be sung to tonight wi' the rest? If her ear is as fine as her face, we shall have enough to do to be up-sides* with her.'

'What about her face?' said young Dewy.

'Well, as to that,' Mr Spinks replied, ''tis a face you can hardly gainsay.* A very good pink face, as far as that do go. Still, only a face, when all is said and done.'

'Come, come, Elias Spinks, say she's a pretty maid and have done wi' her,' said the tranter, again preparing to visit the cider-barrel.

4

GOING THE ROUNDS

Shortly after ten o'clock the singing-boys arrived at the tranter's house, which was invariably the place of meeting, and preparations were made for the start. The older men and musicians wore thick coats, with stiff perpendicular collars, and coloured handkerchiefs wound round and round the neck till the end came to hand, over all which they just showed their ears and noses, like people looking over a wall. The remainder, stalwart ruddy men and boys, were dressed mainly in snow-white smock-frocks, embroidered upon the shoulders and breasts in ornamental forms of hearts, diamonds, and zigzags. The cider-mug was emptied for the ninth time, the music-books were arranged, and the pieces finally decided upon. The boys in the meantime put the old horn-lanterns* in order, cut candles into short lengths to fit the lanterns; and, a thin fleece of snow having fallen since the early part of the evening, those who had no leggings went to the stable and wound wisps of hay round their ankles to keep the insidious flakes from the interior of their boots.

Mellstock was a parish of considerable acreage, the hamlets composing it lying at a much greater distance from each other than is ordinarily the case. Hence several hours were consumed in playing and singing within hearing of every family, even if but a single air were bestowed on each. There was Lower Mellstock, the main village; half a mile from this were the church and vicarage, and a few other houses, the spot being rather lonely now, though in past centuries it had been the most thickly populated quarter of the parish. A mile north-east lay the hamlet of Upper Mellstock, where the tranter lived; and at other points knots of cottages, besides solitary farmsteads and dairies.

Old William Dewy, with the violoncello, played the bass; his grandson Dick the treble violin; and Reuben and Michael Mail the tenor and second violins respectively. The singers consisted of four men and seven boys, upon whom devolved the task of carrying and attending to the lanterns, and holding the books open for the players. Directly music was the theme old William ever and instinctively came to the front.

'Now mind, neighbours,' he said, as they all went out one by one at the door, he himself holding it ajar and regarding them with a critical face as they passed, like a shepherd counting out his sheep. 'You two counter-boys,* keep your ears open to Michael's fingering, and don't ye go straying into the treble part along o' Dick and his set, as ye did last year; and mind this especially when we be in "Arise, and hail". Billy Chimlen, don't you sing quite so raving mad as you fain would; and, all o' ye, whatever ye do, keep from making a great scuffle on the ground when we go in at people's gates; but go quietly, so as to strike up all of a sudden, like spirits.'

'Farmer Ledlow's* first?'

'Farmer Ledlow's first; the rest as usual.'

'And, Voss,' said the tranter terminatively, 'you keep house here till about half-past two; then heat the metheglin* and cider in the warmer* you'll find turned up upon the copper; and bring it wi' the victuals to church-hatch,* as th'st know.'

Just before the clock struck twelve they lighted the lanterns and started. The moon, in her third quarter, had risen since the snowstorm; but the dense accumulation of snow-cloud weakened her power to a faint twilight which was rather pervasive of the landscape than traceable to the sky. The breeze had gone down, and the rustle of their feet and tones of their speech echoed with an alert rebound from every post, boundary-stone, and ancient wall they passed, even where the distance of the echo's origin was less than a few yards. Beyond their own slight noises nothing was to be heard save the occasional bark of foxes in the direction of Yalbury Wood, or the brush of a rabbit among the grass now and then as it scampered out of their way.

Most of the outlying homesteads and hamlets had been visited by about two o'clock; they then passed across the outskirts of a wooded park toward the main village, nobody being at home at the Manor.* Pursuing no recognised track, great care was necessary in walking lest their faces should come in contact with the low-hanging boughs of the old lime-trees, which in many spots formed dense overgrowths of interlaced branches.

'Times have changed from the times they used to be,' said Mail, regarding nobody can tell what interesting old panoramas with an inward eye, and letting his outward glance rest on the ground because it was as convenient a position as any. 'People don't care much about us now! I've been thinking we must be almost the last left in the county of the old string players? Barrel-organs, and the things next door to 'em that you blow wi' your foot, have come in terribly of late years.'

'Ay!' said Bowman shaking his head; and old William on seeing him did the same thing.

'More's the pity,' replied another. 'Time was – long and merry ago now! – when not one of the varmits* was to be heard of; but it served some of the quires right. They should have stuck to strings as we did, and kept out clarinets, and done away with serpents.* If you'd thrive in musical religion, stick to strings, says I.'

'Strings be safe soul-lifters, as far as that do go,' said Mr Spinks.

'Yet there's worse things than serpents,' said Mr Penny. 'Old things pass away, 'tis true; but a serpent was a good old note: a deep rich note was the serpent.'

'Clar'nets, however, be bad, at all times,' said Michael Mail. 'One Christmas – years agone now, years – I went the rounds wi' the Weatherbury quire. 'Twas a hard frosty night, and the keys of all the clar'nets froze – ah, they did freeze! – so that 'twas like drawing a cork every time a key was opened; and the players o' 'em had to go into a hedger-and-ditcher's* chimley-corner, and thaw their clar'nets every now and then. An icicle o' spet hung down from the end of every man's clar'net a span long; and as to fingers – well, there, if ye'll believe me, we had no fingers at all, to our knowing.'

'I can well bring back to my mind,' said Mr Penny, 'what I said to poor Joseph Ryme (who took the treble part in Chalk-Newton Church for two-and-forty year) when they thought of having clar'nets there. "Joseph," I said says I, "depend upon't, if so be you have them tooting clar'nets you'll spoil the whole set-out. Clar'nets were not made for the service of the Lard; you can see it by looking at 'em," I said. And what came o't? Why, souls, the parson set up a barrel-organ on his own account within two years o' the time I spoke, and the old quire went to nothing.'

'As far as look is concerned,' said the tranter, 'I don't for my part see that a fiddle is much nearer heaven than a clar'net. 'Tis further off. There's always a rakish, scampish twist about a fiddle's looks that seems to say the Wicked One* had a hand in making o'en; while angels be supposed to play clar'nets in heaven, or som'at like 'em, if ye may believe picters.'

'Robert Penny, you was in the right,' broke in the eldest Dewy. 'They should ha' stuck to strings. Your brass-man is a rafting* dog – well and good; your reed-man is a dab* at stirring ye – well and good; your drum-man is a rare bowel-shaker – good again. But I don't care who hears me say it, nothing will spak to your heart wi' the sweetness o' the man of strings!'

'Strings for ever!' said little Jimmy.

'Strings alone would have held their ground against all the newcomers in creation.' ('True, true!' said Bowman.) 'But clarinets was death.' ('Death they was!' said Mr Penny.) 'And harmonions,' William continued in a louder voice, and getting excited by these signs of approval, 'harmonions and barrel-organs' ('Ah!' and groans from Spinks) 'be miserable – what shall I call 'em? – miserable—'

'Sinners,' suggested Jimmy, who made large strides like the men and did not lag behind with the other little boys.

'Miserable dumbledores!'*

'Right, William, and so they be – miserable dumbledores!' said the choir with unanimity.

By this time they were crossing to a gate in the direction of the school which, standing on a slight eminence at the junction of three ways, now rose in unvarying and dark flatness against the sky. The instruments were returned, and all the band entered the school enclosure, enjoined by old William to keep upon the grass.

'Number seventy-eight,' he softly gave out as they formed round in a semicircle, the boys opening the lanterns to get a clearer light, and directing their rays on the books.

Then passed forth into the quiet night an ancient and time-worn hymn, embodying a quaint Christianity in words orally transmitted from father to son through several generations down to the present characters, who sang them out right earnestly:

Remember Adam's fall,
  O thou Man:
Remember Adam's fall
  From Heaven to Hell.
Remember Adam's fall;
How he hath condemn'd all
In Hell perpetual
  There for to dwell.

Remember God's goodnesse,
  O thou Man:
Remember God's goodnesse,
  His promise made.
Remember God's goodnesse;
He sent His Son sinlesse
Our ails for to redress;
  Be not afraid!

In Bethlehem He was born,
  O thou Man:
In Bethlehem He was born,
  For mankind's sake.
In Bethlehem He was born,
Christmas-day i' the morn:
Our Saviour thought no scorn
  Our faults to take.

Give thanks to God alway,
  O thou Man:
Give thanks to God alway
  With heart-most joy.
Give thanks to God alway
On this our joyful day:
Let all men sing and say,
  Holy, Holy!

Having concluded the last note they listened for a minute or
two, but found that no sound issued from the schoolhouse.

'Four breaths, and then, "O, what unbounded goodness!"
number fifty-nine,' said William.

This was duly gone through, and no notice whatever seemed
to be taken of the performance.

'Good guide us, surely 'tisn't a' empty house, as befell us in the year thirty-nine and forty-three!'* said old Dewy.

'Perhaps she's jist come from some musical city, and sneers at our doings?' the tranter whispered.

''Od rabbit her!' said Mr Penny, with an annihilating look at a corner of the school chimney, 'I don't quite stomach her, if this is it. Your plain music well done is as worthy as your other sort done bad, a' b'lieve, souls; so say I.'

'Four breaths, and then the last,' said the leader authoritatively. '"Rejoice, ye Tenants of the Earth", number sixty-four.'

At the close, waiting yet another minute, he said in a clear loud voice, as he had said in the village at that hour and season for the previous forty years –

'A merry Christmas to ye!'

5

THE LISTENERS

When the expectant stillness consequent upon the exclamation had nearly died out of them all, an increasing light made itself visible in one of the windows of the upper floor. It came so close to the blind that the exact position of the flame could be perceived from the outside. Remaining steady for an instant, the blind went upward from before it, revealing to thirty concentrated eyes a young girl framed as a picture by the window architrave, and unconsciously illuminating her countenance to a vivid brightness by a candle she held in her left hand, close to her face, her right hand being extended to the side of the window. She was wrapped in a white robe of some kind, whilst down her shoulders fell a twining profusion of marvellously rich hair, in a wild disorder which proclaimed it to be only during the invisible hours of the night that such a condition was discoverable. Her bright eyes were looking into the grey world outside with an uncertain expression, oscillating between courage and shyness, which, as she recognised the semicircular group of dark forms gathered before her, transformed itself into pleasant resolution.

Opening the window, she said lightly and warmly—

'Thank you, singers, thank you!'

Together went the window quickly and quietly, and the blind started downward on its return to its place. Her fair forehead and eyes vanished; her little mouth; her neck and shoulders; all of her. Then the spot of candlelight shone nebulously as before; then it moved away.

'How pretty!' exclaimed Dick Dewy.

'If she'd been rale wexwork she couldn't ha' been comelier,' said Michael Mail.

'As near a thing to a spiritual vision as ever *I* wish to see!' said tranter Dewy.

'O, sich I never, never see!' said Leaf fervently.

All the rest, after clearing their throats and adjusting their hats, agreed that such a sight was worth singing for.

'Now to Farmer Shiner's, and then replenish our insides, father?' said the tranter.

'Wi' all my heart,' said old William, shouldering his bass-viol.

Farmer Shiner's was a queer lump of a house, standing at the corner of a lane that ran into the principal thoroughfare. The upper windows were much wider than they were high, and this feature, together with a broad bay-window where the door might have been expected, gave it by day the aspect of a human countenance turned askance, and wearing a sly and wicked leer. Tonight nothing was visible but the outline of the roof upon the sky.

The front of this building was reached, and the preliminaries arranged as usual.

'Four breaths, and number thirty-two, "Behold the Morning Star",' said old William.

They had reached the end of the second verse, and the fiddlers were doing the up bow-stroke previously to pouring forth the opening chord of the third verse, when, without a light appearing or any signal being given a roaring voice exclaimed—

'Shut up, woll 'ee! Don't make your blaring row here! A feller wi' a headache enough to split his skull likes a quiet night!'

Slam went the window.

'Hullo, that's a' ugly blow for we!' said the tranter, in a keenly appreciative voice, and turning to his companions.

'Finish the carrel, all who be friends of harmony!' commanded old William; and they continued to the end.

'Four breaths, and number nineteen!' said William firmly. 'Give it him well; the quire can't be insulted in this manner!'

A light now flashed into existence, the window opened, and the farmer stood revealed as one in a terrific passion.

'Drown en! – drown en!' the tranter cried, fiddling frantically. 'Play fortissimy, and drown his spaking!'

'Fortissimy!' said Michael Mail, and the music and singing waxed so loud that it was impossible to know what Mr Shiner had said, was saying, or was about to say; but wildly flinging his arms and body about in the forms of capital Xs and Ys, he appeared to utter enough invectives to consign the whole parish to perdition.

'Very onseemly – very!' said old William, as they retired. 'Never such a dreadful scene in the whole round o' my carrel practice – never! And he a churchwarden!'

'Only a drap o' drink got into his head,' said the tranter. 'Man's well enough when he's in his religious frame. He's in his worldly frame now. Must ask en to our bit of a party tomorrow night, I suppose, and so put en in humour again. We bear no mortal man ill-will.'

They now crossed Mellstock Bridge, and went along an embowered path beside the Froom* towards the church and vicarage, meeting Voss with the hot mead and bread-and-cheese as they were approaching the churchyard. This determined them to eat and drink before proceeding further, and they entered the church and ascended to the gallery. The lanterns were opened, and the whole body sat round against the walls on benches and whatever else was available, and made a hearty meal. In the pauses of conversation there could be heard through the floor overhead a little world of undertones and creaks from the halting clockwork, which never spread further than the tower they were born in, and raised in the more meditative minds a fancy that here lay the direct pathway of Time.

Having done eating and drinking they again tuned the instruments, and once more the party emerged into the night air.

'Where's Dick?' said old Dewy.

Every man looked round upon every other man, as if Dick might have been transmuted into one or the other; and then they said they didn't know.

'Well now, that's what I call very nasty of Master Dicky, that I do,' said Michael Mail.

'He've clinked off home-along,* depend upon't,' another suggested, though not quite believing that he had.

'Dick!' exclaimed the tranter, and his voice rolled sonorously forth among the yews.

He suspended his muscles rigid as stone whilst listening for an answer, and finding he listened in vain, turned to the assemblage.

'The treble man* too! Now if he'd been a tenor or counter chap, we might ha' contrived the rest o't without en, you see. But for a quire to lose the treble, why, my sonnies, you may so well lose your . . .' The tranter paused, unable to mention an image vast enough for the occasion.

'Your head at once,' suggested Mr Penny.

The tranter moved a pace as if it were puerile of people to complete sentences when there were more pressing things to be done.

'Was ever heard such a thing as a young man leaving his work half done and turning tail like this!'

'Never,' replied Bowman, in a tone signifying that he was the last man in the world to wish to withhold the formal finish required of him.

'I hope no fatal tragedy has overtook the lad!' said his grandfather.

'O no,' replied tranter Dewy placidly. 'Wonder where he's put that there fiddle of his. Why that fiddle cost thirty shillings, and good words besides. Somewhere in the damp, without doubt; that instrument will be unglued and spoilt in ten minutes – ten! ay, two.'

'What in the name o' righteousness can have happened?' said old William, more uneasily. 'Perhaps he's drownded!'

Leaving their lanterns and instruments in the belfry they retraced their steps along the waterside track. 'A strapping lad like Dick d'know better than let anything happen onawares,' Reuben remarked. 'There's sure to be some poor little scram* reason for't staring us in the face all the while.' He lowered his voice to a mysterious tone: 'Neighbours, have ye noticed any sign of a scornful woman in his head, or suchlike?'

'Not a glimmer of such a body. He's as clear as water yet.'

'And Dicky said he should never marry,' cried Jimmy, 'but live at home always along wi' mother and we!'

'Ay, ay, my sonny; every lad has said that in his time.'

They had now again reached the precincts of Mr Shiner's, but hearing nobody in that direction, one or two went across to the schoolhouse. A light was still burning in the bedroom, and though the blind was down the window had been slightly opened, as if to admit the distant notes of the carollers to the ears of the occupant of the room.

Opposite the window, leaning motionless against a beech tree, was the lost man, his arms folded, his head thrown back, his eyes fixed upon the illuminated lattice.

'Why, Dick, is that thee? What b'st* doing here?' Dick's body instantly flew into a more rational attitude, and his head was seen to turn east and west in the gloom as if endeavouring to discern some proper answer to that question; and at last he said in rather feeble accents—

'Nothing, father.'

'Th'st take long enough time about it then, upon my body,' said the tranter as they all turned anew towards the vicarage.

'I thought you hadn't done having snap* in the gallery,' said Dick.

'Why, we've been traypsing and rambling about, looking everywhere, and thinking you'd done fifty deathly things, and here have you been at nothing at all!'

'The stupidness lies in that point of it being nothing at all,' murmured Mr Spinks.

The vicarage front was their next field of operation, and Mr Maybold, the lately arrived incumbent,* duly received his share of the night's harmonies. It was hoped that by reason of his profession he would have been led to open the window, and an extra carol in quick time was added to draw him forth. But Mr Maybold made no stir.

'A bad sign!' said old William, shaking his head.

However, at that same instant a musical voice was heard exclaiming from inner depths of bedclothes—

'Thanks, villagers!'

'What did he say?' asked Bowman, who was rather dull of hearing. Bowman's voice, being therefore loud, had been heard by the vicar within.

'I said, "Thanks, villagers!"' cried the vicar again.

'Oh, we didn't hear 'ee the first time!' cried Bowman.

'Now don't for heaven's sake spoil the young man's temper by answering like that!' said the tranter.

'You won't do that, my friends!' the vicar shouted.

'Well to be sure, what ears!' said Mr Penny in a whisper. 'Beats any horse or dog in the parish, and depend upon't that's a sign he's a proper clever chap.'

'We shall see that in time,' said the tranter.

Old William, in his gratitude for such thanks from a comparatively new inhabitant, was anxious to play all the tunes over again; but renounced his desire on being reminded by Reuben that it would be best to leave well alone.

'Now putting two and two together,' the tranter continued, as they went their way over the hill, and across to the last remaining houses; 'that is, in the form of that young female vision we zeed just now, and this young tenor-voiced parson, my belief is she'll wind en round her finger, and twist the pore young feller about like the figure of 8 – that she will, my sonnies.'

6

CHRISTMAS MORNING

The choir at last reached their beds, and slept like the rest of the parish. Dick's slumbers, through the three or four hours remaining for rest, were disturbed and slight; an exhaustive variation upon the incidents that had passed that night in connection with the school window going on in his brain every moment of the time.

In the morning, do what he would – go upstairs, downstairs, out of doors, speak of the wind and weather, or what not – he could not refrain from an unceasing renewal, in imagination, of that interesting enactment. Tilted on the edge of one foot he stood beside the fireplace, watching his mother grilling rashers; but there was nothing in grilling, he thought, unless the Vision grilled. The limp rasher hung down between the bars of the gridiron* like a cat in a child's arms; but there was nothing in similes unless She uttered them. He looked at the daylight shadows of a yellow hue, dancing with the firelight shadows in blue on the whitewashed chimney corner, but there was nothing in shadows. 'Perhaps the new young wom—sch—Miss Fancy Day will sing in church with us this morning,' he said.

The tranter looked a long time before he replied, 'I fancy she will; and yet I fancy she won't.'

Dick implied that such a remark was rather to be tolerated than admired; though deliberateness in speech was known to have, as a rule, more to do with the machinery of the tranter's throat than with the matter enunciated.

They made preparations for going to church as usual; Dick with extreme alacrity, though he would not definitely consider why he was so religious. His wonderful nicety in brushing and cleaning his best light boots had features which elevated it to the rank of an art. Every particle and speck of last week's mud was scraped and brushed from toe and heel; new blacking* from the packet was carefully mixed and made use of, regardless of expense. A coat was laid on and polished; then another coat for increased blackness; and lastly a third, to give the perfect and mirror-like jet which the hoped-for rencounter demanded.

It being Christmas Day, the tranter prepared himself with Sunday particularity. Loud sousing and snorting noises were heard to proceed from a tub in the back quarters of the dwelling, proclaiming that he was there performing his great Sunday wash, lasting half-an-hour, to which his washings on working-day mornings were mere flashes in the pan. Vanishing into the outhouse with a large brown towel, and the above-named bubblings and snortings being carried on for about twenty minutes, the tranter would appear round the edge of the door, smelling like a summer fog, and looking as if he had just narrowly escaped a watery grave with the loss of much of his clothes, having since been weeping bitterly till his eyes were red; a crystal drop of water hanging ornamentally at the bottom of each ear, one at the tip of his nose, and others in the form of spangles about his hair.

After a great deal of crunching upon the sanded stone floor by the feet of father, son, and grandson as they moved to and fro in these preparations, the bass-viol and fiddles were taken from their nook, and the strings examined and screwed a little above concert-pitch,* that they might keep their tone when the service began, to obviate the awkward contingency of having to retune them at the back of the gallery during a cough, sneeze, or amen – an inconvenience which had been known to arise in damp wintry weather.

The three left the door and paced down Mellstock Lane and

across the ewe-lease, bearing under their arms the instruments in faded green-baize bags, and old brown music-books* in their hands; Dick continually finding himself in advance of the other two, and the tranter moving on with toes turned outwards to an enormous angle.

At the foot of an incline the church became visible through the north gate, or 'church hatch', as it was called here. Seven agile figures in a clump were observable beyond, which proved to be the choristers waiting; sitting on an altar-tomb* to pass the time, and letting their heels dangle against it. The musicians being now in sight the youthful party scampered off and rattled up the old wooden stairs of the gallery like a regiment of cavalry; the other boys of the parish waiting outside and observing birds, cats, and other creatures till the vicar entered, when they suddenly subsided into sober church-goers, and passed down the aisle with echoing heels.

The gallery of Mellstock Church* had a status and sentiment of its own. A stranger there was regarded with a feeling altogether differing from that of the congregation below towards him. Banished from the nave as an intruder whom no originality could make interesting, he was received above as a curiosity that no unfitness could render dull. The gallery, too, looked down upon and knew the habits of the nave to its remotest peculiarity, and had an extensive stock of exclusive information about it; whilst the nave knew nothing of the gallery folk, as gallery folk, beyond their loud-sounding minims and chest notes. Such topics as that the clerk* was always chewing tobacco except at the moment of crying amen; that he had a dust-hole* in his pew; that during the sermon certain young daughters of the village had left off caring to read anything so mild as the marriage service for some years, and now regularly studied the one which chronologically follows it;* that a pair of lovers touched fingers through a knot-hole between their pews in the manner ordained by their great exemplars, Pyramus and Thisbe;* that Mrs Ledlow, the farmer's wife, counted her money and reckoned her week's marketing expenses during the first lesson – all news to those below – were stale subjects here.

Old William sat in the centre of the front row, his violon cello between his knees and two singers on each hand. Behind him, on the left, came the treble singers and Dick; and on the right the tranter and the tenors. Further back was old Mail with the altos and supernumeraries.

But before they had taken their places, and whilst they were standing in a circle at the back of the gallery practising a psalm or two, Dick cast his eyes over his grandfather's shoulder, and saw the vision of the past night enter the porch-door as methodically as if she had never been a vision at all. A new atmosphere seemed suddenly to be puffed into the ancient edifice by her movement, which made Dick's body and soul tingle with novel sensations. Directed by Shiner, the churchwarden,* she proceeded to the small aisle on the north side of the chancel, a spot now allotted to a throng of Sunday-school girls, and distinctly visible from the gallery-front by looking under the curve of the furthermost arch on that side.

Before this moment the church had seemed comparatively empty – now it was thronged; and as Miss Fancy rose from her knees and looked around her for a permanent place in which to deposit herself – finally choosing the remotest corner – Dick began to breathe more freely the warm new air she had brought with her; to feel rushings of blood, and to have impressions that there was a tie between her and himself visible to all the congregation.

Ever afterwards the young man could recollect individually each part of the service of that bright Christmas morning, and the trifling occurrences which took place as its minutes slowly drew along; the duties of that day dividing themselves by a complete line from the services of other times. The tunes they that morning essayed remained with him for years, apart from all others; also the text; also the appearance of the layer of dust upon the capitals of the piers;* that the holly-bough in the chancel archway was hung a little out of the centre – all the ideas, in short, that creep into the mind when reason is only exercising its lowest activity through the eye.

By chance or by fate, another young man who attended Mellstock Church on that Christmas morning had towards the end of the service the same instinctive perception of an interesting presence, in the shape of the same bright maiden, though his emotion reached a far less developed stage. And there was this difference, too, that the person in question was surprised at his condition, and sedulously endeavoured to reduce himself to his normal state of mind. He was the young vicar, Mr Maybold.

The music on Christmas mornings was frequently below the standard of church-performances at other times. The boys were sleepy from the heavy exertions of the night; the men were slightly wearied; and now, in addition to these constant reasons, there was a dampness in the atmosphere that still further aggravated the evil. Their strings, from the recent long exposure to the night air, rose whole semitones, and snapped with a loud twang at the most silent moment; which necessitated more retiring than ever to the back of the gallery, and made the gallery throats quite husky with the quantity of coughing and hemming required for tuning in. The vicar looked cross.

When the singing was in progress there was suddenly discovered to be a strong and shrill reinforcement from some point, ultimately found to be the school-girls' aisle. At every attempt it grew bolder and more distinct. At the third time of singing, these intrusive feminine voices were as mighty as those of the regular singers; in fact, the flood of sound from this quarter assumed such an individuality, that it had a time, a key, almost a tune of its own, surging upwards when the gallery plunged downwards, and the reverse.

Now this had never happened before within the memory of man. The girls, like the rest of the congregation, had always been humble and respectful followers of the gallery; singing at sixes and sevens* if without gallery leaders; never interfering with the ordinances of these practised artists – having no will, union, power, or proclivity except it was given them from the established choir enthroned above them.

A good deal of desperation became noticeable in the gallery throats and strings, which continued throughout the musical portion of the service. Directly the fiddles were laid down, Mr Penny's spectacles put in their sheath, and the text had been given out, an indignant whispering began.

'Did ye hear that, souls?' Mr Penny said, in a groaning breath.

'Brazen-faced hussies!' said Bowman.

'True; why, they were every note as loud as we, fiddles and all, if not louder!'

'Fiddles and all!' echoed Bowman bitterly.

'Shall anything saucier be found than united 'ooman?' Mr Spinks murmured.

'What I want to know is,' said the tranter (as if he knew already, but that civilisation required the form of words), 'what business people have to tell maidens to sing like that when they don't sit in a gallery, and never have entered one in their lives? That's the question, my sonnies.'

'"Tis the gallery have got to sing, all the world knows,' said Mr Penny. 'Why, souls, what's the use o' the ancients spending scores of pounds to build galleries if people down in the lowest depths of the church sing like that at a moment's notice?'

'Really, I think we useless ones had better march out of church, fiddles and all!' said Mr Spinks, with a laugh which, to a stranger, would have sounded mild and real. Only the initiated body of men he addressed could understand the horrible bitterness of irony that lurked under the quiet words 'useless ones', and the ghastliness of the laughter apparently so natural.

'Never mind! Let 'em sing too – 'twill make it all the louder – hee, hee!' said Leaf.

'Thomas Leaf, Thomas Leaf! Where have you lived all your life?' said grandfather William sternly.

The quailing Leaf tried to look as if he had lived nowhere at all.

'When all's said and done, my sonnies,' Reuben said, 'there'd have been no real harm in their singing if they had let nobody hear 'em, and only jined in now and then.'

'None at all,' said Mr Penny. 'But though I don't wish to accuse people wrongfully, I'd say before my lord judge that I could hear every note o' that last psalm come from 'em as much as from us – every note as if 'twas their own.'

'Know it! ah, I should think I did know it!' Mr Spinks was heard to observe at this moment without reference to his fellow-players – shaking his head at some idea he seemed to see floating before him, and smiling as if he were attending a funeral at the time. 'Ah, do I or don't I know it!'

No one said 'Know what?' because all were aware from experience that what he knew would declare itself in process of time.

'I could fancy last night that we should have some trouble wi' that young man,' said the tranter, pending the continuance of Spinks's speech, and looking towards the unconscious Mr Maybold in the pulpit.

'*I* fancy,' said old William, rather severely, 'I fancy there's too much whispering going on to be of any spiritual use to gentle or simple.'* Then folding his lips and concentrating his glance on the vicar, he implied that none but the ignorant would speak again; and accordingly there was silence in the gallery, Mr Spinks's telling speech remaining for ever unspoken.

Dick had said nothing, and the tranter little, on this episode of the morning; for Mrs Dewy at breakfast expressed it as her intention to invite the youthful leader of the culprits to the small party it was customary with them to have on Christmas night – a piece of knowledge which had given a particular brightness to Dick's reflections since he had received it. And in the tranter's slightly cynical nature, party feeling was weaker than in the other members of the choir, though friendliness and faithful partnership still sustained in him a hearty earnestness on their account.

7

THE TRANTER'S PARTY

During the afternoon unusual activity was seen to prevail about the precincts of tranter Dewy's house. The flagstone floor was swept of dust, and a sprinkling of the finest yellow sand from the innermost stratum of the adjoining sand-pit lightly scattered thereupon. Then were produced large knives and forks, which had been shrouded in darkness and grease since the last occasion of the kind, and bearing upon their sides, 'Shear-steel,* warranted', in such emphatic letters of assurance, that the warranter's name was not required as further proof, and not given. The key was left in the tap of the cider-barrel instead of being carried in a pocket. And finally the tranter had to stand up in the room and let his wife wheel him round like a turnstile, to see if anything discreditable was visible in his appearance.

'Stand still till I've been for the scissors,' said Mrs Dewy.

The tranter stood as still as a sentinel at the challenge.

The only repairs necessary were a trimming of one or two whiskers that had extended beyond the general contour of the mass; a like trimming of a slightly frayed edge visible on his shirt-collar; and a final tug at a grey hair – to all of which operations he submitted in resigned silence, except the last, which produced a mild 'Come, come, Ann,' by way of expostulation.

'Really, Reuben, 'tis quite a disgrace to see such a man,' said Mrs Dewy, with the severity justifiable in a long-tried companion, giving him another turn round, and picking several of Smiler's hairs from the shoulder of his coat. Reuben's thoughts seemed engaged elsewhere, and he yawned. 'And the collar of your coat is a shame to behold – so plastered with dirt, or dust, or grease, or something. Why, wherever could you have got it?'

''Tis my warm nater in summertime, I suppose. I always did get in such a heat when I bustle about.'

'Ay, the Dewys always were such a coarse-skinned family. There's your brother Bob just as bad – as fat as a porpoise – wi' his low, mean "How'st do, Ann?" whenever he meets me. I'd "How'st do" him indeed! If the sun only shines out a minute, there be you all streaming in the face – I never see!'

'If I be hot weekdays, I must be hot Sundays.'

'If any of the girls should turn after* their father 'twill be a bad look-out for 'em, poor things! None of my family was sich vulgar sweaters, not one of 'em. But, Lord-a-mercy, the Dewys! I don't know how ever I cam' into such a family!'

'Your woman's weakness when I asked ye to jine us. That's how it was, I suppose.' But the tranter appeared to have heard some such words from his wife before, and hence his answer had not the energy it might have shown if the inquiry had possessed the charm of novelty.

'You never did look so well in a pair o' trousers as in them,' she continued in the same unimpassioned voice, so that the unfriendly criticism of the Dewy family seemed to have been more normal than spontaneous. 'Such a cheap pair as 'twas too. As big as any man could wish to have, and lined inside, and double-lined in the lower parts, and an extra piece of stiffening at the bottom. And 'tis a nice high cut that comes up right under your armpits, and there's enough turned down inside the seams to make half a pair more, besides a piece of cloth left that will make an honest waistcoat – all by my contriving in buying the stuff at a bargain, and having it made up under my eye. It only shows what may be done by taking a little trouble, and not going straight to the rascally tailors.'

The discourse was cut short by the sudden appearance of Charley on the scene, with a face and hands of hideous blackness, and a nose like a guttering candle. Why, on that particularly cleanly afternoon he should have discovered that the chimney-crook* and chain from which the hams were suspended should have possessed more merits and general interest as playthings than any other articles in the house, is a question for nursing mothers to decide. However, the humour seemed to lie in the result being, as has been seen, that any given player with these articles was in the long-run daubed with soot. The last that was seen of Charley by daylight after this piece of ingenuity was when in the act of vanishing from his father's presence round the corner of the house – looking back over his shoulder with an expression of great sin on his face, like Cain* as the Outcast in Bible pictures.

The guests had all assembled, and the tranter's party had reached that degree of development which accords with ten o'clock p.m. in rural assemblies. At that hour the sound of a fiddle in process of tuning was heard from the inner pantry.

'That's Dick,' said the tranter. 'That lad's crazy for a jig.'

'Dick! Now I cannot – really, I cannot have any dancing at all till Christmas Day is out,' said old William emphatically. 'When the clock ha' done striking twelve, dance as much as ye like.'

'Well, I must say there's reason in that, William,' said Mrs Penny. 'If you do have a party on Christmas night, 'tis only fair and honourable to the Church to have it a sit-still party. Jigging parties be all very well, and this, that, and therefore; but a jigging party looks suspicious now. O yes; stop till the clock strikes, young folk – so say I.'

It happened that some warm mead accidentally got into Mr Spinks's head about this time.

'Dancing,' he said, 'is a most strengthening, livening, and courting movement, 'specially with a little beverage added! And dancing is good. But why disturb what is ordained, Richard and Reuben, and the company zhinerally? Why, I ask, as far as that do go?'

'Then nothing till after twelve,' said William.

Though Reuben and his wife ruled on social points, religious questions were mostly disposed of by the old man, whose firmness on this head quite counterbalanced a certain weakness in his handling of domestic matters. The hopes of the younger members of the household were therefore relegated to a distance of one hour and three quarters – a result that took visible shape in them by a remote and listless look about the eyes – the singing of songs being permitted in the interim.

At five minutes to twelve the soft tuning was again heard in the back quarters; and when at length the clock had whizzed forth the last stroke, Dick appeared ready primed, and the instruments were boldly handled; old William very readily taking the bass-viol from its accustomed nail, and touching the strings as irreligiously as could be desired.

The country-dance called the 'Triumph, or Follow my Lover', was the figure with which they opened. The tranter took for his partner Mrs Penny, and Mrs Dewy was chosen by Mr Penny, who made so much of his limited height by a judicious carriage of the head, straightening of the back, and important flashes of his spectacle-glasses, that he seemed almost as tall as the tranter. Mr Shiner, age about thirty-five, farmer and churchwarden, a character principally composed of a crimson stare, vigorous breath, and a watch-chain, with a mouth hanging on a dark smile but never smiling, had come quite willingly to the party, and showed a wondrous obliviousness of all his antics on the previous night. But the comely, slender, prettily dressed prize Fancy Day fell to Dick's lot, in spite of some private machinations of the farmer, for the reason that Mr Shiner, as a richer man, had shown too much assurance in asking the favour, whilst Dick had been duly courteous.

We gain a good view of our heroine as she advances to her place in the ladies' line. She belonged to the taller division of middle height. Flexibility was her first characteristic, by which she appeared to enjoy the most easeful rest when she was in gliding motion. Her dark eyes – arched by brows of so keen, slender, and soft a curve that they resembled nothing so much as two slurs in music* – showed primarily a bright sparkle each. This was softened by a frequent thoughtfulness, yet not so frequent as to do away, for more than a few minutes at a time, with a certain coquettishness; which in its turn was never so decided as to banish honesty. Her lips imitated her brows in their clearly cut outline and softness of bend; and her nose was well shaped – which is saying a great deal, when it is remembered that there are a hundred pretty mouths and eyes for one pretty nose. Add to this, plentiful knots of dark-brown hair, a gauzy dress of white with blue facings; and the slightest idea may be gained of the young maiden who showed, amidst the rest of the dancing-ladies, like a flower among vegetables. And so the dance proceeded. Mr Shiner, according to the interesting rule laid down, deserted his own partner and made off down the middle with this fair one of Dick's – the pair appearing from the top of the room like two persons tripping down a lane to be married. Dick trotted behind with what was intended to be a look of composure, but which was, in fact, a rather silly expression of feature – implying, with too much earnestness, that such an elopement could not be tolerated. Then they turned and came back, when Dick grew more rigid around his mouth, and blushed with ingenuous ardour as he joined hands with the rival and formed the arch over his lady's head, which presumably gave the figure its name; relinquishing her again at setting to partners, when Mr Shiner's new chain quivered in every link, and all the loose flesh upon the tranter – who here came into action again – shook like jelly. Mrs Penny, being always rather concerned for her personal safety when she danced with the tranter, fixed her face to a chronic smile of timidity the whole time it lasted – a peculiarity which filled her features with wrinkles, and reduced her eyes to little straight lines like hyphens, as she jigged up and down opposite him; repeating in her own person not only his proper movements, but also the minor flourishes which the richness of the tranter's imagination led him to introduce from time to time – an imitation which had about it something of slavish obedience, not unmixed with fear.

The ear-rings of the ladies now flung themselves wildly about, turning violent somersaults, banging this way and that, and then swinging quietly against the ears sustaining them. Mrs Crumpler – a heavy woman, who, for some reason which nobody ever thought worth inquiry, danced in a clean apron – moved so smoothly through the figure that her feet were never seen; conveying to imaginative minds the idea that she rolled on castors.

Minute after minute glided by, and the party reached the period when ladies' back-hair begins to look forgotten and dissipated; when a perceptible dampness makes itself apparent upon the faces even of delicate girls – a ghastly dew having for some time rained from the features of their masculine partners; when skirts begin to be torn out of their gathers; when elderly people, who have stood up to please their juniors, begin to feel sundry small tremblings in the region of the knees, and to wish the interminable dance was at Jericho;* when (at country parties of the thorough sort) waistcoats begin to be unbuttoned, and when the fiddlers' chairs have been wriggled, by the frantic bowing of their occupiers, to a distance of about two feet from where they originally stood.

Fancy was dancing with Mr Shiner. Dick knew that Fancy, by the law of good manners, was bound to dance as pleasantly with one partner as with another; yet he could not help suggesting to himself that she need not have put *quite* so much spirit into her steps, nor smiled *quite* so frequently whilst in the farmer's hands.

'I'm afraid you didn't cast off,'* said Dick mildly to Mr Shiner, before the latter man's watch-chain had done vibrating from a recent whirl.

Fancy made a motion of accepting the correction; but her partner took no notice, and proceeded with the next movement with an affectionate bend towards her.

'That Shiner's too fond of her,' the young man said to himself as he watched them. They came to the top again, Fancy smiling warmly towards her partner, and went to their places.

'Mr Shiner, you didn't cast off,' said Dick, for want of something else to demolish him with; casting off himself, and being put out at the farmer's irregularity.

'Perhaps I shan't cast off for any man,' said Mr Shiner.

'I think you ought to, sir.'

Dick's partner, a young lady of the name of Lizzy – called Lizz for short – tried to mollify.

'I can't say that I myself have much feeling for casting off,' she said.

'Nor I,' said Mrs Penny, following up the argument; 'especially if a friend and neighbour is set against it. Not but that 'tis a terrible tasty thing in good hands and well done; yes, indeed, so say I.'

'All I meant was,' said Dick, rather sorry that he had spoken correctly to a guest, 'that 'tis in the dance; and a man has hardly any right to hack and mangle what was ordained by the regular dance-maker, who, I daresay, got his living by making 'em, and thought of nothing else all his life.'

'I don't like casting off: then very well; I cast off for no dance-maker that ever lived.'

Dick now appeared to be doing mental arithmetic, the act being really an effort to present to himself, in an abstract form, how far an argument with a formidable rival ought to be carried when that rival was his mother's guest. The deadlock was put an end to by the stamping arrival up the middle of the tranter, who, despising minutiae on principle, started a theme of his own.

'I assure you, neighbours,' he said, 'the heat of my frame no tongue can tell!' He looked around and endeavoured to give, by a forcible gaze of self-sympathy, some faint idea of the truth.

Mrs Dewy formed one of the next couple.

'Yes,' she said in an auxiliary tone, 'Reuben always was such a hot man.'

Mrs Penny implied the species of sympathy that such a class of affliction required by trying to smile and to look grieved at the same time.

'If he only walk round the garden of a Sunday morning his shirt-collar is as limp as no starch at all,' continued Mrs Dewy, her countenance lapsing parenthetically into a housewifely expression of concern at the reminiscence.

'Come, come, you women-folk; 'tis hands-across* – come, come!' said the tranter; and the conversation ceased for the present.

8

THEY DANCE MORE WILDLY

Dick had at length secured Fancy for that most delightful of country-dances, opening with six-hands-round.*

'Before we begin,' said the tranter, 'my proposal is, that 'twould be a right and proper plan for every mortal man in the dance to pull off his jacket, considering the heat.'

'Such low notions as you have, Reuben! Nothing but strip will go down with you when you are a-dancing. Such a hot man as he is!'

'Well, now, look here, my sonnies,' he argued to his wife,

whom he often addressed in the plural masculine for economy of epithet merely; 'I don't see that. You dance and get hot as fire; therefore you lighten your clothes. Isn't that nature and reason for gentle and simple? If I strip by myself and not necessary, 'tis rather pot-housey* I own; but if we stout* chaps strip one and all, why, 'tis the native manners of the country, which no man can gainsay? Hey – what did you say, my sonnies?'

'Strip we will!' said the three other heavy men who were in the dance; and their coats were accordingly taken off and hung in the passage, whence the four sufferers from heat soon reappeared marching in close column, with flapping shirt-sleeves, and having as common to them all a general glance of being now a match for any man or dancer in England or Ireland. Dick, fearing to lose ground in Fancy's good opinion, retained his coat like the rest of the thinner men; and Mr Shiner did the same from superior knowledge.

And now a further phase of revelry had disclosed itself. It was the time of night when a guest may write his name in the dust upon the tables and chairs, and a bluish mist pervades the atmosphere, becoming a distinct halo round the candles; when people's nostrils, wrinkles, and crevices in general seem to be getting gradually plastered up; when the very fiddlers as well as the dancers get red in the face, the dancers having advanced further still towards incandescence, and entered the cadaverous phase; the fiddlers no longer sit down, but kick back their chairs and saw madly at the strings with legs firmly spread and eyes closed, regardless of the visible world. Again and again did Dick share his Love's hand with another man, and wheel round; then, more delightfully, promenade in a circle with her all to himself, his arm holding her waist more firmly each time, and his elbow getting further and further behind her back, till the distance reached was rather noticeable; and, most blissful, swinging to places shoulder to shoulder, her breath curling round his neck like a summer zephyr that had strayed from its proper date. Threading the couples one by one they reached the bottom, when there arose in Dick's mind a minor misery lest the tune should end before they could work their way to the top again, and have anew the same exciting run down through. Dick's feelings on actually reaching the top in spite of his doubts were supplemented by a mortal fear that the fiddling might even stop at this supreme moment; which prompted him to convey a stealthy whisper to the far-gone musicians to the effect that they were not to leave off till he and his partner had reached the bottom of the dance once more, which remark was replied to by the nearest of those convulsed and quivering men by a private nod to the anxious young man between two semiquavers of the tune, and a simultaneous 'All right, ay, ay,' without opening the eyes. Fancy was now held so closely that Dick and she were practically one person. The room became to Dick like a picture in a dream; all that he could remember of it afterwards being the look of the fiddlers going to sleep as humming-tops sleep, by increasing their motion and hum, together with the figures of grandfather James and old Simon Crumpler sitting by the chimney-corner talking and nodding in dumb-show, and beating the air to their emphatic sentences like people near a threshing machine.

The dance ended. 'Piph-h-h-h!' said tranter Dewy, blowing out his breath in the very finest stream of vapour that a man's lips could form. 'A regular tightener, that one, sonnies!' He wiped his forehead, and went to the cider and ale mugs on the table.

'Well!' said Mrs Penny, flopping into a chair, 'my heart haven't been in such a thumping state of uproar since I used to sit up on old Midsummer Eves* to see who my husband was going to be.'

'And that's getting on for a good few years ago now, from what I've heard you tell,' said the tranter without lifting his eyes from the cup he was filling. Being now engaged in the business of handing round refreshments he was warranted in keeping his coat off still, though the other heavy men had resumed theirs.

'And a thing I never expected would come to pass, if you'll believe me, came to pass then,' continued Mrs Penny. 'Ah, the first spirit ever I see on a Midsummer Eve was a puzzle to me when he appeared, a hard puzzle, so say I!'

'So I should have fancied,' said Elias Spinks.

'Yes,' said Mrs Penny, throwing her glance into past times and talking on in a running tone of complacent abstraction, as if a listener were not a necessity. 'Yes; never was I in such a taking* as on that Midsummer Eve! I sat up, quite determined to see if John Wildway was going to marry me or no. I put the bread-and-cheese and beer quite ready, as the witch's book ordered, and I opened the door, and I waited till the clock struck twelve, my nerves all alive and so strained that I could feel every one of 'em twitching like bell-wires. Yes, sure! and when the clock had struck, lo and behold I could see through the door a *little small* man in the lane wi' a shoemaker's apron on.'

Here Mr Penny stealthily enlarged himself half an inch.

'Now, John Wildway,' Mrs Penny continued, 'who courted me at that time, was a shoe-maker, you see, but he was a very fair-sized man, and I couldn't believe that any such a little small man had anything to do wi' me, as anybody might. But on he came, and crossed the threshold — not John, but actually the same little small man in the shoemaker's apron—'

'You needn't be so mighty particular about little and small!' said her husband.

'In he walks, and down he sits, and O my goodness me, didn't I flee upstairs, body and soul hardly hanging together! Well, to cut a long story short, by-long and by-late* John Wildway and I had a miff* and parted; and lo and behold, the coming man came! Penny asked me if I'd go snacks* with him, and afore I knew what I was about a'most, the thing was done.'

'I've fancied you never knew better in your life; but I mid* be mistaken,' said Mr Penny in a murmur.

After Mrs Penny had spoken, there being no new occupation for her eyes she still let them stay idling on the past scenes just related, which were apparently visible to her in the centre of the room. Mr Penny's remark received no reply.

During this discourse the tranter and his wife might have been observed standing in an unobtrusive corner in mysterious closeness to each other, a just perceptible current of intelligence passing from each to each, which had apparently no relation whatever to the conversation of their guests, but much to their sustenance. A conclusion of some kind having at length been drawn, the palpable confederacy of man and wife was once more obliterated, the tranter marching off into the pantry humming a tune that he couldn't quite recollect, and then breaking into the words of a song of which he could remember about one line and a quarter. Mrs Dewy spoke a few words about preparations for a bit of supper.

That elder portion of the company which loved eating and drinking put on a look to signify that till that moment they had quite forgotten that it was customary to expect suppers on these occasions; going even further than this politeness of feature, and starting irrelevant subjects, the exceeding flatness and forced tone of which rather betrayed their object. The younger members said they were quite hungry, and that supper would be delightful though it was so late.

Good luck attended Dick's love-passes during the meal. He sat next Fancy, and had the thrilling pleasure of using permanently a glass which had been taken by Fancy in mistake; of letting the outer edge of the sole of his boot touch the lower verge of her skirt; and to add to these delights the cat, which had lain unobserved in her lap for several minutes, crept across into his own, touching him with fur that had touched her hand a moment before. There were, besides, some little pleasures in the shape of helping her to vegetable she didn't want, and when it had nearly alighted on her plate taking it across for his own use, on the plea of waste not, want not. He also, from time to time, sipped sweet sly glances at her profile; noticing the set of her head, the curve of her throat, and other artistic properties of the lively goddess, who the while kept up a rather free, not to say too free, conversation with Mr Shiner sitting opposite; which, after some uneasy criticism, and much shifting of argument backwards and forwards in Dick's mind, he decided not to consider of alarming significance.

'A new music greets our ears now,' said Miss Fancy, alluding, with the sharpness that her position as village sharpener* demanded, to the contrast between the rattle of knives and forks and the late notes of the fiddlers.

'Ay; and I don't know but what 'tis sweeter in tone when you get above forty,' said the tranter; 'except, in faith, as regards father there. Never such a mortal man as he for tunes. They do move his soul; don't 'em, father?'

The eldest Dewy smiled across from his distant chair an assent to Reuben's remark.

'Spaking of being moved in soul,' said Mr, Penny, 'I shall never forget the first time I heard the "Dead March".* 'Twas at poor Corp'l Nineman's funeral at Casterbridge. It fairly made my hair creep and fidget about like a vlock of sheep – ah, it did, souls! And when they had done, and the last trump* had sounded, and the guns was fired over the dead hero's grave, a' icy-cold drop o' moist sweat hung upon my forehead, and another upon my jawbone. Ah, 'tis a very solemn thing!'

'Well, as to father in the corner there,' the tranter said; pointing to old William, who was in the act of filling his mouth, 'he'd starve to death for music's sake now, as much as when he was a boy-chap of fifteen.'

'Truly, now,' said Michael Mail, clearing the corner of his throat in the manner of a man who meant to be convincing; 'there's a friendly tie of some sort between music and eating.' He lifted the cup to his mouth, and drank himself gradually backwards from a perpendicular position to a slanting one, during which time his looks performed a circuit from the wall opposite him to the ceiling overhead. Then clearing the other corner of his throat: 'Once I was a-setting in the little kitchen of the Dree Mariners* at Casterbridge, having a bit of dinner, and a brass band struck up in the street. Such a beautiful band as that were! I was setting eating fried liver and lights,* I well can mind – ah, I was! and to save my life, I couldn't help chawing* to the tune. Band played six-eight time; six-eight chaws I, willynilly. Band plays common; common time* went my teeth among the liver and lights as true as a hair. Beautiful 'twere! Ah, I shall never forget that there band!'

'That's as tuneful a thing as ever I heard of,' said grandfather James, with the absent gaze which accompanies profound criticism.

'I don't like Michael's tuneful stories then,' said Mrs Dewy. They are quite coarse to a person o' decent taste.'

Old Michael's mouth twitched here and there, as if he wanted to smile but didn't know where to begin, which gradually settled to an expression that it was not displeasing for a nice woman like the tranter's wife to correct him.

'Well, now,' said Reuben, with decisive earnestness, 'that sort o' coarse touch that's so upsetting to Ann's feelings is to my mind a recommendation; for it do always prove a story to be true. And for the same reason, I like a story with a bad moral. My sonnies, all true stories have a coarse touch or a bad moral, depend upon't. If the story-tellers could ha' got decency and good morals from true stories, who'd have troubled to invent parables?' Saying this the tranter arose to fetch a new stock of cider, ale, mead, and home-made wines.

Mrs Dewy sighed and appended a remark (ostensibly behind her husband's back, though that the words should reach his ears distinctly was understood by both): 'Such a man as Dewy is!

Nobody do know the trouble I have to keep that man barely respectable. And did you ever hear too – just now at supper-time – talking about "taties" with Michael in such a work-folk way. Well, 'tis what I was never brought up to! With our family 'twas never less than "taters", and very often "pertatoes" outright; mother was so particular and nice with us girls: there was no family in the parish that kept themselves up more than we.'

The hour of parting came. Fancy could not remain for the night because she had engaged a woman to wait up for her. She disappeared temporarily from the flagging party of dancers, and then came downstairs wrapped up and looking altogether a different person from whom she had been hitherto, in fact (to Dick's sadness and disappointment), a woman somewhat reserved and of a phlegmatic temperament – nothing left in her of the romping girl that she had seemed but a short quarter-hour before, who had not minded the weight of Dick's hand upon her waist, nor shirked the purlieus of the mistletoe.

'What a difference!' thought the young man – hoary cynic *pro tem.** What a miserable deceiving difference between the manners of a maid's life at dancing times and at others! Look at this lovely Fancy! Through the whole past evening touchable, squeezable – even kissable! For whole half-hours I held her so close to me that not a sheet of paper could have been slipped between us; and I could feel her heart only just outside my own, her life beating on so close to mine, that I was aware of every breath in it. A flit is made upstairs – a hat and a cloak put on – and I no more dare to touch her than – ' Thought failed him, and he returned to realities.

But this was an endurable misery in comparison with what followed. Mr Shiner and his watch-chain, taking the intrusive advantage that ardent bachelors who are going homeward along the same road as a pretty young woman always do take of that circumstance, came forward to assure Fancy – with a total disregard of Dick's emotions, and in tones which were certainly not frigid – that he (Shiner) was not the man to go to bed before seeing his Lady Fair safe within her own door – not he, nobody should say he was that; and that he would not leave her side an inch till the thing was done – drown him if he would. The proposal was assented to by Miss Day, in Dick's foreboding judgment, with one degree – or at any rate, an appreciable fraction of a degree – of warmth beyond that required by a disinterested desire for protection from the dangers of the night.

All was over; and Dick surveyed the chair she had last occupied, looking now like a setting from which the gem has been torn. There stood her glass, and the romantic teaspoonful of elder wine at the bottom that she couldn't drink by trying ever so hard, in obedience to the mighty arguments of the tranter (his hand coming down upon her shoulder the while like a Nasmyth hammer);* but the drinker was there no longer. There were the nine or ten pretty little crumbs she had left on her plate; but the eater was no more seen.

There seemed a disagreeable closeness of relationship between himself and the members of his family now that they were left alone again face to face. His father seemed quite offensive for appearing to be in just as high spirits as when the guests were there; and as for grandfather James (who had not yet left), he was quite fiendish in being rather glad they were gone.

'Really,' said the tranter, in a tone of placid satisfaction, 'I've had so little time to attend to myself all the evenen that I mean to enjoy a quiet meal now! A slice of this here ham – neither too fat nor too lean – so; and then a drop of this vinegar and pickles – there, that's it – and I shall be as fresh as a lark again! And to tell the truth, my sonny, my inside has been as dry as a lime-basket* all night.'

'I like a party very well once in a while,' said Mrs Dewy, leaving off the adorned tones she had been bound to use throughout the evening and returning to the natural marriage voice, 'but, Lord, 'tis such a sight of heavy work next day! What with the dirty plates, and knives and forks, and dust and smother, and bits kicked off your furniture, and I don't know what all, why a body could a'most wish there were no such things as Christmases ... Ah-h dear!' she yawned, till the clock in the corner had ticked several beats. She cast her eyes round upon the displaced, dust-laden furniture, and sat down over-powered at the sight.

'Well, I be getting all right by degrees, thank the Lord for't!' said the tranter cheerfully through a mangled mass of ham and bread, without lifting his eyes from his plate, and chopping away with his knife and fork as if he were felling trees. 'Ann, you may as well go on to bed at once, and not bide there making such sleepy faces; you look as long-favoured as a fiddle,* upon my life, Ann. There, you must be wearied out 'tis true. I'll do the doors and wind up the clock;* and you go on, or you'll be as white as a sheet tomorrow.'

'Ay; I don't know whether I shan't or no.' The matron passed her hand across her eyes to brush away the film of sleep till she got upstairs.

Dick wondered how it was that when people were married they could be so blind to romance; and was quite certain that if he ever took to wife that dear impossible Fancy, he and she would never be so dreadfully practical and undemonstrative of the Passion as his father and mother were. The most extraordinary thing was that all the fathers and mothers he knew were just as undemonstrative as his own.

9

DICK CALLS AT THE SCHOOL

The early days of the year drew on, and Fancy, having spent the holiday weeks at home, returned again to Mellstock.

Every spare minute of the week following her return was used by Dick in accidentally passing the schoolhouse in his journeys about the neighbourhood; but not once did she make herself visible. A handkerchief belonging to her had been providentially found by his mother in clearing the rooms the day after that of the dance; and by much contrivance Dick got it handed over to him, to leave with her at any time he should be near the school after her return. But he delayed taking the extreme measure of calling with it lest, had she really no sentiment of interest in him, it might be regarded as a slightly absurd errand, the reason guessed, and the sense of the ludicrous, which was rather keen in her, do his dignity considerable injury in her eyes; and what she thought of him, even apart from the question of her loving, was all the world to him now.

But the hour came when the patience of love at twenty-one could endure no longer. One Saturday he approached the school with a mild air of indifference, and had the satisfaction of seeing the object of his quest at the further end of her garden, trying, by the aid of a spade and gloves, to root a bramble that had intruded itself there.

He disguised his feelings from some suspicious-looking cottage windows opposite by endeavouring to appear like a man in a great hurry of business, who wished to leave the handkerchief and have done with such trifling errands.

This endeavour signally failed; for on approaching the gate he found it locked to keep the children, who were playing 'crossdadder'* in the front, from running into her private grounds.

She did not see him; and he could only think of one thing to be done, which was to shout her name.

'Miss Day!'

The words were uttered with a jerk and a look meant to imply to the cottages opposite that he was now simply one who liked shouting as a pleasant way of passing his time, without any reference to persons in gardens. The name died away, and the unconscious Miss Day continued digging and pulling as before.

He screwed himself up to enduring the cottage windows yet more stoically, and shouted again. Fancy took no notice whatever.

He shouted the third time, with desperate vehemence, turning suddenly about and retiring a little distance as if it were by no means for his own pleasure that he had come.

This time she heard him, came down the garden, and entered the school at the back. Footsteps echoed across the interior, the door opened, and three-quarters of the blooming young schoolmistress's face and figure stood revealed before him; a slice on her left-hand side being cut off by the edge of the door. Having surveyed and recognised him she came to the gate.

At sight of him had the pink of her cheeks increased, lessened, or did it continue to cover its normal area of ground? It was a question meditated several hundreds of times by her visitor in after-hours – the meditation, after wearying involutions, always ending in one way, that it was impossible to say.

'Your handkerchief: Miss Day: I called with.' He held it out spasmodically and awkwardly. 'Mother found it: under a chair.'

'O, thank you very much for bringing it, Mr Dewy. I couldn't think where I had dropped it.'

Now Dick, not being an experienced lover – indeed, never before having been engaged in the practice of love-making at all, except in a small schoolboy way – could not take advantage of the situation; and out came the blunder which afterwards cost him so many bitter moments and a sleepless night:

'Good morning, Miss Day.'

'Good morning, Mr Dewy.'

The gate was closed; she was gone; and Dick was standing outside, unchanged in his condition from what he had been before he called. Of course the Angel was not to blame – a young woman living alone in a house could not ask him indoors unless she had known him better – he should have kept her outside before floundering into that fatal farewell. He wished that before he called he had realised more fully than he did the pleasure of being about to call; and turned away.

PART II
SPRING

I

PASSING BY THE SCHOOL

It followed that as the spring advanced Dick walked abroad much more frequently than had hitherto been usual with him, and was continually finding that his nearest way to or from home lay by the road which skirted the garden of the school. The first-fruits of his perseverance were that, on turning the angle on the nineteenth journey by that track, he saw Miss Fancy's figure, clothed in a dark-grey dress, looking from a high open window upon the crown of his hat. The friendly greeting resulting from this rencounter was considered so valuable an elixir that Dick passed still oftener; and by the time he had almost trodden a little path under the fence where never a path was before, he was rewarded with an actual meeting face to face on the open road before her gate. This brought another meeting, and another, Fancy faintly showing by her bearing that it was a pleasure to her of some kind to see him there; but the sort of pleasure she derived, whether exultation at the hope her exceeding fairness inspired, or the true feeling which was alone Dick's concern, he could not anyhow decide, although he meditated on her every little movement for hours after it was made.

2

A MEETING OF THE QUIRE

It was the evening of a fine spring day. The descending sun appeared as a nebulous blaze of amber light, its outline being lost in cloudy masses hanging round it like wild locks of hair.

The chief members of Mellstock parish choir were standing in a group in front of Mr Penny's workshop in the lower village. They were all brightly illuminated, and each was backed up by a shadow as long as a steeple; the lowness of the source of light rendering the brims of their hats of no use at all as a protection to the eyes.

Mr Penny's was the last house in that part of the parish, and stood in a hollow by the roadside; so that cartwheels and horses' legs were about level with the sill of his shop window. This was low and wide, and was open from morning till evening, Mr Penny himself being invariably seen working inside like a framed portrait of a shoemaker by some modern Moroni.* He sat facing the road, with a boot on his knees and the awl in his hand, only looking up for a moment as he stretched out his arms and bent forward at the pull, when his spectacles flashed in the passer's face with a shine of flat whiteness, and then returned again to the boot as usual. Rows of lasts, small and large, stout and slender, covered the wall which formed the background, in the extreme shadow of which a kind of dummy was seen sitting, in the shape of an apprentice with a string tied round his hair (probably to keep it out of his eyes). He smiled at remarks that floated in from without, but was never known to answer them in Mr Penny's presence. Outside the window the upper-leather of a Wellington-boot was usually hung, pegged to a board as if to dry. No sign was over his door; in fact – as with old banks and mercantile houses – advertising in any shape was scorned, and it would have been felt as beneath his dignity to paint up, for the benefit of strangers, the name of an establish-ment whose trade came solely by connection based on personal respect.

His visitors now came and stood on the outside of his window, sometimes leaning against the sill, sometimes moving a pace or two backwards and forwards in front of it. They talked with deliberate gesticulations to Mr Penny, enthroned in the shadow of the interior.

'I do like a man to stick to men who be in the same line o' life – o' Sundays, anyway – that I do so.'

''Tis like all the doings of folk who don't know what a day's work is, that's what I say.'

'My belief is the man's not to blame; 'tis *she* – she's the bitter weed!'

'No, not altogether. He's a poor gawk-hammer.* Look at his sermon yesterday.'

'His sermon was well enough, a very good guessable sermon, only he couldn't put it into words and speak it. That's all was the matter wi' the sermon. He hadn't been able to get it past his pen.'

'Well – ay, the sermon might have been good; for, 'tis true, the sermon of Old Eccl'iastes* himself lay in Eccl'iastes's ink-bottle afore he got it out.'

Mr Penny, being in the act of drawing the last stitch tight, could afford time to look up and throw in a word at this point.

'He's no spouter* – that must be said, 'a b'lieve.'

''Tis a terrible muddle sometimes with the man, as far as spout do go,' said Spinks.

'Well, we'll say nothing about that,' the tranter answered; 'for I don't believe 'twill make a penneth o' difference to we poor martels here or hereafter whether his sermons be good or bad, my sonnies.'

Mr Penny made another hole with his awl, pushed in the thread, and looked up and spoke again at the extension of arms.

''Tis his goings-on, souls, that's what it is.' He clenched his features for an Herculean* addition to the ordinary pull, and continued, 'The first thing he done when he came here was to be hot and strong about church business.'

'True,' said Spinks; 'that was the very first thing he done.'

Mr Penny, having now been offered the ear of the assembly, accepted it, ceased stitching, swallowed an unimportant quantity of air as if it were a pill, and continued:

'The next thing he do do is to think about altering the church, until he found 'twould be a matter o' cost and what not, and then not to think no more about it.'

'True: that was the next thing he done.'

'And the next thing was to tell the young chaps that they were not on no account to put their hats in the christening font during service.'

'True.'

'And then 'twas this, and then 'twas that, and now 'tis – '

Words were not forcible enough to conclude the sentence, and Mr Penny gave a huge pull to signify the concluding word.

'Now 'tis to turn us out of the quire neck and crop,' said the tranter after an interval of half a minute, not by way of explaining the pause and pull, which had been quite understood, but as a means of keeping the subject well before the meeting.

Mrs Penny came to the door at this point in the discussion. Like all good wives, however much she was inclined to play the Tory to her husband's Whiggism,* and *vice versa*, in times of peace, she coalesced with him heartily enough in time of war.

'It must be owned he's not all there,' she replied in a general way to the fragments of talk she had heard from indoors. 'Far below poor Mr Grinham' (the late vicar).

'Ay, there was this to be said for he, that you were quite sure he'd never come mumbudgeting* to see ye, just as you were in the middle of your work, and put you out with his fuss and trouble about ye.'

'Never. But as for this new Mr Maybold, though he mid be a very well-intending party in that respect, he's unbearable; for as to sifting your cinders, scrubbing your floors, or emptying your slops, why, you can't do it. I assure you I've not been able to empt them for several days, unless I throw 'em up the chimley or out of winder; for as sure as the sun you meet him at the door, coming to ask how you are, and 'tis such a confusing thing to meet a gentleman at the door when ye are in the mess o' washing.'

''Tis only for want of knowing better, poor gentleman,' said the tranter. 'His meaning's good enough. Ay, your pa'son comes by fate: 'tis heads or tails, like pitch-halfpenny,* and no choosing; so we must take en as he is, my sonnies, and thank God he's no worse, I suppose.'

'I fancy I've seen him look across at Miss Day in a warmer way than Christianity asked for,' said Mrs Penny musingly; 'but I don't quite like to say it.'

'O no; there's nothing in that,' said grandfather William.

'If there's nothing, we shall see nothing,' Mrs Penny replied in the tone of a woman who might possibly have private opinions still.

'Ah, Mr Grinham was the man!' said Bowman. 'Why, he never troubled us wi' a visit from year's end to year's end. You might go anywhere, do anything: you'd be sure never to see him.'

'Yes; he was a right sensible pa'son,' said Michael. 'He never entered our door but once in his life, and that was to tell my poor wife – ay, poor soul, dead and gone now, as we all shall! – that as she was such a' old aged person, and lived so far from the church, he didn't at all expect her to come any more to the service.'

'And 'a was a very jinerous gentleman about choosing the psalms and hymns o' Sundays. "Confound ye," says he, "blare and scrape what ye will; but don't bother me!"'

'And he was a very honourable man in not wanting any of us to come and hear him if we were all on-end for a jaunt or spree, or to bring the babies to be christened if they were inclined to squalling. There's good in a man's not putting a parish to unnecessary trouble.'

'And there's this here man never letting us have a bit o' peace; but keeping on about being good and upright till 'tis carried to such a pitch as I never see the like afore nor since!'

'No sooner had he got here than he found the font wouldn't hold water, as it hadn't for years off and on; and when I told him that Mr Grinham never minded it, but used to spet upon his vinger and christen 'em just as well, 'a said, "Good Heavens! Send for a workman immediate. What place have I come to!" Which was no compliment to us, come to that.'

'Still, for my part,' said old William, 'though he's arrayed against us, I like the hearty borus-snorus* ways of the new pa'son.'

'You, ready to die for the quire,' said Bowman reproachfully, 'to stick up for the quire's enemy, William!'

'Nobody will feel the loss of our church-work so much as I,' said the old man firmly, 'That you d'all know. I've a-been in the quire man and boy ever since I was a chiel of eleven. But for all that 'tisn't in me to call the man a bad man, because I truly and sincerely believe en to be a good young feller.'

Some of the youthful sparkle that used to reside there animated William's eye as he uttered the words, and a certain nobility of aspect was also imparted to him by the setting sun, which gave him a Titanic* shadow at least thirty feet in length, stretching away to the east in outlines of imposing magnitude, his head finally terminating upon the trunk of a grand old oak-tree.

'Mayble's a hearty feller enough,' the tranter replied, 'and will spak to you be you dirty or be you clane. The first time I met en was in a drong,* and though 'a didn't know me no more than the dead 'a passed the time of day. "D'ye do!" he said says he, nodding his head. "A fine day." Then the second time I met en was full-buff* in town street, when my breeches were tore into a long strent* by getting through a copse of thorns and brimbles for a short cut home-along; and not wanting to disgrace the man by spaking in that state, I fixed my eye on the weathercock to let en pass me as a stranger. But no: "How d'ye do, Reuben?"

says he, right hearty, and shook my hand. If I'd been dressed in silver spangles from top to toe the man couldn't have been civiller.'

At this moment Dick was seen coming up the village street, and they turned and watched him.

3

A TURN IN THE DISCUSSION

'I'm afraid Dick's a lost man,' said the tranter.

'What? – no!' said Mail, implying by his manner that it was a far commoner thing for his ears to report what was not said than that his judgment should be at fault.

'Ay,' said the tranter, still gazing at Dick's unconscious advance. 'I don't at all like what I see! There's too many o' them looks out of the winder without noticing anything; too much shining of boots; too much peeping round corners; too much looking at the clock; telling about clever things *she* did till you be sick of it, and then upon a hint to that effect a horrible silence about her. I've walked the path once in my life and know the country, neighbours; and Dick's a lost man!' The tranter turned a quarter round and smiled a smile of miserable satire at the setting new moon, which happened to catch his eye.

The others became far too serious at this announcement to allow them to speak; and they still regarded Dick in the distance.

''Twas his mother's fault,' the tranter continued, 'in asking the young woman to our party last Christmas. When I eyed the blue frock and light heels o' the maid, I had my thoughts directly. "God bless thee, Dicky my sonny," I said to myself, "there's a delusion for thee!"'

'They seemed to be rather distant in manner last Sunday, I thought?' Mail tentatively observed, as became one who was not a member of the family.

'Ay, that's a part of the zickness. Distance belongs to it, slyness belongs to it, queerest things on earth belongs to it! There, 'tmay as well come early as late s'far as I know. The sooner begun, the sooner over; for come it will.'

'The question I ask is,' said Mr Spinks, connecting into one thread the two subjects of discourse, as became a man learned in rhetoric, and beating with his hand in a way which signified that the manner rather than the matter of his speech was to be observed, 'how did Mr Maybold know she could play the organ? You know we had it from her own lips, as far as lips go, that she has never, first or last, breathed such a thing to him; much less that she ever would play.'

In the midst of this puzzle Dick joined the party, and the news which had caused such a convulsion among the ancient musicians was unfolded to him. Well,' he said, blushing at the allusion to Miss Day, 'I know by some words of hers that she has a particular wish not to play, because she is a friend of ours; and how the alteration comes I don't know.'

'Now, this is my plan,' said the tranter, reviving the spirit of the discussion by the infusion of new ideas, as was his custom – 'this is my plan; if you don't like it, no harm's done. We all know one another very well, don't we, neighbours?'

That they knew one another very well was received as a statement which, though familiar, should not be omitted in introductory speeches.

'Then I say this' – and the tranter in his emphasis slapped down his hand on Mr Spinks's shoulder with a momentum of several pounds, upon which Mr Spinks tried to look not in the least startled – 'I say that we all move down-along straight as a line to Pa'son Mayble's when the clock has gone six tomorrow night. There we one and all stand in the passage; then one or two of us go in and spak to en, man and man, and say, "Pa'son Mayble, every tradesman d'like to have his own way in his workshop, and Mellstock Church is yours. Instead of turning us out neck and crop, let us stay on till Christmas, and we'll gie way to the young woman, Mr Mayble, and make no more ado about it. And we shall always be quite willing to touch our hats when we meet ye, Mr Mayble, just as before." That sounds very well? Hey?'

'Proper well, in faith, Reuben Dewy.'

'And we won't sit down in his house; 'twould be looking too familiar when only just reconciled?'

'No need at all to sit down. Just do our duty man and man, turn round, and march out – he'll think all the more of us for it.'

'I hardly think Leaf had better go wi' us?' said Michael,

turning to Leaf and taking his measure from top to bottom by the eye. 'He's so terrible silly that he might ruin the concern.'

'He don't want to go much; do ye, Thomas Leaf?' said William.

'Hee-hee! no; I don't want to.'

'I be mortal afeard, Leaf, that you'll never be able to tell how many cuts d'take to sharpen a spar,'* said Mail.

'I never had no head, never! that's how it happened to happen, hee-hee!'

They all assented to this, not with any sense of humiliating Leaf by disparaging him after an open confession, but because it was an accepted thing that Leaf didn't in the least mind having no head, that deficiency of his being an unimpassioned matter of parish history.

'But I can sing my treble!' continued Thomas Leaf, quite delighted at being called a fool in such a friendly way; 'I can sing my treble as well as any maid, or married woman either, and better! And if Jim had lived, I should have had a clever brother! Tomorrow is poor Jim's birthday. He'd ha' been twenty-six if he'd lived till tomorrow.'

'You always seem very sorry for Jim,' said old William musingly.

'Ah! I do. Such a stay to Mother as he'd always have been! She'd never have had to work in her old age if he had continued strong, poor Jim!'

'What was his age when 'a died?'

'Four hours and twenty minutes, poor Jim. 'A was born as might be at night; and 'a didn't last as might be till the morning. No, 'a didn't last. Mother called en Jim on the day that would ha' been his christening day if he had lived; and she's always thinking about en. You see he died so very young.'

'Well, 'twas rather youthful,' said Michael.

'Now to my mind that woman is very romantical on the matter o' children?' said the tranter, his eye sweeping his audience.

'Ah, well she mid be,' said Leaf. 'She had twelve regular one after another, and they all, except myself, died very young; either before they was born or just afterwards.'

'Pore feller, too. I suppose th'st want to come wi' us?' the tranter murmured.

'Well, Leaf, you shall come wi' us as yours is such a melancholy family,' said old William rather sadly.

'I never see such a melancholy family as that afore in my life,' said Reuben. 'There's Leaf's mother, poor woman! Every morning I see her eyes mooning out through the panes of glass like a pot-sick winder-flower; and as Leaf sings a very high treble, and we don't know what we should do without en for upper G, we'll let en come as a trate, poor feller.'

'Ay, we'll let en come, 'a b'lieve,' said Mr Penny, looking up, as the pull happened to be at that moment.

'Now,' continued the tranter, dispersing by a new tone of voice these digressions about Leaf, 'as to going to see the pa'son, one of us might call and ask en his meaning, and 'twould be just as well done; but it will add a bit of a flourish to the cause if the quire waits on him as a body. Then the great thing to mind is, not for any of our fellers to be nervous; so before starting we'll one and all come to my house and have a rasher of bacon; then every man-jack het* a pint of cider into his inside; then we'll warm up an extra drop wi' some mead and a bit of ginger; every one take a thimbleful – just a glimmer of a drop, mind ye, no more, to finish off his inner man – and march off to Pa'son Mayble. Why, sonnies, a man's not himself till he is fortified wi' a bit and a drop? We shall be able to look any gentleman in the face then without shrink or shame.'

Mail recovered from a deep meditation and downward glance into the earth in time to give a cordial approval to this line of action, and the meeting adjourned.

4

THE INTERVIEW WITH THE VICAR

At six o'clock next day the whole body of men in the choir emerged from the tranter's door, and advanced with a firm step down the lane. This dignity of march gradually became obliterated as they went on, and by the time they reached the hill behind the vicarage a faint resemblance to a flock of sheep might have been discerned in the venerable party. A word from the tranter, however, set them right again; and as they descended the hill, the regular tramp, tramp, tramp of the united feet was clearly audible from the vicarage garden. At the opening of the gate there was another short interval of irregular shuffling, caused by a rather peculiar habit the gate had, when swung open quickly, of striking against the bank and slamming back into the opener's face.

'Now keep step again, will ye?' said the tranter. It looks better, and more becomes the high class of arrant* which has brought us here.' Thus they advanced to the door.

At Reuben's ring the more modest of the group turned aside, adjusted their hats, and looked critically at any shrub that happened to lie in the line of vision; endeavouring thus to give a person who chanced to look out of the windows the impression that their request, whatever it was going to be, was rather a casual thought occurring whilst they were inspecting the vicar's shrubbery and grass-plot than a predetermined thing. The tranter who, coming frequently to the vicarage with luggage, coals, firewood, etc., had none of the awe for its precincts that filled the breasts of most of the others, fixed his eyes firmly on the knocker during this interval of waiting. The knocker having no characteristic worthy of notice he relinquished it for a knot in one of the door-panels, and studied the winding lines of the grain.

'O, sir, please, here's Tranter Dewy, and old William Dewy, and young Richard Dewy, O, and all the quire too, sir, except the boys, a-come to see you!' said Mr Maybold's maid-servant to Mr Maybold, the pupils of her eyes dilating like circles in a pond.

'All the choir?' said the astonished vicar (who may be shortly described as a good-looking young man with courageous eyes, timid mouth, and neutral nose), abandoning his writing and looking at his parlour-maid after speaking, like a man who fancied he had seen her face before but couldn't recollect where.

'And they looks very firm, and Tranter Dewy do turn neither to the right hand nor to the left,* but stares quite straight and solemn with his mind made up!'

'O, all the choir,' repeated the vicar to himself, trying by that simple device to trot out his thoughts on what the choir could come for.

'Yes; every man-jack of 'em, as I be alive!' (The parlour-maid was rather local in manner, having in fact been raised in the same village.) 'Really, sir, 'tis thoughted by many in town and country that—'

'Town and country! – Heavens, I had no idea that I was public property in this way!' said the vicar, his face acquiring a hue somewhere between that of the rose and the peony. 'Well, "It is thought in town and country that—"'

'It is thought that you be going to get it hot and strong! – excusen my incivility, sir.'

The vicar suddenly recalled to his recollection that he had long ago settled it to be decidedly a mistake to encourage his servant Jane in giving personal opinions. The servant Jane saw by the vicar's face that he recalled this fact to his mind; and removing her forehead from the edge of the door, and rubbing away the indent that edge had made, vanished into the passage as Mr Maybold remarked, 'Show them in, Jane.'

A few minutes later a shuffling and jostling (reduced to as refined a form as was compatible with the nature of shuffles and jostles) was heard in the passage; then an earnest and prolonged wiping of shoes, conveying the notion that volumes of mud had to be removed; but the roads being so clean that not a particle of dirt appeared on the choir's boots (those of all the elder members being newly oiled, and Dick's brightly polished), this wiping might have been set down simply as a desire to show that respectable men had no wish to take a mean advantage of clean roads for curtailing proper ceremonies. Next there came a powerful whisper from the same quarter: –

'Now stand stock-still there, my sonnies, one and all! And don't make no noise; and keep your backs close to the wall, that company may pass in and out easy if they want to without squeezing through ye: and we two are enough to go in . . .' The voice was the tranter's.

'I wish I could go in too and see the sight!' said a reedy voice – that of Leaf.

''Tis a pity Leaf is so terrible silly, or else he might,' another said.

'I never in my life seed a quire go into a study to have it out about the playing and singing,' pleaded Leaf, 'and I should like to see it just once!'

'Very well; we'll let en come in,' said the tranter. 'You'll be like chips in porridge,[1]* Leaf – neither good nor hurt. All right, my sonny, come along;' and immediately himself, old William, and Leaf appeared in the room.

'We took the liberty to come and see 'ee, sir,' said Reuben, letting his hat hang in his left hand, and touching with his right the brim of an imaginary one on his head. 'We've come to see 'ee, sir, man and man, and no offence, I hope?'

'None at all,' said Mr Maybold.

'This old aged man standing by my side is Father; William Dewy by name, sir.'

'Yes; I see it is,' said the vicar, nodding aside to old William, who smiled.

'I thought ye mightn't know en without his bass-viol,' the tranter apologised. You see, he always wears his best clothes and his bass-viol a-Sundays, and it do make such a difference in a' old man's look.'

'And who's that young man?' the vicar said.

'Tell the pa'son yer name,' said the tranter, turning to Leaf, who stood with his elbows nailed back to a bookcase.

'Please, Thomas Leaf, your holiness!' said Leaf, trembling.

'I hope you'll excuse his looks being so very thin,' continued the tranter deprecatingly, turning to the vicar again. 'But 'tisn't his fault, poor feller. He's rather silly by nature, and could never get fat; though he's a' excellent treble, and so we keep him on.'

'I never had no head, sir,' said Leaf, eagerly grasping at this opportunity for being forgiven his existence.

'Ah, poor young man!' said Mr Maybold.

'Bless you, he don't mind it a bit, if you don't, sir,' said the tranter assuringly. 'Do ye, Leaf?'

'Not I – not a morsel – hee, hee! I was afeard it mightn't please your holiness, sir, that's all.'

The tranter, finding Leaf get on so very well through his negative qualities, was tempted in a fit of generosity to advance him still higher, by giving him credit for positive ones. 'He's very clever for a silly chap, good-now,* sir. You never knowed a young feller keep his smock-frocks so clane; very honest too. His ghastly looks is all there is against en, poor feller; but we can't help our looks, you know, sir.'

---

[1] This, a local expression, must be a corruption of something less questionable.

'True: we cannot. You live with your mother, I think, Leaf?'

The tranter looked at Leaf to express that the most friendly assistant to his tongue could do no more for him now, and that he must be left to his own resources.

'Yes, sir: a widder, sir. Ah, if brother Jim had lived she'd have had a clever son to keep her without work!'

'Indeed! poor woman. Give her this half-crown. I'll call and see your mother.'

'Say, "Thank you, sir,"' the tranter whispered imperatively towards Leaf.

'Thank you, sir!' said Leaf.

'That's it, then; sit down, Leaf,' said Mr Maybold.

'Y-yes, sir!'

The tranter cleared his throat after this accidental parenthesis about Leaf, rectified his bodily position, and began his speech.

'Mr Mayble,' he said, 'I hope you'll excuse my common way, but I always like to look things in the face.'

Reuben made a point of fixing this sentence in the vicar's mind by gazing hard at him at the conclusion of it, and then out of the window.

Mr Maybold and old William looked in the same direction, apparently under the impression that the things' faces alluded to were there visible.

'What I have been thinking' – the tranter implied by this use of the past tense that he was hardly so discourteous as to be positively thinking it then – 'is that the quire ought to be gie'd a little time, and not done away wi' till Christmas, as a fair thing between man and man. And, Mr Mayble, I hope you'll excuse my common way?'

'I will, I will. Till Christmas,' the vicar murmured, stretching the two words to a great length, as if the distance to Christmas might be measured in that way. 'Well, I want you all to understand that I have no personal fault to find, and that I don't wish to change the church music by forcible means, or in a way which should hurt the feelings of any parishioners. Why I have at last spoken definitely on the subject is that a player has been brought under – I may say pressed upon – my notice several times by one of the churchwardens. And as the organ I brought with me is here waiting' (pointing to a cabinet-organ standing in the study), 'there is no reason for longer delay.'

'We made a mistake I suppose then, sir? But we understood

the young woman didn't want to play particularly?' The tranter arranged his countenance to signify that he did not want to be inquisitive in the least.

'No, nor did she. Nor did I definitely wish her to just yet; for your playing is very good. But, as I said, one of the churchwardens has been so anxious for a change that, as matters stand, I couldn't consistently refuse my consent.'

Now for some reason or other the vicar at this point seemed to have an idea that he had prevaricated; and as an honest vicar it was a thing he determined not to do. He corrected himself, blushing as he did so, though why he should blush was not known to Reuben.

'Understand me rightly,' he said: 'the churchwarden proposed it to me, but I had thought myself of getting – Miss Day to play.'

'Which churchwarden might that be who proposed her, sir? – excusing my common way.' The tranter intimated by his tone that so far from being inquisitive he did not even wish to ask a single question.

'Mr Shiner, I believe.'

'Clk, my sonny! – beg your pardon, sir, that's only a form of words of mine, and slipped out accidental – he nourishes enmity against us for some reason or another; perhaps because we played rather hard upon en Christmas night. Anyhow 'tis certain sure that Mr Shiner's real love for music of a particular kind isn't his reason. He've no more ear than that chair. But let that be.'

'I don't think you should conclude that, because Mr Shiner wants a different music, he has any ill-feeling for you. I myself, I must own, prefer organ music to any other. I consider it most proper, and feel justified in endeavouring to introduce it; but then, although other music is better, I don't say yours is not good.'

'Well then, Mr Mayble, since death's to be, we'll die like men any day you name (excusing my common way).'

Mr Maybold bowed his head.

'All we thought was, that for us old ancient singers to be choked off quiet at no time in particular, as now, in the Sundays after Easter, would seem rather mean in the eyes of other parishes, sir. But if we fell glorious with a bit of a flourish at Christmas, we should have a respectable end, and not dwindle away at some nameless paltry second-Sunday-after or Sunday-next-before something, that's got no name of his own.'

'Yes, yes, that's reasonable; I own it's reasonable.'

'You see, Mr Mayble, we've got – do I keep you inconvenient long, sir?'

'No, no.'

'We've got our feelings – father there especially.'

The tranter, in his earnestness, had advanced his person to within six inches of the vicar's.'

'Certainly, certainly!' said Mr Maybold, retreating a little for convenience of seeing. 'You are all enthusiastic on the subject, and I am all the more gratified to find you so. A Laodicean* lukewarmness is worse than wrongheadedness itself.'

'Exactly, sir. In fact now, Mr Mayble,' Reuben continued more impressively, and advancing a little closer still to the vicar, 'father there is a perfect figure o' wonder, in the way of being fond of music!'

The vicar drew back a little further, the tranter suddenly also standing back a foot or two to throw open the view of his father, and pointing to him at the same time.

Old William moved uneasily in the large chair, and with a minute smile on the mere edge of his lips for good manners, said he was indeed very fond of tunes.

'Now, you see exactly how it is,' Reuben continued, appealing to Mr Maybold's sense of justice by looking sideways into his eyes. The vicar seemed to see how it was so well that the gratified tranter walked up to him again with even vehement eagerness, so that his waistcoat-buttons almost rubbed against the vicar's as he continued: 'As to father, if you or I, or any man or woman of the present generation, at the time music is a-playing, was to shake your fist in father's face, as may be this way, and say, "Don't you be delighted with that music!"' – the tranter went back to where Leaf was sitting, and held his fist so close to Leaf's face that the latter pressed his head back against the wall: 'All right, Leaf, my sonny, I won't hurt you; 'tis just to show my meaning to Mr Mayble. – As I was saying, if you or I, or any man, was to shake your fist in father's face this way, and say, "William, your life or your music!" he'd say, "My life!" Now that's father's nature all over; and you see, sir, it must hurt the feelings of a man of that kind for him and his bass-viol to be done away wi' neck and crop.'

The tranter went back to the vicar's front and again looked earnestly at his face.

'True, true, Dewy,' Mr Maybold answered, trying to withdraw his head and shoulders without moving his feet; but finding this impracticable edging back another inch. These frequent retreats had at last jammed Mr Maybold between his easy-chair and the edge of the table.

And at the moment of the announcement of the choir Mr Maybold had just redipped the pen he was using; at their entry, instead of wiping it, he had laid it on the table with the nib overhanging. At the last retreat his coat-tails came in contact with the pen, and down it rolled, first against the back of the chair, thence turning a somersault into the seat, thence falling to the floor with a rattle.

The vicar stooped for his pen, and the tranter, wishing to show that, however great their ecclesiastical differences, his mind was not so small as to let this affect his social feelings, stooped also.

'And have you anything else you want to explain to me, Dewy?' said Mr Maybold from under the table.

'Nothing, sir. And, Mr Mayble, you be not offended? I hope you see our desire is reason?' said the tranter from under the chair.

'Quite, quite; and I shouldn't think of refusing to listen to such a reasonable request,' the vicar replied. Seeing that Reuben had secured the pen he resumed his vertical position, and added, 'You know, Dewy, it is often said how difficult a matter it is to act up to our convictions and please all parties. It may be said with equal truth, that it is difficult for a man of any appreciativeness to have convictions at all. Now in my case, I see right in you, and right in Shiner. I see that violins are good, and that an organ is good; and when we introduce the organ it will not be that fiddles were bad, but that an organ was better. That you'll clearly understand, Dewy?'

'I will; and thank you very much for such feelings, sir. Piph-h-h-h! How the blood do get into my head, to be sure, whenever I quat* down like that!' said Reuben, who having also risen to his feet stuck the pen vertically in the inkstand and almost through the bottom, that it might not roll down again under any circumstances whatever.

Now the ancient body of minstrels in the passage felt their curiosity surging higher and higher as the minutes passed. Dick, not having much affection for this errand, soon grew tired, and went away in the direction of the school. Yet their sense of propriety would probably have restrained them from any attempt to discover what was going on in the study had not the vicar's pen fallen to the floor. The conviction that the movement of chairs, etc., necessitated by the search, could only have been caused by the catastrophe of a bloody fight beginning, overpowered all other considerations; and they advanced to the door, which had only just fallen to. Thus, when Mr Maybold raised his eyes after the stooping he beheld glaring through the door Mr Penny in full-length portraiture, Mail's face and shoulders above Mr Penny's head, Spinks's forehead and eyes over Mail's crown, and a fractional part of Bowman's countenance under Spinks's arm – crescent-shaped portions of other heads and faces being visible behind these – the whole dozen and odd eyes bristling with eager inquiry.

Mr Penny, as is the case with excitable bootmakers and men, seeing the vicar look at him and hearing no word spoken, thought it incumbent upon himself to say something of any kind. Nothing suggested itself till he had looked for about half a minute at the vicar.

'You'll excuse my naming of it, sir,' he said, regarding with much commiseration the mere surface of the vicar's face; 'but perhaps you don't know that your chin have bust out a-bleeding where you cut yourself a-shaving this morning, sir.'

'Now, that was the stooping, depend upon't,' the tranter suggested, also looking with much interest at the vicar's chin. 'Blood always will bust out again if you hang down the member that's been bleeding.'

Old William raised his eyes and watched the vicar's bleeding chin likewise; and Leaf advanced two or three paces from the bookcase, absorbed in the contemplation of the same phenomenon with parted lips and delighted eyes.

'Dear me, dear me!' said Mr Maybold hastily, looking very red and brushing his chin with his hand, then taking out his handkerchief and wiping the place.

'That's it, sir; all right again now, 'a b'lieve – a mere nothing,' said Mr Penny. 'A little bit of fur off your hat will stop it in a minute if it should bust out again.'

'I'll let 'ee have a bit off mine,' said Reuben, to show his good feeling; 'my hat isn't so new as yours, sir, and 'twon't hurt mine a bit.'

'No, no; thank you, thank you,' Mr Maybold again nervously replied.

"Twas rather a deep cut seemingly?' said Reuben, feeling these to be the kindest and best remarks he could make.

'O, no; not particularly.'

'Well, sir, your hand will shake sometimes a-shaving, and just when it comes into your head that you may cut yourself, there's the blood.'

'I have been revolving in my mind that question of the time at which we make the change,' said Mr Maybold, 'and I know you'll meet me halfway. I think Christmas Day as much too late for me as the present time is too early for you. I suggest Michaelmas* or thereabout as a convenient time for both parties; for I think your objection to a Sunday which has no name is not one of any real weight.'

'Very good, sir. I suppose mortal men mustn't expect their own way entirely; and I express in all our names that we'll make shift and be satisfied with what you say.' The tranter touched the brim of his imaginary hat again, and all the choir did the same. 'About Michaelmas, then, as far as you are concerned, sir, and then we make room for the next generation.'

'About Michaelmas,' said the vicar.

5

RETURNING HOMEWARD

"A took it very well, then?' said Mail, as they all walked up the hill.

'He behaved like a man; 'a did so,' said the tranter. 'And I'm glad we've let en know our minds. And though, beyond that, we ha'n't got much by going, 'twas worth while. He won't forget it. Yes, he took it very well. Supposing this tree here was Pa'son Mayble, and I standing here, and thik gr't* stone is father sitting in the easy-chair. "Dewy," says he, "I don't wish to change the church music in a forcible way."'

'That was very nice o' the man, even though words be wind.'

'Proper nice – out and out nice. The fact is,' said Reuben confidentially, "tis how you take a man. Everybody must be managed. Queens must be managed: kings must be managed; for men want managing almost as much as women, and that's saying a good deal.'

''Tis truly!' murmured the husbands.

'Pa'son Mayble and I were as good friends all through it as if we'd been sworn brothers. Ay, the man's well enough; 'tis what's put in his head that spoils him, and that's why we've got to go.'

'There's really no believing half you hear about people nowadays.'

'Bless ye, my sonnies, 'tisn't the pa'son's move at all. That gentleman over there' (the tranter nodded in the direction of Shiner's farm) 'is at the root of the mischty.'*

'What! Shiner?'

'Ay; and I see what the pa'son don't see. Why, Shiner is for putting forward that young woman that only last night I was saying was our Dick's sweetheart, but I suppose can't be, and making much of her in the sight of the congregation, and thinking he'll win her by showing her off. Well, perhaps 'a woll.'

'Then the music is second to the woman, the other church-warden is second to Shiner, the pa'son is second to the church-wardens, and God A'mighty is nowhere at all.'

'That's true; and you see,' continued Reuben, 'at the very beginning it put me in a stud* as to how to quarrel wi' en. In short, to save my soul, I couldn't quarrel wi' such a civil man without belying my conscience. Says he to father there, in a voice as quiet as a lamb's, "William, you are a' old aged man, as all shall be, so sit down in my easy-chair, and rest yourself." And down Father zot. I could fain ha' laughed at thee, father, for thou'st take it so unconcerned at first, and then looked so frightened when the chair-bottom sunk in.'

'You see,' said old William, hastening to explain, 'I was scared to find the bottom gie way – what should I know o' spring bottoms? – and thought I had broke it down: and of course as to breaking down a man's chair, I didn't wish any such thing.'

'And, neighbours, when a feller, ever so much up for a miff, d'see his own father sitting in his enemy's easy-chair, and a poor chap like Leaf made the best of, as if he almost had brains – why, it knocks all the wind out of his sail at once: it did out of mine.'

'If that young figure of fun – Fance Day, I mean, said

Bowman, 'hadn't been so mighty forward wi' showing herself off to Shiner and Dick and the rest, 'tis my belief we should never ha' left the gallery.'

''Tis my belief that though Shiner fired the bullets, the parson made 'em,' said Mr Penny. 'My wife sticks to it that he's in love wi' her.'

'That's a thing we shall never know. I can't onriddle her,* nohow.'

'Thou'st ought to be able to onriddle such a little chiel as she,' the tranter observed.

'The littler the maid, the bigger the riddle, to my mind. And coming of such a stock, too, she may well be a twister.'*

'Yes; Geoffrey Day is a clever man if ever there was one. Never says anything: not he.'

'Never.'

'You might live wi' that man, my sonnies, a hundred years, and never know there was anything in him.'

'Ay; one o' these up-country London ink-bottle chaps* would call Geoffrey a fool.'

'Ye never find out what's in that man: never,' said Spinks. 'Close? ah, he is close! He can hold his tongue well. That man's dumbness is wonderful to listen to.'

'There's so much sense in it. Every moment of it is brimmen over wi' sound understanding.'

''A can hold his tongue very clever – very clever truly,' echoed Leaf. ''A do look at me as if 'a could see my thoughts running round like the works of a clock.'

'Well, all will agree that the man can halt well in his talk, be it a long time or be it a short time. And though we can't expect his daughter to inherit his closeness, she may have a few dribble its from his sense.'

'And his pocket, perhaps.'

'Yes; the nine hundred pound that everybody says he's worth; but I call it four hundred and fifty; for I never believe more than half I hear.'

'Well, he've made a pound or two, and I suppose the maid will have it, since there's nobody else. But 'tis rather sharp upon her, if she's born to fortune, to bring her up as if not born for it, and letting her work so hard.'

''Tis all upon his principle. A long-headed feller!'

'Ah,' murmured Spinks, ''twould be sharper upon her if she were born for fortune, and not to it! I suffer from that affliction.'

6

YALBURY WOOD AND THE
KEEPER'S HOUSE

A mood of blitheness rarely experienced even by young men was Dick's on the following Monday morning. It was the week after the Easter holidays, and he was journeying along with Smart the mare and the light spring-cart,* watching the damp slopes of the hillsides as they streamed in the warmth of the sun, which at this unsettled season shone on the grass with the freshness of an occasional inspector rather than as an accustomed proprietor. His errand was to fetch Fancy, and some additional household goods, from her father's house in the neighbouring parish to her dwelling at Mellstock. The distant view was darkly shaded with clouds; but the nearer parts of the landscape were whitely illumined by the visible rays of the sun streaming down across the heavy grey shade behind.

The tranter had not yet told his son of the state of Shiner's heart that had been suggested to him by Shiner's movements. He preferred to let such delicate affairs right themselves; experience having taught him that the uncertain phenomenon of love, as it existed in other people, was not a groundwork upon which a single action of his own life could be founded.

Geoffrey Day lived in the depths of Yalbury Wood,* which formed portion of one of the outlying estates of the Earl of Wessex, to whom Day was head gamekeeper, timber-steward, and general overlooker for this district. The wood was intersected by the highway from Casterbridge* to London at a place not far from the house, and some trees had of late years been felled between its windows and the ascent of Yalbury Hill, to give the solitary cottager a glimpse of the passers-by.

It was a satisfaction to walk into the keeper's house, even as a stranger, on a fine spring morning like the present. A curl of wood-smoke came from the chimney and drooped over the roof like a blue feather in a lady's hat; and the sun shone obliquely upon the patch of grass in front, which reflected its brightness through the open doorway and up the staircase opposite, lighting up each riser* with a shiny green radiance and leaving the top of each step in shade.

The window-sill of the front room was between four and five feet from the floor, dropping inwardly to a broad low bench, over which, as well as over the whole surface of the wall beneath, there always hung a deep shade, which was considered objectionable on every ground save one, namely, that the perpetual sprinkling of seeds and water by the caged canary above was not noticed as an eyesore by visitors. The window was set with thickly leaded diamond glazing, formed, especially in the lower panes, of knotty glass of various shades of green. Nothing was better known to Fancy than the extravagant manner in which these circular knots or eyes distorted every-thing seen through them from the outside – lifting hats from heads, shoulders from bodies; scattering the spokes of cart-wheels, and bending the straight fir-trunks into semicircles. The ceiling was carried by a beam traversing its midst, from the side of which projected a large nail, used solely and constantly as a peg for Geoffrey's hat; the nail was arched by a rainbow-shaped stain, imprinted by the brim of the said hat when it was hung there dripping wet.

The most striking point about the room was the furniture. This was a repetition upon inanimate objects of the old principle introduced by Noah,* consisting for the most part of two articles of every sort. The duplicate system of furnishing owed its existence to the forethought of Fancy's mother, exercised from the date of Fancy's birthday onwards. The arrangement spoke for itself: nobody who knew the tone of the household could look at the goods without being aware that the second set was a provision for Fancy when she should marry and have a house of her own. The most noticeable instance was a pair of green-faced eight-day clocks ticking alternately, which were severally two-and-a-half minutes and three minutes striking the hour of twelve, one proclaiming, in Italian flourishes, Thomas Wood as the name of its maker, and the other – arched at the top, and altogether of more cynical appearance – that of Ezekiel Saunders. They were two departed clockmakers of Casterbridge, whose desperate rivalry throughout their lives was nowhere more emphatically perpetuated than here at Geoffrey's. These chief specimens of the marriage provision were supported on the right by a couple of kitchen dressers, each fitted complete with their cups, dishes, and plates, in their turn followed by two dumb-waiters,* two family Bibles, two warming-pans,* and two intermixed sets of chairs.

But the position last reached – the chimney-corner – was, after all, the most attractive side of the parallelogram. It was large enough to admit, in addition to Geoffrey himself, Geoffrey's wife, her chair, and her work-table, entirely within the line of the mantel, without danger or even inconvenience from the heat of the fire; and was spacious enough overhead to allow of the insertion of wood poles for the hanging of bacon, which were cloaked with long shreds of soot floating on the draught like the tattered banners on the walls of ancient aisles.

These points were common to most chimney-corners of the neighbourhood; but one feature there was which made Geoffrey's fireside not only an object of interest to casual aristocratic visitors – to whom every cottage fireside was more or less a curiosity – but the admiration of friends who were accustomed to fireplaces of the ordinary hamlet model. This peculiarity was a little window in the chimney-back, almost over the fire, around which the smoke crept caressingly when it left the perpendicular course. The window-board was curiously stamped with black circles, burnt thereon by the heated bottoms of drinking-cups which had rested there after previously standing on the hot ashes of the hearth for the purpose of warming their contents, the result giving to the ledge the look of an envelope which has passed through innumerable post-offices.

Fancy was gliding about the room preparing dinner, her head inclining now to the right, now to the left, and singing the tips and ends of tunes that sprang up in her mind like mushrooms. The footsteps of Mrs Day could be heard in the room overhead. Fancy went finally to the door.

'Father! Dinner.'

A tall spare figure was seen advancing by the window with periodical steps, and the keeper entered from the garden. He appeared to be a man who was always looking down as if trying to recollect something he said yesterday. The surface of his face was fissured rather than wrinkled, and over and under his eyes were folds which seemed as a kind of exterior eyelids. His nose had been thrown backwards by a blow in a poaching fray, so that when the sun was low and shining in his face people could see far into his head. There was in him a quiet grimness which would in his moments of displeasure have become surliness, had it not been tempered by honesty of soul, and which was often wrongheadedness because not allied with subtlety.

Although not an extraordinarily taciturn man among friends slightly richer than himself, he never wasted words upon outsiders, and to his trapper Enoch his ideas were seldom conveyed by any other means than nods and shakes of the head. Their long acquaintance with each other's ways, and the nature of their labours, rendered words between them almost superfluous as vehicles of thought, whilst the coincidence of their horizons, and the astonishing equality of their social views, by startling the keeper from time to time as very damaging to the theory of master and man, strictly forbade any indulgence in words as courtesies.

Behind the keeper came Enoch (who had been assisting in the garden) at the well-considered chronological distance of three minutes – an interval of non-appearance on the trapper's art not arrived at without some reflection. Four minutes had been found to express indifference to indoor arrangements, and simultaneousness had implied too great an anxiety about meals.

'A little earlier than usual, Fancy,' the keeper said, as he sat down and looked at the clocks. 'That Ezekiel Saunders o' thine is tearing on afore Thomas Wood again.'

'I kept in the middle between them,' said Fancy, also looking at the two clocks.

'Better stick to Thomas,' said her father. 'There's a healthy beat in Thomas that would lead a man to swear by en offhand. He is as true as the town time. How is it your stap-mother isn't here?'

As Fancy was about to reply the rattle of wheels was heard, and 'Weh-hey, Smart!' in Mr Richard Dewy's voice rolled into the cottage from round the corner of the house.

'Hullo! there's Dewy's cart come for thee, Fancy – Dick driving – afore time, too. Well, ask the lad to have pot-luck* with us.'

Dick on entering made a point of implying by his general bearing that he took an interest in Fancy simply as in one of the same race and country as himself; and they all sat down. Dick could have wished her manner had not been so entirely free from all apparent consciousness of those accidental meetings of theirs; but he let the thought pass. Enoch sat diagonally at a table afar off under the corner cupboard, and drank his cider from a long perpendicular pint cup having tall fir-trees done in brown on its sides. He threw occasional remarks into the general tide of conversation, and with this advantage to himself, that he participated in the pleasures of a talk (slight as it was) at meal-times, without saddling himself with the responsibility of sustaining it.

'Why don't your stap-mother come down, Fancy?' said Geoffrey. 'You'll excuse her, Mister Dick, she's a little queer sometimes.'

'O yes – quite,' said Richard, as if he were in the habit of excusing people every day.

'She d'belong to that class of womankind that become second wives: a rum class rather.'

'Indeed,' said Dick, with sympathy for an indefinite something.

'Yes; and 'tis trying to a female, especially if you've been a first wife, as she have.'

'Very trying it must be.'

'Yes: you see her first husband was a young man who let her go too far; in fact, she used to kick up Bob's-a-dying* at the least thing in the world. And when I'd married her and found it out, I thought, thinks I, "'Tis too late now to begin to cure 'ee," and so I let her bide. But she's queer – very queer, at times!'

'I'm sorry to hear that.'

'Yes: there; wives be such a provoking class of society because, though they be never right, they be never more than half wrong.'

Fancy seemed uneasy under the infliction of this household moralising, which might tend to damage the airy-fairy nature that Dick, as maiden shrewdness told her, had accredited her with. Her dead silence impressed Geoffrey with the notion that something in his words did not agree with her educated ideas, and he changed the conversation.

'Did Fred Shiner send the cask o' drink, Fancy?'

'I think he did: O yes, he did.'

'Nice solid feller, Fred Shiner!' said Geoffrey to Dick as he helped himself to gravy, bringing the spoon round to his plate by way of the potato-dish, to obviate a stain on the cloth in the event of a spill.

Now Geoffrey's eyes had been fixed upon his plate for the previous four or five minutes, and in removing them he had only carried them to the spoon, which, from its fullness and the distance of its transit, necessitated a steady watching through the whole of the route. Just as intently as the keeper's eyes had been fixed on the spoon Fancy's had been fixed on her father's, without premeditation or the slightest phase of furtiveness; but there they were fastened. This was the reason why:

Dick was sitting next to her on the right side, and on the side of the table opposite to her father. Fancy had laid her right hand lightly down upon the table-cloth for an instant, and to her alarm Dick, after dropping his fork and brushing his forehead as a reason, flung down his own left hand, overlapping a third of Fancy's with it, and keeping it there. So the innocent Fancy, instead of pulling her hand from the trap, settled her eyes on her father's, to guard against his discovery of this perilous game of Dick's. Dick finished his mouthful; Fancy finished her crumb, and nothing was done beyond watching Geoffrey's eyes. Then the hands slid apart; Fancy's going over six inches of cloth, Dick's over one. Geoffrey's eye had risen.

'I said Fred Shiner is a nice solid feller,' he repeated more emphatically.

'He is; yes, he is,' stammered Dick; 'but to me he is little more than a stranger.'

'O, sure. Now I know en as well as any man can be known. And you know en very well too, don't ye, Fancy?'

Geoffrey put on a tone expressing that these words signified at present about one hundred times the amount of meaning they conveyed literally.

Dick looked anxious.

'Will you pass me some bread?' said Fancy in a flurry, the red of her face becoming slightly disordered, and looking as solicitous as a human being could look about a piece of bread.

'Ay, that I will,' replied the unconscious Geoffrey. 'Ay,' he continued, returning to the displaced idea, 'we are likely to remain friendly wi' Mr Shiner if the wheels d'run smooth.'

'An excellent thing – a very capital thing, as I should say,' the youth answered with exceeding relevance, considering that his thoughts, instead of following Geoffrey's remark, were nestling at a distance of about two feet on his left the whole time.

'A young woman's face will turn the north wind, Master

Richard: my heart if 'twon't.' Dick looked more anxious and was attentive in earnest at these words. 'Yes; turn the north wind,' added Geoffrey after an impressive pause. 'And though she's one of my own flesh and blood . . .'

'Will you fetch down a bit of raw-mil' cheese* from pantry-shelf?' Fancy interrupted as if she were famishing.

'Ay, that I will, chiel; chiel, says I, and Mr Shiner only asking last Saturday night . . . cheese you said, Fancy?'

Dick controlled his emotion at these mysterious allusions to Mr Shiner – the better enabled to do so by perceiving that Fancy's heart went not with her father's – and spoke like a stranger to the affairs of the neighbourhood. 'Yes, there's a great deal to be said upon the power of maiden faces in settling your courses,' he ventured, as the keeper retreated for the cheese.

'The conversation is taking a very strange turn: nothing that *I* have ever done warrants such things being said!' murmured Fancy with emphasis just loud enough to reach Dick's ears.

'You think to yourself, 'twas to be,' cried Enoch from his distant corner, by way of filling up the vacancy caused by Geoffrey's momentary absence. 'And so you marry her, Master Dewy, and there's an end o't.'

'Pray don't say such things, Enoch,' came from Fancy severely, upon which Enoch relapsed into servitude.

'If we be doomed to marry, we marry; if we be doomed to remain single, we do,' replied Dick.

Geoffrey had by this time sat down again, and he now made his lips thin by severely straining them across his gums, and looked out of the window along the vista to the distant highway up Yalbury Hill. That's not the case with some folk,' he said at length, as if he read the words on a board at the further end of the vista.

Fancy looked interested, and Dick said, 'No?'

'There's that wife o' mine. It was her doom to be nobody's wife at all in the wide universe. But she made up her mind that she would, and did it twice over. Doom? Doom is nothing beside a elderly woman – quite a chiel in her hands!'

A movement was now heard along the upstairs passage, and footsteps descending. The door at the foot of the stairs opened and the second Mrs Day appeared in view, looking fixedly at the table as she advanced towards it, with apparent obliviousness of the presence of any other human being than herself. In short, if the table had been the personages, and the persons the table, her glance would have been the most natural imaginable.

She showed herself to possess an ordinary woman's face, iron-grey hair, hardly any hips, and a great deal of cleanliness in a broad white apron-string as it appeared upon the waist of her dark stuff dress.

'People will run away with a story now, I suppose,' she began saying, 'that Jane Day's tablecloths are as poor and ragged as any union* beggar's!'

Dick now perceived that the tablecloth was a little the worse for wear, and reflecting for a moment concluded that 'people' in step-mother language probably meant himself. On lifting his eyes he found that Mrs Day had vanished again upstairs, and presently returned with an armful of new damask-linen table-cloths folded square and hard as boards by long compression. These she flounced down into a chair; then took one, shook it out from its folds, and spread it on the table by instalments, transferring the plates and dishes one by one from the old to the new cloth.

'And I suppose they'll say, too, that she ha'n't a decent knife and fork in her house!'

'I shouldn't say any such ill-natured thing, I am sure—' began Dick. But Mrs Day had vanished into the next room. Fancy appeared distressed.

'Very strange woman, isn't she?' said Geoffrey, quietly going on with his dinner. But 'tis too late to attempt curing. My heart! 'tis so growed into her that 'twould kill her to take it out. Ay, she's very queer: you'd be amazed to see what valuable goods we've got stowed away upstairs.'

Back again came Mrs Day with a box of bright steel horn-handled knives, silver-plated forks, carver, and all complete. These were wiped of the preservative oil which coated them, and then a knife and fork were laid down to each individual with a bang, the carving knife and fork thrust into the meat dish, and the old ones they had hitherto used tossed away.

Geoffrey placidly cut a slice with the new knife and fork, and asked Dick if he wanted any more.

The table had been spread for the mixed midday meal of dinner and tea which was common among frugal countryfolk. 'The parishioners about here,' continued Mrs Day, not looking at any living being, but snatching up the brown delf* tea-things, 'are the laziest, gossipest, poachest, jailest* set of any ever I came among. And they'll talk about my teapot and tea-things next, I suppose!' She vanished with the teapot, cups, and saucers, and reappeared with a tea service in white china, and a packet wrapped in brown paper. This was removed, together with folds of tissue-paper underneath; and a brilliant silver teapot appeared.

'I'll help to put the things right,' said Fancy soothingly, and rising from her seat. 'I ought to have laid out better things, I suppose. But' (here she enlarged her looks so as to include Dick) 'I have been away from home a good deal, and I make shocking blunders in my housekeeping.' Smiles and suavity were then dispensed all around by this bright little bird.

After a little more preparation and modification Mrs Day took her seat at the head of the table, and during the latter or tea division of the meal presided with much composure. It may cause some surprise to learn that, now her vagary was over, she showed herself to be an excellent person with much common sense, and even a religious seriousness of tone on matters pertaining to her afflictions.

7

DICK MAKES HIMSELF USEFUL

The effect of Geoffrey's incidental allusions to Mr Shiner was to restrain a considerable flow of spontaneous chat that would otherwise have burst from young Dewy along the drive homeward. And a certain remark he had hazarded to her, in rather too blunt and eager a manner, kept the young lady herself even more silent than Dick. On both sides there was an unwillingness to talk on any but the most trivial subjects, and their sentences rarely took a larger form than could be expressed in two or three words.

Owing to Fancy being later in the day than she had promised the charwoman* had given up expecting her; whereupon Dick could do no less than stay and see her comfortably tided over the disagreeable time of entering and establishing herself in an empty house after an absence of a week. The additional furniture and utensils that had been brought (a canary and cage among the rest) were taken out of the vehicle, and the horse was unharnessed and put in the plot opposite, where there was some tender grass. Dick lighted the fire already laid; and activity began to loosen their tongues a little.

'There!' said Fancy, 'we forgot to bring the fire-irons!'*

She had originally found in her sitting-room, to bear out the expression 'nearly furnished' which the school-manager had used in his letter to her, a table, three chairs, a fender, and a piece of carpet. This 'nearly' had been supplemented hitherto by a kind friend, who had lent her fire-irons and crockery until she should fetch some from home.

Dick attended to the young lady's fire, using his whip-handle for a poker till it was spoilt, and then flourishing a hurdle stick for the remainder of the time.

'The kettle boils; now you shall have a cup of tea,' said Fancy, diving into the hamper she had brought.

'Thank you,' said Dick, whose drive had made him ready for some, especially in her company.

'Well, here's only one cup and saucer, as I breathe! Whatever could Mother be thinking about? Do you mind making shift, Mr Dewy?'

'Not at all, Miss Day,' said that civil person.

' – And only having a cup by itself? or a saucer by itself?'

'Don't mind in the least.'

'Which do you mean by that?'

'I mean the cup if you like the saucer.'

'And the saucer if I like the cup?'

'Exactly, Miss Day.'

'Thank you, Mr Dewy, for I like the cup decidedly. Stop a minute; there are no spoons now!'

She dived into the hamper again, and at the end of two or three minutes looked up and said, 'I suppose you don't mind if I can't find a spoon?'

'Not at all,' said the agreeable Richard.

'The fact is the spoons have slipped down somewhere; right under the other things. O yes, here's one, and only one. You would rather have one than not I suppose, Mr Dewy?'

'Rather not. I never did care much about spoons.'

'Then I'll have it. I do care about them. You must stir up your tea with a knife. Would you mind lifting the kettle off, that it may not boil dry?'

Dick leapt to the fireplace, and earnestly removed the kettle.

'There! you did it so wildly that you have made your hand black. We always use kettle-holders; didn't you learn housewifery as far as that, Mr Dewy? Well, never mind the soot on your hand. Come here. I am going to rinse mine, too.'

They went to a basin she had placed in the back room. 'This is the only basin I have,' she said. 'Turn up your sleeves, and by that time my hands will be washed, and you can come.'

Her hands were in the water now. 'O, how vexing!' she exclaimed. 'There's not a drop of water left for you unless you draw it, and the well is I don't know how many furlongs deep; all that was in the pitcher* I used for the kettle and this basin. Do you mind dipping the tips of your fingers in the same?'

'Not at all. And to save time I won't wait till you have done, if you have no objection?'

Thereupon he plunged in his hands, and they paddled together. It being the first time in his life that he had touched female fingers under water, Dick duly registered the sensation as rather a nice one.

'Really, I hardly know which are my own hands and which are yours, they have got so mixed up together,' she said, withdrawing her own very suddenly.

'It doesn't matter at all,' said Dick, 'at least as far as I am concerned.'

'There! no towel! Whoever thinks of a towel till the hands are wet?'

'Nobody.'

'"Nobody." How very dull it is when people are so friendly! Come here, Mr Dewy. Now do you think you could lift the lid of that box with your elbow, and then, with something or other, take out a towel you will find under the clean clothes? Be *sure* don't touch any of them with your wet hands, for the things at the top are all starched and ironed.'

Dick managed by the aid of a knife and fork to extract a towel from under a muslin* dress without wetting the latter; and for a moment he ventured to assume a tone of criticism.

'I fear for that dress,' he said, as they wiped their hands together.

'What?' said Miss Day, looking into the box at the dress

alluded to. 'O, I know what you mean – that the vicar will never let me wear muslin?'

'Yes.'

'Well, I know it is condemned by all orders in the church as flaunting, and unfit for common wear for girls who've their living to get; but we'll see.'

'In the interest of the church I hope you don't speak seriously.'

'Yes, I do; but we'll see.' There was a comely determination on her lip, very pleasant to a beholder who was neither bishop, priest, nor deacon. 'I think I can manage any vicar's views about me if he's under forty.'

Dick rather wished she had never thought of managing vicars.

'I certainly shall be glad to get some of your delicious tea,' he said in rather a free way, yet modestly, as became one in a position between that of visitor and inmate, and looking wistfully at his lonely saucer.

'So shall I. Now is there anything else we want, Mr Dewy?'

'I really think there's nothing else, Miss Day.'

She prepared to sit down, looking musingly out of the window at Smart's enjoyment of the rich grass. 'Nobody seems to care about me,' she murmured, with large lost eyes fixed upon the sky beyond Smart.

'Perhaps Mr Shiner does,' said Dick, in the tone of a slightly injured man.

'Yes, I forgot – he does, I know.' Dick precipitately regretted that he had suggested Shiner since it had produced such a miserable result as this.

'I'll warrant you'll care for somebody very much indeed another day, won't you, Mr Dewy?' she continued, looking very feelingly into the mathematical centre of his eyes.

'Ah, I'll warrant I shall,' said Dick, feelingly too, and looking back into her dark pupils, whereupon they were turned aside.

'I meant,' she went on, preventing him from speaking just as he was going to narrate a forcible story about his feelings, I meant that nobody comes to see if I have returned – not even the vicar.'

'If you want to see him, I'll call at the vicarage directly we have had some tea.'

'No, no! Don't let him come down here, whatever you do, whilst I am in such a state of disarrangement. Parsons look so miserable and awkward when one's house is in a muddle;

walking about and making impossible suggestions in quaint academic phrases till your flesh creeps and you wish them dead. Do you take sugar?'

Mr Maybold was at this instant seen coming up the path.

'There! That's he coming! How I wish you were not here! – that is, how awkward – dear, dear!' she exclaimed, with a quick ascent of blood to her face, and irritated with Dick rather than the vicar, as it seemed.

'Pray don't be alarmed on my account, Miss Day – good afternoon!' said Dick in a huff, putting on his hat and leaving the room hastily by the back door.

The horse was caught and put in, and on mounting the shafts to start he saw through the window the vicar, standing upon some books piled in a chair, and driving a nail into the wall; Fancy, with a demure glance, holding the canary-cage up to him as if she had never in her life thought of anything but vicars and canaries.

8

DICK MEETS HIS FATHER

For several minutes Dick drove along homeward, with the inner eye of reflection so anxiously set on his passages at arms with Fancy that the road and scenery were as a thin mist over the real pictures of his mind. Was she a coquette? The balance between the evidence that she did love him and that she did not was so nicely struck that his opinion had no stability. She had let him put his hand upon hers; she had allowed her gaze to drop plumb into the depths of his – his into hers – three or four times; her manner had been very free with regard to the basin and towel; she had appeared vexed at the mention of Shiner. On the other hand, she had driven him about the house like a quiet dog or cat, said Shiner cared for her, and seemed anxious that Mr Maybold should do the same.

Thinking thus as he neared the handpost* at Mellstock Cross, sitting on the front board of the spring cart – his legs on the outside, and his whole frame jigging up and down like a candle-flame to the time of Smart's trotting – who should he see coming down the hill but his father in the light wagon, quivering up and down on a smaller scale of shakes, those merely caused by the stones in the road. They were soon crossing each other's front.

'Weh-hey!' said the tranter to Smiler.

'Weh-hey!' said Dick to Smart, in an echo of the same voice.

'Th'st hauled her back, I suppose?' Reuben inquired peaceably.

'Yes,' said Dick, with such a clinching period at the end that it seemed he was never going to add another word. Smiler, thinking this the close of the conversation, prepared to move on.

'Weh-hey!' said the tranter. 'I tell thee what it is, Dick. That there maid is taking up thy thoughts more than's good for thee, my sonny. Thou'rt, never happy now unless th'rt making thyself miserable about her in one way or another.'

'I don't know about that, Father,' said Dick rather stupidly.

'But I do – Wey, Smiler! – 'Od rot* the women, 'tis nothing else wi' 'em nowadays but getting young men and leading 'em astray.'

'Pooh, Father! you just repeat what all the common world says; that's all you do.'

'The world's a very sensible feller on things in jineral, Dick; very sensible indeed.'

Dick looked into the distance at a vast expanse of mortgaged estate. 'I wish I was as rich as a squire when he's as poor as a crow,' he murmured. 'I'd soon ask Fancy something.'

'I wish so too, wi' all my heart, sonny; that I do. Well, mind what beest about, that's all.'

Smart moved on a step or two. 'Supposing now, Father, – We-hey, Smart! – I did think a little about her, and I had a chance, which I ha'n't; don't you think she's a very good sort of – of – one?'

'Ay, good; she's good enough. When you've made up your mind to marry, take the first respectable body that comes to hand – she's as good as any other; they be all alike in the groundwork; 'tis only in the flourishes* there's a difference. She's good enough; but I can't see what the nation* a young feller like you – wi' a comfortable house and home, and father and mother to take care o' thee, and who sent 'ee to a school so good that 'twas hardly fair to the other children – should want to go hollering after a young woman for, when she's quietly making a husband in her pocket, and not troubled by chick nor chiel, to make a poverty-stric' wife and family of her, and neither hat, cap, wig, nor waistcoat to set 'em up with: be drowned if I can see it, and that's the long and short o't, my sonny!'

Dick looked at Smart's ears, then up the hill; but no reason was suggested by any object that met his gaze.

'For about the same reason that you did, father, I suppose.'

'Dang it, my sonny, thou'st got me there!' And the tranter gave vent to a grim admiration, with the mien of a man who was too magnanimous not to appreciate artistically a slight rap on the knuckles, even if they were his own.

'Whether or no,' said Dick, 'I asked her a thing going along the road.'

'Come to that, is it? Turk!* won't thy mother be in a taking! Well, she's ready, I don't doubt?'

'I didn't ask her anything about having me; and if you'll let me speak, I'll tell 'ee what I want to know. I just said, Did she care about me?'

'Piph-ph-ph!'

'And then she said nothing for a quarter of a mile, and then she said she didn't know. Now, what I want to know is, what was the meaning of that speech?' The latter words were spoken resolutely, as if he didn't care for the ridicule of all the fathers in creation.

'The meaning of that speech is,' the tranter replied deliberately, 'that the meaning is meant to be rather hid at present. Well, Dick, as an honest father to thee, I don't pretend to deny what you d'know well enough; that is, that her father being rather better in the pocket than we, I should welcome her ready enough if it must be somebody.'

'But what d'ye think she really did mean?' said the unsatisfied Dick.

'I'm afeard I am not o' much account in guessing, especially as I was not there when she said it, and seeing that your mother was the only 'ooman I ever cam' into such close quarters as that with.'

'And what did mother say to you when you asked her?' said Dick musingly.

'I don't see that that will help 'ee.'

'The principle is the same.'

'Well – ay: what did she say? Let's see. I was oiling my

working-day boots without taking 'em off, and wi' my head
hanging down, when she just brushed on by the garden hatch*
like a flittering leaf. "Ann," I said says I, and then, – but, Dick,
I'm afeard 'twill be no help to thee; for we were such a rum
couple, your mother and I, leastways one half was, that is myself
– and your mother's charms was more in the manner than the
material.'

'Never mind! "Ann," said you.'

' "Ann," said I, as I was saying . . . "Ann," I said to her when
I was oiling my working-day boots wi' my head hanging down,
"Woot hae me?" . . . What came next I can't quite call up at
this distance o' time. Perhaps your mother would know – she's
got a better memory for her little triumphs than I. However, the
long and the short o' the story is that we were married somehow
as I found afterwards. 'Twas on White Tuesday* – Mellstock
Club walked* the same day, every man two and two, and a fine
day 'twas, – hot as fire; how the sun did strike down upon my
back going to church! I well can mind what a bath o' sweating I
was in, body and soul! But Fance will ha' thee, Dick – she won't
walk with another chap – no such good luck.'

'I don't know about that,' said Dick, whipping at Smart's
flank in a fanciful way which, as Smart knew, meant nothing in
connection with going on. 'There's Pa'son Maybold, too – that's
all against me.'

'What about he? She's never been stuffing into thy innocent
heart that he's in love with her? Lord, the vanity o' maidens!'

'No, no. But he called, and she looked at him in such a way,
and at me in such a way – quite different the ways were – and
as I was coming off there was he hanging up her birdcage.'

'Well, why shouldn't the man hang up her birdcage? Turk
seize it all, what's that got to do wi' it? Dick, that thou beest a
white-lyvered* chap I don't say, but if thou beestn't as mad as a
cappel-faced* bull let me smile no more.'

'O, ay.'

'And what's think now, Dick?'

'I don't know.'

'Here's another pretty kettle o' fish for thee. Who d'ye think's
the bitter weed* in our being turned out? Did our party tell 'ee?'

'No. Why, Pa'son Maybold, I suppose.'

'Shiner – because he's in love with thy young woman, and

d'want to see her young figure sitting up at that queer instrument, and her young fingers rum-strumming upon the keys.'

A sharp ado of sweet and bitter was going on in Dick during this communication from his father. 'Shiner's a fool! – no, that's not it; I don't believe any such thing, father. Why, Shiner would never take a bold step like that unless she'd been a little made up to, and had taken it kindly. Pooh!'

'Who's to say she didn't?'

'I do.'

'The more fool you.'

'Why, father of me?'

'Has she ever done more to thee?'

'No.'

'Then she has done as much to he – rot 'em! Now, Dick, this is how a maid is. She'll swear she's dying for thee, and she is dying for thee, and she will die for thee; but she'll fling a look over t'other shoulder at another young feller, though never leaving off dying for thee just the same.'

'She's not dying for me, and so she didn't fling a look at him.'

'But she may be dying for him, for she looked at thee.'

'I don't know what to make of it at all,' said Dick gloomily.

'All I can make of it is,' the tranter said, raising his whip, arranging his different joints and muscles, and motioning to the horse to move on, 'that if you can't read a maid's mind by her motions, nature d'seem to say thou'st ought to be a bachelor. Clk, clk! Smiler!' And the tranter moved on.

Dick held Smart's rein firmly, and the whole concern of horse, cart, and man remained rooted in the lane. How long this condition would have lasted is unknown, had not Dick's thoughts, after adding up numerous items of misery, gradually wandered round to the fact that as something must be done it could not be done by staying there all night.

Reaching home he went up to his bedroom, shut the door as if he were going to be seen no more in this life, and taking a sheet of paper and uncorking the ink-bottle he began a letter. The dignity of the writer's mind was so powerfully apparent in every line of this effusion that it obscured the logical sequence of facts and intentions to an appreciable degree; and it was not at all clear to a reader whether he there and then left off loving Miss Fancy Day; whether he had never loved her seriously and never meant to; whether he had been dying up to the present moment and now intended to get well again; or whether he had hitherto been in good health and intended to die for her forthwith.

He put this letter in an envelope, sealed it up, directed it in a stern handwriting of straight dashes – easy flourishes being rigorously excluded. He walked with it in his pocket down the lane in strides not an inch less than three feet long. Reaching her gate he put on a resolute expression – then put it off again, turned back homeward, tore up his letter, and sat down.

That letter was altogether in a wrong tone – that he must own. A heartless man-of-the-world tone was what the juncture required. That he rather wanted her, and rather did not want her – the latter for choice; but that as a member of society he didn't mind making a query in jaunty terms, which could only be answered in the same way: did she mean anything by her bearing towards him, or did she not?

This letter was considered so satisfactory in every way that, being put into the hands of a little boy and the order given that he was to run with it to the school, he was told in addition not to look behind him if Dick called after him to bring it back, but to run along with it just the same. Having taken this precaution against vacillation Dick watched his messenger down the road, and turned into the house whistling an air in such ghastly jerks and starts that whistling seemed to be the act the very furthest removed from that which was instinctive in such a youth.

The letter was left as ordered: the next morning came and passed – and no answer. The next. The next. Friday night came. Dick resolved that if no answer or sign were given by her the next day, on Sunday he would meet her face to face, and have it all out by word of mouth.

'Dick,' said his father, coming in from the garden at that moment – in each hand a hive of bees tied in a cloth to prevent their egress – 'I think you'd better take these two swarms of bees to Mrs Maybold's tomorrow, instead o' me, and I'll go wi, Smiler and the wagon.'

It was a relief; for Mrs Maybold, the vicar's mother, who had just taken into her head a fancy for keeping bees (pleasantly disguised under the pretence of its being an economical wish to produce her own honey), lived near the watering-place of Budmouth Regis,* ten miles off, and the business of transporting the hives thither would occupy the whole day, and to some extent annihilate the vacant time between this evening and the coming Sunday. The best spring-cart was washed throughout, the axles oiled, and the bees placed therein for the journey.

PART III
SUMMER

DRIVING OUT OF BUDMOUTH

An easy bend of neck and graceful set of head; full and wavy bundles of dark-brown hair; light fall of little feet; pretty devices on the skirt of the dress; clear deep eyes; in short, a bunch of sweets: it was Fancy! Dick's heart went round to her with a rush.

The scene was the corner of Mary Street in Budmouth Regis,* near the King's statue,* at which point the white angle of the last house in the row cut perpendicularly an embayed and nearly motionless expanse of salt water projected from the outer ocean – today lit in bright tones of green and opal. Dick and Smart had just emerged from the street, and there on the right, against the brilliant sheet of liquid colour, stood Fancy Day; and she turned and recognized him.

Dick suspended his thoughts of the letter and wonder at how she came there by driving close to the chains of the Esplanade – incontinently displacing two chairmen,* who had just come to life for the summer in new clean shirts and revivified clothes, and being almost displaced in turn by a rigid boy rattling along with a baker's cart and looking neither to the right nor the left. He asked if she were going to Mellstock that night.

'Yes, I'm waiting for the carrier,' she replied, seeming, too, to suspend thoughts of the letter.

'Now I can drive you home nicely, and you save half an hour. Will ye come with me?'

As Fancy's power to will anything seemed to have departed in some mysterious manner at that moment, Dick settled the matter by getting out and assisting her into the vehicle without another word.

The temporary flush upon her cheek changed to a lesser hue which was permanent, and at length their eyes met; there was present between them a certain feeling of embarrassment, which arises at such moments when all the instinctive acts dictated by the position have been performed. Dick, being engaged with the reins, thought less of this awkwardness than did Fancy, who had nothing to do but to feel his presence, and to be more and more conscious of the fact that by accepting a seat beside him in this way she succumbed to the tone of his note. Smart jogged along, and Dick jogged, and the helpless Fancy necessarily jogged too; and she felt that she was in a measure captured and made a prisoner.

'I am so much obliged to you for your company, Miss Day,' he observed, as they drove past the two semicircular bays of the Old Royal Hotel, where His Majesty King George the Third had many a time attended the balls of the burgesses.*

To Miss Day, crediting him with the same consciousness of mastery – a consciousness of which he was perfectly innocent – this remark sounded like a magnanimous intention to soothe her, the captive.

'I didn't come for the pleasure of obliging you with my company,' she said.

The answer had an unexpected manner of incivility in it that must have been rather surprising to young Dewy. At the same time it may be observed that when a young woman returns a rude answer to a young man's civil remark her heart is in a state which argues rather hopefully for his case than otherwise.

There was silence between them till they had left the sea-front and passed about twenty of the trees that ornamented the road leading up out of the town towards Casterbridge and Mellstock.

'Though I didn't come for that purpose either, I would have done it,' said Dick at the twenty-first tree.

'Now, Mr Dewy, no flirtation, because it's wrong, and I don't wish it.'

Dick seated himself afresh just as he had been sitting before, arranged his looks very emphatically, and cleared his throat.

'Really, anybody would think you had met me on business and were just going to commence,' said the lady intractably.

'Yes, they would.'

'Why, you never have, to be sure!'

This was a shaky beginning. He chopped round and said cheerily, as a man who had resolved never to spoil his jollity by loving one of womankind—

'Well, how are you getting on Miss Day at the present time? Gaily, I don't doubt for a moment.'

'I am not gay, Dick; you know that.'

'Gaily doesn't mean decked in gay dresses.'

'I didn't suppose gaily was gaily dressed. Mighty me, what a scholar you've grown!'

'Lots of things have happened to you this spring, I see.'

'What have you seen?'

'O, nothing, I've heard, I mean!'

'What have you heard?'

'The name of a pretty man with brass studs, and a copper ring, and a tin watch-chain, a little mixed up with your own. That's all.'

'That's a very unkind picture of Mr Shiner, for that's who you mean! The studs are gold as you know, and it's a real silver chain; the ring I can't conscientiously defend, and he only wore it once.'

'He might have worn it a hundred times without showing it half so much.'

'Well, he's nothing to me,' she serenely observed.

'Not any more than I am?'

'Now, Mr Dewy,' said Fancy severely, 'certainly he isn't any more to me than you are!'

'Not so much?'

She looked aside to consider the precise compass of that question. 'That I can't exactly answer,' she replied with soft archness.

As they were going rather slowly another spring-cart, containing a farmer, farmer's wife, and farmer's man, jogged past them; and the farmer's wife and farmer's man eyed the couple very curiously. The farmer never looked up from the horse's tail.

'Why can't you exactly answer?' said Dick, quickening Smart a little, and jogging on just behind the farmer and farmer's wife and man.

As no answer came, and as their eyes had nothing else to do, they both contemplated the picture presented in front, and noticed how the farmer's wife sat flattened between the two men, who bulged over each end of the seat to give her room till they almost sat upon their respective wheels; and they looked too at the farmer's wife's silk mantle* inflating itself between her shoulders like a balloon and sinking flat again at each jog of the horse. The farmer's wife, feeling their eyes sticking into her back, looked over her shoulder. Dick dropped ten yards further behind.

'Fancy, why can't you answer?' he repeated.

'Because how much you are to me depends upon how much I am to you,' said she in low tones.

'Everything,' said Dick, putting his hand towards hers and casting emphatic eyes upon the upper curve of her cheek.

'Now, Richard Dewy, no touching me! I didn't say in what way your thinking of me affected the question – perhaps inversely, don't you see? No touching, sir! Look; goodness me, don't, Dick!'

The cause of her sudden start was the unpleasant appearance over Dick's right shoulder of an empty timber-wagon and four journeymen-carpenters* reclining in lazy postures inside it, their eyes directed upwards at various oblique angles into the surrounding world, the chief object of their existence being apparently to criticise to the very backbone and marrow every animate object that came within the compass of their vision. This difficulty of Dick's was overcome by trotting on till the wagon and carpenters were beginning to look rather misty by reason of a film of dust that accompanied their wagon-wheels and rose around their heads like a fog.

'Say you love me, Fancy.'

'No, Dick, certainly not; 'tisn't time to do that yet.'

'Why, Fancy?'

' "Miss Day" is better at present – don't mind my saying so; and I ought not to have called you Dick.'

'Nonsense! when you know that I would do anything on earth for your love. Why, you make anyone think that loving is a thing that can be done and undone, and put on and put off at a mere whim.'

'No, no, I don't,' she said gently; 'but there are things which tell me I ought not to give way to much thinking about you, even if—'

'But you want to, don't you? Yes, say you do; it is best to be truthful. Whatever they may say about a woman's right to conceal where her love lies, and pretend it doesn't exist, and things like that, it is not best; I do know it, Fancy. And an honest woman in that, as well as in all her daily concerns, shines most brightly, and is thought most of in the long run.'

'Well then, perhaps, Dick, I do love you a little,' she whispered tenderly; 'but I wish you wouldn't say any more now.'

'I won't say any more now, then, if you don't like it, dear. But you do love me a little, don't you?'

'Now you ought not to want me to keep saying things twice. I can't say any more now, and you must be content with what you have.'

'I may at any rate call you Fancy? There's no harm in that.'

'Yes, you may.'

'And you'll not call me Mr Dewy any more?'

'Very well.'

2

FURTHER ALONG THE ROAD

Dick's spirits having risen in the course of these admissions of his sweetheart he now touched Smart with the whip; and on Smart's neck, not far behind his ears. Smart, who had been lost in thought for some time, never dreaming that Dick could reach so far with a whip which, on this particular journey, had never been extended further than his flank, tossed his head and scampered along with exceeding briskness, which was very pleasant to the young couple behind him till, turning a bend in the road, they came instantly upon the farmer, farmer's man, and farmer's wife with the flapping mantle, all jogging on just the same as ever.

'Bother those people! Here we are upon them again.'

'Well, of course. They have as much right to the road as we.'

'Yes, but it is provoking to be overlooked so. I like a road all to myself. Look what a lumbering affair theirs is!' The wheels of the farmer's cart just at that moment jogged into a depression running across the road, giving the cart a twist, whereupon all three nodded to the left, and on coming out of it all three nodded to the right, and went on jerking their backs in and out as usual. 'We'll pass them when the road gets wider.'

When an opportunity seemed to offer itself for carrying this intention into effect they heard light flying wheels behind, and on their quartering* there whizzed along past them a brand-new gig,* so brightly polished that the spokes of the wheels sent forth a continual quivering light at one point in their circle, and all the panels glared like mirrors in Dick and Fancy's eyes. The driver, and owner as it appeared, was really a handsome man;

his companion was Shiner. Both turned round as they passed Dick and Fancy and stared with bold admiration in her face till they were obliged to attend to the operation of passing the farmer. Dick glanced for an instant at Fancy while she was undergoing their scrutiny; then returned to his driving with rather a sad countenance.

'Why are you so silent?' she said after a while, with real concern.

'Nothing.'

'Yes, it is, Dick. I couldn't help those people passing.'

'I know that.'

'You look offended with me. What have I done?'

'I can't tell without offending you.'

'Better out.'

'Well,' said Dick, who seemed longing to tell even at the risk of offending her, 'I was thinking how different you in love are from me in love. Whilst those men were staring you dismissed me from your thoughts altogether and—'

'You can't offend me further now; tell all!'

'And showed upon your face a pleased sense of being attractive to 'em.'

'Don't be silly, Dick! You know very well I didn't.'

Dick shook his head sceptically and smiled.

'Dick, I always believe flattery *if possible* – and it was possible then. Now there's an open confession of weakness. But I showed no consciousness of it.'

Dick, perceiving by her look that she would adhere to her statement, charitably forbore saying anything that could make her prevaricate. The sight of Shiner, too, had recalled another branch of the subject to his mind; that which had been his greatest trouble till her company and words had obscured its probability.

'By the way, Fancy, do you know why our quire is to be dismissed?'

'No: except that it is Mr Maybold's wish for me to play the organ.'

'Do you know how it came to be his wish?'

'That I don't.'

'Mr Shiner, being churchwarden, has persuaded the vicar; who, however, was willing enough before. Shiner, I know, is crazy to see you playing every Sunday; I suppose he'll turn over your music, for the organ will be close to his pew. But – I know you have never encouraged him?'

'Never once!' said Fancy emphatically, and with eyes full of earnest truth. 'I don't like him indeed, and I never heard of his doing this before! I have always felt that I should like to play in a church, but I never wished to turn you and your choir out; and I never even said that I could play till I was asked. You don't think for a moment that I did, surely, do you?'

'I know you didn't, dear.'

'Or that I care the least morsel of a bit for him?'

'I know you don't.'

The distance between Budmouth and Mellstock was ten or eleven miles, and there being a good inn, the Ship,* four miles out of Budmouth, with a mast and cross-trees in front, Dick's custom in driving thither was to divide his journey into three stages by resting at this inn going and coming, and not troubling the Budmouth stables at all, whenever his visit to the town was a mere call and deposit, as today.

Fancy was ushered into a little tea-room and Dick went to the stables to see to the feeding of Smart. In face of the significant twitches of feature that were visible in the ostler and labouring men idling around, Dick endeavoured to look unconscious of the fact that there was any sentiment between him and Fancy beyond a tranter's desire to carry a passenger home. He presently entered the inn and opened the door of Fancy's room.

'Dick, do you know, it has struck me that it is rather awkward my being here alone with you like this. I don't think you had better come in with me.'

'That's rather unpleasant, dear.'

'Yes, it is, and I wanted you to have some tea as well as myself too, because you must be tired.'

'Well, let me have some with you, then. I was denied once before, if you recollect, Fancy.'

'Yes, yes, never mind! And it seems unfriendly of me now, but I don't know what to do.'

'It shall be as you say, then.' Dick began to retreat with a dissatisfied wrinkling of face, and a farewell glance at the cosy tea-tray.

'But you don't see how it is, Dick, when you speak like that,' she said with more earnestness than she had ever shown before. 'You do know that even if I care very much for you I must remember that I have a difficult position to maintain. The vicar would not like me, as his schoolmistress, to indulge in a *tête-à-tête** anywhere with anybody.'

'But I am not *any*body!' exclaimed Dick.

'No, no, I mean with a young man;' and she added softly, 'unless I were really engaged to be married to him.'

'Is that all? Then, dearest, dearest, why we'll be engaged at once, to be sure we will, and down I sit! There it is, as easy as a glove!'

'Ah! but suppose I won't! And, goodness me, what have I done!' she faltered, getting very red. 'Positively, it seems as if I meant you to say that!'

'Let's do it! I mean get engaged,' said Dick. 'Now, Fancy, will you be my wife?'

'Do you know, Dick, it was rather unkind of you to say what you did coming along the road,' she remarked as if she had not heard the latter part of his speech; though an acute observer might have noticed about her breast as the word 'wife' fell from Dick's lips a soft silent escape of breaths, with very short rests between each.

'What did I say?'

'About my trying to look attractive to those men in the gig.'

'You couldn't help looking so, whether you tried or no. And, Fancy, you do care for me?'

'Yes.'

'Very much?'

'Yes.'

'And you'll be my own wife?'

Her heart quickened, adding to and withdrawing from her cheek varying tones of red to match each varying thought. Dick looked expectantly at the ripe tint of her delicate mouth, waiting for what was coming forth.

'Yes – if father will let me.'

Dick drew himself close to her, compressing his lips and pouting them out as if he were about to whistle the softest melody known.

'O no!' said Fancy solemnly.

The modest Dick drew back a little.

'Dick, Dick, kiss me and let me go instantly! – here's somebody coming!' she whisperingly exclaimed.

*

Half an hour afterwards Dick emerged from the inn, and if Fancy's lips had been real cherries probably Dick's would have appeared deeply stained. The landlord was standing in the yard.

'Heu-heu! hay-hay, Master Dewy! Ho-ho!' he laughed, letting the laugh slip out gently and by degrees that it might make little noise in its exit, and smiting Dick under the fifth rib at the same time. 'This will never do, upon my life, Master Dewy! Calling for tay for a feymel passenger, and then going in and sitting down and having some too, and biding such a fine long time!'

'But surely you know?' said Dick, with great apparent surprise. 'Yes, yes! Ha-ha!' smiting the landlord under the ribs in return.

'Why, what? Yes, yes; ha-ha!'

'You know, of course!'

'Yes, of course! But – that is – I don't.'

'Why about – between that young lady and me?' nodding to the window of the room that Fancy occupied.

'No; not I!' said the innkeeper, bringing his eyes into circles.

'And you don't!'

'Not a word, I'll take my oath!'

'But you laughed when I laughed.'

'Ay, that was me sympathy; so did you when I laughed!'

'Really, you don't know? Goodness – not knowing that!'

'I'll take my oath I don't!'

'O yes,' said Dick, with frigid rhetoric of pitying astonishment, 'we're engaged to be married, you see, and I naturally look after her.'

'Of course, of course! I didn't know that, and I hope ye'll excuse any little freedom of mine, Mr Dewy. But it is a very odd thing; I was talking to your father very intimate about family matters only last Friday in the world, and who should come in but Keeper Day, and we all then fell a-talking o' family matters; but neither one o' them said a mortal word about it; knowen me too so many years, and I at your father's own wedding. 'Tisn't what I should have expected from an old neighbour!'

'Well, to say the truth, we hadn't told Father of the engagement at that time; in fact, 'twasn't settled.'

'Ah! The business was done Sunday. Yes, yes, Sunday's the courting day. Heu-heu!'

'No, 'twasn't done Sunday in particular.'

'After school-hours this week? Well, a very good time, a very proper good time.'

'O no, 'twasn't done then.'

'Coming along the road today then, I suppose?'

'Not at all; I wouldn't think of getting engaged in a dog-cart.'*

'Dammy – might as well have said at once the *when* be blowed! Anyhow, 'tis a fine day, and I hope next time you'll come as one.'

Fancy was duly brought out and assisted into the vehicle, and the newly affianced youth and maiden passed up the steep hill to the Ridgeway, and vanished in the direction of Mellstock.

3

A CONFESSION

It was a morning of the latter summertime; a morning of lingering dews, when the grass is never dry in the shade. Fuchsias and dahlias were laden till eleven o'clock with small drops and dashes of water changing the colour of their sparkle at every movement of the air; and elsewhere hanging on twigs like small silver fruit. The threads of garden-spiders appeared thick and polished. In the dry and sunny places dozens of long-legged crane-flies* whizzed off the grass at every step the passer took.

Fancy Day and her friend Susan Dewy the tranter's daughter were in such a spot as this, pulling down a bough laden with early apples. Three months had elapsed since Dick and Fancy had journeyed together from Budmouth, and the course of their love had run on vigorously during the whole time. There had been just enough difficulty attending its development, and just enough finesse required in keeping it private, to lend the passion an ever-increasing freshness on Fancy's part, whilst, whether from these accessories or not, Dick's heart had been at all times as fond as could be desired. But there was a cloud on Fancy's horizon now.

'She is so well off – better than any of us,' Susan Dewy was saying. 'Her father farms five hundred acres, and she might marry a doctor or curate or anything of that kind if she contrived a little.'

'I don't think Dick ought to have gone to that gipsy-party at all when he knew I couldn't go,' replied Fancy uneasily.

'He didn't know that you would not be there till it was too late to refuse the invitation,' said Susan.

'And what was she like? Tell me.'

'Well, she was rather pretty, I must own.'

'Tell straight on about her, can't you! Come, do, Susan. How many times did you say he danced with her?'

'Once.'

'Twice, I think you said?'

'Indeed I'm sure I didn't.'

'Well, and he wanted to again, I expect.'

'No; I don't think he did. She wanted to dance with him again bad enough, I know. Everybody does with Dick, because he's so handsome and such a clever courter.'

'O, I wish! – How did you say she wore her hair?'

'In long curls, – and her hair is light, and it curls without being put in paper: that's how it is she's so attractive.'

'She's trying to get him away! Yes, yes, she is! And through keeping this miserable school I mustn't wear my hair in curls! But I will; I don't care if I leave the school and go home, I will wear my curls! Look, Susan, do! is her hair as soft and long as this?' Fancy pulled from its coil under her hat a twine of her own hair and stretched it down her shoulder to show its length, looking at Susan to catch her opinion from her eyes.

'It is about the same length as that, I think,' said Miss Dewy.

Fancy paused hopelessly. 'I wish mine was lighter, like hers!' she continued mournfully. 'But hers isn't so soft, is it? Tell me, now.'

'I don't know.'

Fancy abstractedly extended her vision to survey a yellow butterfly and a red-and-black butterfly that were flitting along in company, and then became aware that Dick was advancing up the garden.

'Susan, here's Dick coming; I suppose that's because we've been talking about him.'

'Well, then, I shall go indoors now – you won't want me;' and Susan turned practically and walked off.

Enter the single-minded Dick, whose only fault at the

gipsying, or picnic, had been that of loving Fancy too exclusively and depriving himself of the innocent pleasure the gathering might have afforded him, by sighing regretfully at her absence, – who had danced with the rival in sheer despair of ever being able to get through that stale, flat, and unprofitable* afternoon in any other way; but this she would not believe.

Fancy had settled her plan of emotion. To reproach Dick? O no, no. 'I am in great trouble,' said she, taking what was intended to be a hopelessly melancholy survey of a few small apples lying under the tree; yet a critical ear might have noticed in her voice a tentative tone as to the effect of the words upon Dick when she uttered them.

'What are you in trouble about? Tell me of it,' said Dick earnestly. 'Darling, I will share it with 'ee and help 'ee.'

'No, no: you can't! Nobody can!'

'Why not? You don't deserve it, whatever it is. Tell me, dear.'

'O, it isn't what you think! It is dreadful: my own sin!'

'Sin, Fancy! as if you could sin! I know it can't be.'

''Tis, 'tis!' said the young lady, in a pretty little frenzy of sorrow. 'I have done wrong, and I don't like to tell it! Nobody will forgive me, nobody! and you above all will not! . . . I have allowed myself to – to – fl—'

'What – not flirt!' he said, controlling his emotion as it were by a sudden pressure inward from his surface. And you said only the day before yesterday that you hadn't flirted in your life!'

'Yes, I did; and that was a wicked story! I have let another love me, and – '

'Good G—! Well, I'll forgive you – yes, if you couldn't help it – yes, I will!' said the now dismal Dick. 'Did you encourage him?'

'O, – I don't know – yes – no. O, I think so!'

'Who was it?'

A pause.

'Tell me!'

'Mr Shiner.'

After a silence that was only disturbed by the fall of an apple,* a long-checked sigh from Dick, and a sob from Fancy, he said with real austerity—

'Tell it all; – every word!'

'He looked at me, and I looked at him, and he said, "Will you let me show you how to catch bullfinches down here by the stream?" And I – wanted to know very much – I did so long to have a bullfinch! I couldn't help that! – And I said, "Yes!" and then he said, "Come here." And I went with him down to the lovely river, and then he said to me, "Look and see how I do it, and then you'll know: I put this bird-lime* round this twig, and then I go here," he said, "and hide away under a bush; and presently clever Mister Bird comes and perches upon the twig, and flaps his wings, and you've got him before you can say Jack" – something; O, O, O, I forget what!'

'Jack Sprat,' mournfully suggested Dick through the cloud of his misery.

'No, not Jack Sprat,' she sobbed.

'Then 'twas Jack Robinson!' he said with the emphasis of a man who had resolved to discover every iota of the truth or die.

'Yes, that was it! And then I put my hand upon the rail of the bridge to get across, and – That's all.'

'Well, that isn't much, either,' said Dick critically and more cheerfully. 'Not that I see what business Shiner has to take upon himself to teach you anything. But it seems – it do seem there must have been more than that to set you up in such a dreadful taking?'

He looked into Fancy's eyes. Misery of miseries! – guilt was written there still.

'Now, Fancy, you've not told me all!' said Dick, rather sternly for a quiet young man.

'O, don't speak so cruelly! I am afraid to tell now! If you hadn't been harsh I was going on to tell all; now I can't!'

'Come, dear Fancy, tell: come. I'll forgive; I must, – by heaven and earth, I must, whether I will or no; I love you so!'

'Well, when I put my hand on the bridge, he touched it – '

'A scamp!' said Dick, grinding an imaginary human frame to powder.

'And then he looked at me, and at last he said, "Are you in love with Dick Dewy?" And I said, "Perhaps I am!" and then he said, "I wish you weren't then, for I want to marry you, with all my soul."'

'There's a villain now! Want to marry you!' And Dick quivered with the bitterness of satirical laughter. Then suddenly remembering that he might be reckoning without his host:

'Unless, to be sure, you are willing to have him – perhaps you are,' he said, with the wretched indifference of a castaway.

'No, indeed I am not!' she said, her sobs just beginning to take a favourable turn towards cure.

'Well, then,' said Dick, coming a little to his senses, 'you've been stretching it very much in giving such a dreadful beginning to such a mere nothing. And I know what you've done it for – just because of that gipsy-party!' He turned away from her and took five paces decisively, as if he were tired of an ungrateful country, including herself. You did it to make me jealous, and I won't stand it!' He flung the words to her over his shoulder and then stalked on, apparently very anxious to walk to the remotest of the Colonies that very minute.

'O, O, O, Dick – Dick!' she cried, trotting after him like a pet lamb and really seriously alarmed at last. 'You'll kill me! My impulses are bad – miserably wicked, – and I can't help it; forgive me, Dick! And I love you always; and those times when you look silly and don't seem quite good enough for me, – just the same, I do, Dick! And there is something more serious, though not concerning that walk with him.'

'Well, what is it?' said Dick, altering his mind about walking to the Colonies; in fact, passing to the other extreme, and standing so rooted to the road that he was apparently not even going home.

'Why this,' she said, drying the beginning of a new flood of tears she had been going to shed, 'this is the serious part. Father has told Mr Shiner that he would like him for a son-in-law if he could get me; – that he has his right hearty consent to come courting me!'

4
AN ARRANGEMENT

'That *is* serious,' said Dick, more intellectually than he had spoken for a long time.

The truth was that Geoffrey knew nothing about his daughter's continued walks and meetings with Dick. When a hint that there were symptoms of an attachment between them had first reached Geoffrey's ears he stated so emphatically that he must think the matter over before any such thing could be allowed that, rather unwisely on Dick's part, whatever it might have been on the lady's, the lovers were careful to be seen together no more in public; and Geoffrey, forgetting the report, did not think over the matter at all. So Mr Shiner resumed his old position in Geoffrey's brain by mere flux of time. Even Shiner began to believe that Dick existed for Fancy no more, – though that remarkably easy-going man had taken no active steps on his own account as yet.

'And father has not only told Mr Shiner that,' continued Fancy, 'but he has written me a letter to say he should wish me to encourage Mr Shiner if 'twas convenient!'

'I must start off and see your father at once!' said Dick, taking two or three vehement steps to the south, recollecting that Mr Day lived to the north, and coming back again.

'I think we had better see him together. Not tell him what you come for, or anything of the kind, until he likes you, and so win his brain through his heart, which is always the way to manage people. I mean in this way: I am going home on Saturday week to help them in the honey-taking. You might come there to me, have something to eat and drink, and let him guess what your coming signifies, without saying it in so many words.'

'We'll do it, dearest. But I shall ask him for you, flat and plain; not wait for his guessing.' And the lover then stepped close to her, and attempted to give her one little kiss on the cheek, his lips alighting, however, on an outlying tract of her back hair by reason of an impulse that had caused her to turn her head with a jerk. 'Yes, and I'll put on my second-best suit and a clean shirt and collar, and black my boots as if 'twas a Sunday. 'Twill have a good appearance, you see, and that's a great deal to start with.'

'You won't wear that old waistcoat, will you, Dick?'

'Bless you, no! Why I – '

'I didn't mean to be personal, dear Dick,' she said, fearing she had hurt his feelings. "Tis a very nice waistcoat, but what I meant was, that though it is an excellent waistcoat for a settled-down man, it is not quite one for' (she waited, and a blush expanded over her face, and then she went on again) – 'for going courting in.'

'No, I'll wear my best winter one, with the leather lining, that

Mother made. It is a beautiful, handsome waistcoat inside, yes, as ever anybody saw. In fact, only the other day, I unbuttoned it to show a chap that very lining, and he said it was the strongest, handsomest lining you could wish to see on the king's waistcoat himself.'

'*I* don't quite know what to wear,' she said, as if her habitual indifference alone to dress had kept back so important a subject till now.

'Why, that blue frock you wore last week.'

'Doesn't set well round the neck. I couldn't wear that.'

'But I shan't care.'

'No, you won't mind.'

'Well, then it's all right. Because you only care how you look to me, do you, dear? I only dress for you, that's certain.'

'Yes, but you see I couldn't appear in it again very well.'

'Any strange gentleman you mid meet in your journey might notice the set of it, I suppose. Fancy, men in love don't think so much about how they look to other women.' It is difficult to say whether a tone of playful banter or of gentle reproach prevailed in the speech.

'Well then, Dick,' she said, with good-humoured frankness, 'I'll own it. I shouldn't like a stranger to see me dressed badly even though I am in love. 'Tis our nature, I suppose.'

'You perfect woman!'

'Yes; if you lay the stress on "woman",' she murmured, looking at a group of hollyhocks in flower, round which a crowd of butterflies had gathered like female idlers round a bonnet-shop.*

'But about the dress. Why not wear the one you wore at our party?'

'That sets well, but a girl of the name of Bet Tallor, who lives near our house, has had one made almost like it (only in pattern, though of miserably cheap stuff), and I couldn't wear it on that account. Dear me, I am afraid I can't go now.'

'O yes, you must; I know you will!' said Dick, with dismay. 'Why not wear what you've got on?'

'What! this old one! After all, I think that by wearing my grey one Saturday, I can make the blue one do for Sunday. Yes, I will. A hat or a bonnet, which shall it be? Which do I look best in?'

'Well, I think the bonnet is nicest, more quiet and matronly.'

'What's the objection to the hat? Does it make me look old?'

'O no; the hat is well enough; but it makes you look rather too – you won't mind me saying it, dear?'

'Not at all, for I shall wear the bonnet.'

' – Rather too coquettish and flirty for an engaged young woman.'

She reflected a minute. 'Yes; yes. Still, after all, the hat would do best; hats *are* best, you see. Yes, I must wear the hat, dear Dicky, because I ought to wear a hat, you know.'

PART IV
AUTUMN

Dick, dressed in his second-best suit, burst into Fancy's sitting-room with a glow of pleasure on his face.

It was two o'clock on Friday, the day before her contemplated visit to her father, and for some reason connected with cleaning the school the children had been given this Friday afternoon for pastime, in addition to the usual Saturday.

'Fancy! it happens just right that it is a leisure half day with you. Smart is lame in his near-foot-afore,* and so, as I can't do anything, I've made a holiday afternoon of it, and am come for you to go nutting with me!'

She was sitting by the parlour window with a blue frock lying across her lap and scissors in her hand.

'Go nutting! Yes. But I'm afraid I can't go for an hour or so.'

'Why not? 'Tis the only spare afternoon we may both have together for weeks.'

'This dress of mine, that I am going to wear on Sunday at Yalbury; – I find it fits so badly that I must alter it a little, after all. I told the dressmaker to make it by a pattern I gave her at the time; instead of that, she did it her own way, and made me look a perfect fright.'

'How long will you be?' he inquired, looking rather disappointed.

'Not long. Do wait and talk to me; come, do, dear.'

Dick sat down. The talking progressed very favourably amid the snipping and sewing till about half-past two, at which time his conversation began to be varied by a slight tapping upon his toe with a walking-stick he had cut from the hedge as he came along. Fancy talked and answered him, but sometimes the answers were so negligently given that it was evident her thoughts lay for the greater part in her lap with the blue dress.

The clock struck three. Dick arose from his seat, walked round the room with his hands behind him, examined all the furniture, then sounded a few notes on the harmonium, then looked inside all the books he could find, then smoothed Fancy's head with his hand. Still the snipping and sewing went on.

The clock struck four. Dick fidgeted about, yawned privately; counted the knots in the table, yawned publicly; counted the flies on the ceiling, yawned horribly; went into the kitchen and scullery* and so thoroughly studied the principle upon which the pump was constructed that he could have delivered a lecture on the subject. Stepping back to Fancy, and finding still that she had not done, he went into her garden and looked at her cabbages and potatoes, and reminded himself that they seemed to him to wear a decidedly feminine aspect; then pulled up several weeds and came in again. The clock struck five, and still the snipping and sewing went on.

Dick attempted to kill a fly, peeled all the rind off his walking-stick, then threw the stick into the scullery because it was spoilt, produced hideous discords from the harmonium, and accidentally overturned a vase of flowers, the water from which ran in a rill across the table and dribbled to the floor, where it formed a lake, the shape of which, after the lapse of a few minutes, he began to modify considerably with his foot till it was like a map of England and Wales.

'Well, Dick, you needn't have made quite such a mess.'

'Well, I needn't, I suppose.' He walked up to the blue dress, and looked at it with a rigid gaze. Then an idea seemed to cross his brain.

'Fancy.'

'Yes.'

'I thought you said you were going to wear your grey gown all day tomorrow on your trip to Yalbury, and in the evening too, when I shall be with you, and ask your father for you?'

'So I am.'

'And the blue one only on Sunday?'

'And the blue one Sunday.'

'Well, dear, I shan't be at Yalbury Sunday to see it.'

'No, but I shall walk to Longpuddle church in the afternoon with father, and such lots of people will be looking at me there, you know; and it did set so badly round the neck.'

'I never noticed it, and 'tis like nobody else would.'

'They might.'

'Then why not wear the grey one on Sunday as well? 'Tis as pretty as the blue one.'

'I might make the grey one do, certainly. But it isn't so good;

it didn't cost half so much as this one, and besides, it would be the same I wore Saturday.'

'Then wear the striped one, dear.'

'I might.'

'Or the dark one.'

'Yes, I might; but I want to wear a fresh one they haven't seen.'

'I see, I see,' said Dick, in a voice in which the tones of love were decidedly inconvenienced by a considerable emphasis, his thoughts meanwhile running as follows: 'I, the man she loves best in the world, as she says, am to understand that my poor half-holiday is to be lost, because she wants to wear on Sunday a gown there is not the slightest necessity for wearing, simply, in fact, to appear more striking than usual in the eyes of the Longpuddle young men; and I not there, either.'

'Then there are three dresses good enough for my eyes, but neither is good enough for the youths of Longpuddle,' he said.

'No, not that exactly, Dick. Still, you see, I do want – to look pretty to them – there, that's honest! But I shan't be much longer.'

'How much?'

'A quarter of an hour.'

'Very well; I'll come in in a quarter of an hour.'

'Why go away?'

'I mid as well.'

He went out, walked down the road, and sat upon a gate. Here he meditated and meditated, and the more he meditated the more decidedly did he begin to fume, and the more positive was he that his time had been scandalously trifled with by Miss Fancy Day – that, so far from being the simple girl who had never had a sweetheart before, as she had solemnly assured him time after time, she was, if not a flirt, a woman who had had no end of admirers; a girl most certainly too anxious about her frocks; a girl, whose feelings, though warm, were not deep; a girl who cared a great deal too much how she appeared in the eyes of other men. 'What she loves best in the world,' he thought, with an incipient spice of his father's grimness, 'is her hair and complexion. What she loves next best, her gowns and hats; what she loves next best, myself, perhaps!'

Suffering great anguish at this disloyalty in himself and

harshness to his darling, yet disposed to persevere in it, a horribly cruel thought crossed his mind. He would not call for her, as he had promised, at the end of a quarter of an hour! Yes, it would be a punishment she well deserved. Although the best part of the afternoon had been wasted he would go nutting as he had intended, and go by himself.

He leaped over the gate, and pushed up the lane for nearly two miles, till a winding path called Snail-Creep sloped up a hill and entered a hazel copse by a hole like a rabbit's burrow. In he plunged, vanished among the bushes, and in a short time there was no sign of his existence upon earth save an occasional rustling of boughs and snapping of twigs in divers points of Grey's Wood.

Never man nutted as Dick nutted that afternoon. He worked like a galley slave. Half-hour after half-hour passed away, and still he gathered without ceasing. At last, when the sun had set, and bunches of nuts could not be distinguished from the leaves which nourished them, he shouldered his bag, containing quite two pecks* of the finest produce of the wood, about as much use to him as two pecks of stones from the road, strolled down the woodland track, crossed the highway and entered the homeward lane, whistling as he went.

Probably, Miss Fancy Day never before or after stood so low in Mr Dewy's opinion as on that afternoon. In fact, it is just possible that a few more blue dresses on the Longpuddle young men's account would have clarified Dick's brain entirely, and made him once more a free man.

But Venus* had planned other developments, at any rate for the present. Cuckoo-Lane, the way he pursued, passed over a ridge which rose keenly against the sky about fifty yards in his van. Here, upon the bright after-glow about the horizon, was now visible an irregular shape, which at first he conceived to be a bough standing a little beyond the line of its neighbours. Then it seemed to move, and, as he advanced still further, there was no doubt that it was a living being sitting in the bank, head bowed on hand. The grassy margin entirely prevented his footsteps from being heard, and it was not till he was close that the figure recognised him. Up it sprang, and he was face to face with Fancy.

'Dick, Dick! O, is it you, Dick!'

'Yes, Fancy,' said Dick, in a rather repentant tone, and lowering his nuts.

She ran up to him, flung her parasol on the grass, put her little head against his breast, and then there began a narrative disjointed by such a hysterical weeping as was never surpassed for intensity in the whole history of love.

'O Dick,' she sobbed out, where have you been away from me? O, I have suffered agony, and thought you would never come any more! 'Tis cruel, Dick; no 'tisn't, it is justice! I've been walking miles and miles up and down Grey's Wood, trying to find you, till I was wearied and worn out, and I could walk no further, and had come back this far! O Dick, directly you were gone I thought I had offended you and I put down the dress; 'tisn't finished now, and I never will finish it, and I'll wear an old one Sunday! Yes, Dick, I will, because I don't care what I wear when you are not by my side – ha, you think I do, but I don't! – and I ran after you, and I saw you go up Snail-Creep and not look back once, and then you plunged in, and I after you; but I was too far behind. O, I did wish the horrid bushes had been cut down so that I could see your dear shape again! And then I called out to you and nobody answered, and I was afraid to call very loud lest anybody else should hear me. Then I kept wandering and wandering about, and it was dreadful misery, Dick. And then I shut my eyes and fell to picturing you looking at some other woman, very pretty and nice, but with no affection or truth in her at all, and then imagined you saying to yourself, "Ah, she's as good as Fancy, for Fancy told me a story, and was a flirt, and cared for herself more than me, so now I'll have this one for my sweetheart." O, you won't, will you, Dick, for I do love you so!'

It is scarcely necessary to add that Dick renounced his freedom there and then, and kissed her ten times over, and promised that no pretty woman of the kind alluded to should ever engross his thoughts; in short, that though he had been vexed with her all such vexation was past, and that henceforth and for ever it was simply Fancy or death for him. And then they set about proceeding homewards, very slowly on account of Fancy's weariness, she leaning upon his shoulder and in addition receiving support from his arm round her waist; though she had sufficiently recovered from her desperate condition to sing to him, 'Why are you wandering here, I pray?'* during the latter part of their walk. Nor is it necessary to describe in detail how the bag of nuts was quite forgotten until three days later, when it was found among the brambles and restored empty to Mrs Dewy, her initials being marked thereon in red cotton; and how she puzzled herself till her head ached upon the question of how on earth her meal-bag could have got into Cuckoo-Lane.

2

HONEY-TAKING, AND AFTERWARDS

Saturday evening saw Dick Dewy journeying on foot to Yalbury Wood, according to the arrangement with Fancy.

The landscape being concave, at the going down of the sun* everything suddenly assumed a uniform robe of shade. The evening advanced from sunset to dusk long before Dick's arrival, and his progress during the latter portion of his walk through the trees was indicated by the flutter of terrified birds that had been roosting over the path. And in crossing the glades, masses of hot dry air that had been formed on the hills during the day greeted his cheeks alternately with clouds of damp night air from the valleys. He reached the keeper-steward's house, where the grass-plot and the garden in front appeared light and pale against the unbroken darkness of the grove from which he had emerged, and paused at the garden gate.

He had scarcely been there a minute when he beheld a sort of procession advancing from the door in his front. It consisted first of Enoch the trapper, carrying a spade on his shoulder and a lantern dangling in his hand; then came Mrs Day, the light of the lantern revealing that she bore in her arms curious objects about a foot long in the form of Latin crosses* (made of lath and brown paper dipped in brimstone – called matches by bee-masters); next came Miss Day with a shawl thrown over her head; and behind all, in the gloom, Mr Frederic Shiner.

Dick in his consternation at finding Shiner present was at a loss how to proceed, and retired under a tree to collect his thoughts.

'Here I be, Enoch,' said a voice; and the procession advancing further, the lantern's rays illuminated the figure of Geoffrey awaiting their arrival beside a row of bee-hives in front of the path. Taking the spade from Enoch he proceeded to dig two holes in the earth beside the hives, the others standing round in a circle except Mrs Day, who deposited her matches in the fork of an apple tree and returned to the house. The party remaining were now lit up in front by the lantern in their midst, their shadows radiating each way upon the garden-plot like the spokes of a wheel. An apparent embarrassment of Fancy at the presence of Shiner caused a silence in the assembly, during which the preliminaries of execution were arranged, the matches fixed, the stake kindled, the two hives placed over the two holes, and the earth stopped round the edges. Geoffrey then stood erect, and rather more, to straighten his backbone after the digging.

'They were a peculiar family,' said Mr Shiner, regarding the hives reflectively.

Geoffrey nodded.

'Those holes will be the grave of thousands!' said Fancy. 'I think 'tis rather a cruel thing to do.'

Her father shook his head. 'No,' he said, tapping the hives to shake the dead bees from their cells, 'if you suffocate 'em this way, they only die once: if you fumigate 'em in the new way, they come to life again, and die o' starvation; so the pangs o' death be twice upon 'em.'

'I incline to Fancy's notion,' said Mr Shiner, laughing lightly.

'The proper way to take honey, so that the bees be neither starved nor murdered, is a puzzling matter,' said the keeper steadily.

'I should like never to take it from them,' said Fancy.

'But 'tis the money,' said Enoch musingly. 'For without money man is a shadder!'

The lantern-light had disturbed many bees that had escaped from hives destroyed some days earlier, and, demoralised by affliction, were now getting a living as marauders about the doors of other hives. Several flew round the head and neck of Geoffrey, then darted upon him with an irritated bizz.

Enoch threw down the lantern and ran off and pushed his head into a currant bush; Fancy scudded up the path; and Mr Shiner floundered away helter-skelter among the cabbages. Geoffrey stood his ground, unmoved and firm as a rock. Fancy was the first to return, followed by Enoch picking up the lantern. Mr Shiner still remained invisible.

'Have the craters stung ye?' said Enoch to Geoffrey.

'No, not much – on'y a little here and there,' he said with leisurely solemnity, shaking one bee out of his shirt sleeve, pulling another from among his hair, and two or three more from his neck. The rest looked on during this proceeding with a complacent sense of being out of it – much as a European nation in a state of internal commotion is watched by its neighbours.

'Are those all of them, Father?' said Fancy, when Geoffrey had pulled away five.

'Almost all – though I feel one or two more sticking into my shoulder and side. Ah! there's another just begun again upon my backbone. You lively young mortals, how did you get inside there? However, they can't sting me many times more, poor things, for they must be getting weak. They mid as well stay in me till bedtime now, I suppose.'

As he himself was the only person affected by this arrangement it seemed satisfactory enough; and after a noise of feet kicking against cabbages in a blundering progress among them the voice of Mr Shiner was heard from the darkness in that direction.

'Is all quite safe again?'

No answer being returned to this query he apparently assumed that he might venture forth, and gradually drew near the lantern again. The hives were now removed from their position over the holes, one being handed to Enoch to carry indoors, and one being taken by Geoffrey himself.

'Bring hither the lantern, Fancy: the spade can bide.'*

Geoffrey and Enoch then went towards the house, leaving Shiner and Fancy standing side by side on the garden-plot.

'Allow me,' said Shiner, stooping for the lantern and seizing it at the same time with Fancy.

'I can carry it,' said Fancy, religiously repressing all inclination to trifle. She had thoroughly considered that subject after the tearful explanation of the bird-catching adventure to Dick, and had decided that it would be dishonest in her as an engaged young woman to trifle with men's eyes and hands any more. Finding that Shiner still retained his hold of the lantern she relinquished it, and he, having found her retaining it, also let go. The lantern fell and was extinguished. Fancy moved on.

'Where is the path?' said Mr Shiner.

'Here,' said Fancy. 'Your eyes will get used to the dark in a minute or two.'

'Till that time will ye lend me your hand?'

Fancy gave him the extreme tips of her fingers and they stepped from the plot into the path.

'You don't accept attentions very freely.'

'It depends upon who offers them.'

'A fellow like me, for instance.'

A dead silence.

'Well, what do you say, Missie?'

'It then depends upon how they are offered.'

'Not wildly, and yet not careless-like; not purposely, and yet not by chance; not too quick nor yet too slow.'

'How then?' said Fancy.

'Coolly and practically,' he said. 'How would that kind of love be taken?'

'Not anxiously, and yet not indifferently; neither blushing nor pale; nor religiously nor yet quite wickedly.'

'Well, how?'

'Not at all.'

Geoffrey Day's storehouse at the back of his dwelling was hung with bunches of dried horehound,* mint, and sage; brown-paper bags of thyme and lavender; and long ropes of clean onions. On shelves were spread large red and yellow apples, and choice selections of early potatoes for seed next year; – vulgar crowds of commoner kind lying beneath in heaps. A few empty beehives were clustered around a nail in one corner, under which stood two or three barrels of new cider of the first crop, each bubbling and squirting forth from the yet open bunghole.

Fancy was now kneeling beside the two inverted hives, one of which rested against her lap for convenience in operating upon the contents. She thrust her sleeves above her elbows, and inserted her small pink hand edgewise between each white lobe of honeycomb, performing the act so adroitly and gently as not to unseal a single cell. Then cracking the piece off at the crown of the hive by a slight backward and forward movement she lifted each portion as it was loosened into a large blue platter placed on a bench at her side.

'Bother these little mortals!' said Geoffrey, who was holding the light to her and giving his back an uneasy twist. I really think I may as well go indoors and take 'em out, poor things! for they won't let me alone. There's two a stinging wi' all their might now. I'm sure I wonder their strength can last so long.'

'All right, friend; I'll hold the candle whilst you are gone,' said Mr Shiner, leisurely taking the light and allowing Geoffrey to depart, which he did with his usual long paces.

He could hardly have gone round to the house-door when other footsteps were heard approaching the outbuilding; the tip of a finger appeared in the hole through which the wood latch was lifted, and Dick Dewy came in, having been all this time walking up and down the wood vainly waiting for Shiner's departure.

Fancy looked up and welcomed him rather confusedly. Shiner grasped the candlestick more firmly, and, lest doing this in silence should not imply to Dick with sufficient force that he was quite at home and cool, he sang invincibly –

King Arthur he had three sons.*

'Father here?' said Dick.

'Indoors, I think,' said Fancy, looking pleasantly at him.

Dick surveyed the scene and did not seem inclined to hurry off just at that moment. Shiner went on singing –

> The miller was drown'd in his pond,
>   The weaver was hung in his yarn,
> And the d— ran away with the little tail-or,
>   With the broadcloth* under his arm.

'That's a terrible crippled rhyme, if that's your rhyme!' said Dick, with a grain of superciliousness in his tone.

'It's no use your complaining to me about the rhyme!' said Mr Shiner. 'You must go to the man that made it.'

Fancy by this time had acquired confidence.

'Taste a bit, Mr Dewy,' she said, holding up to him a small circular piece of honeycomb that had been the last in the row of layers, remaining still on her knees and flinging back her head to look in his face; 'and then I'll taste a bit too.'

'And I, if you please,' said Mr Shiner. Nevertheless the farmer looked superior, as if he could even now hardly join the trifling from very importance of station; and after receiving the honey-comb from Fancy he turned it over in his hand till the cells began to be crushed, and the liquid honey ran down from his fingers in a thin string.

Suddenly a faint cry from Fancy caused them to gaze at her.

'What's the matter, dear?' said Dick.

'It is nothing, but – O-o! – a bee has stung the inside of my lip! He was in one of the cells I was eating!'

'We must keep down the swelling or it may be serious!' said Shiner, stepping up and kneeling beside her. 'Let me see it.'

'No, no!'

'Just let *me* see it,' said Dick kneeling on the other side; and after some hesitation she pressed down her lip with one finger to show the place. 'O, I hope 'twill soon be better! I don't mind a sting in ordinary places, but it is so bad upon your lip,' she added with tears in her eyes, and writhing a little from the pain.

Shiner held the light above his head and pushed his face close to Fancy's, as if the lip had been shown exclusively to himself, upon which Dick pushed closer, as if Shiner were not there at all.

'It is swelling,' said Dick to her right aspect.

'It isn't swelling,' said Shiner to her left aspect.

'Is it dangerous on the lip?' cried Fancy. 'I know it is dangerous on the tongue.'

'O no, not dangerous,' answered Dick.

'Rather dangerous,' had answered Shiner simultaneously.

'I must try to bear it!' said Fancy, turning again to the hives.

'Hartshorn*-and-oil is a good thing to put to it, Miss Day,' said Shiner with great concern.

'Sweet-oil-and-hartshorn I've found to be a good thing to cure stings, Miss Day,' said Dick with greater concern.

'We have some mixed indoors; would you kindly run and get it for me?' she said.

Now whether by inadvertence or whether by mischievous intention, the individuality of the *you* was so carelessly denoted that both Dick and Shiner sprang to their feet like twin acrobats, and marched abreast to the door; both seized the latch and lifted it, and continued marching on shoulder to shoulder in the same manner to the dwelling-house. Not only so but, entering the room, they marched as before straight up to Mrs Day's chair, letting the door in the oak partition slam so forcibly that the rows of pewter on the dresser rang like a bell.

'Mrs Day, Fancy has stung her lip and wants you to give me

the hartshorn, please,' said Mr Shiner, very close to Mrs Day's face.

'O, Mrs Day, Fancy has asked me to bring out the hartshorn, please, because she has stung her lip!' said Dick, a little closer to Mrs Day's face.

'Well, men alive! that's no reason why you should eat me, I suppose!' said Mrs Day, drawing back.

She searched in the corner-cupboard, produced the bottle, and began to dust the cork, the rim, and every other part very carefully, Dick's hand and Shiner's hand waiting side by side.

'Which is head man?' said Mrs Day. 'Now, don't come mumbudgeting so close again. Which is head man?'

Neither spoke; and the bottle was inclined towards Shiner. Shiner, as a high-class man, would not look in the least triumphant, and turned to go off with it as Geoffrey came downstairs after the search in his linen for concealed bees.

'O – that you, Master Dewy?'

Dick assured the keeper that it was; and the young man then determined upon a bold stroke for the attainment of his end, forgetting that the worst of bold strokes is the disastrous consequences they involve if they fail.

'I've come on purpose to speak to you very particular, Mr Day,' he said, with a crushing emphasis intended for the ears of Mr Shiner, who was vanishing round the door-post at that moment.

'Well, I've been forced to go upstairs and unrind* myself, and shake some bees out o' me,' said Geoffrey, walking slowly towards the open door and standing on the threshold. 'The young rascals got into my shirt and wouldn't be quiet nohow.'

Dick followed him to the door.

'I've come to speak a word to you,' he repeated, looking out at the pale mist creeping up from the gloom of the valley. 'You may perhaps guess what it is about.'

The keeper lowered his hands into the depths of his pockets, twirled his eyes, balanced himself on his toes, looked as perpendicularly downward as if his glance were a plumb-line, then horizontally, collecting together the cracks that lay about his face till they were all in the neighbourhood of his eyes.

'Maybe I don't know,' he replied.

Dick said nothing; and the stillness was disturbed only by some small bird that was being killed by an owl in the adjoining wood, whose cry passed into the silence without mingling with it.

'I've left my hat up in chammer,' said Geoffrey; 'wait while I step up and get en.'

'I'll be in the garden,' said Dick.

He went round by a side wicket into the garden, and Geoffrey went upstairs. It was the custom in Mellstock and its vicinity to discuss matters of pleasure and ordinary business inside the house, and to reserve the garden for very important affairs: a custom which, as is supposed, originated in the desirability of getting away at such times from the other members of the family when there was only one room for living in, though it was now quite as frequently practised by those who suffered from no such limitation to the size of their domiciles.

The head-keeper's form appeared in the dusky garden, and Dick walked towards him. The elder paused and leant over the rail of a piggery that stood on the left of the path, upon which Dick did the same; and they both contemplated a whitish shadowy shape that was moving about and grunting among the straw of the interior.

'I've come to ask for Fancy,' said Dick.

'I'd as lief* you hadn't.'

'Why should that be, Mr Day?'

'Because it makes me say that you've come to ask what ye be'n't likely to have. Have ye come for anything else?'

'Nothing.'

'Then I'll just tell 'ee you've come on a very foolish errand. D'ye know what her mother was?'

'No.'

'A teacher in a landed family's nursery,* who was foolish enough to marry the keeper* of the same establishment; for I was only a keeper then, though now I've a dozen other irons in the fire* as steward here for my lord, what with the timber sales and the yearly fellings, and the gravel and sand sales, and one thing and t'other. However, d'ye think Fancy picked up her good manners, the smooth turn of her tongue, her musical notes, and her knowledge of books, in a homely hole like this?'

'No.'

'D'ye know where?'

'No.'

'Well, when I went a-wandering after her mother's death she

lived with her aunt, who kept a boarding-school, till her aunt married Lawyer Green – a man as sharp as a needle – and the school was broke up. Did ye know that then she went to the training-school, and that her name stood first among the Queen's scholars* of her year?'

'I've heard so.'

'And that when she sat for her certificate as Government teacher, she had the highest of the first class?'

'Yes.'

'Well, and do ye know what I live in such a miserly way for when I've got enough to do without it, and why I make her work as a schoolmistress instead of living here?'

'No.'

'That if any gentleman, who sees her to be his equal in polish, should want to marry her, and she want to marry him, he shan't be superior to her in pocket. Now do ye think after this that you be good enough for her?'

'No.'

'Then good night t'ee, Master Dewy.'

'Good night, Mr Day.'

Modest Dick's reply had faltered upon his tongue, and he turned away wondering at his presumption in asking for a woman whom he had seen from the beginning to be so superior to him.

3
FANCY IN THE RAIN

The next scene is a tempestuous afternoon in the following month, and Fancy Day is discovered walking from her father's home towards Mellstock.

A single vast grey cloud covered the country, from which the small rain and mist had just begun to blow down in wavy sheets, alternately thick and thin. The trees of the fields and plantations writhed like miserable men as the air wound its way swiftly among them: the lowest portions of their trunks, that had hardly ever been known to move, were visibly rocked by the fiercer gusts, distressing the mind by its painful unwontedness, as when a strong man is seen to shed tears. Low-hanging boughs went up and down; high and erect boughs went to and fro; the blasts being so irregular, and divided into so many cross-currents, that neighbouring branches of the same tree swept the skies in independent motions, crossed each other, or became entangled. Across the open spaces flew flocks of green and yellowish leaves which, after travelling a long distance from their parent trees, reached the ground and lay there with their undersides upward.

As the rain and wind increased, and Fancy's bonnet-ribbons leapt more and more snappishly against her chin, she paused on entering Mellstock Lane to consider her latitude, and the distance to a place of shelter. The nearest house was Elizabeth Endorfield's* in Higher Mellstock, whose cottage and garden stood not far from the junction of that hamlet with the road she followed. Fancy hastened onward, and in five minutes entered a gate which shed upon her toes a flood of water-drops as she opened it.

'Come in, chiel!' a voice exclaimed before Fancy had knocked: a promptness that would have surprised her had she not known that Mrs Endorfield was an exceedingly and exceptionally sharp woman in the use of her eyes and ears.

Fancy went in and sat down. Elizabeth was paring potatoes for her husband's supper.

Scrape, scrape, scrape; then a toss, and splash went a potato into a bucket of water.

Now as Fancy listlessly noted these proceedings of the dame she began to reconsider an old subject that lay uppermost in her heart. Since the interview between her father and Dick the days had been melancholy days for her. Geoffrey's firm opposition to the notion of Dick as a son-in-law was more than she had expected. She had frequently seen her lover since that time, it is true, and had loved him more for the opposition than she would have otherwise dreamt of doing – which was a happiness of a certain kind. Yet, though love is thus an end in itself it must be believed to be the means to another end if it is to assume the rosy hues of an unalloyed pleasure. And such a belief Fancy and Dick were emphatically denied just now.

Elizabeth Endorfield had a repute among women which was in its nature something between distinction and notoriety. It was founded on the following items of character. She was shrewd and penetrating; her house stood in a lonely place; she never went to church; she wore a red cloak; she always retained her bonnet indoors; and she had a pointed chin. Thus far her attributes were distinctly Satanic; and those who looked no further called her, in plain terms, a witch. But she was not gaunt, nor ugly in the upper part of her face, nor particularly strange in manner; so that, when her more intimate acquaintances spoke of her the term was softened, and she became simply a Deep Body, who was as long-headed as she was high. It may be stated that Elizabeth belonged to a class of suspects who were gradually losing their mysterious characteristics under the administration of the young vicar; though during the long reign of Mr Grinham the parish of Mellstock had proved extremely favourable to the growth of witches.

While Fancy was revolving all this in her mind, and putting it to herself whether it was worth while to tell her troubles to Elizabeth, and ask her advice in getting out of them the witch spoke.

'You be down – proper down,' she said suddenly, dropping another potato into the bucket.

Fancy took no notice.

'About your young man.'

Fancy reddened. Elizabeth seemed to be watching her thoughts. Really one would almost think she must have the powers people ascribed to her.

'Father not in the humour for't, hey?' Another potato was finished and flung in. 'Ah, I know about it. Little birds tell me things that people don't dream of my knowing.'

Fancy was desperate about Dick, and here was a chance – O, such a wicked chance! – of getting help; and what was goodness beside love!

'I wish you'd tell me how to put him in the humour for it?' she said.

'That I could soon do,' said the witch quietly.

'Really? O, do; anyhow – I don't care – so that it is done! How could I do it, Mrs Endorfield?'

'Nothing so mighty wonderful in it.'

'Well, but how?'

'By witchery, of course!' said Elizabeth.

'No!' said Fancy.

''Tis, I assure ye. Didn't you ever hear I was a witch?'

'Well,' hesitated Fancy, 'I have heard you called so.'

'And you believed it?'

'I can't say that I did exactly believe it, for 'tis very horrible and wicked; but, O, how I do wish it was possible for you to be one!'

'So I am. And I'll tell you how to bewitch your father to let you marry Dick Dewy.'

'Will it hurt him, poor thing?'

'Hurt who?'

'Father.'

'No; the charm is worked by common sense, and the spell can only be broke by your acting stupidly.'

Fancy looked rather perplexed, and Elizabeth went on:

> This fear of Lizz – whatever 'tis –
>   By great and small,
> She makes pretence to common sense,
>   And that's all.

'You must do it like this.' The witch laid down her knife and potato, and then poured into Fancy's ear a long and detailed list of directions, glancing up from the corner of her eye into Fancy's face with an expression of sinister humour. Fancy's face brightened, clouded, rose and sank, as the narrative proceeded. 'There,' said Elizabeth at length, stooping for the knife and another potato, 'do that, and you'll have him by-long and by-late, my dear.'

'And do it I will!' said Fancy.

She then turned her attention to the external world once more. The rain continued as usual, but the wind had abated considerably during the discourse. Judging that it was now possible to keep an umbrella erect she pulled her hood again over her bonnet, bade the witch goodbye, and went her way.

4
THE SPELL

Mrs Endorfield's advice was duly followed.

'I be proper sorry that your daughter isn't so well as she might be,' said a Mellstock man to Geoffrey one morning.

'But is there anything in it?' said Geoffrey uneasily, as he shifted his hat to the right. 'I can't understand the report. She didn't complain to me a bit when I saw her.'

'No appetite at all, they say.'

Geoffrey crossed to Mellstock and called at the school that afternoon. Fancy welcomed him as usual, and asked him to stay and take tea with her.

'I be'n't much for tea this time o' day,' he said, but stayed.

During the meal he watched her narrowly. And to his great consternation discovered the following unprecedented change in the healthy girl – that she cut herself only a diaphanous* slice of bread and butter, and, laying it on her plate, passed the meal-time in breaking it into pieces, but eating no more than about one-tenth of the slice. Geoffrey hoped she would say something about Dick and finish up by weeping, as she had done after the decision against him a few days subsequent to the interview in the garden. But nothing was said, and in due time Geoffrey departed again for Yalbury Wood.

''Tis to be hoped poor Miss Fancy will be able to keep on her school,' said Geoffrey's man Enoch to Geoffrey the following week, as they were shovelling up ant-hills in the wood.

Geoffrey stuck in the shovel, swept seven or eight ants from his sleeve, and killed another that was prowling round his ear, then looked perpendicularly into the earth, as usual, waiting for Enoch to say more. 'Well, why shouldn't she?' said the keeper at last.

'The baker told me yesterday,' continued Enoch, shaking out another emmet* that had run merrily up his thigh, 'that the bread he've left at that there school-house this last month would starve any mouse in the three creations;* that 'twould so! And afterwards I had a pint o' small* down at Morrs's, and there I heard more.'

'What might that ha' been?'

'That she used to have a pound o' the best rolled butter a week, regular as clockwork, from Dairyman Viney's for herself, as well as just so much salted for the helping girl, and the 'ooman she calls in; but now the same quantity d'last her three weeks, and then 'tis thoughted she throws it away sour.'

'Finish doing the emmets, and carry the bag home-along.' The keeper resumed his gun, tucked it under his arm, and went on without whistling to the dogs, who however followed with a bearing meant to imply that they did not expect any such attentions when their master was reflecting.

On Saturday morning a note came from Fancy. He was not to trouble about sending her the couple of rabbits as was intended, because she feared she should not want them. Later in the day Geoffrey went to Casterbridge and called upon the butcher who served Fancy with fresh meat, which was put down to her father's account.

'I've called to pay up our little bill, Neighbour Haylock, and you can gie me the chiel's account at the same time.'

Mr Haylock turned round three-quarters of a circle in the midst of a heap of joints, altered the expression of his face from meat to money, went into a little office consisting only of a door and a window, looked very vigorously into a book which possessed length but no breadth; and then, seizing a piece of paper and scribbling thereupon, handed the bill.

Probably it was the first time in the history of commercial transactions that the quality of shortness in a butcher's bill was a cause of tribulation to the debtor. 'Why, this isn't all she've had in a whole month!' said Geoffrey.

'Every mossel,' said the butcher – '(now, Dan, take that leg and shoulder to Mrs White's, and this eleven pound here to Mr Martin's) – you've been treating her to smaller joints lately, to my thinking, Mr Day?'

'Only two or three little scram rabbits this last week, as I am alive – I wish I had!'

'Well, my wife said to me – (Dan! Not too much, not too much on that tray at a time; better go twice) – my wife said to me as she posted up the books: "Haylock," she says, "Miss Day must have been affronted* this summer during that hot muggy weather that spoilt so much for us; for depend upon't," she says, "she've been trying John Grimmett unknown to us: see her account else." 'Tis little, of course, at the best of times, being only for one, but now 'tis next kin to nothing.'

'I'll inquire,' said Geoffrey despondingly.

He returned by way of Mellstock, and called upon Fancy in fulfilment of a promise. It being Saturday the children were enjoying a holiday, and on entering the residence Fancy was nowhere to be seen. Nan the charwoman was sweeping the kitchen.

'Where's my da'ter?' said the keeper.

'Well, you see she was tired with the week's teaching, and this morning she said, "Nan, I shan't get up till the evening." You see, Mr Day, if people don't eat they can't work; and as she've gie'd up eating she must gie up working.'

'Have ye carried up any dinner to her?'

'No; she don't want any. There, we all know that such things don't come without good reason – not that I wish to say anything about a broken heart, or anything of the kind.'

Geoffrey's own heart felt inconveniently large just then. He went to the staircase and ascended to his daughter's door.

'Fancy!'

'Come in, father.'

To see a person in bed from any cause whatever on a fine afternoon is depressing enough; and here was his only child Fancy not only in bed, but looking very pale. Geoffrey was visibly disturbed.

'Fancy, I didn't expect to see thee here, chiel,' he said. 'What's the matter?'

'I'm not well, father.'

'How's that?'

'Because I think of things.'

'What things can you have to think o' so mortal much?'

'You know, father.'

'You think I've been cruel to thee in saying that that penniless Dick o' thine shan't marry thee, I suppose.'

No answer.

'Well, you know, Fancy, I do it for the best, and he isn't good enough for thee. You know that well enough.' Here he again looked at her as she lay. Well, Fancy, I can't let my only chiel die; and if you can't live without en, you must ha' en, I suppose.'

'O, I don't want him like that; all against your will, and everything so disobedient!' sighed the invalid.

'No, no, 'tisn't against my will. My wish is, now I d'see how 'tis hurten thee to live without en, that he shall marry thee as soon as we've considered a little. That's my wish flat and plain, Fancy. There, never cry, my little maid! You ought to have cried afore; no need o' crying now 'tis all over. Well, howsoever, try to step over and see me and Mother-law* tomorrow, and ha' a bit of dinner wi' us.'

'And – Dick too?'

'Ay, Dick too, 'far's I know.'

'And *when* do you think you'll have considered, Father, and he may marry me?' she coaxed.

'Well, there, say next Midsummer; that's not a day too long to wait.'

On leaving the school Geoffrey went to the tranter's. Old William opened the door.

'Is your grandson Dick in 'ithin, William?'

'No, not just now, Mr Day. Though he've been at home a good deal lately.'

'O, how's that?'

'What wi' one thing, and what wi' t'other, he's all in a mope, as might be said. Don't seem the feller he used to. Ay, 'a will sit studding* and thinking as if 'a were going to turn chapel-member,* and then do nothing but traypse and wamble* about. Used to be such a chatty boy, too, Dick did; and now 'a don't speak at all. But won't ye step inside? Reuben will be home soon, 'a b'lieve.'

'No, thank you, I can't stay now. Will ye just ask Dick if he'll do me the kindness to step over to Yalbury tomorrow with my da'ter Fancy, if she's well enough? I don't like her to come by herself, now she's not so terrible topping in health.'

'So I've heard. Ay, sure, I'll tell him without fail.'

5

AFTER GAINING HER POINT

The visit to Geoffrey passed off as delightfully as a visit might have been expected to pass off when it was the first day of smooth experience in a hitherto obstructed love-course. And then came a series of several happy days of the same undisturbed serenity. Dick could court her when he chose; stay away when he chose – which was never; walk with her by winding streams and waterfalls and autumn scenery till dews and twilight sent them home. And thus they drew near the day of the Harvest Thanksgiving, which was also the time chosen for opening the organ in Mellstock Church.

It chanced that Dick on that very day was called away from Mellstock. A young acquaintance had died of consumption at

Charmley, a neighbouring village, on the previous Monday, and Dick in fulfilment of a long-standing promise was to assist in carrying him to the grave. When on Tuesday Dick went towards the school to acquaint Fancy with the fact it is difficult to say whether his own disappointment at being denied the sight of her triumphant *début* as organist, was greater than his vexation that his pet should on this great occasion be deprived of the pleasure of his presence. However, the intelligence was communicated. She bore it as she best could not without many expressions of regret and convictions that her performance would be nothing to her now.

Just before eleven o'clock on Sunday he set out upon his sad errand. The funeral was to be immediately after the morning service, and as there were four good miles to walk, driving being inconvenient, it became necessary to start comparatively early. Half an hour later would certainly have answered his purpose quite as well, yet at the last moment nothing would content his ardent mind but that he must go a mile out of his way in the direction of the school, in the hope of getting a glimpse of his Love as she started for church.

Striking therefore into the lane towards the school, instead of across the ewelease direct to Charmley, he arrived opposite her door as his goddess emerged.

If ever a woman looked a divinity Fancy Day appeared one that morning as she floated down those school steps, in the form of a nebulous collection of colours inclining to blue. With an audacity unparalleled in the whole history of village schoolmistresses at this date – partly owing, no doubt, to papa's respectable accumulation of cash, which rendered her profession not altogether one of necessity – she had actually donned a hat and feather and lowered her hitherto plainly looped-up hair, which now fell about her shoulders in a profusion of curls. Poor Dick was astonished: he had never seen her look so distractingly beautiful before save on Christmas Eve, when her hair was in the same luxuriant condition of freedom. But his first burst of delighted surprise was followed by less comfortable feelings as soon as his brain recovered its power to think.

Fancy had blushed; – was it with confusion? She had also involuntarily pressed back her curls. She had not expected him.

'Fancy, you didn't know me for a moment in my funeral clothes, did you?'

'Good morning, Dick – no, really, I didn't know you for an instant in such a sad suit.'

He looked again at the gay tresses and hat. 'You've never dressed so charming before, dearest.'

'I like to hear you praise me in that way, Dick,' she said, smiling archly. 'It is meat and drink to a woman. Do I look nice really?'

'Fie! you know it. Did you remember – I mean didn't you remember about my going away today?'

'Well, yes, I did, Dick; but, you know, I wanted to look well; – forgive me.'

'Yes, darling; yes, of course – there's nothing to forgive. No, I was only thinking that when we talked on Tuesday and Wednesday and Thursday and Friday about my absence today, and I was so sorry for it, you said, Fancy, so were you sorry, and almost cried, and said it would be no pleasure to you to be the attraction of the church today since I could not be there.'

'My dear one, neither will it be so much pleasure to me . . . But I do take a little delight in my life, I suppose,' she pouted.

'Apart from mine?'

She looked at him with perplexed eyes. 'I know you are vexed with me, Dick, and it is because the first Sunday I have curls and a hat and feather since I have been here happens to be the very day you are away and won't be with me. Yes, say it is, for that is it! And you think that all this week I ought to have remembered you wouldn't be here today, and not have cared to be better dressed than usual. Yes, you do, Dick, and it is rather unkind!'

'No, no,' said Dick earnestly and simply, 'I didn't think so badly of you as that. I only thought that – if *you* had been going away, I shouldn't have tried new attractions for the eyes of other people. But then of course you and I are different, naturally.'

'Well, perhaps we are.'

'Whatever will the vicar say, Fancy?'

'I don't fear what he says in the least!' she answered proudly. 'But he won't say anything of the sort you think. No, no.'

'He can hardly have conscience to, indeed.'

'Now come, you say, Dick, that you quite forgive me, for I must go,' she said with sudden gaiety, and skipped backwards into the porch. 'Come here, sir – say you forgive me, and then you shall kiss me – you never have yet when I have worn curls, you know. Yes, just where you want to so much – yes, you may!'

Dick followed her into the inner corner, where he was probably not slow in availing himself of the privilege offered.

'Now that's a treat for you, isn't it?' she continued. 'Goodbye, or I shall be late. Come and see me tomorrow: you'll be tired tonight.'

Thus they parted, and Fancy proceeded to the church. The organ stood on one side of the chancel, close to and under the immediate eye of the vicar when he was in the pulpit and also in full view of the congregation. Here she sat down, for the first time in such a conspicuous position, her seat having previously been in a remote spot in the aisle.

'Good heavens – disgraceful! Curls and a hat and feather!' said the daughters of the small gentry, who had either only curly hair without a hat and feather, or a hat and feather without curly hair. 'A bonnet for church always!' said sober matrons.

That Mr Maybold was conscious of her presence close beside him during his sermon; that he was not at all angry at her development of costume; that he admired her, she perceived. But she did not see that he loved her during that sermon-time as he had never loved a woman before; that her proximity was a strange delight to him; and that he gloried in her musical success that morning in a spirit quite beyond a mere cleric's glory at the inauguration of a new order of things.

The old choir, with humbled hearts, no longer took their seats in the gallery as heretofore (which was now given up to the school-children who were not singers, and a pupil-teacher), but were scattered about with their wives in different parts of the church. Having nothing to do with conducting the service for almost the first time in their lives they all felt awkward, out of place, abashed, and inconvenienced by their hands. The tranter had proposed that they should stay away today and go nutting, but grandfather William would not hear of such a thing for a moment. 'No,' he replied reproachfully, and quoted a verse: ' "Though this has come upon us let not our hearts be turned back, or our steps go out of the way." '*

So they stood and watched the curls of hair trailing down the back of the successful rival, and the waving of her feather as she swayed her head. After a few timid notes and uncertain touches her playing became markedly correct, and towards the end full and free. But, whether from prejudice or unbiased judgment, the venerable body of musicians could not help thinking that the simpler notes they had been wont to bring forth were more in keeping with the simplicity of their old church than the crowded chords and interludes it was her pleasure to produce.

6

INTO TEMPTATION

The day was done, and Fancy was again in the school-house. About five o'clock it began to rain, and in rather a dull frame of mind she wandered into the schoolroom for want of something better to do. She was thinking – of her lover Dick Dewy? Not precisely. Of how weary she was of living alone; how unbearable it would be to return to Yalbury under the rule of her strange-tempered step-mother; that it was far better to be married to anybody than do that; that eight or nine long months had yet to be lived through ere the wedding could take place.

At the side of the room were high windows of Ham-hill stone,* upon either sill of which she could sit by first mounting a desk and using it as a footstool. As the evening advanced here she perched herself, as was her custom on such wet and gloomy occasions, put on a light shawl and bonnet, opened the window, and looked out at the rain.

The window overlooked a field called the Grove, and it was the position from which she used to survey the crown of Dick's passing hat in the early days of their acquaintance and meetings. Not a living soul was now visible anywhere; the rain kept all people indoors who were not forced abroad by necessity, and necessity was less importunate on Sundays than during the week.

Sitting here and thinking again – of her lover, or of the sensation she had created at church that day? – well, it is unknown – thinking and thinking she saw a dark masculine figure arising into distinctness at the further end of the Grove – a man without an umbrella. Nearer and nearer he came, and she perceived that he was in deep mourning, and then that it was Dick. Yes, in the fondness and foolishness of his young heart, after walking four miles in a drizzling rain without overcoat or umbrella and in face of a remark from his love that he was not to come because he would be tired, he had made it his business to wander this mile out of his way again from sheer wish of spending ten minutes in her presence.

'O Dick, how wet you are!' she said, as he drew up under the window. 'Why, your coat shines as if it had been varnished, and your hat – my goodness, there's a streaming hat!'

'O, I don't mind, darling!' said Dick cheerfully. 'Wet never hurts me, though I am rather sorry for my best clothes. However, it couldn't be helped; we lent all the umbrellas to the women. I don't know when I shall get mine back.'

'And look, there's a nasty patch of something just on your shoulder.'

'Ah, that's japanning;* it rubbed off the clamps of poor Jack's coffin when we lowered him from our shoulders upon the bier! I don't care about that, for 'twas the last deed I could do for him; and 'tis hard if you can't afford a coat for an old friend.'

Fancy put her hand to her mouth for half a minute. Underneath the palm of that little hand there existed for that half-minute a little yawn.

'Dick, I don't like you to stand there in the wet. And you mustn't sit down. Go home and change your things. Don't stay another minute.'

'One kiss after coming so far,' he pleaded.

'If I can reach, then.'

He looked rather disappointed at not being invited round to the door. She twisted from her seated position and bent herself downwards, but not even by standing on the plinth was it possible for Dick to get his lips into contact with hers as she held them. By great exertion she might have reached a little lower; but then she would have exposed her head to the rain.

'Never mind, Dick; kiss my hand,' she said, flinging it down to him. 'Now, goodbye.'

'Goodbye.'

He walked slowly away, turning and turning again to look at her till he was out of sight. During the retreat she said to herself, almost involuntarily, and still conscious of that morning's triumph—

'I like Dick, and I love him; but how plain and sorry a man looks in the rain, with no umbrella, and wet through!'

As he vanished she made as if to descend from her seat; but

glancing in the other direction she saw another form coming along the same track. It was also that of a man. He, too, was in black from top to toe; but he carried an umbrella.

He drew nearer, and the direction of the rain caused him so to slant his umbrella that from her height above the ground his head was invisible, as she was also to him. He passed in due time directly beneath her, and in looking down upon the exterior of his umbrella her feminine eyes perceived it to be of superior silk – less common at that date than since – and of elegant make. He reached the entrance to the building, and Fancy suddenly lost sight of him. Instead of pursuing the roadway as Dick had done he had turned sharply round into her own porch.

She jumped to the floor, hastily flung off her shawl and bonnet, smoothed and patted her hair till the curls hung in passable condition, and listened. No knock. Nearly a minute passed, and still there was no knock. Then there arose a soft series of raps no louder than the tapping of a distant wood-pecker, and barely distinct enough to reach her ears. She composed herself and flung open the door.

In the porch stood Mr Maybold.

There was a warm flush upon his face and a bright flash in his eyes which made him look handsomer than she had ever seen him before.

'Good evening, Miss Day.'

'Good evening, Mr Maybold,' she said, in a strange state of mind. She had noticed, beyond the ardent hue of his face, that his voice had a singular tremor in it, and that his hand shook like an aspen leaf when he laid his umbrella in the corner of the porch. Without another word being spoken by either he came into the schoolroom, shut the door, and moved close to her. Once inside the expression of his face was no more discernible by reason of the increasing dusk of evening.

'I want to speak to you,' he then said; 'seriously – on a perhaps unexpected subject, but one which is all the world to me – I don't know what it may be to you, Miss Day.'

No reply.

'Fancy, I have come to ask you if you will be my wife?'

As a person who has been idly amusing himself with rolling a snowball might start at finding he had set in motion an avalanche, so did Fancy start at these words from the young vicar. And in the dead silence which followed them the breathings of the man and of the woman could be distinctly and separately heard; and there was this difference between them – his respirations gradually grew quieter and less rapid after the enunciation; hers, from having been low and regular, increased in quickness and force till she almost panted.

'I cannot, I cannot, Mr Maybold – I cannot! Don't ask me!' she said.

'Don't answer in a hurry!' he entreated. 'And do listen to me. This is no sudden feeling on my part. I have loved you for more than six months! Perhaps my late interest in teaching the children here has not been so single-minded as it seemed. You will understand my motive – like me better, perhaps, for honestly telling you that I have struggled against my emotion continually, because I have thought that it was not well for me to love you! But I resolved to struggle no longer; I have examined the feeling; and the love I bear you is as genuine as that I could bear any woman! I see your great charm; I respect your natural talents, and the refinement they have brought into your nature – they are quite enough, and more than enough for me! They are equal to anything ever required of the mistress of a quiet parsonage-house – the place in which I shall pass my days, wherever it may be situated. O Fancy, I have watched you, criticised you even severely, brought my feelings to the light of judgment, and still have found them rational, and such as any man might have expected to be inspired with by a woman like you! So there is nothing hurried, secret, or untoward in my desire to do this. Fancy, will you marry me?'

No answer was returned.

'Don't refuse; don't,' he implored. 'It would be foolish of you – I mean cruel! Of course we would not live here, Fancy. I have had for a long time the offer of an exchange of livings with a friend in Yorkshire, but I have hitherto refused on account of my mother. There we would go. Your musical powers shall be still further developed; you shall have whatever pianoforte you like; you shall have anything, Fancy, anything to make you happy – pony-carriage, flowers, birds, pleasant society; yes, you have enough in you for any society, after a few months of travel with me! Will you, Fancy, marry me?'

Another pause ensued, varied only by the surging of the rain against the window-panes, and then Fancy spoke, in a faint and broken voice.

'Yes, I will,' she said.

'God bless you, my own!' He advanced quickly, and put his arm out to embrace her. She drew back hastily. 'No no, not now!' she said in an agitated whisper. 'There are things – but the temptation is, O, too strong, and I can't resist it; I can't tell you now, but I must tell you! Don't, please, don't come near me now! I want to think. I can scarcely get myself used to the idea of what I have promised yet.' The next minute she turned to a desk, buried her face in her hands, and burst into a hysterical fit of weeping. 'O, leave me to myself!' she sobbed; 'leave me! O, leave me!'

'Don't be distressed; don't, dearest!' It was with visible difficulty that he restrained himself from approaching her. 'You shall tell me at your leisure what it is that grieves you so; I am happy – beyond all measure happy! – at having your simple promise.'

'And do go and leave me now!'

'But I must not, in justice to you, leave for a minute, until you are yourself again.'

'There then,' she said, controlling her emotion, and standing up; 'I am not disturbed now.'

He reluctantly moved towards the door. 'Goodbye!' he murmured tenderly. 'I'll come tomorrow about this time.'

7
SECOND THOUGHTS

The next morning the vicar rose early. The first thing he did was to write a long and careful letter to his friend in Yorkshire. Then, eating a little breakfast, he crossed the meadows in the direction of Casterbridge, bearing his letter in his pocket, that he might post it at the town office, and obviate the loss of one day in its transmission that would have resulted had he left it for the foot-post* through the village.

It was a foggy morning, and the trees shed in noisy water-drops the moisture they had collected from the thick air, an acorn occasionally falling from its cup to the ground in company with the drippings. In the meads sheets of spiders' web, almost opaque with wet, hung in folds over the fences, and the falling leaves appeared in every variety of brown, green, and yellow hue.

A low and merry whistling was heard on the highway he was approaching, then the light footsteps of a man going in the same direction as himself. On reaching the junction of his path with the road the vicar beheld Dick Dewy's open and cheerful face. Dick lifted his hat, and the vicar came out into the highway that Dick was pursuing.

'Good morning, Dewy. How well you are looking!' said Mr Maybold.

'Yes, sir, I am well – quite well! I am going to Casterbridge now, to get Smart's collar; we left it there Saturday to be repaired.'

'I am going to Casterbridge, so we'll walk together,' the vicar said. Dick gave a hop with one foot to put himself in step with Mr Maybold, who proceeded: 'I fancy I didn't see you at church yesterday, Dewy. Or were you behind the pier?'

'No; I went to Charmley. Poor John Dunford chose me to be one of his bearers a long time before he died, and yesterday was the funeral. Of course I couldn't refuse, though I should have liked particularly to have been at home as 'twas the day of the new music.'

'Yes, you should have been. The musical portion of the service was successful – very successful indeed, and what is more to the purpose no ill-feeling whatever was evinced by any of the members of the old choir. They joined in the singing with the greatest goodwill.'

''Twas natural enough that I should want to be there, I suppose,' said Dick, smiling a private smile; 'considering who the organ-player was.'

At this the vicar reddened a little, and said, 'Yes, yes,' though not at all comprehending Dick's true meaning, who, as he received no further reply, continued hesitatingly, and with another smile denoting his pride as a lover –

'I suppose you know what I mean, sir? You've heard about me and – Miss Day?'

The red in Maybold's countenance went away: he turned and looked Dick in the face.

'No,' he said constrainedly, 'I've heard nothing whatever about you and Miss Day.'

'Why, she's my sweetheart, and we are going to be married next Midsummer. We are keeping it rather close just at present, because 'tis a good many months to wait; but it is her father's wish that we don't marry before, and of course we must submit. But the time 'ill soon slip along.'

'Yes, the time, will soon slip along – Time glides away every day – yes.'

Maybold said these words, but he had no idea of what they were. He was conscious of a cold and sickly thrill throughout him; and all he reasoned was this that the young creature whose graces had intoxicated him into making the most imprudent resolution of his life was less an angel than a woman.

'You see, sir,' continued the ingenuous Dick, ''twill be better in one sense. I shall by that time be the regular manager of a branch o' Father's business which we think of starting elsewhere. It has very much increased lately, and we expect next year to keep a' extra couple of horses. We've already our eye on one – brown as a berry, neck like a rainbow, fifteen hands,* and not a grey hair in her – offered us at twenty-five want a crown.* And to kip pace with the times I have had some cards prented, and I beg leave to hand you one, sir.'

'Certainly,' said the vicar, mechanically taking the card that Dick offered him.

'I turn in here by Grey's Bridge,* said Dick. 'I suppose you go straight on and up town?'

'Yes.'

'Good morning, sir.'

'Good morning, Dewy.'

Maybold stood still upon the bridge, holding the card as it had been put into his hand, and Dick's footsteps died away towards Durnover Mill. The vicar's first voluntary action was to read the card: –

DEWY AND SON
TRANTERS AND HAULIERS
MELLSTOCK

N.B. – Furniture, Coals, Potatoes, Live and Dead Stock, removed to any distance on the shortest notice.

Mr Maybold leant over the parapet of the bridge and looked into the river. He saw – without heeding – how the water came rapidly from beneath the arches, glided down a little steep, then spread itself over a pool in which dace, trout, and minnows sported at ease among the long green locks of weed that lay heaving and sinking with their roots towards the current. At the end of ten minutes spent leaning thus he drew from his pocket the letter to his friend, tore it deliberately into such minute fragments that scarcely two syllables remained in juxtaposition, and sent the whole handful of shreds fluttering into the water. Here he watched them eddy, dart, and turn, as they were carried downwards towards the ocean and gradually disappeared from his view. Finally he moved off, and pursued his way at a rapid pace back again to Mellstock Vicarage.

Nerving himself by a long and intense effort he sat down in his study and wrote as follows:

DEAR MISS DAY,

The meaning of your words, 'the temptation is too strong', of your sadness and your tears, has been brought home to me by an accident. I know today what I did not know yesterday – that you are not a free woman.

Why did you not tell me – why didn't you? Did you suppose I knew? No. Had I known, my conduct in coming to you as I did would have been reprehensible.

But I don't chide you! Perhaps no blame attaches to you – I can't tell. Fancy, though my opinion of you is assailed and disturbed in a way which cannot be expressed, I love you still, and my word to you holds good yet. But will you, in justice to an honest man who relies upon your word to him, consider whether, under the circumstances, you can honourably forsake him? – Yours ever sincerely,

ARTHUR MAYBOLD

He rang the bell. 'Tell Charles to take these copybooks and this note to the school at once.'

The maid took the parcel and the letter, and in a few minutes a boy was seen to leave the vicarage gate with the one under his arm and the other in his hand. The vicar sat with his hand to his brow, watching the lad as he descended Church Lane and entered the waterside path which intervened between that spot and the school.

Here he was met by another boy, and after a free salutation and pugilistic frisk had passed between the two the second boy came on his way to the vicarage, and the other vanished out of sight.

The boy came to the door, and a note for Mr Maybold was brought in.

He knew the writing. Opening the envelope with an unsteady hand he read the subjoined words:

DEAR MR MAYBOLD,

I have been thinking seriously and sadly through the whole of the night of the question you I put to me last evening; and of my answer. That answer, as an honest woman, I had no right to give.

It is my nature – perhaps all women's – to love refinement of mind and manners; but even more than this, to be ever fascinated with the idea of surroundings more elegant and pleasing than those which have been customary. And you praised me, and praise is life to me. It was alone my sensations at these things which prompted my reply. Ambition and vanity they would be called; perhaps they are so.

After this explanation I hope you will generously allow me to withdraw the answer I too hastily gave.

And one more request. To keep the meeting of last night, and all that passed between us there, forever a secret. Were it to become known it would utterly blight the happiness of a trusting and generous man, whom I love still, and shall love always. – Yours sincerely,

FANCY DAY

The last written communication that ever passed from the vicar to Fancy was a note containing these words only:

'Tell him everything; it is best. He will forgive you.'

PART V
CONCLUSION

I

'THE KNOT THERE'S
NO UNTYING'*

The last day of the story is dated just subsequent to that point in the development of the seasons when country people go to bed among nearly naked trees, are lulled to sleep by a fall of rain, and awake next morning among green ones; when the landscape appears embarrassed with the sudden weight and brilliancy of its leaves; when the night-jar comes and strikes up for the summer his tune of one note; when the apple trees have bloomed, and the roads and orchard-grass become spotted with fallen petals; when the faces of the delicate flowers are darkened and their heads weighed down by the throng of honey-bees, which increase their humming till humming is too mild a term for the all-pervading sound; and when cuckoos, blackbirds, and sparrows, that have hitherto been merry and respectful neighbours, become noisy and persistent intimates.

The exterior of Geoffrey Day's house in Yalbury Wood appeared exactly as was usual at that season, but a frantic barking of the dogs at the back told of unwonted movements somewhere within. Inside the door the eyes beheld a gathering which was a rarity indeed for the dwelling of the solitary wood-steward and keeper.

About the room were sitting and standing, in various gnarled attitudes, our old acquaintance grandfathers James and William, the tranter, Mr Penny, two or three children, including Jimmy and Charley, besides three or four country ladies and gentlemen from a greater distance who do not require any distinction by name. Geoffrey was seen and heard stamping about the out-house and among the bushes of the garden, attending to details of daily routine before the proper time arrived for their perform-ance, in order that they might be off his hands for the day. He appeared with his shirt-sleeves rolled up; his best new nether garments, in which he had arrayed himself that morning, being temporarily disguised under a weekday apron whilst these proceedings were in operation. He occasionally glanced at the hives in passing to see if his wife's bees were swarming, ultimately rolling down his shirt-sleeves and going indoors, talking to tranter Dewy whilst buttoning the wristbands, to save time; next going upstairs for his best waistcoat, and coming down again to make another remark whilst buttoning that, during the time looking fixedly in the tranter's face as if he were a looking-glass.

The furniture had undergone attenuation to an alarming extent, every duplicate piece having been removed, including the clock by Thomas Wood; Ezekiel Saunders being at last left sole referee in matters of time.

Fancy was stationary upstairs, receiving her layers of clothes and adornments and answering by short fragments of laughter which had more fidgetiness than mirth in them, remarks that were made from time to time by Mrs Dewy and Mrs Penny, who were assisting her at the toilet, Mrs Day having pleaded a queerness in her head as a reason for shutting herself up in an inner bedroom for the whole morning. Mrs Penny appeared with nine corkscrew curls on each side of her temples, and a back comb stuck upon her crown like a castle on a steep.

The conversation just now going on was concerning the banns,* the last publication of which had been on the Sunday previous.

'And how did they sound?' Fancy subtly inquired.

'Very beautiful indeed,' said Mrs' Penny. 'I never heard any sound better.'

'But *how*?'

'O, *so* natural and elegant, didn't they, Reuben!' she cried through the chinks of the unceiled floor to the tranter downstairs.

'What's that?' said the tranter, looking up inquiringly at the floor above him for an answer.

'Didn't Dick and Fancy sound well when they were called home* in church last Sunday?' came downwards again in Mrs Penny's voice.

'Ay, that they did, my sonnies! – especially the first time. There was a terrible whispering piece of work in the congregation, wasn't there, neighbour Penny?' said the tranter, taking up the thread of conversation on his own account and, in order to be heard in the room above, speaking very loud to Mr Penny, who sat at the distance of three feet from him, or rather less.

'I never can mind seeing such a whispering as there was,' said

Mr Penny, also loudly, to the room above. 'And such sorrowful envy on the maidens' faces; really, I never did see such envy as there was!'

Fancy's lineaments varied in innumerable little flushes and her heart palpitated innumerable little tremors of pleasure. 'But perhaps,' she said, with assumed indifference, 'it was only because no religion was going on just then?'

'O, no; nothing to do with that. 'Twas because of your high standing in the parish. It was just as if they had one and all caught Dick kissing and coling* ye to death, wasn't it, Mrs Dewy?'

'Ay; that 'twas.'

'How people will talk about one's doings!' Fancy exclaimed.

'Well, if you make songs about yourself, my dear, you can't blame other people for singing 'em.'

'Mercy me! how shall I go through it?' said the young lady again, but merely to those in the bedroom, with a breathing of a kind between a sigh and a pant, round shining eyes, and warm face.

'O, you'll get through it well enough, child,' said Mrs Dewy placidly. 'The edge of the performance is took off at the calling home; and when once you get up to the chancel end o' the church you feel as saucy as you please. I'm sure I felt as brave as a sodger all through the deed – though of course I dropped my face and looked modest, as was becoming to a maid. Mind you do that, Fancy.'

'And I walked into the church as quiet as a lamb, I'm sure,' subjoined Mrs Penny. 'There, you see Penny is such a little small man. But certainly I was flurried in the inside o' me. Well, thinks I, 'tis to be, and here goes! And do you do the same: say, "'Tis to be, and here goes!"'

'Is there such wonderful virtue in "'Tis to be, and here goes!"' inquired Fancy.

'Wonderful! 'Twill carry a body through it all from wedding to churching,* if you only let it out with spirit enough.'

'Very well, then,' said Fancy, blushing. "'Tis to be, and here goes!'

'That's a girl for a husband!' said Mrs Dewy.

'I do hope he'll come in time!' continued the bride-elect, inventing a new cause of affright now that the other was demolished.

'"Twould be a thousand pities if he didn't come, now you be so brave,' said Mrs Penny.

Grandfather James, having overheard some of these remarks, said downstairs with mischievous loudness –

'I've known some would-be weddings when the men didn't come.'

'They've happened not to come, before now, certainly,' said Mr Penny, cleaning one of the glasses of his spectacles.

'O, do hear what they are saying downstairs,' whispered Fancy. 'Hush, hush!'

She listened.

'They have, haven't they, Geoffrey?' continued grim grandfather James, as Geoffrey entered.

'Have what?' said Geoffrey.

'The men have been known not to come.'

'That they have,' said the keeper.

'Ay; I've knowed times when the wedding had to be put off through his not appearing, being tired of the woman. And another case I knowed was when the man was catched in a mantrap crossing Oaker's Wood, and the three months had run out before he got well, and the banns had to be published ever again.'

'How horrible!' said Fancy.

'They only say it on purpose to tease 'ee, my dear,' said Mrs Dewy.

'"Tis quite sad to think what wretched shifts poor maids have been put to,' came again from downstairs. 'Ye should hear Clerk Wilkins, my brother-law, tell his experiences in marrying couples these last thirty year: sometimes one thing, sometimes another – 'tis quite heart-rending – enough to make your hair stand on end.'

'Those things don't happen very often, I know,' said Fancy with smouldering uneasiness.

'Well, really 'tis time Dick was here,' said the tranter.

'Don't keep on at me so, grandfather James and Mr Dewy, and all you down there!' Fancy broke out, unable to endure any longer. 'I am sure I shall die, or do something, if you do!'

'Never you hearken to these old chaps, Miss Day!' cried Nat Callcome the best man, who had just entered, and threw his voice upward through the chinks of the floor as the others had done. '"Tis all right; Dick's coming on like a wild feller; he'll be here in a minute. The hive o' bees his mother gie'd en for his new garden swarmed jist as he was starting, and he said, "I can't afford to lose a stock o' bees; no, that I can't, though I fain would; and Fancy wouldn't wish it on any account." So he jist stopped to ting* 'em and shake 'em.'

'A genuine wise man,' said Geoffrey.

'To be sure what a day's work we had yesterday!' Mr Callcome continued, lowering his voice as if it were not necessary any longer to include those in the room above among his audience, and selecting a remote corner of his best clean handkerchief for wiping his face. 'To be sure!'

'Things so heavy, I suppose,' said Geoffrey, as if reading through the chimney-window from the far end of the vista.

'Ay,' said Nat, looking round the room at points from which furniture had been removed. 'And so awkward to carry, too. 'Twas ath'art and across Dick's garden; in and out Dick's door; up and down Dick's stairs; round and round Dick's chammers till legs were worn to stumps: and Dick is so particular, too. And the stores of victuals and drink that lad has laid in: why, 'tis enough for Noah's ark! I'm sure I never wish to see a choicer half-dozen of hams than he's got there in his chimley; and the cider I tasted was a very pretty drop, indeed – none could desire a prettier cider.'

'They be for the love and the stalled ox both.* Ah, the greedy martels!' said grandfather James.

'Well, maybe they be. "Surely," says I, "that couple between 'em have heaped up so much furniture and victuals that anybody would think they were going to take hold the big end of married life first, and begin wi' a grown-up family." Ah, what a bath of heat we two chaps were in, to be sure, a-getting that furniture in order!'

'I do so wish the room below was ceiled,'* said Fancy as the dressing went on, 'we can hear all they say and do down there.'

'Hark! Who's that?' exclaimed a small pupil-teacher, who also assisted this morning to her great delight. She ran halfway down the stairs and peeped round the banister. 'O, you should, you should, you should!' she exclaimed, scrambling up to the room again.

'What?' said Fancy.

'See the bridesmaids! They've just a-come! 'Tis wonderful, really! 'tis wonderful how muslin can be brought to it. There, they don't look a bit like themselves, but like some very rich sisters o' theirs that nobody knew they had!'

'Make them come up to me, make them come up!' cried Fancy ecstatically; and the four damsels appointed, namely, Miss Susan Dewy, Miss Bessie Dewy, Miss Vashti Sniff, and Miss Mercy Onmey surged upstairs and floated along the passage.

'I wish Dick would come!' was again the burden of Fancy.

The same instant a small twig and flower from the creeper outside the door flew in at the open window, and a masculine voice said, 'Ready, Fancy dearest?'

'There he is, he is!' cried Fancy, tittering spasmodically and breathing as it were for the first time that morning.

The bridesmaids crowded to the window and turned their heads in the direction pointed out, at which motion eight earrings all swung as one: – not looking at Dick because they particularly wanted to see him, but with an important sense of their duty as obedient ministers of the will of that apotheosised* being – the Bride.

'He looks very taking!' said Miss Vashti Sniff, a young lady who blushed cream-colour and wore yellow bonnet-ribbons.

Dick was advancing to the door in a painfully new coat of shining cloth, primrose-coloured waistcoat, hat of the same painful style of newness, and with an extra quantity of whiskers shaved off his face and hair cut to an unwonted shortness in honour of the occasion.

'Now I'll run down,' said Fancy, looking at herself over her shoulder in the glass, and flitting off.

'O Dick!' she exclaimed, 'I am so glad you are come! I knew you would, of course, but I thought, O, if you shouldn't!'

'Not come, Fancy! Het or wet, blow or snow, here come I today! Why, what's possessing your little soul? You never used to mind such things a bit.'

'Ah, Mr Dick, I hadn't hoisted my colours and committed myself then!' said Fancy.

''Tis a pity I can't marry the whole five of ye!' said Dick, surveying them all round.

'Heh-heh-heh!' laughed the four bridesmaids, and Fancy privately touched Dick and smoothed him down behind his shoulder as if to assure herself that he was there in flesh and blood as her own property.

'Well, whoever would have thought such a thing?' said Dick,

taking off his hat, sinking into a chair, and turning to the elder members of the company.

The latter arranged their eyes and lips to signify that in their opinion nobody could have thought such a thing, whatever it was.

'That my bees should ha' swarmed just then, of all times and seasons!' continued Dick, throwing a comprehensive glance like a net over the whole auditory. 'And 'tis a fine swarm, too: I haven't seen such a fine swarm for these ten years.'

'A' excellent sign,' said Mrs Penny, from the depths of experience. 'A' excellent sign.'

'I am glad everything seems so right,' said Fancy with a breath of relief.

'And so am I,' said the four bridesmaids with much sympathy.

'Well, bees can't be put off,' observed the inharmonious grandfather James. 'Marrying a woman is a thing you can do at any moment but a swarm o' bees won't come for the asking.'

Dick fanned himself with his hat. 'I can't think,' he said thoughtfully, 'whatever 'twas I did to offend Mr Maybold, – a man I like so much, too. He rather took to me when he came first, and used to say he should like to see me married, and that he'd marry me, whether the young woman I chose lived in his parish or no. I just hinted to him of it when I put in the banns, but he didn't seem to take kindly to the notion now, and so I said no more. I wonder how it was.'

'I wonder!' said Fancy, looking into vacancy with those beautiful eyes of hers – too refined and beautiful for a tranter's wife; but, perhaps, not too good.

'Altered his mind, as folks will, I suppose,' said the tranter. 'Well, my sonnies, there'll be a good strong party looking at us today as we go along.'

'And the body of the church,' said Geoffrey, 'will be lined with females, and a row of young fellers' heads, as far down as the eyes, will be noticed just above the sills of the chancel-winders.'

'Ay, you've been through it twice,' said Reuben, 'and well mid know.'

'I can put up with it for once,' said Dick, 'or twice either, or a dozen times.'

'O Dick!' said Fancy reproachfully.

'Why, dear, that's nothing – only just a bit of a flourish. You be as nervous as a cat today.'

'And then, of course, when 'tis all over,' continued the tranter, 'we shall march two and two* round the parish.'

'Yes, sure,' said Mr Penny, 'two and two: every man hitched up to his woman, 'a b'lieve.'

'I never can make a show of myself in that way!' said Fancy, looking at Dick to ascertain if he could.

'I'm agreed to anything you and the company like, my dear!' said Mr Richard Dewy heartily.

'Why, we did when we were married, didn't we, Ann?' said the tranter, 'and so do everybody, my sonnies.'

'And so did we,' said Fancy's father.

'And so did Penny and I,' said Mrs Penny: 'I wore my best Bath clogs,* I remember, and Penny was cross because it made me look so tall.'

'And so did Father and Mother,' said Miss Mercy Onmey.

'And I mean to, come next Christmas!' said Nat the groomsman vigorously, and looking towards the person of Miss Vashti Sniff.

'Respectable people don't nowadays,' said Fancy. 'Still, since poor mother did, I will.'

'Ay,' resumed the tranter, ''twas on a White Tuesday when I committed it. Mellstock Club walked the same day, and we new-married folk went a-gaying round the parish behind 'em. Everybody used to wear something white at Whitsuntide in them days. My sonnies, I've got the very white trousers that I wore, at home in box now. Ha'n't I, Ann?'

'You had till I cut 'em up for Jimmy,' said Mrs Dewy.

'And we ought, by rights, after doing this parish, to go round Higher and Lower Mellstock, and call at Viney's, and so work our way hither again across He'th,' said Mr Penny, recovering scent of the matter in hand. 'Dairyman Viney is a very respectable man, and so is Farmer Kex, and we ought to show ourselves to them.'

'True,' said the tranter, 'we ought to go round Mellstock to do the thing well. We shall form a very striking object walking along in rotation, good-now, neighbours?'

'That we shall: a proper pretty sight for the nation,' said Mrs Penny.

'Hullo!' said the tranter, suddenly catching sight of a singular human figure standing in the doorway, and wearing a long smock-frock of pillowcase cut and of snowy whiteness. Why, Leaf! whatever dost thou do here?'

'I've come to know if so be I can come to the wedding – hee-hee!' said Leaf in a voice of timidity.

'Now, Leaf,' said the tranter reproachfully, 'you know we don't want 'ee here today: we've got no room for 'ee, Leaf.'

'Thomas Leaf, Thomas Leaf, fie upon 'ee for prying!' said old William.

'I know I've got no head, but I thought, if I washed and put on a clane shirt and smock-frock, I might just call,' said Leaf, turning away disappointed and trembling.

'Poor feller!' said the tranter, turning to Geoffrey. 'Suppose we must let en come? His looks are rather against en, and he is terrible silly; but 'a have never been in jail, and 'a won't do no harm.'

Leaf looked with gratitude at the tranter for these praises, and then anxiously at Geoffrey, to see what effect they would have in helping his cause.

'Ay, let en come,' said Geoffrey decisively. 'Leaf, th'rt welcome, 'st know;' and Leaf accordingly remained.

They were now all ready for leaving the house, and began to form a procession in the following order: Fancy and her father, Dick and Susan Dewy, Nat Callcome and Vashti Sniff, Ted Waywood and Mercy Onmey, and Jimmy and Bessie Dewy. These formed the executive, and all appeared in strict wedding attire. Then came the tranter and Mrs Dewy, and last of all Mr and Mrs Penny; – the tranter conspicuous by his enormous gloves, size eleven and three-quarters, which appeared at a distance like boxing gloves bleached and sat rather awkwardly upon his brown hands; this hallmark of respectability having been set upon himself today (by Fancy's special request) for the first time in his life.

'The proper way is for the bridesmaids to walk together,' suggested Fancy.

'What? 'Twas always young man and young woman, arm in crook, in my time!' said Geoffrey, astounded.

'And in mine!' said the tranter.

'And in ours!' said Mr and Mrs Penny.

'Never heard o' such a thing as woman and woman!' said old

William; who, with grandfather James and Mrs Day, was to stay at home.

'Whichever way you and the company like, my dear!' said Dick, who, being on the point of securing his right to Fancy, seemed willing to renounce all other rights in the world with the greatest pleasure. The decision was left to Fancy.

'Well, I think I'd rather have it the way mother had it,' she said, and the couples moved along under the trees, every man to his maid.

'Ah!' said grandfather James to grandfather William as they retired, 'I wonder which she thinks most about, Dick or her wedding raiment!'

'Well, 'tis their nature,' said grandfather William. 'Remember the words of the prophet Jeremiah: "Can a maid forget her ornaments, or a bride her attire?"'*

Now among dark perpendicular firs, like the shafted columns of a cathedral; now through a hazel copse, matted with prim-roses and wild hyacinths; now under broad beeches in bright young leaves they threaded their way into the high road over Yalbury Hill, which dipped at that point directly into the village of Geoffrey Day's parish; and in the space of a quarter of an hour Fancy found herself to be Mrs Richard Dewy, though, much to her surprise, feeling no other than Fancy Day still.

On the circuitous return walk through the lanes and fields, amid much chattering and laughter, especially when they came to stiles, Dick discerned a brown spot far up a turnip field.

'Why, 'tis Enoch!' he said to Fancy. 'I thought I missed him at the house this morning. How is it he's left you?'

'He drank too much cider, and it got into his head, and they put him in Weatherbury stocks* for it. Father was obliged to get somebody else for a day or two, and Enoch hasn't had anything to do with the woods since.'

'We might ask him to call down tonight. Stocks are nothing for once, considering 'tis our wedding day.' The bridal party was ordered to halt.

'Eno-o-o-o-ch!' cried Dick at the top of his voice.

'Y-a-a-a-a-a-as!' said Enoch from the distance.

'D'ye know who I be-e-e-e-e-e?'

'No-o-o-o-o-o-o!'

'Dick Dew-w-w-w-wy!'

'O-h-h-h-h-h!'

'Just a-ma-a-a-a-a-arried!'

'O-h-h-h-h-h!'

'This is my wife, Fa-a-a-a-a-ancy!' (holding her up to Enoch's view as if she had been a nosegay).

'O-h-h-h-h-h!'

'Will ye come across to the party to-ni-i-i-i-i-ight!'

'Ca-a-a-a-a-an't!'

'Why n-o-o-o-o-ot?'

'Don't work for the family no-o-o-o-ow!'

'Not nice of Master Enoch,' said Dick as they resumed their walk.

'You mustn't blame en,' said Geoffrey, 'the man's not hisself now; he's in his morning frame of mind. When he's had a gallon o' cider or ale, or a pint or two of mead, the man's well enough, and his manners be as good as anybody's in the kingdom.'

2

UNDER THE GREENWOOD TREE

The point in Yalbury Wood which abutted on the end of Geoffrey Day's premises was closed with an ancient tree, horizontally of enormous extent, though having no great pretensions to height. Many hundreds of birds had been born amidst the boughs of this single tree; tribes of rabbits and hares had nibbled at its bark from year to year; quaint tufts of fungi had sprung from the cavities of its forks; and countless families of moles and earthworms had crept about its roots. Beneath and beyond its shade spread a carefully tended grass-plot, its purpose being to supply a healthy exercise-ground for young chickens and pheasants: the hens, their mothers, being enclosed in coops placed upon the same green flooring.

All these encumbrances were now removed, and as the afternoon advanced the guests gathered on the spot, where music, dancing, and the singing of songs went forward with great spirit throughout the evening. The propriety of every one was intense, by reason of the influence of Fancy, who, as an additional precaution in this direction had strictly charged her father and the tranter to carefully avoid saying 'thee' and 'thou'* in their conversation, on the plea that those ancient words sounded so very humiliating to persons of newer taste; also that they were never to be seen drawing the back of the hand across the mouth after drinking – a local English custom of extraordinary antiquity, but stated by Fancy to be decidedly dying out among the better classes of society.

In addition to the local musicians present a man who had a thorough knowledge of the tambourine was invited from the village of Tantrum Clangley,* – a place long celebrated for the skill of its inhabitants as performers on instruments of percussion. These important members of the assembly were relegated to a height of two or three feet from the ground, upon a temporary erection of planks supported by barrels. Whilst the dancing progressed the older persons sat in a group under the trunk of the tree – the space being allotted to them somewhat grudgingly by the young ones, who were greedy of pirouetting room – and fortified by a table against the heels of the dancers. Here the gaffers and gammers* whose dancing days were over told stories of great impressiveness, and at intervals surveyed the advancing and retiring couples from the same retreat, as people on shore might be supposed to survey a naval engagement in the bay beyond; returning again to their tales when the pause was over. Those of the whirling throng who, during the rests between each figure, turned their eyes in the direction of these seated ones, were only able to discover, on account of the music and bustle, that a very striking circumstance was in course of narration – denoted by an emphatic sweep of the hand, snapping of the fingers, close of the lips, and fixed look into the centre of the listener's eye for the space of a quarter of a minute, which raised in that listener such a reciprocating working of face as to sometimes make the distant dancers half wish to know what such an interesting tale could refer to.

Fancy caused her looks to wear as much matronly expression as was obtainable out of six hours' experience as a wife, in order that the contrast between her own state of life and that of the unmarried young women present might be duly impressed upon the company: occasionally stealing glances of admiration at her left hand, but this quite privately; for her ostensible bearing concerning the matter was intended to show that, though she undoubtedly occupied the most wondrous position in the eyes of the world that had ever been attained, she was almost unconscious of the circumstance, and that the somewhat prominent position in which that wonderfully emblazoned left hand was continually found to be placed when handing cups and saucers, knives, forks, and glasses, was quite the result of accident. As to wishing to excite envy in the bosoms of her maiden companions by the exhibition of the shining ring, everyone was to know it was quite foreign to the dignity of such an experienced married woman. Dick's imagination in the meantime was far less capable of drawing so much wontedness from his new condition. He had been for two or three hours trying to feel himself merely a newly married man, but had been able to get no further in the attempt than to realize that he was Dick Dewy, the tranter's son, at a party given by Lord Wessex's head man-in-charge, on the outlying Yalbury estate, dancing and chatting with Fancy Day.

Five country dances, including 'Haste to the Wedding', two reels, and three fragments of hornpipes, brought them to the time for supper which, on account of the dampness of the grass from the immaturity of the summer season, was spread indoors. At the conclusion of the meal Dick went out to put the horse in; and Fancy, with the elder half of the four bridesmaids, retired upstairs to dress for the journey to Dick's new cottage near Mellstock.

'How long will you be putting on your bonnet, Fancy?' Dick inquired at the foot of the staircase. Being now a man of business and married he was strong on the importance of time, and doubled the emphasis of his words in conversing, and added vigour to his nods.

'Only a minute.'

'How long is that?'

'Well, dear, five.'

'Ah, sonnies!' said the tranter, as Dick retired, "tis a talent of the female race that low numbers should stand for high, more especially in matters of waiting, matters of age, and matters of money.'

'True, true, upon my body,' said Geoffrey.

'Ye spak with feeling, Geoffrey, seemingly.'

'Anybody that d'know my experience might guess that.'

'What's she doing now, Geoffrey?'

'Claning out all the upstairs drawers and cupboards, and dusting the second-best chainey* – a thing that's only done once a year. "If there's work to be done I must do it," says she, "wedding or no."'

''Tis my belief she's a very good woman at bottom.'

'She's terrible deep, then.'

Mrs Penny turned round. 'Well, 'tis humps and hollers with the best of us; but still and for all that, Dick and Fancy stand as fair a chance of having a bit of sunsheen as any married pair in the land.'

'Ay, there's no gainsaying it.'

Mrs Dewy came up, talking to one person and looking at another. 'Happy, yes,' she said. ''Tis always so when a couple is so exactly in tune with one another as Dick and she.'

'When they be'n't too poor to have time to sing,' said grandfather James.

'I tell ye, neighbours, when the pinch comes,' said the tranter: 'when the oldest daughter's boots be only a size less than her mother's, and the rest o' the flock close behind her. A sharp time for a man that, my sonnies; a very sharp time! Chanticleer's comb is a-cut* then, 'a believe.'

'That's about the form o't', said Mr Penny.

'That'll put the stuns upon* a man, when you must measure mother and daughters' lasts to tell 'em apart.'

'You've no cause to complain, Reuben, of such a close-coming flock,' said Mrs, Dewy; 'for ours was a straggling lot enough, God knows!'

'I d'know it, I d'know it,' said the tranter. 'You be a well-enough woman, Ann.'

Mrs Dewy put her mouth in the form of a smile and put it back again without smiling.

'And if they come together, they go together,' said Mrs Penny, whose family had been the reverse of the tranter's; 'and a little money will make either fate tolerable. And money can be made by our young couple, I know.'

'Yes, that it can!' said the impulsive voice of Leaf, who had hitherto humbly admired the proceedings from a corner. 'It can be done – all that's wanted is a few pounds to begin with. That's all! I know a story about it!'

'Let's hear thy story, Leaf,' said the tranter. 'I never knew you were clever enough to tell a story. Silence, all of ye! Mr Leaf will tell a story.'

'Tell your story, Thomas Leaf,' said grandfather William in the tone of a schoolmaster.

'Once,' said the delighted Leaf, in an uncertain voice, 'there was a man who lived in a house! Well, this man went thinking and thinking night and day. At last, he said to himself, as I might, "If I had only ten pound, I'd make a fortune." At last by hook or by crook, behold he got the ten pounds!'

'Only think of that!' said Nat Callcome satirically.

'Silence!' said the tranter.

'Well, now comes the interesting part of the story! In a little time he made that ten pounds twenty. Then a little time after that he doubled it, and made it forty. Well, he went on, and a good while after that he made it eighty, and on to a hundred. Well, by-and-by he made it two hundred! Well, you'd never believe it, but – he went on and made it four hundred! He went on, and what did he do? Why, he made it eight hundred! Yes, he did,' continued Leaf in the highest pitch of excitement, bringing down his fist upon his knee with such force that he quivered with the pain; 'yes, and he went on and made it A THOUSAND!'

'Hear, hear!' said the tranter. 'Better than the history of England, my sonnies!'

'Thank you for your story, Thomas Leaf,' said grandfather William; and then Leaf gradually sank into nothingness again.

Amid a medley of laughter, old shoes, and elder-wine,* Dick and his bride took their departure side by side in the excellent new spring-cart which the young tranter now possessed. The moon was just over the full, rendering any light from lamps or their own beauties quite unnecessary to the pair. They drove slowly along Yalbury Bottom, where the road passed between two copses. Dick was talking to his companion.

'Fancy,' he said, 'why we are so happy is because there is such full confidence between us. Ever since that time you confessed to that little flirtation with Shiner by the river (which was really no flirtation at all), I have thought how artless and good you must be to tell me o' such a trifling thing, and to be so frightened about it as you were. It has won me to tell you my every deed and word since then. We'll have no secrets from each other, darling, will we ever? – no secret at all.'

'None from today,' said Fancy. 'Hark! what's that?'

From a neighbouring thicket was suddenly heard to issue in a loud, musical, and liquid voice –

'Tippiwit! swe-e-et! ki-ki-ki! Come hither, come hither, come hither!'

'O, 'tis the nightingale,'* murmured she, and thought of a secret she would never tell.

OUR EXPLOITS AT WEST POLEY

CONTENTS

I

HOW WE WENT EXPLORING UNDERGROUND

On a certain fine evening of early autumn – I will not say how many years ago – I alighted from a green gig, before the door of a farmhouse at West Poley, a village in Somersetshire. I had reached the age of thirteen, and though rather small for my age, I was robust and active. My father was a schoolmaster, living about twenty miles off. I had arrived on a visit to my Aunt Draycot, a farmer's widow, who, with her son Stephen, or Steve, as he was invariably called by his friends, still managed the farm, which had been left on her hands by her deceased husband.

Steve promptly came out to welcome me. He was two or three years my senior, tall, lithe, ruddy, and somewhat masterful withal. There was that force about him which was less suggestive of intellectual power than (as Carlyle said of Cromwell)* 'Doughtiness – the courage and faculty to do'.

When the first greetings were over, he informed me that his mother was not indoors just then, but that she would soon be home. 'And, do you know, Leonard,' he continued, rather mournfully, 'she wants me to be a farmer all my life, like my father.'

'And why not be a farmer all your life, like your father?' said a voice behind us.

We turned our heads, and a thoughtful man in a threadbare, yet well-fitting suit of clothes, stood near, as he paused for a moment on his way down to the village.

'The straight course is generally the best for boys,' the speaker continued, with a smile. 'Be sure that professions you know little of have as many drudgeries attaching to them as those you know well – it is only their remoteness that lends them their charm.' Saying this he nodded and went on.

'Who is he?' I asked.

'Oh – he's nobody,' said Steve. 'He's a man who has been all over the world, and tried all sorts of lives, but he has never got rich, and now he has retired to this place for quietness. He calls himself the Man who has Failed.'

After this explanation I thought no more of the Man who had Failed than Steve himself did: neither of us was at that time old enough to know that the losers in the world's battle are often the very men who, too late for themselves, have the clearest perception of what constitutes success; while the successful men are frequently blinded to the same by the tumult of their own progress.

To change the subject, I said something about the village and Steve's farmhouse – that I was glad to see the latter was close under the hills, which I hoped we might climb before I returned home. I had expected to find these hills much higher, and I told Steve so without disguise.

'They may not be very high, but there's a good deal inside 'em,' said my cousin as we entered the house, as if he thought me hypercritical, 'a good deal more than you think.'

'Inside 'em?' said I. 'Stone and earth, I suppose.'

'More than that,' said he. 'You have heard of the Mendip Caves, haven't you?'

'But they are nearer Cheddar,' I said.

'There are one or two in this place, likewise,' Steve answered me. 'I can show them to you tomorrow. People say there are many more, only there is no way of getting into them.'

Being disappointed in the height of the hills, I was rather incredulous about the number of the caves; but on my saying so, Steve rejoined, 'Whatever you may think, I went the other day into one of 'em – Nick's Pocket – that's the cavern nearest here, and found that what was called the end was not really the end at all. Ever since then I've wanted to be an explorer, and not a farmer; and in spite of that old man, I think I am right.'

At this moment my aunt came in, and soon after we were summoned to supper; and during the remainder of the evening nothing more was said about the Mendip Caves. It would have been just as well for us two boys if nothing more had been said about them at all; but it was fated to be otherwise, as I have reason to remember.

Steve did not forget my remarks, which, to him, no doubt, seemed to show a want of appreciation for the features of his native district. The next morning he returned to the subject, saying, as he came indoors to me suddenly, 'I mean to show ye a little of what the Mendips contain, Leonard, if you'll come with me. But we must go quietly, for my mother does not like me to prowl about such places, because I get muddy. Come here, and see the preparations I have made.'

He took me into the stable, and showed me a goodly supply of loose candle ends; also a bit of board perforated with holes, into which the candles would fit, and shaped to a handle at one extremity. He had provided, too, some slices of bread and cheese, and several apples. I was at once convinced that caverns which demanded such preparations must be something larger than the mere gravel-pits I had imagined; but I said nothing beyond assenting to the excursion.

It being the time after harvest, while there was not much to be attended to on the farm, Steve's mother could easily spare him, 'to show me the neighbourhood', as he expressed it, and off we went, with our provisions and candles.

A quarter of a mile, or possibly a little more – for my recollections on matters of distance are not precise – brought us to the mouth of the cave called Nick's Pocket, the way thither being past the village houses, and the mill, and across the mill-stream, which came from a copious spring in the hillside some distance farther up. I seem to hear the pattering of that mill-wheel when we walked by it, as well as if it were going now; and yet how many years have passed since the sound beat last upon my ears.

The mouth of the cave was screened by bushes, the face of the hill behind being, to the best of my remembrance, almost vertical. The spot was obviously well known to the inhabitants, and was the haunt of many boys, as I could see by footprints; though the cave, at this time, with others thereabouts, had been but little examined by tourists and men of science.

We entered unobserved, and no sooner were we inside, than Steve lit a couple of candles and stuck them into the board. With these he showed the way. We walked on over a somewhat uneven floor, the novelty of the proceeding impressing me, at first, very agreeably; the light of the candles was sufficient, at first, to reveal only the nearer stalactites,* remote nooks of the cavern being left in well nigh their original, mystic shadows. Steve would occasionally turn and accuse me, in arch tones, of being afraid, which accusation I (as a boy would naturally do) steadfastly denied; though even now I can recollect that I experienced more than once some sort of misgiving.

'As for me – I have been there hundreds of times,' Steve said proudly. 'We West Poley boys come here continually to play "I spy", and think nothing of running in with no light of any sort. Come along, it is home to me. I said I would show you the inside of the Mendips, and so I will.'

Thus we went onward. We were now in the bowels of the Mendip hills – a range of limestone rocks stretching from the shores of the Bristol Channel into the middle of Somersetshire. Skeletons of great extinct beasts and the remains of prehistoric men have been found thereabouts since that time; but at the date of which I write science was not so ardent as she is now, in the pursuit of the unknown; and we boys could only conjecture on subjects in which the boys of the present generation are well informed.

The dim sparkle of stalactites, which had continually appeared above us, now ranged lower and lower over our heads, till at last the walls of the cave seemed to bar further progress.

'There, this spot is what everybody calls the end of Nick's Pocket,' observed Steve, halting upon a mount of stalagmite,* and throwing the beams of the candles around. 'But let me tell you,' he added, 'that here is a little arch, which I and some more boys found the other day. We did not go under it, but if you are agreed we will go in now and see how far we can get, for the fun of the thing. I brought these pieces of candle on purpose.' Steve looked what he felt – that there was a certain grandeur in a person like himself, to whom such mysteries as caves were mere playthings, because he had been born close alongside them. To do him justice, he was not altogether wrong, for he was a truly courageous fellow, and could look dangers in the face without flinching.

'I think we may as well leave fun out of the question,' I said, laughing; 'but we will go in.'

Accordingly he went forward, stooped. and entered the low archway, which, at first sight, appeared to be no more than a slight recess. I kept close at his heels. The arch gave access to a narrow tunnel or gallery, sloping downwards, and presently terminating in another cave, the floor of which spread out into a beautiful level of sand and shingle, interspersed with pieces of rock. Across the middle of this subterranean shore, as it might have been called, flowed a pellucid stream. Had my thoughts been in my books, I might have supposed we had descended to the nether regions, and had reached the Stygian* shore; but it was out of sight, out of mind, with my classical studies then.

Beyond the stream, at some elevation, we could see a delightful recess in the crystallized stonework, like the apse of a Gothic church.

'How tantalizing!' exclaimed Steve, as he held the candles above his head, and peered across. 'If it were not for this trickling riband of water, we could get over and climb up into that arched nook, and sit there like kings on a crystal throne!'

'Perhaps it would not look so wonderful if we got close to it,' I suggested. 'But, for that matter, if you had a spade, you could soon turn the water out of the way, and into that hole.' The fact was, that just at that moment I had discovered a low opening on the left hand, like a human mouth, into which the stream would naturally flow if a slight barrier of sand and pebbles were removed.

On looking there, also, Steve complimented me on the sharpness of my eyes. 'Yes,' he said, 'we could scrape away that bank, and the water would go straight into the hole surely enough. And we will. Let us go for a spade!'

I had not expected him to put the idea into practice; but it was no sooner said than done. We retraced our steps, and in a few minutes found ourselves again in the open air, where the sudden light overpowered our eyes for a while.

'Stay here, while I run home,' he said. 'I'll not be long.'

I agreed, and he disappeared. In a very short space he came back with the spade in his hand, and we again plunged in. This time the candles had been committed to my charge. When we had passed down the gallery into the second cave, Steve directed me to light a couple more of the candles, and stick them against a piece of rock, that he might have plenty of light to work by. This I did, and my stalwart cousin began to use the spade with a will, upon the breakwater of sand and stones.

The obstacle, which had been sufficient to turn the stream at a right angle, possibly for centuries, was of the most fragile description. Such instances of a slight obstruction diverting a sustained onset often occur in nature on a much larger scale. The Chesil Bank, for example, connecting the peninsula of Portland, in Dorsetshire, with the mainland, is a mere string of loose pebbles; yet it resists, by its shelving surface and easy curve, the mighty roll of the channel seas, when urged upon the bank by the most furious south-west gales.

In a minute or two a portion of the purling* stream discovered the opening Steve's spade was making in the sand, and began to flow through. The water assisted him in his remaining labours, supplementing every spadeful that he threw back, by washing aside ten. I remember that I was child enough, at that time, to clap my hands at the sight of larger and larger quantities of the brook tumbling in the form of a cascade down the dark chasm, where it had possibly never flowed before, or at any rate, never within the human period of the earth's history. In less than twenty minutes the whole stream trended off in this new direction, as calmly as if it had coursed there always. What had before been its bed now gradually drained dry, and we saw that we could walk across dryshod,* with ease.

We speedily put the possibility into practice, and so reached the beautiful, glistening niche, that had tempted us to our engineering. We brought up into it the candles we had stuck against the rockwork farther down, placed them with the others around the niche, and prepared to rest awhile, the spot being quite dry.

'That's the way to overcome obstructions!' said Steve triumphantly. 'I warrant nobody ever got so far as this before – at least, without wading up to his knees, in crossing that watercourse.'

My attention was so much attracted by the beautiful natural ornaments of the niche, that I hardly heeded his remark. These covered the greater part of the sides and roof; they were flesh-coloured, and assumed the form of pills, lace, coats of mail; in many places they quaintly resembled the skin of geese after plucking, and in others the wattles of turkeys. All were decorated with water crystals.

'Well,' exclaimed I, 'I could stay here always!'

'So could I,' said Steve, 'if I had victuals enough. And some we'll have at once.'

Our bread and cheese and apples were unfolded, and we speedily devoured the whole. We then tried to chip pieces from the rock, and but indifferently succeeded, though while doing this we discovered some curious stones, like axe- and arrow-heads, at the bottom of the niche; but they had become partially attached to the floor by the limestone deposit, and could not be extracted.

'This is a long enough visit for today,' said my cousin, jumping up as one of the candles went out. 'We shall be left in the dark if we don't mind, and it would be no easy matter to find our way out without a light.'

Accordingly we gathered up the candles that remained, descended from the niche, recrossed the deserted bed of the stream, and found our way to the open air, well pleased enough with the adventure, and promising each other to repeat it at an early date. On which account, instead of bringing away the unburnt candles, and the wood candlestick, and the spade, we laid these articles on a hidden shelf near the entrance, to be ready at hand at any time.

Having cleaned the telltale mud from our boots, we were on the point of entering the village, when our ears were attracted by a great commotion in the road below.

'What is it?' said I, standing still.

'Voices, I think,' replied Steve. 'Listen!'.

It seemed to be a man in a violent frenzy.

'I think it is somebody out of his mind,' continued my cousin. 'I never heard a man rave so in my life.'

'Let us draw nearer,' said I.

'We moved on, and soon came in sight of an individual, who, standing in the midst of the street, was gesticulating distractedly, and uttering invectives against something or other, to several villagers that had gathered around.

'Why, 'tis the miller!' said Steve. 'What can be the matter with him?'

We were not kept long in suspense, for we could soon hear his words distinctly. 'The money I've sunk here!' he was saying; 'the time – the honest labour – all for nothing! Only beggary afore me now! One month it was a new pair of mill-stones; then the back wall was cracked with the shaking, and had to be repaired; then I made a bad speculation in corn and dropped money that way! But 'tis nothing to this! My own freehold* – the only staff and dependence o' my family – all useless now – all of us ruined!'

'Don't you take on so, Miller Griffin,' soothingly said one who proved to be the Man who had Failed. 'Take the ups with the downs, and maybe 'twill come right again.'

'Right again!' raved the miller; 'how can what's gone for ever come back again as 'twere afore – that's what I ask my wretched self – how can it?'

'We'll get up a subscription for ye,' said a local dairyman.

'I don't drink hard; I don't stay away from church, and I only grind into Sabbath* hours when there's no getting through the work otherwise, and I pay my way like a man!'

'Yes – you do that,' corroborated the others.

'And yet, I be brought to ruinous despair, on this sixth day of September, Hannah Dominy;* as if I were a villain! Oh, my mill, my mill-wheel – you'll never go round any more – never more!' The miller flung his arms upon the rail of the bridge, and buried his face in his hands.

'This raving is but making a bad job worse,' said the Man who had Failed. 'But who will listen to counsel on such matters.'

By this time we had drawn near, and Steve said, 'What's the cause of all this?'

'The river has dried up – all on a sudden,' said the dairyman, 'and so his mill won't go any more.'

I gazed instantly towards the stream, or rather what had been the stream. It was gone; and the mill-wheel, which had pattered so persistently when we entered the cavern, was silent. Steve and I instinctively stepped aside.

'The river gone dry!' Steve whispered.

'Yes,' said I. 'Why, Steve, don't you know why?'

My thoughts had instantly flown to our performance of turning the stream out of its channel in the cave, and I knew in a moment that this was the cause. Steve's silence showed me that he divined the same thing, and we stood gazing at each other in consternation.

2

HOW WE SHONE IN THE EYES
OF THE PUBLIC

As soon as we had recovered ourselves we walked away, unconsciously approaching the river-bed, in whose hollows lay the dead and dying bodies of loach, sticklebacks, dace,* and other small fry, which before our entrance into Nick's Pocket had raced merrily up and down the waterway. Farther on we perceived numbers of people ascending to the upper part of the village, with pitchers on their heads, and buckets yoked to their shoulders.

'Where are you going?' said Steve to one of these.

'To your mother's well for water,' was the answer. 'The river we have always been used to dip from is dried up. Oh, mercy me, what with the washing and cooking and brewing I don't know what we shall do to live, for 'tis killing work to bring water on your back so far!'

As may be supposed, all this gave me still greater concern than before, and I hurriedly said to Steve that I was strongly of opinion that we ought to go back to the cave immediately, and turn the water into the old channel, seeing what harm we had unintentionally done by our manœuvre.

'Of course we'll go back – that's just what I was going to say,' returned Steve. 'We can set it all right again in half an hour, and the river will run the same as ever. Hullo – now you are frightened at what has happened! I can see you are.'

I told him that I was not exactly frightened, but that it seemed to me that we had caused a very serious catastrophe in the village, in driving the miller almost crazy, and killing the fish, and worrying the poor people into supposing they would never have enough water again for their daily use without fetching it from afar. 'Let us tell them how it came to pass,' I suggested, 'and then go and set it right.'

'Tell 'em – not I!' said Steve. 'We'll go back and put it right, and say nothing about it to anyone, and they will simply think it was caused by a temporary earthquake, or something of that sort.' He then broke into a vigorous whistle, and we retraced our steps together.

It occupied us but a few minutes to rekindle a light inside the cave, take out the spade from its nook, and penetrate to the scene of our morning exploit. Steve then fell to, and first rolling down a few large pieces of stone into the current, dexterously banked them up with clay from the other side of the cave, which caused the brook to swerve back into its original bed almost immediately. 'There,' said he, 'it is all just as it was when we first saw it – now let's be off.'

We did not dally long in the cavern; but when we gained the

exterior we decided to wait there a little time till the villagers should have discovered the restoration of their stream, to watch the effect. Our waiting was but temporary; for in quick succession there burst upon our ears a shout, and then the starting of the mill-wheel patter.

At once we walked into the village street with an air of unconcern. The miller's face was creased with wrinkles of satisfaction; the countenances of the blacksmith, shoemaker, grocer and dairyman were perceptibly brighter. These, and many others of West Poley, were gathered on the bridge over the mill-tail, and they were all holding a conversation with the parson of the parish, as to the strange occurrence.

Matters remained in a quiet state during the next two days. Then there was a remarkably fine and warm morning, and we proposed to cross the hills and descend into East Poley, the next village, which I had never seen. My aunt made no objection to the excursion, and we departed, ascending the hill in a straight line, without much regard to paths. When we had reached the summit, and were about halfway between the two villages, we sat down to recover breath. While we sat a man overtook us, and Steve recognized him as a neighbour.

'A bad job again for West Poley folks!' cried the man, without halting.

'What's the matter now?' said Steve, and I started with curiosity.

'Oh, the river is dry again. It happened at a quarter past ten this morning, and it is thought it will never flow any more. The miller he's gone crazy, or all but so. And the washerwoman, she will have to be kept by the parish, because she can't get water to wash with; aye, 'tis a terrible time that's come. I'm off to try to hire a water-cart, but I fear I shan't hear of one.'

The speaker passed by, and on turning to Steve I found he was looking on the ground. 'I know how that's happened,' he presently said. 'We didn't make our embankment so strong as it was before, and so the water has washed it away.'

'Let's go back and mend it,' said I; and I proposed that we should reveal where the mischief lay, and get some of the labourers to build the bank up strong, that this might not happen again.

'No,' said Steve, 'since we are halfway we will have our day's pleasure. It won't hurt the West Poley people to be out of water for one day. We'll return home a little earlier than we intended, and put it all in order again, either ourselves, or by the help of some men.'

Having gone about a mile and a half farther we reached the brow of the descent into East Poley, the place we had come to visit. Here we beheld advancing towards us a stranger whose actions we could not at first interpret. But as the distance between us and him lessened we discerned, to our surprise, that he was in convulsions of laughter. He would laugh until he was tired, then he would stand still gazing on the ground, as if quite preoccupied, then he would burst out laughing again and walk on. No sooner did he see us two boys than he placed his hat upon his walking-stick, twirled it and cried 'Hurrah!'

I was so amused that I could not help laughing with him; and when he came abreast of us Steve said, 'Good morning; may I ask what it is that makes you laugh so?'

But the man was either too self-absorbed or too supercilious to vouchsafe to us any lucid explanation 'What makes me laugh?' he said. 'Why, good luck, my boys! Perhaps when you are as lucky, you will laugh too.' Saying which he walked on and left us; and we could hear him exclaiming to himself, 'Well done – hurrah!' as he sank behind the ridge

Without pausing longer we descended towards the village, and soon reached its outlying homesteads. Our path intersected a green field dotted with trees, on the other side of which was an inn. As we drew near we heard the strains of a fiddle, and presently perceived a fiddler standing on a chair outside the inn door; whilst on the green in front were several people seated at a table eating and drinking, and some younger members of the assembly dancing a reel* in the background.

We naturally felt much curiosity as to the cause of the merriment, which we mentally connected with that of the man we had met just before. Turning to one of the old men feasting at the table, I said to him as civilly as I could, 'Why are you all so lively in this parish, sir?'

'Because we are in luck's way just now, for we don't get a new river every day. Hurrah!'

'A new river?' said Steve and I in one breath.

'Yes,' said one of our interlocutors, waving over the table a ham-bone he had been polishing. 'Yesterday afternoon a river of beautiful water burst out of the quarry at the higher end of this bottom; in an hour or so it stopped again. This morning, about a quarter past ten, it burst out again, and it is running now as if it would run always.'

'It will make all land and houses in this parish worth double as much as afore,' said another; 'for want of water is the one thing that has always troubled us, forcing us to sink deep wells, and even then being hard put to, to get enough for our cattle. Now, we have got a river, and the place will grow to a town.'

'It is as good as two hundred pounds to me!' said one who looked like a grazier.

'And two hundred and fifty to me!' cried another, who seemed to be a brewer.

'And sixty pound a year to me, and to every man here in the building trade!' said a third.

As soon as we could withdraw from the company, our thoughts found vent in words.

'I ought to have seen it!' said Steve. 'Of course if you stop a stream from flowing in one direction, it must force its way out in another.'

'I wonder where their new stream is,' said I.

We looked round. After some examination we saw a depression in the centre of a pasture, and, approaching it, beheld the stream meandering along over the grass, the current not having had as yet sufficient time to scour a bed. Walking down to the brink, we were lost in wonder at what we had unwittingly done, and quite bewildered at the strange events we had caused. Feeling, now, that we had walked far enough from home for one day, we turned, and, in a brief time, entered a road pointed out by Steve, as one that would take us to West Poley by a shorter cut than our outward route.

As we ascended the hill, Steve looked round at me. I suppose my face revealed my thoughts, for he said, 'You are amazed, Leonard, at the wonders we have accomplished without knowing it. To tell the truth, so am I.'

I said that what staggered me was this – that we could not turn back the water into its old bed now, without doing as much harm to the people of East Poley by taking it away, as we should do good to the people of West Poley by restoring it.

'True,' said Steve, 'that's what bothers me. Though I think we have done more good to these people than we have done harm to the others; and I think these are rather nicer people than those in our village, don't you?'

I objected that even if this were so, we could have no right to take water away from one set of villagers and give it to another set without consulting them.

Steve seemed to feel the force of the argument; but as his mother had a well of her own he was less inclined to side with his native place than he might have been if his own household had been deprived of water, for the benefit of the East Poleyites. The matter was still in suspense, when, weary with our day's pilgrimage, we reached the mill.

The mill-pond was drained to its bed; the wheel stood motionless; yet a noise came from the interior. It was not the noise of machinery, but of the nature of blows, followed by bitter expostulations. On looking in, we were grieved to see that the miller, in a great rage, was holding his apprentice by the collar, and beating him with a strap.

The miller was a heavy, powerful man, and more than a match for his apprentice and us two boys besides, but Steve reddened with indignation, and asked the miller, with some spirit, why he served the poor fellow so badly.

'He says he'll leave,' stormed the frantic miller. 'What right hev he to say he'll leave, I should like to know!'

'There is no work for me to do, now the mill won't go,' said the apprentice, meekly;' and the agreement was that I should be at liberty to leave if work failed in the mill. He keeps me here and don't pay me; and I be at my wits' end how to live.'

'Just shut up!' said the miller. 'Go and work in the garden! Mill-work or no mill-work, you'll stay on.'

Job, as the miller's boy was called, had won the goodwill of Steve, and Steve was now ardent to do him a good turn. Looking over the bridge, we saw, passing by, the Man who had Failed. He was considered an authority on such matters as these, and we begged him to come in. In a few minutes the miller was set down, and it was proved to him that, by the terms of Job's indentures,* he was no longer bound to remain.

'I have to thank you for this,' said the miller, savagely, to Steve. 'Ruined in every way! I may as well die!'

But my cousin cared little for the miller's opinion, and we came away, thanking the Man who had Failed for his interference, and receiving the warmest expressions of gratitude from poor Job; who, it appeared, had suffered much ill-treatment from his irascible master, and was overjoyed to escape to some other employment.

We went to bed early that night, on account of our long walk; but we were far too excited to sleep at once. It was scarcely dark as yet, and the nights being still warm the window was left open as it had been left during the summer. Thus we could hear everything that passed without. People were continually coming to dip water from my aunt's well; they gathered round it in groups, and discussed the remarkable event which had latterly occurred for the first time in parish history.

'My belief is that witchcraft have done it,' said the shoemaker, 'and the only remedy that I can think o', is for one of us to cut across to Bartholomew Gann, the white wizard,* and get him to tell us how to counteract it. 'Tis a long pull to his house for a little man, such as I be, but I'll walk it if nobody else will.'

'Well, there's no harm in your going,' said another. 'We can manage by drawing from Mrs Draycot's well for a few days; but something must be done, or the miller'll be ruined, and the washerwoman can't hold out long.'

When these personages had drawn water and retired, Steve spoke across from his bed to me in mine. 'We've done more good than harm, that I'll maintain. The miller is the only man seriously upset, and he's not a man to deserve consideration. It has been the means of freeing poor Job, which is another good thing. Then, the people in East Poley that we've made happy are two hundred and fifty, and there are only a hundred in this parish, even if all of 'em are made miserable.'

I returned some reply, though the state of affairs was, in truth, one rather suited to the genius of Jeremy Bentham* than to me. But the problem in utilitarian philosophy was shelved by Steve exclaiming, 'I have it! I see how to get some real glory out of this!'

I demanded how, with much curiosity.

'You'll swear not to tell anybody, or let it be known anyhow that we are at the bottom of it all?'

I am sorry to say that my weak compunctions gave way under stress of this temptation; and I solemnly declared that I would reveal nothing, unless he agreed with me that it would be best to do so. Steve made me swear, in the tone of Hamlet to the

Ghost,* and when I had done this, he sat up in his bed to announce his scheme.

'First, we'll go to Job,' said Steve. 'Take him into the secret; show him the cave; give him a spade and pickaxe; and tell him to turn off the water from East Poley at, say, twelve o'clock, for a little while. Then we'll go to the East Poley boys and declare ourselves to be magicians.'

'Magicians?' I said.

'Magicians, able to dry up rivers, or to make 'em run at will,' he repeated.

'I see it!' I almost screamed, in my delight.

'To show our power, we'll name an hour for drying up theirs, and making it run again after a short time. Of course, we'll say the hour we've told Job to turn the water in the cave. Won't they think something of us then?'

I was enchanted. The question of mischief or not mischief was as indifferent to me now as it was to Steve – for which indifference we got rich deserts, as will be seen in the sequel.

'And to look grand and magical,' continued he, 'we'll get some gold lace that I know of in the garret, on an old coat my grandfather wore in the Yeomanry Cavalry,* and put it round our caps, and make ourselves great beards with horse-hair. They will look just like real ones at a little distance off.'

'And we must each have a wand!' said I, explaining that I knew how to make excellent wands, white as snow, by peeling a couple of straight willows; and that I could do all that in the morning while he was preparing the beards.

Thus we discussed and settled the matter, and at length fell asleep – to dream of tomorrow's triumphs among the boys of East Poley, till the sun of that morrow shone in upon our faces and woke us. We arose promptly and made our preparations, having *carte blanche** from my Aunt Draycot to spend the days of my visit as we chose.

Our first object on leaving the farmhouse was to find Job Tray, apprise him of what it was necessary that he should know, and induce him to act as confederate. We found him outside the garden of his lodging; he told us he had nothing to do till the following Monday, when a farmer had agreed to hire him. On learning the secret of the river-head, and what we proposed to do, he expressed his glee by a low laugh of amazed delight, and readily promised to assist as bidden. It took us some little time to show him the inner cave, the tools, and to arrange candles for him, so that he might enter without difficulty just after eleven and do the trick. When this was all settled we put Steve's watch on a ledge in the cave, that Job might know the exact time, and came out to ascend the hills that divided the eastern from the western village.

For obvious reasons we did not appear in magician's guise till we had left the western vale some way behind us. Seated on the limestone ridge, removed from all observation, we set to work at preparing ourselves. I peeled the two willows we had brought with us to be used as magic wands, and Steve pinned the pieces of old lace round our caps, congratulating himself on the fact of the lace not being new, which would thus convey the impression that we had exercised the wizard's calling for some years. Our last adornments were the beards; and, finally equipped, we descended on the other side.

Our plan was now to avoid the upper part of East Poley, which we had traversed on the preceding day, and to strike into the parish at a point farther down, where the humble cottages stood, and where we were both absolutely unknown. An hour's additional walking brought us to this spot, which, as the crow flies, was not more than half so far from West Poley as the road made it.

The first boys we saw were some playing in an orchard near the new stream, which novelty had evidently been the attraction that had brought them there. It was an opportunity for opening the campaign, especially as the hour was long after eleven, and the cessation of water consequent on Job's performance at a quarter past might be expected to take place as near as possible to twelve allowing the five and forty minutes from eleven-fifteen, as the probable time that would be occupied by the stream in travelling to the point we had reached.

I forget at this long distance of years the exact words used by Steve in addressing the strangers; but to the best of my recollection they were, 'How d'ye do, gentlemen, and how does the world use ye?' I distinctly remember the sublimity he threw into his gait, and how slavishly I imitated him in the same.

The boys made some indifferent answer, and Steve continued, 'You will kindly present us with some of those apples, I presume, considering what we are?'

They regarded us dubiously, and at last one of them said, 'What are you, that you should expect apples from us?'

'We are travelling magicians,' replied Steve. You may have heard of us, for by our power this new river has begun to flow. Rhombustas is my name, and this is my familiar, Balcazar.'

'I don't believe it,' said an incredulous one from behind.

'Very well, gentlemen; we can't help that. But if you give us some apples we'll prove our right to the title.'

'Be hanged if we will give you any apples,' said the boy who held the basket; 'since it is already proved that magicians are impossible.'

'In that case,' said Steve, 'we – we—'

'Will perform just the same,' interrupted I, for I feared Steve had forgotten that the time was at hand when the stream would be interrupted by Job, whether he willed it or not.

'We will stop the water of your new river at twelve o'clock this day, when the sun crosses the meridian,' said Rhombustas, 'as a punishment for your want of generosity.'

'Do it!' said the boys incredulously.

'Come here, Balcazar,' said Steve. We walked together to the edge of the stream; then we muttered, *Hi, hae, haec, horum, harum, horum*,* and stood waving our wands.

'The river do run just the same,' said the strangers derisively.

'The spell takes time to work,' said Rhombustas, adding in an aside to me, 'I hope that fellow Job has not forgotten, or we shall be hooted out of the place.'

There we stood, waving and waving our white sticks, hoping and hoping that we should succeed; while still the river flowed. Seven or ten minutes passed thus; and then, when we were nearly broken down by ridicule, the stream diminished its volume. All eyes were instantly bent on the water, which sank so low as to be in a short time but a narrow rivulet. The faithful Job had performed his task. By the time that the clock of the church tower struck twelve the river was almost dry.

The boys looked at each other in amazement, and at us with awe. They were too greatly concerned to speak except in murmurs to each other.

'You see the result of your conduct, unbelieving strangers,' said Steve, drawing boldly up to them. 'And I seriously ask that you hand over those apples before we bring further troubles upon you and your village. We give you five minutes to consider.'

'We decide at once!' cried the boys. 'The apples be yours and welcome.'

'Thank you, gentlemen,' said Steve, while I added, 'For your readiness the river shall run again in two or three minutes' time.'

'Oh – ah, yes,' said Steve, adding heartily in undertones, 'I had forgotten that!'

Almost as soon as the words were spoken we perceived a little increase in the mere dribble of water which now flowed, whereupon he waved his wand and murmured more words. The liquid thread swelled and rose; and in a few minutes was the same as before. Our triumph was complete; and the suspension had been so temporary that probably nobody in the village had noticed it but ourselves and the boys.

3

HOW WE WERE CAUGHT IN

OUR OWN TRAP

At this acme of our glory who should come past but a hedger whom Steve recognized as an inhabitant of West Poley; unluckily for our greatness the hedger also recognized Steve.

'Well, Maister Stevey, what be you doing over in these parts then? And yer little cousin, too, upon my word! And beards – why ye've made yerselves ornamental! haw, haw!'

In great trepidation Steve moved on with the man, endeavouring, thus, to get him out of hearing of the boys.

'Look here,' said Steve to me on leaving that outspoken rustic, 'I think this is enough for one day. We'd better go farther before they guess all.'

'With all my heart,' said I. And we walked on.

'But what's going on here?' said Steve, when, turning a corner of the hedge, we perceived an altercation in progress hard by. The parties proved to be a poor widow and a corn-factor, who had been planning a water-wheel lower down the stream. The latter had dammed the water for his purpose to such an extent as to submerge the poor woman's garden, turning it into a lake.

'Indeed, sir, you need not ruin my premises so!' she said with tears in her eyes. 'The mill-pond can be kept from overflowing my garden by a little banking and digging; it will be just as well for your purpose to keep it lower down, as to let it spread out into a great pool here. The house and garden are yours by law, sir; that's true. But my father built the house, and, oh, sir, I was born here, and I should like to end my days under its roof!'

'Can't help it, mis'ess,' said the corn-factor. 'Your garden is a mill-pond already made, and to get a hollow farther down I should have to dig at great expense. There is a very nice cottage up the hill, where you can live as well as here. When your father died the house came into my hands; and I can do what I like with my own.'

The woman went sadly away indoors. As for Steve and myself, we were deeply moved, as we looked at the pitiable sight of the poor woman's garden, the tops of the gooseberry bushes forming small islands in the water, and her few apple trees standing immersed halfway up their stems.

'The man is a rascal,' said Steve. 'I perceive that it is next to impossible, in this world, to do good to one set of folks without doing harm to another.'

'Since we have not done all good to these people of East Poley,' said I, 'there is a reason for restoring the river to its old course through West Poley.'

'But then,' said Steve, 'if we turn back the stream, we shall be starting Miller Griffin's mill; and then, by the terms of his 'prenticeship, poor Job will have to go back to him and be beaten again! It takes good brains no less than a good heart to do what's right towards all.'

Quite unable to solve the problem into which we had drifted, we retraced our steps, till, at a stile, within half a mile of West Poley, we beheld Job awaiting us.

'Well, how did it act?' he asked with great eagerness. 'Just as the hands of your watch got to a quarter-past eleven, I began to shovel away, and turned the water in no time. But I didn't turn it where you expected – not I – 'twould have started the mill for a few minutes, and I wasn't going to do that.'

'Then where did you turn it?' cried Steve.

'I found another hole,' said Job.

'A third one?'

'Ay, hee, hee! a third one! So I pulled the stones aside from this new hole, and shovelled the clay, and down the water went with a gush. When it had run down there a few minutes, I turned it back to the East Poley hole, as you ordered me to do. But as to getting it back to the old West Poley hole, that I'd never do.'

Steve then explained that we no more wished the East village to have the river than the West village, on account of our discovery that equal persecution was going on in the one place as in the other. Job's news of a third channel solved our difficulty. 'So we'll go at once and send it down this third channel,' concluded he.

We walked back to the village, and, as it was getting late, and we were tired, we decided to do nothing that night, but told Job to meet us in the cave on the following evening, to complete our work there.

All next day my cousin was away from home, at market for his mother, and he had arranged with me that if he did not return soon enough to join me before going to Nick's Pocket, I should proceed thither, where he would meet me on his way back from the market-town. The day passed anxiously enough with me, for I had some doubts of a very grave kind as to our right to deprive two parishes of water on our own judgment, even though that should be, as it was, honestly based on our aversion to tyranny. However, dusk came on at last, and Steve not appearing from market, I concluded that I was to meet him at the cave's mouth.

To this end I strolled out in that direction, and there being as yet no hurry, I allowed myself to be tempted out of my path by a young rabbit, which, however, I failed to capture. This divergence had brought me inside a field, behind a hedge, and before I could resume my walk along the main road, I heard some persons passing along the other side. The words of their conversation arrested me in a moment.

''Tis a strange story if it's true,' came through the hedge in the tones of Miller Griffin. 'We know that East Poley folk will say queer things; but the boys wouldn't say that it was the work of magicians if they hadn't some ground for it.'

'And how do they explain it?' asked the shoemaker.

'They say that these two young fellows passed down their lane about twelve o'clock, dressed like magicians, and offered to show their power by stopping the river. The East Poley boys challenged 'em; when, by George, they did stop the river! They said a few words, and it dried up like magic. Now mark my words, my suspicion is this: these two gamesters have somehow got at the river-head, and been tampering with it in some way. The water that runs down East Poley bottom is the water that ought, by rights, to be running through my mill.'

'A very pretty piece of mischief, if that's the case!' said the shoemaker. 'I've never liked them lads, particularly that Steve – for not a boot or shoe hev he had o' me since he's been old enough to choose for himself – not a pair, or even a mending. But I don't see how they could do all this, even if they had got at the river-head. 'Tis a spring out of the hill, isn't it? And how could they stop the spring?'

It seemed that the miller could offer no explanation, for no answer was returned. My course was clear: to join Job and Steve at Nick's Pocket immediately; tell them that we were suspected, and to get them to give over further proceeding, till we had stated our difficulties to some person of experience – say the Man who had Failed.

I accordingly ran like a hare over the clover inside the hedge, and soon was far away from the interlocutors.* Drawing near the cave, I was relieved to see Steve's head against the sky. I joined him at once, and recounted to him, in haste, what had passed.

He meditated. 'They don't even now suspect that the secret lies in the cavern,' said he.

'But they will soon,' said I.

'Well, perhaps they may,' he answered. 'But there will be time for us to finish our undertaking, and turn the stream down the third hole. When we've done that we can consider which of the villages is most worthy to have the river, and act accordingly.'

'Do let us take a good wise man into our confidence,' I said.

After a little demurring, he agreed that as soon as we had completed the scheme we would state the case to a competent adviser, and let it be settled fairly. 'And now,' he said, 'where's Job? Inside the cave, no doubt, as it is past the time I promised to be here.'

Stepping inside the cave's mouth, we found that the candles and other things which had been deposited there were removed. The probability being that Job had arrived and taken them in with him, we groped our way along in the dark, helped by an occasional match which Steve struck from a box he carried. Descending the gallery at the farther end of the outer cavern, we discerned a glimmer at the remote extremity, and soon beheld Job working with all his might by the light of one of the candles.

'I've almost got it into the hole that leads to neither of the Poleys, but I wouldn't actually turn it till you came,' he said, wiping his face.

We told him that the neighbours were on our track, and might soon guess that we performed our tricks in Nick's Pocket, and come there, and find that the stream flowed through the cave before rising in the spring at the top of the village; and asked him to turn the water at once, and be off with us.

'Ah!' said Job, mournfully, 'then 'tis over with me! They will be here tomorrow, and will turn back the stream, and the mill will go again, and I shall have to finish my time as 'prentice to the man who did this!' He pulled up his shirt sleeve, and showed us on his arm several stripes and bruises – black and blue and green – the tell-tale relics of old blows from the miller.

Steve reddened with indignation. 'I would give anything to stop up the channels to the two Poleys so close that they couldn't be found again!' he said. 'Couldn't we do it with stones and clay? Then, if they come here 'twould make no difference, and the water would flow down the third hole for ever, and we should save Job and the widow after all.'

'We can but try it,' said Job, willing to fall in with anything that would hinder his recall to the mill. 'Let's set to work.'

Steve took the spade, and Job the pickaxe. First they finished what Job had begun – the turning of the stream into the third tunnel or crevice, which led to neither of the Poleys. This done, they set to work jamming stones into the other two openings, treading earth and clay around them, and smoothing over the whole in such a manner that nobody should notice they had ever existed. So intent were we on completing it that – to our utter disaster we did not notice what was going on behind us.

I was the first to look round, and I well remember why. My ears had been attracted by a slight change of tone in the purl of the water down the new crevice discovered by Job, and I was curious to learn the reason of it. The sight that met my gaze might well have appalled a stouter and older heart than mine. Instead of pouring down out of sight, as it had been doing when we last looked, the stream was choked by a rising pool into which it boiled, showing at a glance that what we had innocently believed to be another outlet for the stream was only a blind passage or cul-de-sac, which the water, when first turned that way by Job, had not been left long enough to fill before it was turned back again.

'Oh, Steve – Job!' I cried, and could say no more.

They gazed round at once, and saw the situation. Nick's Pocket had become a cauldron. The surface of the rising pool stood, already, far above the mouth of the gallery by which we had entered, and which was our only way out – stood far above the old exit of the stream to West Poley, now sealed up; far above the second outlet to East Poley, discovered by Steve, and also sealed up by our fatal ingenuity. We had been spending the evening in making a close bottle of the cave, in which the water was now rising to drown us.

'There is one chance for us – only one,' said Steve in a dry voice.

'What one?' we asked in a breath.

'To open the old channel leading to the mill,' said Steve.

'I would almost as soon be drowned as do that,' murmured Job gloomily. 'But there's more lives than my own, so I'll work with a will. Yet how be we to open any channel at all?'

The question was, indeed, of awful aptness. It was extremely improbable that we should have power to reopen either conduit now. Both those exits had been funnel-shaped cavities, narrowing down to mere fissures at the bottom; and the stones and earth we had hurled into these cavities had wedged themselves together by their own weight. Moreover – and here was the rub – it might have been possible to pull the stones out while they remained unsubmerged, but the whole mass was now under water, which enlarged the task of reopening the channel to Herculean dimensions.

But we did not know my cousin Steve as yet.

'You will help me here,' he said authoritatively to Job, pointing to the West Poley conduit. 'Lenny, my poor cousin,' he went on, turning to me, 'we are in a bad way. All you can do is to stand in the niche, and make the most of the candles by keeping them from the draught with your hat, and burning only one at a time. How many have we, Job?'

'Ten ends, some long, some short,' said Job.

'They will burn many hours,' said Steve. 'And now we must dive, and begin to get out the stones.'

They had soon stripped off all but their drawers, and, laying their clothes on the dry floor of the niche behind me, stepped down into the middle of the cave. The water here was already above their waists, and at the original gulley-hole leading to West Poley spring was proportionately deeper. Into this part, nevertheless, Steve dived. I have recalled his appearance a hundred – aye, a thousand times since that day, as he came up – his crown bobbing into the dim candlelight like a floating apple. He stood upright, bearing in his arms a stone as big as his head.

'That's one of 'em!' he said as soon as he could speak. 'But there are many, many more!'

He threw the stone behind; while Job, wasting no time, had already dived in at the same point. Job was not such a good diver as Steve, in the sense of getting easily at the bottom; but he could hold his breath longer, and it was an extraordinary length of time before his head emerged above the surface, though his feet were kicking in the air more than once. Clutched to his chest, when he rose, was a second large stone, and a couple of small ones with it. He threw the whole to a distance; and Steve, having now recovered breath, plunged again into the hole.

But I can hardly bear to recall this terrible hour even now, at a distance of many years. My suspense was, perhaps, more trying than that of the others, for, unlike them, I could not escape reflection by superhuman physical efforts. My task of economizing the candles, by shading them with my hat, was not to be compared, in difficulty, to theirs; but I would gladly have changed places, if it had been possible to such a small boy, with Steve and Job, so intolerable was it to remain motionless in the desperate circumstances.

Thus I watched the rising of the waters, inch by inch, and on that account was in a better position than they to draw an inference as to the probable end of the adventure.

There were a dozen, or perhaps twenty, stones to extract before we could hope for an escape of the pent mass of water; and the difficulty of extracting them increased with each successive attempt, in two ways, by the greater actual remoteness of stone after stone, and by its greater relative remoteness through the rising of the pool. However, the sustained, gallant struggles of my two comrades succeeded, at last, in raising the number of stones extracted to seven. Then we fancied that some slight passage had been obtained for the stream; for, though the terrible pool still rose higher, it seemed to rise less rapidly.

After several attempts, in which Steve and Job brought up nothing, there came a declaration from them that they could do no more. The lower stones were so tightly jammed between the sides of the fissure that no human strength seemed able to pull them out.

Job and Steve both came up from the water. They were exhausted and shivering, and well they might be. 'We must try some other way,' said Steve.

'What way?' asked I.

Steve looked at me. 'You are a very good little fellow to stand this so well!' he said, with something like tears in his eyes.

They soon got on their clothes; and, having given up all hope of escape downward, we turned our eyes to the roof of the cave, on the chance of discovering some outlet there.

There was not enough light from our solitary candle to show us all the features of the vault in detail; but we could see enough to gather that it formed anything but a perfect dome. The roof was rather a series of rifts and projections, and high on one side, almost lost in the shades, there was a larger and deeper rift than elsewhere, forming a sort of loft, the back parts of which were invisible, extending we knew not how far. It was through this overhanging rift that the draught seemed to come which had caused our candle to gutter and flare.

To think of reaching an opening so far above our heads, so advanced into the ceiling of the cave as to require a fly's power of walking upside down to approach it, was mere waste of time. We bent our gaze elsewhere. On the same side with the niche in which we stood there was a small narrow ledge quite near at hand, and to gain it my two stalwart companions now exerted all their strength.

By cutting a sort of step with the pickaxe, Job was enabled to obtain a footing about three feet above the level of our present floor, and then he called to me.

'Now, Leonard, you be the lightest. Do you hop up here, and climb upon my shoulder, and then I think you will be tall enough to scramble to the ledge, so as to help us up after you.'

I leapt up beside him, clambered upon his stout back as he bade me, and, springing from his shoulder, reached the ledge.

He then handed up the pickaxe, directed me how to make its point firm into one of the crevices on the top of the ledge; next, to lie down, hold on to the handle of the pickaxe and give him my other hand. I obediently acted, when he sprang up, and turning, assisted Steve to do likewise.

We had now reached the highest possible coign of vantage left to us, and there remained nothing more to do but wait and hope that the encroaching water would find some unseen outlet before reaching our level.

Job and Steve were so weary from their exertions that they seemed almost indifferent as to what happened, provided they might only be allowed to rest. However, they tried to devise new schemes, and looked wistfully over the surface of the pool.

'I wonder if it rises still?' I said. 'Perhaps not, after all.'

'Then we shall only exchange drowning for starving,' said Steve.

Job, instead of speaking, had endeavoured to answer my query by stooping down and stretching over the ledge with his arm. His face was very calm as he rose again. 'It will be drowning,' he said almost inaudibly, and held up his hand, which was wet.

4

HOW OLDER HEADS THAN OURS
BECAME CONCERNED

The water had risen so high that Job could touch its surface from our retreat.

We now, in spite of Job's remark, indulged in the dream that, provided the water would stop rising, we might, in the course of time, find a way out somehow, and Job by-and-by said, 'Perhaps round there in the dark may be places where we could crawl out, if we could only see them well enough to swim across to them. Couldn't we send a candle round that way?'

'How?' said I and Steve.

'By a plan I have thought of,' said he. Taking off his hat, which was of straw, he cut with his pocket-knife a little hole in the middle of the crown. Into this he stuck a piece of candle, lighted it, and lying down to reach the surface of the water as before, lowered the hat till it rested afloat.

There was, as Job had suspected, a slight circular current in the apparently still water, and the hat moved on slowly. Our six eyes became riveted on the voyaging candle as if it were a thing of fascination. It travelled away from us, lighting up in its progress unsuspected protuberances and hollows, but revealing to our eager stare no spot of safety or of egress. It went farther and yet farther into darkness, till it became like a star alone in a sky. Then it crossed from left to right. Then it gradually turned and enlarged, was lost behind jutting crags, reappeared, and journeyed back towards us, till it again floated under the ledge on which we stood, and we gathered it in. It had made a complete circuit of the cavern, the circular motion of the water being caused by the inpour of the spring, and it had showed us no means of escape at all.

Steve spoke, saying solemnly, 'This is all my fault!'

'No,' said Job. 'For you would not have tried to stop the millstream if it had not been to save me.'

'But I began it all,' said Steve, bitterly. 'I see now the foolishness of presumption. What right had I to take upon myself the ordering of a stream of water that scores of men three times my age get their living by?'

'I thought overmuch of myself, too,' said Job. 'It was hardly right to stop the grinding of flour that made bread for a whole parish, for my poor sake. We ought to ha' got the advice of someone wi' more experience than ourselves.'

We then stood silent. The impossibility of doing more pressed in upon our senses like a chill, and I suggested that we should say our prayers.

'I think we ought,' said Steve, and Job assenting, we all three knelt down. After this a sad sense of resignation fell on us all, and there being now no hopeful attempt which they could make for deliverance, the sleep that excitement had hitherto withstood overcame both Steve and Job. They leant back and were soon unconscious.

Not having exerted myself to the extent they had done, I felt no sleepiness whatever. So I sat beside them with my eyes wide open, holding and protecting the candle mechanically, and wondering if it could really be possible that we were doomed to die.

I do not know how or why, but there came into my mind during this suspense the words I had read somewhere at school, as being those of Flaminius, the consul,* when he was penned up at Thrasymene: 'Friends, we must not hope to get out of this by vows and prayers alone. 'Tis by fortitude and strength we must escape.' The futility of any such resolve in my case was apparent enough, and yet the words were sufficient to lead me to scan the roof of the cave once more.

When the opening up there met my eye I said to myself, 'I wonder where that hole leads to?' Picking up a stone about the size of my fist I threw it with indifference though with a good aim, towards the spot. The stone passed through the gaping orifice, and I heard it alight within like a tennis ball.

But its noise did not cease with its impact. The fall was succeeded by a helter-skelter kind of rattle which, though it receded in the distance, I could hear for a long time with distinctness, owing, I suppose, to the reflection or echo from the top and sides of the cave. It denoted that on the other side of that dark mouth yawning above me there was a slope downward – possibly into another cave, and that the stone had ricocheted down the incline. 'I wonder where it leads?' I murmured again aloud.

Something greeted my ears at that moment of my pronouncing the words 'where it leads' that caused me well nigh to leap out of my shoes. Even now I cannot think of it without experiencing a thrill. It came from the gaping hole.

If my readers can imagine for themselves the sensations of a timid bird, who, while watching the approach of his captors to strangle him, feels his wings loosening from the tenacious snare, and flight again possible, they may conceive my emotions when I realized that what greeted my ears from above were the words of a human tongue, direct from the cavity.

'Where, in the name of fortune, did that stone come from?'

The voice was the voice of the miller.

'Be dazed if I know – but 'a nearly broke my head!' The reply was that of the shoemaker.

'Steve – Job!' said I. They awoke with a start and exclamation. I tried to shout, but could not. 'They have found us – up there – the miller – shoemaker!' I whispered, pointing to the hole aloft.

Steve and Job understood. Perhaps the sole ingredient, in this sudden revival of our hopes, which could save us from fainting with joy, was the one actually present – that our discoverer was the adversary whom we had been working to circumvent. But such antagonism as his weighed little in the scale with our present despairing circumstances.

We all three combined our voices in one shout – a shout which roused echoes in the cavern that probably had never been awakened since the upheaval of the Mendips, in whose heart we stood. When the shout died away we listened with parted lips.

Then we heard the miller speak again. 'Faith, and believe me – 'tis the rascals themselves! A-throwing stones – a-trying to terrify us off the premises! Did man ever know the like impudence? We have found the clue to the water mystery at last – may be at their pranks at this very moment! Clamber up here; and if I don't put about their backs the greenest stick that ever growed, I'm no grinder o' corn!'

Then we heard a creeping movement from the orifice over our heads, as of persons on their hands and knees; a puffing, as of fat men out of breath; sudden interjections, such as can be found in a list in any boys' grammar-book, and, therefore, need not be repeated here. All this was followed by a faint glimmer, about equal to that from our own candle, bursting from the gap on high, and the cautious appearance of a head over the ledge.

It was the visage of the shoemaker. Beside it rose another in haste, exclaiming, 'Urrr – r! The rascals!' and waving a stick. Almost before we had recognized this as the miller, he, climbing forward with too great impetuosity, and not perceiving that the edge of the orifice was so near, was unable to check himself. He fell over headlong, and was precipitated a distance of some thirty feet into the whirling pool beneath.

Job's face, which, until this catastrophe, had been quite white and rigid at sight of his old enemy, instantly put on a more humane expression. 'We mustn't let him drown,' he said. 'No,' said Steve, 'but how can we save him in such an awkward place?'

There was, for the moment, however, no great cause for anxiety. The miller was a stout man, and could swim, though but badly – his power to keep afloat being due rather to the adipose* tissues which composed his person, than to skill. But his immersion had been deep, and when he rose to the surface he was bubbling and spluttering wildly.

'Hu, hu, hu, hu! O, ho – I am drownded!' he gasped. 'I am a

dead man and miller – all on account of those villainous – I mean good boys! If Job would only help me out I would give him such a dressing – blessing I would say – as he never felt the force of before. Oh, bub, bub, hu, hu, hu!'

Job had listened to this with attention. 'Now, will you let me rule in this matter?' he said to Steve.

'With all my heart,' said Steve.

'Look here, Miller Griffin,' then said Job, speaking over the pool, 'you can't expect me or my comrades to help ye until you treat us civilly. No mixed words o' that sort will we stand. Fair and square, or not at all. You must give us straightforward assurance that you will do us no harm; and that if the water runs in your stream again, and the mill goes, and I finish out my 'prenticeship, you treat me well. If you won't promise this, you are a dead man in that water tonight.'

'A master has a right over his 'prentice, body and soul!'* cried the miller, desperately, as he swam round, 'and I have a right over you – and I won't be drownded!'

'I fancy you will,' said Job, quietly. 'Your friends be too high above to get at ye.'

'What must I promise ye, then, Job – hu – hu – hu – bub, bub, bub!'

'Say, if I ever strike Job Tray again, he shall be at liberty to leave my service forthwith, and go to some other employ, and this is the solemn oath of me, Miller Griffin. Say that in the presence of these witnesses.'

'Very well – I say it – bub, bub – I say it.' And the miller repeated the words.

'Now I'll help ye out,' said Job. Lying down on his stomach, he held out the handle of the shovel to the floating miller, and hauled him towards the ledge on which we stood. Then Steve took one of the miller's hands, and Job the other, and he mounted up beside us.

'Saved – saved!' cried Miller Griffin.

'You must stand close in,' said Steve, 'for there isn't much room on this narrow shelf.'

'Ay, yes I will,' replied the saved man gladly. 'And now, let's get out of this dark place as soon as we can – Ho! – Cobbler Jones! – here we be coming up to ye – but I don't see him!'

'Nor I,' said Steve. 'Where is he?'

The whole four of us stared with all our vision at the opening the miller had fallen from. But his companion had vanished.

'Well – never mind,' said Miller Griffin, genially; 'we'll follow. Which is the way?'

'There's no way – we can't follow,' answered Steve.

'*Can't follow!*' echoed the miller, staring round, and perceiving for the first time that the ledge was a prison. 'What – *not saved*!' he shrieked. 'Not able to get out from here?'

'We be not saved unless your friend comes back to save us,' said Job. 'We've been calculating upon his help – otherwise things be as bad as they were before. We three have clung here waiting for death these two hours, and now there's one more to wait for death – unless the shoemaker comes back.'

Job spoke stoically in the face of the cobbler's disappearance, and Steve tried to look cool also; but I think they felt as much discouraged as I, and almost as much as the miller, at the unaccountable vanishing of Cobbler Jones.

On reflection, however, there was no reason to suppose that he had basely deserted us. Probably he had only gone to bring further assistance. But the bare possibility of disappointment at such times is enough to take the nerve from any man or boy.

'He *must* mean to come back!' the miller murmured lugubriously, as we all stood in a row on the ledge, like sparrows on the moulding of a chimney.

'I should think so,' said Steve, 'if he's a man.'

'Yes – he must!' the miller anxiously repeated. 'I once said he was a two-penny sort of workman to his face – I wish I hadn't said it, oh – how I wish I hadn't; but 'twas years and years ago, and pray heaven he's forgot it! I once called him a stingy varmint – that I did! But we've made that up, and been friends ever since. And yet there's men who'll carry a snub in their buzzoms; and perhaps he's going to punish me now!'

''Twould be very wrong of him,' said I, 'to leave us three to die because you've been a wicked man in your time, miller.'

'Quite true,' said Job.

'Zounds* take your saucy tongues!' said Griffin. 'If I had elbow room on this miserable perch I'd – I'd—'

'Just do nothing,' said Job at his elbow. 'Have you no more sense of decency, Mr Griffin, than to go on like that, and the waters rising to drown us minute by minute?'

'Rising to drown us – hey?' said the miller.

'Yes, indeed,' broke in Steve. 'It has reached my feet.'

5

HOW WE BECAME CLOSE ALLIES
WITH THE VILLAGERS

Sure enough, the water – to which we had given less attention since the miller's arrival – had kept on rising with silent and pitiless regularity. To feel it actually lapping over the ledge was enough to paralyse us all. We listened and looked, but no shoemaker appeared. In no very long time it ran into our boots, and coldly encircled our ankles.

Miller Griffin trembled so much that he could scarcely keep his standing. 'If I do get out of this,' he said, 'I'll do good – lots of good – to everybody! Oh, oh – the water!'

'Surely you can hold your tongue if this little boy can bear it without crying out!' said Job, alluding to me.

Thus rebuked, the miller was silent; and nothing more happened till we heard a slight sound from the opening which was our only hope, and saw a slight light. We watched, and the light grew stronger, flickering about the orifice like a smile on parted lips. Then hats and heads broke above the edge of the same – one, two, three, four – then candles, arms and shoulders; and it could be seen then that our deliverers were provided with ropes.

'Ahoy – all right!' they shouted, and you may be sure we shouted back a reply.

'Quick, in the name o' goodness!' cried the miller.

A consultation took place among those above, and one of them shouted, 'We'll throw you a rope's end and you must catch it. If you can make it fast, and so climb up one at a time, do it.'

'If not, tie it round the first one, let him jump into the water; we'll tow him across by the rope till he's underneath us, and then haul him up.'

'Yes, yes, that's the way!' said the miller. 'But do be quick – I'm dead drowned up to my thighs. Let me have the rope.'

'Now, miller, that's not fair!' said one of the group above –

Man who had Failed, for he was with them. 'Of course you'll send up the boys first – the little boy first of all.'

'I will – I will – 'twas a mistake,' Griffin replied with contrition.

The rope was then thrown; Job caught it, and tied it round me. It was with some misgiving that I flung myself on the water; but I did it, and, upheld by the rope, I floated across to the spot in the pool that was perpendicularly under the opening, when the men all heaved, and I felt myself swinging in the air, till I was received into the arms of half the parish. For the alarm having been given, the attempt at rescue was known all over the lower part of West Poley.

My cousin Steve was now hauled up. When he had gone the miller burst into a sudden terror at the thought of being left till the last, fearing he might not be able to catch the rope. He implored Job to let him go up first.

'Well,' said Job, 'so you shall – on one condition.'

'Tell it, and I agree.'

Job searched his pockets, and drew out a little floury pocket-book, in which he had been accustomed to enter sales of meal and bran. Without replying to the miller, he stooped to the candle and wrote. This done he said, 'Sign this, and I'll let ye go.'

The miller read: I hereby certify that I release from this time forth Job Tray, my apprentice, by his wish, and demand no further service from him whatever. 'Very well – have your way,' he said; and taking the pencil subscribed his name. By this time they had untied Steve and were flinging the rope a third time; Job caught it as before, attached it to the miller's portly person, shoved him off, and saw him hoisted. The dragging up on this occasion was a test to the muscles of those above; but it was accomplished. Then the rope was flung back for the last time, and fortunate it was that the delay was no longer. Job could only manage to secure himself with great difficulty, owing to the numbness which was creeping over him from his heavy labours and immersions. More dead than alive he was pulled to the top with the rest.

The people assembled above began questioning us, as well they might, upon how we had managed to get into our perilous position. Before we had explained, a gurgling sound was heard from the pool. Several looked over. The water whose rising had nearly caused our death was sinking suddenly; and the light of the candle, which had been left to burn itself out on the ledge, revealed a whirlpool on the surface. Steve, the only one of our trio who was in a condition to observe anything, knew in a moment what the phenomenon meant.

The weight of accumulated water had completed the task of reopening the closed tunnel or fissure which Job's and Steve's diving had begun; and the stream was rushing rapidly down the old West Poley outlet, through which it had run from geological times. In a few minutes – as I was told, for I was not an eye-witness of further events this night – the water had drained itself out, and the stream could be heard trickling across the floor of the lower cave as before the check.

In the explanations which followed our adventure, the following facts were disclosed as to our discovery by the neighbours.

The miller and the shoemaker, after a little further discussion in the road where I overheard them, decided to investigate the caves one by one. With this object in view they got a lantern, and proceeded, not to Nick's Pocket, but to a well-known cave nearer at hand called Grim Billy, which to them seemed a likely source for the river.

This cave was very well known up to a certain point. The floor sloped upwards, and eventually led to the margin of the hole in the dome of Nick's Pocket; but nobody was aware that it was the inner part of Nick's Pocket which the treacherous opening revealed. Rather was the unplumbed depth beneath supposed to be the mouth of an abyss into which no human being could venture. Thus when a stone ascended from this abyss (the stone I threw) the searchers were amazed, till the miller's intuition suggested to him that we were there. And, what was most curious, when we were all delivered, and had gone home, and had been put into warm beds, neither the miller nor the shoemaker knew for certain that they had lighted upon the source of the millstream. Much less did they suspect the contrivance we had discovered for turning the water to East or West Poley, at pleasure.

By a piece of good fortune, Steve's mother heard nothing of what had happened to us till we appeared dripping at the door, and could testify to our deliverance before explaining our perils.

The result which might have been expected to all of us,

followed in the case of Steve. He caught cold from his prolonged duckings, and the cold was followed by a serious illness.

The illness of Steve was attended with slight fever, which left him very weak, though neither Job nor I suffered any evil effects from our immersion.

The mill-stream having flowed back to its course, the mill was again started, and the miller troubled himself no further about the river-head; but Job, thanks to his ingenuity, was no longer the miller's apprentice. He had been lucky enough to get a place in another mill many miles off, the very next day after our escape.

I frequently visited Steve in his bedroom, and, on one of these occasions, he said to me, 'Suppose I were to die, and you were to go away home, and Job were always to stay away in another part of England, the secret of that mill-stream head would be lost to our village; so that if by chance the vent this way were to choke, and the water run into the East Poley channel, our people would not know how to recover it. They saved our lives, and we ought to make them the handsome return of telling them the whole manœuvre.'

This was quite my way of thinking, and it was decided that Steve should tell all as soon as he was well enough. But I soon found that his anxiety on the matter seriously affected his recovery. He had a scheme, he said, for preventing such a loss of the stream again.

Discovering that Steve was uneasy in his mind, the doctor – to whom I explained that Steve desired to make personal reparation – insisted that his wish be gratified at once – namely, that some of the leading inhabitants of West Poley should be brought up to his bedroom, and learn what he had to say. His mother assented, and messages were sent to them at once.

The villagers were ready enough to come, for they guessed the object of the summons, and they were anxious, too, to know more particulars of our adventures than we had as yet had opportunity to tell them. Accordingly, at a little past six that evening, when the sun was going down, we heard their footsteps ascending the stairs, and they entered. Among them there were the blacksmith, the shoemaker, the dairyman, the Man who had Failed, a couple of farmers; and some men who worked on the farms were also admitted.

Some chairs were brought up from below, and, when our

visitors had settled down, Steve's mother, who was very anxious about him, said, 'Now, my boy, we are all here. What have you to tell?'

Steve began at once, explaining first how we had originally discovered the inner cave, and how we walked on till we came to a stream.

'What we want to know is this,' said the shoemaker, 'is that great pool we fetched you out of, the head of the mill-stream?'

Steve explained that it was not a natural pool, and other things which the reader already knows. He then came to the description of the grand manœuvre by which the stream could be turned into either the east or the west valley.

'But how did you get down there?' asked one. 'Did you walk in through Giant's Ear, or Goblin's Cellar, or Grim Billy?'

'We did not enter by any of these,' said Steve. 'We entered by Nick's Pocket.'

'Ha!' said the company, 'that explains all the mystery.'

''Tis amazing,' said the miller, who had entered, 'that folks should have lived and died here for generations, and never ha' found out that Nick's Pocket led to the river spring!'

'Well, that isn't all I want to say,' resumed Steve. 'Suppose any people belonging to East Poley should find out the secret, they would go there and turn the water into their own vale; and, perhaps, close up the other channel in such a way that we could scarcely open it again. But didn't somebody leave the room a minute ago? – who is it that's going away?'

'I fancy a man went out,' said the dairyman looking round. One or two others said the same, but dusk having closed in it was not apparent which of the company had gone away.

Steve continued: 'Therefore before the secret is known, let somebody of our village go and close up the little gallery we entered by, and the upper mouth you looked in from. Then there'll be no danger of our losing the water again.'

The proposal was received with unanimous commendation, and after a little more consultation, and the best wishes of the neighbours for Steve's complete recovery, they took their leave, arranging to go and stop the cave entrances the next evening.

As the doctor had thought, so it happened. No sooner was his sense of responsibility gone, than Steve began to mend with miraculous rapidity. Four and twenty hours made such a difference in him that he said to me, with animation, the next evening: 'Do, Leonard, go and bring me word what they are doing at Nick's Pocket. They ought to be going up there about this time to close up the gallery. But 'tis quite dark – you'll be afraid.'

'No – not I,' I replied, and off I went, having told my aunt my mission.

It was, indeed, quite dark, and it was not till I got quite close to the mill that I found several West Poley men had gathered in the road opposite thereto. The miller was not among them, being too much shaken by his fright for any active enterprise. They had spades, pickaxes, and other tools, and were just preparing for the start to the caves.

I followed behind, and as soon as we reached the outskirts of West Poley, I found they all made straight for Nick's Pocket as planned. Arrived there, they lit their candles and we went into the interior. Though they had been most precisely informed by Steve how to find the connecting gallery with the inner cavern, so cunningly was it hidden by Nature's hand that they probably would have occupied no small time in lighting on it, if I had not gone forward and pointed out the nook.

They thanked me, and the dairyman, as one of the most active of the group, taking a spade in one hand, and a light in the other, prepared to creep in first and foremost. He had not advanced many steps before he reappeared in the outer cave, looking as pale as death.

6

HOW ALL OUR DIFFICULTIES
CAME TO AN END

'What's the matter!' said the shoemaker.

'Somebody's there!' he gasped.

'It can't be,' said a farmer. 'Till those boys found the hole, not a being in the world knew of such a way in.'

'Well, come and harken for yourselves,' said the dairyman.

We crept close to the gallery mouth and listened. Peck, peck, peck; scrape, scrape, scrape, could be heard distinctly inside.

'Whoever they call themselves, they are at work like the busy bee!' said the farmer.

It was ultimately agreed that some of the party should go softly round into Grim Billy, creep up the ascent within the cave, and peer through the opening that looked down through the roof of the cave before us. By this means they might learn, unobserved, what was going on.

It was no sooner proposed than carried out. The baker and shoemaker were the ones that went round, and, as there was nothing to be seen where the others waited, I thought I would bear them company. To get to Grim Billy, a circuit of considerable extent was necessary; moreover, we had to cross the millstream. The mill had been stopped for the night, some time before, and, hence, it was by a pure chance we noticed that the river was gradually draining itself out. The misfortune initiated by Steve was again upon the village.

'I wonder if the miller knows it?' murmured the shoemaker. 'If not, we won't tell him, or he may lose his senses outright.'

'Then the folks in the cave are enemies!' said the farmer.

'True,' said the baker, 'for nobody else can have done this – let's push on.'

Grim Billy being entered, we crawled on our hands and knees up the slope, which eventually terminated at the hole above Nick's Pocket – a hole that probably no human being had passed through before we were hoisted up through it on the evening of our marvellous escape. We were careful to make no noise in ascending, and, at the edge, we gazed cautiously over.

A striking sight met our view. A number of East Poley men were assembled below on the floor, which had been for a while submerged by our exploit; and they were working with all their might to build and close up the old outlet of the stream towards West Poley, having already, as it appeared, opened the new opening towards their own village, discovered by Steve. We understood it in a moment, and, descending with the same softness as before, we returned to where our comrades were waiting for us in the other cave, where we told them the strange sight we had seen.

'How did they find out the secret?' the shoemaker inquired under his breath. 'We have guarded it as we would ha' guarded our lives.'

'I can guess!' replied the baker. 'Have you forgot how

somebody went away from Master Steve Draycot's bedroom in the dusk last night, and we didn't know who it was? Half an hour after, such a man was seen crossing the hill to East Poley; I was told so today. We've been surprised, and must hold our own by main force, since we can no longer do it by stealth.'

'How, main force?' asked the blacksmith and a farmer simultaneously.

'By closing the gallery they went in by,' said the baker. 'Then we shall have them in prison, and bring them to book rarely.'

The rest being all irritated at having been circumvented so slyly and selfishly by the East Poley men, the baker's plan met with ready acceptance. Five of our body at once chose hard boulders from the outer cave, of such a bulk that they would roll about halfway into the passage or gallery – where there was a slight enlargement – but which would pass no further. These being put in position, they were easily wedged there, and is was impossible to remove them from within, owing to the diminishing size of the passage, except by more powerful tools than they had, which were only spades. We now felt sure of our antagonists, and in a far better position to argue with them than if they had been free. No longer taking the trouble to preserve silence, we, of West Poley, walked in a body round to the other cave – Grim Billy – ascended the inclined floor like a flock of goats, and arranged ourselves in a group at the opening that impended over Nick's Pocket.

The East Poley men were still working on, absorbed in their labour, and were unconscious that twenty eyes regarded them from above like stars.

'Let's halloo!' said the baker.

Halloo we did with such vigour that the East Poley men, taken absolutely unawares, well nigh sprang into the air at the shock it produced on their nerves. Their spades flew from their hands, and they stared around in dire alarm, for the echoes confused them as to the direction whence the hallooing came. They finally turned their eyes upwards, and saw us individuals of the rival village far above them, illuminated with candles, and with countenances grave and stern as a bench of unmerciful judges.

'Men of East Poley,' said the baker, 'we have caught ye in the execution of a most unfair piece of work. Because of a temporary turning of our water into your vale by a couple of meddlesome boys – a piece of mischief that was speedily repaired – you have thought fit to covet our stream. You have sent a spy to find out its secret, and have meanfully come here to steal the stream for yourselves forever. This cavern is in our parish, and you have no right here at all.'

'The waters of the earth be as much ours as yours,' said one from beneath. But the remainder were thunderstruck, for they knew that their chance had lain entirely in strategy and not in argument.

The shoemaker then spoke: 'Ye have entered upon our property, and diverted the water, and made our parish mill useless, and caused us other losses. Do ye agree to restore it to its old course, close up the new course ye have been at such labour to widen – in short, to leave things as they have been from time immemorial?'

'No-o-o-o!' was shouted from below in a yell of defiance.

'Very well, then,' said the baker, 'we must make you. Gentlemen, ye are prisoners. Until you restore that water to us, you will bide where you be.'

The East Poley men rushed to escape by the way they had entered. But halfway up the tunnel a barricade of adamantine blocks barred their footsteps. 'Bring spades!' shouted the foremost. But the stones were so well wedged, and the passage so small, that, as we had anticipated, no engineering force at their disposal could make the least impression upon the blocks. They returned to the inner cave disconsolately.

'D'ye give in?' we asked them.

'Never!' said they doggedly.

'Let 'em sweat – let 'em sweat,' said the shoemaker, placidly. 'They'll tell a different tale by tomorrow morning. Let 'em bide for the night, and say no more.'

In pursuance of this idea we withdrew from our position, and, passing out of Grim Billy, went straight home. Steve was excited by the length of my stay, and still more when I told him the cause of it. 'What – got them prisoners in the cave?' he said. 'I must go myself tomorrow and see the end of this!'

Whether it was partly due to the excitement of the occasion, or solely to the recuperative powers of a strong constitution, cannot be said; but certain it is that next morning, on hearing the villagers shouting and gathering together, Steve sprang out of bed, declaring that he must go with me to see what was happening to the prisoners. The doctor was hastily called in, and gave it as his opinion that the outing would do Steve no harm, if he were warmly wrapped up; and soon away we went, just in time to overtake the men who had started on their way.

With breathless curiosity we entered Grim Billy, lit our candles and clambered up the incline. Almost before we reached the top, exclamations ascended through the chasm to Nick's Pocket, there being such words as, 'We give in!' 'Let us out!' 'We give up the water for ever!'

Looking in upon them, we found their aspect to be very different from what it had been the night before. Some had extemporized a couch with smock-frocks and gaiters, and jumped up from a sound sleep thereon; while others had their spades in their hands, as if undoing what they had been at such pains to build up, as was proved in a moment by their saying eagerly, 'We have begun to put it right, and shall finish soon – we are restoring the river to his old bed – give us your word, good gentlemen, that when it is done we shall be free!'

'Certainly,' replied our side with great dignity. 'We have said so already.'

Our arrival stimulated them in the work of repair, which had hitherto been somewhat desultory. Then shovels entered the clay and rubble like giants' tongues; they lit up more candles, and in half an hour had completely demolished the structure raised the night before with such labour and amazing solidity that it might have been expected to last for ever. The final stone rolled away, the much tantalized river withdrew its last drop from the new channel, and resumed its original course once more.

While the East Poley men had been completing this task, some of our party had gone back to Nick's Pocket, and there, after much exertion, succeeded in unpacking the boulders from the horizontal passage admitting to the inner cave. By the time this was done, the prisoners within had finished their work of penance, and we West Poley men, who had remained to watch them, rejoined our companions. Then we all stood back, while those of East Poley came out, walking between their vanquishers, like the Romans under the Caudine Forks, when they surrendered to the Samnites.* They glared at us with suppressed rage, and passed without saying a word.

'I see from their manner that we have not heard the last of

this,' said the Man who had Failed, thoughtfully. He had just joined us, and learnt the state of the case.

'I was thinking as much,' said the shoemaker. 'As long as that cave is known in Poley, so long will they bother us about the stream.'

'I wish it had never been found out,' said the baker bitterly. 'If not now upon us, they will be playing that trick upon our children when we are dead and gone.'

Steve glanced at me, and there was sadness in his look.

We walked home considerably in the rear of the rest, by no means at ease. It was impossible to disguise from ourselves that Steve had lost the good feeling of his fellow parishioners by his explorations and their results.

As the West Poley men had predicted, so it turned out. Some months afterwards, when I had gone back to my home and school, and Steve was learning to superintend his mother's farm, I heard that another midnight entry had been made into the cave by the rougher characters of East Poley. They diverted the stream as before, and when the miller and other inhabitants of the west village rose in the morning, behold, their stream was dry! The West Poley folk were furious, and rushed to Nick's Pocket. The mischief-makers were gone, and there was no legal proof as to their identity, though it was indirectly clear enough where they had come from. With some difficulty the water was again restored, but not till Steve had again been spoken of as the original cause of the misfortunes.

About this time I paid another visit to my cousin and aunt. Steve seemed to have grown a good deal older than when I had last seen him, and, almost as soon as we were alone, he began to speak on the subject of the mill-stream.

'I am glad you have come, Leonard,' he said, 'for I want to talk to you. I have never been happy, you know, since the adventure, I don't like the idea that by a freak of mine our village should be placed at the mercy of the East Poleyites, I shall never be liked again unless I make that river as secure from interruption as it was before.'

'But that can't be,' said I.

'Well, I have a scheme,' said Steve musingly. 'I am not so sure that the river may not be made as secure as it was before.'

'But how? What is the scheme based on?' I asked, incredulously.

'I cannot reveal to you at present,' said he. 'All I can say is, that I have injured my native village, that I owe it amends, and that I'll pay the debt if it's a possibility.'

I soon perceived from my cousin's manner at meals and elsewhere that the scheme, whatever it might be, occupied him to the exclusion of all other thoughts. But he would not speak to me about it. I frequently missed him for spaces of an hour or two, and soon conjectured that these hours of absence were spent in furtherance of his plan.

The last day of my visit came round, and to tell the truth I was not sorry, for Steve was so preoccupied as to be anything but a pleasant companion. I walked up to the village alone, and soon became aware that something had happened.

During the night another raid had been made upon the river-head – with but partial success, it is true; but the stream was so much reduced that the mill-wheel would not turn, and the dipping pools were nearly empty. It was resolved to repair the mischief in the evening, but the disturbance in the village was very great, for the attempt proved that the more unscrupulous characters of East Poley were not inclined to desist.

Before I had gone much farther, I was surprised to discern in the distance a figure which seemed to be Steve's, though I thought I had left him at the rear of his mother's premises.

He was making for Nick's Pocket, and following thither I reached the mouth of the cave just in time to see him enter.

'Steve!' I called out. He heard me and came back. He was pale, and there seemed to be something in his face which I had never seen there before.

'Ah – Leonard,' he said, 'you have traced me. Well, you are just in time. The folks think of coming to mend this mischief as soon as their day's work is over, but perhaps it won't be necessary. My scheme may do instead.'

'How – do instead?' asked I.

'Well, save them the trouble,' he said with assumed careless-ness. 'I had almost decided not to carry it out, though I have got the materials in readiness, but the doings of the night have stung me; I carry out my plan.'

'When?'

'Now – this hour – this moment. The stream must flow into its right channel, and stay there, and no man's hands must be able to turn it elsewhere. Now goodbye, in case of accidents.'

To my surprise, Steve shook hands with me solemnly, and wringing from me a promise not to follow, disappeared into the blackness of the cave.

For some moments I stood motionless where Steve had left me, not quite knowing what to do. Hearing footsteps behind my back, I looked round. To my great pleasure I saw Job approaching, dressed up in his best clothes, and with him the Man who had Failed.

Job was glad to see me. He had come to West Poley for a holiday, from the situation with the farmer which, as I now learned for the first time, the Man who had Failed had been the means of his obtaining. Observing, I suppose, the perplexity upon my face, they asked me what was the matter, and I, after some hesitation, told them of Steve. The Man who had Failed looked grave.

'Is it serious?' I asked him.

'It may be,' said he, in that poetico-philosophic strain which, under more favouring circumstances, might have led him on to the intellectual eminence of a Coleridge or an Emerson.* 'Your cousin, like all such natures, is rushing into another extreme, that may be worse than the first. The opposite of error is error still; from careless adventuring at other people's expense he may have flown to rash self-sacrifice. He contemplates some violent remedy, I make no doubt. How long has he been in the cave? We had better follow him.'

Before I could reply, we were startled by a jet of smoke, like that from the muzzle of a gun, bursting from the mouth of Nick's Pocket; and this was immediately followed by a deadened rumble like thunder underground. In another moment a duplicate of the noise reached our ears from over the hill in the precise direction of Grim Billy.

'Oh – what can it be?' said I.

'Gunpowder,' said the Man who had Failed, slowly.

'Ah – yes – I know what he's done – he has blasted the rocks inside!' cried Job. 'Depend upon it, that's his plan for closing up the way to the river-head.'

'And for losing his life into the bargain,' said our companion. 'But no – he may be alive. We must go in at once – or as soon as we can breathe there.'

Job ran for lights, and before he had returned we heard a familiar sound from the direction of the village. It was the patter of the mill-wheel. Job came up almost at the moment, and with him a crowd of the village people.

'The river is right again,' they shouted. 'Water runs better than ever – a full, steady stream, all on a sudden – just when we heard the rumble underground.'

'Steve has done it!' I said.

'A brave fellow,' said the Man who had Failed. 'Pray that he is not hurt.'

Job had lighted the candles, and, when we were entering, some more villagers, who at the noise of the explosion had run to Grim Billy, joined us. 'Grim Billy is partly closed up inside!' they told us. 'Where you used to climb up the slope to look over into Nick's Pocket, 'tis all altered. There's no longer any opening there; the whole rock has crumbled down as if the mountain had sunk bodily.'

Without waiting to answer, we, who were about to enter Nick's Pocket, proceeded on our way. We soon had penetrated to the outer approaches, though nearly suffocated by the sulphurous atmosphere; but we could get no farther than the first cavern. At a point somewhat in advance of the little gallery to the inner cave, Nick's Pocket ceased to exist. Its roof had sunk. The whole superimposed mountain, as it seemed, had quietly settled down upon the hollow places beneath it, closing like a pair of bellows, and barring all human entrance.

But alas, where was Steve? 'I would liever* have had no water in West Poley for ever more than have lost Steve!' said Job.

'And so would I!' said many of us.

To add to our terror, news was brought into the cave at that moment that Steve's mother was approaching; and how to meet my poor aunt was more than we could think.

But suddenly a shout was heard. A few of the party, who had not penetrated so far into the cave as we had done, were exclaiming, 'Here he is!' We hastened back, and found they were in a small, side hollow, close to the entrance, which we had passed by unheeded. The Man who had Failed was there, and he and the baker were carrying something into the light. It was Steve – apparently dead, or unconscious.

'Don't be frightened,' said the baker to me. 'He's not dead; perhaps not much hurt.'

As he had declared, so it turned out. No sooner was Steve in the open air, than he unclosed his eyes, looked round with a stupefied expression, and sat up.

'Steve – Steve!' said Job and I, simultaneously.

'All right,' said Steve, recovering his senses by degrees. 'I'll tell – how it happened – in a minute or two.'

Then his mother came up, and was at first terrified enough, but on seeing Steve gradually get upon his legs, she recovered her equanimity. He soon was able to explain all. He said that the damage to the village by his tampering with the stream had weighed upon his mind, and led him to revolve many schemes for its cure. With this in view he had privately made examination of the cave; when he discovered that the whole superincumbent mass, forming the roof of the inner cave, was divided from the walls of the same by a vein of sand, and that it was only kept in its place by a slim support at one corner. It seemed to him that if this support could be removed, the upper mass would descend by its own weight, like the brick of a brick-trap when the peg is withdrawn.

He laid his plans accordingly; procuring gunpowder, and scooping out holes for the same, at central points in the rock. When all this was done, he waited a while, in doubt, as to the effect; and might possibly never have completed his labours, but for the renewed attempt upon the river. He then made up his mind, and attached the fuse. After lighting it, he would have reached the outside safely enough but for the accident of stumbling as he ran, which threw him so heavily on the ground, that, before he could recover himself and go forward, the explosion had occurred.

All of us congratulated him, and the whole village was joyful, for no less than three thousand, four hundred and fifty tons of rock and earth – according to calculations made by an experienced engineer a short time afterwards – had descended between the river's head and all human interference, so that there was not much fear of any more East Poley manœuvres for turning the stream into their valley.

The inhabitants of the parish, gentle and simple,* said that Steve had made ample amends for the harm he had done; and their goodwill was further evidenced by his being invited to no less than nineteen Christmas and New Year's parties during the following holidays.

As we left the cave, Steve, Job, Mrs Draycot and I walked behind the Man who had Failed.

'Though this has worked well,' he said to Steve, 'it is by the merest chance in the world. Your courage is praiseworthy, but you see the risks that are incurred when people go out of their way to meddle with what they don't understand. Exceptionally smart actions, such as you delight in, should be carefully weighed with a view to their utility before they are begun. Quiet perseverance in clearly defined courses is, as a rule, better than the erratic exploits that may do much harm.'

Steve listened respectfully enough to this, but he said to his mother afterwards, 'He has failed in life, and how can his opinions be worth anything?'

'For this reason,' said she. 'He is one who has failed, not from want of sense, but from want of energy; and people of that sort, when kindly, are better worth attending to than those successful ones, who have never seen the seamy side of things. I would advise you to listen to him.'

Steve probably did; for he is now the largest gentleman-farmer of those parts, remarkable for his avoidance of anything like speculative exploits.

FOUR SHORT STORIES

Note; These four stories are told by characters travelling by carrier-van (the omnibus of that time) from Casterbridge to Longpuddle. They have been joined by someone who emigrated from their village thirty-five years before and who asks them about the people he knew then.

TONY KYTES, THE ARCH-DECEIVER

(told by the carrier)

'I shall never forget Tony's face. 'Twas a little, round, firm, tight face, with a seam here and there left by the smallpox, but not enough to hurt his looks in a woman's eye, though he'd had it badish when he was a boy. So very serious looking and unsmiling 'a was, that young man, that it really seemed as if he couldn't laugh at all without great pain to his conscience. He looked very hard at a small speck in your eye when talking to 'ee. And there was no more sign of a whisker or beard on Tony Kytes's face than on the palm of my hand. He used to sing "The Tailor's Breeches"* with a religious manner, as if it were a hymn:

> O the petticoats went off, and the breeches they went on!

and all the rest of the scandalous stuff. He was quite the women's favourite, and in return for their likings he loved 'em in shoals.

'But in course of time Tony got fixed down to one in particular, Milly Richards, a nice, light, small, tender little thing; and it was soon said that they were engaged to be married. One Saturday he had been to market to do business for his father, and was driving home the wagon in the afternoon. When he reached the foot of the very hill we shall be going over in ten minutes who should he see waiting for him at the top but Unity Sallet, a handsome girl, one of the young women he'd been very tender towards before he'd got engaged to Milly.

'As soon as Tony came up to her she said, "My dear Tony, will you give me a lift home?"

'"That I will, darling," said Tony. "You don't suppose I could refuse 'ee?"

'She smiled a smile, and up she hopped, and on drove Tony.

'"Tony," she says, in a sort of tender chide, "why did ye desert me for that other one? In what is she better than I? I should have made 'ee a finer wife, and a more loving one, too. 'Tisn't girls that are so easily won at first that are the best. Think how long we've known each other – ever since we were children almost – now haven't we, Tony?"'

'"Yes, that we have," says Tony, a-struck with the truth o't.

'"And you've never seen anything in me to complain of, have ye, Tony? Now tell the truth to me!"

'"I never have, upon my life," says Tony.

'"And – can you say I'm not pretty, Tony? Now look at me!"

'He let his eyes light upon her for a long while. "I really can't," says he. "In fact, I never knowed you was so pretty before!"

'"Prettier than she?"

'What Tony would have said to that nobody knows, for before he could speak, what should he see ahead, over the hedge past the turning, but a feather he knew well – the feather in Milly's hat – she to whom he had been thinking of putting the question as to giving out the banns that very week.

'"Unity," says he, as mild as he could, "here's Milly coming. Now I shall catch it mightily if she sees 'ee riding here with me; and if you get down she'll be turning the corner in a moment, and, seeing 'ee in the road, she'll know we've been coming on together. Now, dearest Unity, will ye, to avoid all unpleasantness, which I know ye can't bear any more than I, will ye lie down in the back part of the wagon, and let me cover you over with the tarpaulin till Milly has passed? It will all be done in a minute. Do! – and I'll think over what we've said, and perhaps I shall put a loving question to you after all, instead of to Milly. 'Tisn't true that it is all settled between her and me."

'Well, Unity Sallet agreed, and lay down at the back end of the wagon, and Tony covered her over, so that the wagon seemed to be empty but for the loose tarpaulin; and then he drove on to meet Milly.

'"My dear Tony!" cries Milly, looking up with a little pout at him as he came near. "How long you've been coming home! Just as if I didn't live at Upper Longpuddle* at all! And I've come to meet you as you asked me to do, and to ride back with you, and talk over our future home – since you asked me, and I promised. But I shouldn't have come else, Mr Tony!"

'"Ay, my dear, I did ask 'ee – to be sure I did, now I think of it – but I had quite forgot it. To ride back with me, did you say, dear Milly?"

'"Well, of course! What can I do else? Surely you don't want me to walk, now I've come all this way?"

'"O no, no! I was thinking you might be going on to town to meet your mother. I saw her there – and she looked as if she might be expecting 'ee."

'"O no; she's just home. She came across the fields, and so got back before you."

'"Ah! I didn't know that," says Tony. And there was no help for it but to take her up beside him.

'They talked on very pleasantly, and looked at the trees, and beasts, and birds, and insects, and at the ploughmen at work in the fields, till presently who should they see looking out of the upper window of a house that stood beside the road they were following, but Hannah Jolliver, another young beauty of the place at that time, and the very first woman that Tony had fallen in love with – before Milly and before Unity, in fact – the one that he had almost arranged to marry instead of Milly. She was a much more dashing girl than Milly Richards, though he'd not thought much of her of late. The house Hannah was looking from was her aunt's.

'"My dear Milly – my coming wife, as I may call 'ee," says Tony in his modest way, and not so loud that Unity could overhear, "I see a young woman a-looking out of window, who I think may accost me. The fact is, Milly, she had a notion that I was wishing to marry her, and since she's discovered I've promised another, and a prettier than she, I'm rather afeared of her temper if she sees us together. Now, Milly, would you do me a favour – my coming wife, as I may say?"

'"Certainly, dearest Tony," says she.

'"Then would ye creep under the empty sacks just here in the front of the wagon, and hide there out of sight till we've passed the house? She hasn't seen us yet. You see, we ought to live in peace and goodwill since 'tis almost Christmas, and 'twill prevent angry passions rising, which we always should do."

'"I don't mind, to oblige you, Tony," Milly said; and though she didn't care much about doing it, she crept under, and crouched down just behind the seat, Unity being snug at the other end. So they drove on till they got near the roadside cottage. Hannah had soon seen him coming, and waited at the window, looking down upon him. She tossed her head a little disdainful and smiled off-hand.

'"Well, aren't you going to be civil enough to ask me to ride home with you!" she says, seeing that he was for driving past with a nod and a smile.

'"Ah, to be sure! What was I thinking of?" said Tony, in a flutter. "But you seem as if you was staying at your aunt's?"

'"No, I am not," she said. "Don't you see I have my bonnet and jacket on? I have only called to see her on my way home. How can you be so stupid, Tony?"

'"In that case – ah – of course you must come along wi' me," says Tony, feeling a dim sort of sweat rising up inside his clothes. And he reined in the horse, and waited till she'd come downstairs, and then helped her up beside him, her feet outside. He drove on again, his face as long as a face that was a round one by nature well could be.

'Hannah looked round sideways into his eyes. "This is nice, isn't it, Tony?" she says. "I like riding with you."

'Tony looked back into her eyes. "And I with you," he said after a while. In short, having considered her, he warmed up, and the more he looked at her the more he liked her, till he couldn't for the life of him think why he had ever said a word about marriage to Milly or Unity while Hannah Jolliver was in question. So they sat a little closer and closer, their feet upon the foot-board and their shoulders touching, and Tony thought over and over again how handsome Hannah was. He spoke tenderer and tenderer, and called her "dear Hannah" in a whisper at last.

'"You've settled it with Milly by this time, I suppose?" said she.

'"N-no, not exactly."

'"What? How low you talk, Tony."

'"Yes – I've a kind of hoarseness. I said, not exactly."

'"I suppose you mean to?"

'"Well, as to that— " His eyes rested on her face, and hers on his. He wondered how he could have been such a fool as not to follow up Hannah. "My sweet Hannah!" he bursts out, taking her hand, not being really able to help it, and forgetting Milly and Unity, and all the world besides. "Settled it? I don't think I have!"

'"Hark!" says Hannah.

'"What?" says Tony, letting go her hand.

'"Surely I heard a sort of little screaming squeak under those sacks? Why, you've been carrying corn, and there's mice in this wagon, I declare!" She began to haul up the tails of her gown.

'"O no, 'tis the axle," said Tony in an assuring way. "It do go like that sometimes in dry weather."

'"Perhaps it was ... Well, now, to be quite honest, dear Tony, do you like her better than me? Because – because, although I've held off so independent, I'll own at last that I do like 'ee, Tony, to tell the truth; and I wouldn't say no if you asked me – you know what."

'Tony was so won over by this pretty offering mood of a girl who had been quite the reverse (Hannah had a backward way with her at times, if you can mind) that he just glanced behind, and then whispered very soft, "I haven't quite promised her, and I think I can get out of it, and ask you that question you speak of."

'"Throw over Milly? – all to marry me! How delightful!" broke out Hannah, quite loud, clapping her hands.

'At this there was a real squeak – an angry, spiteful squeak, and afterward a long moan, as if something had broke its heart, and a movement of the empty sacks.

'"Something's there!" said Hannah, starting up.

'"It's nothing really," says Tony in a soothing voice, and praying inwardly for a way out of this. "I wouldn't tell 'ee at first, because I wouldn't frighten 'ee. But, Hannah, I've really a couple of ferrets in a bag under there, for rabbiting, and they quarrel sometimes. I don't wish it knowed, as 'twould be called poaching. Oh, they can't get out, bless 'ee – you are quite safe! And – and – what a fine day it is, isn't it, Hannah, for this time of year? Be you going to market next Saturday? How is your aunt now?" And so on, says Tony, to keep her from talking any more about love in Milly's hearing.

'But he found his work cut out for him, and wondering again how he should get out of this ticklish business, he looked about for a chance. Nearing home he saw his father in a field not far off, holding up his hand as if he wished to speak to Tony.

'"Would you mind taking the reins a moment, Hannah," he said, much relieved, "while I go and find out what Father wants?"

'She consented, and away he hastened into the field, only too glad to get breathing time. He found that his father was looking at him with rather a stern eye.

'"Come, come, Tony," says old Mr Kytes, as soon as his son was alongside him, "this won't do, you know."

'"What?" says Tony.

'"Why, if you mean to marry Milly Richards, do it, and there's an end o't. But don't go driving about the country with Jolliver's daughter and making a scandal. I won't have such things done."

'"I only asked her – that is, she asked me, to ride home."

'"She? Why, now, if it had been Milly, 'twould have been quite proper; but you and Hannah Jolliver going about by yourselves—"

'"Milly's there, too, father."

'"Milly? Where?"

'"Under the corn-sacks! Yes, the truth is, Father, I've got rather into a nunnywatch,* I'm afeared! Unity Sallet is there, too – yes, at the other end, under the tarpaulin. All three are in that wagon, and what to do with 'em I know no more than the dead! The best plan is, as I'm thinking, to speak out loud and plain to one of 'em before the rest, and that will settle it; not but what 'twill cause 'em to kick up a bit of a miff, for certain. Now which would you marry, Father, if you was in my place?"

'"Whichever of 'em did *not* ask to ride with thee."

'"That was Milly, I'm bound to say, as she only mounted by my invitation. But Milly—"

'"Then stick to Milly, she's the best . . . But look at that!"

'His father pointed toward the wagon. "She can't hold that horse in. You shouldn't have left the reins in her hands. Run on and take the horse's head, or there'll be some accident to them maids!"

'Tony's horse, in fact, in spite of Hannah's tugging at the reins, had started on his way at a brisk walking pace, being very anxious to get back to the stable, for he had had a long day out. Without another word Tony rushed away from his father to overtake the horse.

'Now of all things that could have happened to wean him from Milly there was nothing so powerful as his father's recommending her. No; it could not be Milly, after all. Hannah must be the one, since he could not marry all three as he longed to do. This he thought while running after the waggon. But queer things were happening inside it.

'It was, of course, Milly who had screamed under the sack-bags, being obliged to let off her bitter rage and shame in that way at what Tony was saying, and never daring to show, for very pride and dread o' being laughed at, that she was in hiding. She became more and more restless, and in twisting herself about, what did she see but another woman's foot and white stocking close to her head. It quite frightened her, not knowing that Unity Sallet was in the wagon likewise. But after the fright was over she determined to get to the bottom of all this, and she crept and crept along the bed of the wagon, under the tarpaulin, like a snake, when lo and behold she came face to face with Unity.

'"Well, if this isn't disgraceful!" says Milly in a raging whisper to Unity.

'"'Tis," says Unity, "to see you hiding in a young man's wagon like this, and no great character belonging to either of ye!"

'"Mind what you are saying!" replied Milly, getting louder. "I am engaged to be married to him, and haven't I a right to be here? What right have you, I should like to know? What has he been promising you? A pretty lot of nonsense, I expect! But what Tony says to other women is all mere wind, and no concern to me!"

'"Don't you be too sure!" says Unity. "He's going to have Hannah, and not you, nor me either; I could hear that."

'Now at these strange voices sounding from under the cloth Hannah was thunderstruck a'most into a swound;*and it was just at this time that the horse moved on. Hannah tugged away wildly, not knowing what she was doing; and as the quarrel rose louder and louder Hannah got so horrified that she let go the reins altogether. The horse went on at his own pace, and coming to the corner where we turn round to drop down the hill to Lower Longpuddle* he turned too quick, the off wheels went up the bank, the wagon rose sideways till it was quite on edge upon the near axles, and out rolled the three maidens into the road in a heap. The horse looked round and stood still.

'When Tony came up, frightened and breathless, he was relieved enough to see that neither of his darlings was hurt, beyond a few scratches from the brambles of the hedge. But he was rather alarmed when he heard how they were going on at one another.

'"Don't ye quarrel, my dears – don't ye!" says he, taking off his hat out of respect to 'em. And then he would have kissed them all round, as fair and square as a man could, but they were in too much of a taking to let him, and screeched and sobbed till they was quite spent.

'"Now I'll speak out honest, because I ought to," says Tony, as soon as he could get heard. "And this is the truth," says he. "I've asked Hannah to be mine, and she is willing, and we are going to put up the banns next—"

'Tony had not noticed that Hannah's father was coming up behind, nor had he noticed that Hannah's face was beginning to bleed from the scratch of a bramble. Hannah had seen her father, and had run to him, crying worse than ever.

'"My daughter is *not* willing, sir!" says Mr Jolliver hot and strong. "Be you willing, Hannah? I ask ye to have spirit enough to refuse him, if yer virtue is left to 'ee and you run no risk?"*

'"She's as sound as a bell for me, that I'll swear!" says Tony, flaring up. "And so's the others, come to that, though you may think it an onusual thing in me!"

'"I have spirit, and I do refuse him!" says Hannah, partly because her father was there, and partly, too, in a tantrum because of the discovery, and the scar that might be left on her face. "Little did I think when I was so soft with him just now that I was talking to such a false deceiver!"

'"What, you won't have me, Hannah?" says Tony, his jaw hanging down like a dead man's.

'"Never – I would sooner marry no – nobody at all!" she gasped out, though with her heart in her throat, for she would not have refused Tony if he had asked her quietly, and her father had not been there, and her face had not been scratched by the bramble. And having said that, away she walked upon her father's arm, thinking and hoping he would ask her again.

'Tony didn't know what to say next. Milly was sobbing her heart out; but as his father had strongly recommended her he couldn't feel inclined that way. So he turned to Unity.

'"Well, will you, Unity dear, be mine?" he says.

'"Take her leavings? Not I!" says Unity. "I'd scorn it!" And away walks Unity Sallet likewise, though she looked back when she'd gone some way, to see if he was following her.

'So there at last were left Milly and Tony by themselves, she crying in watery streams, and Tony looking like a tree struck by lightning.

'"Well, Milly," he says at last, going up to her, "it do seem as if fate had ordained that it should be you and I, or nobody. And what must be must be, I suppose. Hey, Milly?"

'"If you like, Tony. You didn't really mean what you said to them?"

'"Not a word of it!" declares Tony, bringing down his fist upon his palm.

'And then he kissed her, and put the wagon to rights, and they mounted together; and their banns were put up the very next Sunday. I was not able to go to their wedding, but it was a rare party they had, by all account . . .'

ANDREY SATCHEL AND THE
PARSON AND CLERK

(told by the master-thatcher)

'It all arose, you must know, from Andrey being fond of a drop of drink at that time – though he's a sober enough man now by all account, so much the better for him. Jane, his bride, you see, was somewhat older than Andrey; how much older I don't pretend to say; she was not one of our parish, and the register alone may be able to tell that. But, at any rate, her being a little ahead of her young man in mortal years, coupled with other bodily circumstances* owing to that young man—'

('Ah, poor thing!' sighed the women.)

' – made her very anxious to get the thing done before he changed his mind; and 'twas with a joyful countenance (they say) that she, with Andrey and his brother and sister-in-law, marched off to church one November morning as soon as 'twas day a'most to be made one with Andrey for the rest of her life. He had left our place long before it was light, and the folks that were up all waved their lanterns at him, and flung up their hats as he went.

'The church of her parish was a mile and more from where she lived, and, as it was a wonderful fine day for the time of year, the plan was that as soon as they were married they would make out a holiday by driving straight off to Port Bredy,* to see the ships and the sea and the sojers, instead of coming back to a meal at the house of the distant relation she lived wi', and moping about there all the afternoon.

'Well, some folks noticed that Andrey walked with rather wambling* steps to church that morning; the truth o't was that his nearest neighbour's child had been christened the day before, and Andrey, having stood godfather, had stayed all night keeping up* the christening, for he had said to himself, "Not if I live to be a thousand shall I again be made a godfather one day, and a husband the next, and perhaps a father the next, and therefore I'll make the most of the blessing." So that when he started from home in the morning he had not been in bed at all. The result was, as I say, that when he and his bride-to-be walked up the church to get married, the pa'son (who was a very strict man inside the church, whatever he was outside) looked hard at Andrey, and said, very sharp:

' "How's this, my man? You are in liquor. And so early, too. I'm ashamed of you!"

' "Well, that's true, sir," says Andrey. "But I can walk straight enough for practical purposes. I can walk a chalk line," he says (meaning no offence) "as well as some other folk: and" – (getting hotter) – "I reckon that if you, Pa'son Billy Toogood, had kept up a christening all night so thoroughly as I have done, you wouldn't be able to stand at all; d—me if you would!"

'This answer made Pa'son Billy – as they used to call him – rather spitish, not to say hot, for he was a warm-tempered man if provoked, and he said, very decidedly: "Well, I cannot marry you in this state; and I will not! Go home and get sober!" And he slapped the book* together like a rat-trap.

'Then the bride burst out crying as if her heart would break, for very fear that she would lose Andrey after all her hard work to get him, and begged and implored the pa'son to go on with the ceremony. But no.

' "I won't be a party to your solemnizing matrimony with a tipsy man," says Mr Toogood. "It is not right and decent. I am sorry for you, my young woman, seeing the condition you are in, but you'd better go home again. I wonder how you could think of bringing him here drunk like this!"

' "But if-if he don't come drunk he won't come at all, sir!" she says, through her sobs.

' "I can't help that," says the pa'son; and plead as she might, it did not move him. Then she tried him another way.

'"Well, then, if you'll go home, sir, and leave us here, and come back to the church in an hour or two, I'll undertake to say that he shall be as sober as a judge," she cries. "We'll bide here, with your permission; for if he once goes out of this here church unmarried, all Van Amburgh's horses* won't drag him back again!"

'"Very well," says the parson. "I'll give you two hours, and then I'll return."

'"And please, sir, lock the door, so that we can't escape!" says she.

'"Yes," says the parson.

'"And let nobody know that we are here."

'The pa'son then took off his clane white surplice, and went away; and the others consulted upon the best means for keeping the matter a secret, which it was not a very hard thing to do, the place being so lonely, and the hour so early. The witnesses, Andrey's brother and brother's wife, neither one o' which cared about Andrey's marrying Jane, and had come rather against their will, said they couldn't wait two hours in that hole of a place, wishing to get home to Longpuddle before dinner-time. They were altogether so crusty that the clerk said there was no difficulty in their doing as they wished. They could go home as if their brother's wedding had actually taken place and the married couple had gone onward for their day's pleasure jaunt to Port Bredy as intended. He, the clerk, and any casual passer-by would act as witnesses when the pa'son came back.

'This was agreed to, and away Andrey's relations went, nothing loath, and the clerk shut the church door and prepared to lock in the couple. The bride went up and whispered to him, with her eyes a-streaming still.

'"My dear good clerk," she says, "if we bide here in the church, folk may see us through the windows, and find out what has happened; and 'twould cause such a talk and scandal that I never should get over it: and perhaps, too, dear Andrey might try to get out and leave me! Will ye lock us up in the tower, my dear good clerk?" she says. "I'll tole* him in there if you will."

'The clerk had no objection to do this to oblige the poor young woman, and they toled Andrey into the tower, and the clerk locked 'em both up straightway, and then went home, to return at the end of the two hours.

'Pa'son Toogood had not been long in his house after leaving

the church when he saw a gentleman in pink and top-boots*
ride past his windows, and with a sudden flash of heat he called
to mind that the hounds met that day just on the edge of his
parish. The pa'son was one who dearly loved sport, and much
he longed to be there.

'In short, except o' Sundays and at tide-times* in the week,
Pa'son Billy was the life o' the hunt. 'Tis true that he was poor,
and that he rode all of a heap, and that his black mare was rat-
tailed and old, and his tops* older, and all over of one colour,
whitey-brown, and full o' cracks. But he'd been in at the death
of three thousand foxes. And – being a bachelor man – every
time he went to bed in summer he used to open the bed at
bottom and crawl up head foremost, to mind en of the coming
winter and the good sport he'd have, and the foxes going to
earth.* And whenever there was a christening at the Squire's,
and he had dinner there afterwards, as he always did, he never
failed to christen the chiel over again in a bottle of port wine.

'Now the clerk was the pa'son's groom and gardener and
general manager, and had just got back to his work in the
garden when he, too, saw the hunting man pass, and presently
saw lots more of 'em, noblemen and gentry, and then he saw
the hounds, the huntsman, Jim Treadhedge, the whipper-in,*
and I don't know who besides. The clerk loved going to cover*
as frantical* as the pa'son, so much so that whenever he saw or
heard the pack he could no more rule his feelings than if they
were the winds of heaven. He might be bedding,* or he might
be sowing – all was forgot. So he throws down his spade and
rushes in to the pa'son, who was by this time as frantical to go
as he.

'"That there mare of yours, sir, do want exercise bad, very
bad, this morning!" the clerk says, all of a tremble. "Don't ye
think I'd better trot her round the downs for an hour, sir?"

'"To be sure, she does want exercise badly. I'll trot her round
myself," says the pa'son.

'"Oh – you'll trot her yerself? Well, there's the cob,* sir.
Really that cob is getting oncontrollable through biding in a stable
so long! If you wouldn't mind my putting on the saddle—"

'"Very well. Take him out, certainly," says the pa'son, never
caring what the clerk did so long as he himself could get off
immediately. So, scrambling into his riding-boots and breeches
as quick as he could, he rode off towards the meet,* intending

to be back in an hour. No sooner was he gone than the clerk mounted the cob, and was off after him. When the pa'son got to the meet he found a lot of friends, and was as jolly as he could be: the hounds found* a'most as soon as they threw off,* and there was great excitement. So, forgetting that he had meant to go back at once, away rides the pa'son with the rest o' the hunt, all across the fallow ground that lies between Lippet Wood and Green's Copse; and as he galloped he looked behind for a moment, and there was the clerk close to his heels.

'"Ha, ha, clerk – you here?" he says.

'"Yes, sir, here be I," says t'other.

'"Fine exercise for the horses!"

'"Ay, sir – hee, hee!" says the clerk.

'So they went on and on, into Green's Copse, then across to Higher Jirton; then on across this very turnpike-road to Waterston Ridge, then away towards Yalbury Wood: up hill and down dale, like the very wind, the clerk close to the pa'son, and the pa'son not far from the hounds. Never was there a finer run knowed with that pack than they had that day; and neither pa'son nor clerk thought one word about the unmarried couple locked up in the church tower waiting to get j'ined.

'"These hosses of yours, sir, will be much improved by this!" says the clerk as he rode along, just a neck behind the pa'son. "'Twas a happy thought of your reverent mind to bring 'em out today. Why, it may be frosty and slippery in a day or two, and then the poor things mid not be able to leave the stable for weeks."

'"They may not, they may not, it is true. A merciful man is merciful to his beast," says the pa'son.

'"Hee, hee!" says the clerk, glancing sly into the pa'son's eye.

'"Ha, ha!" says the pa'son, a-glancing back into the clerk's. "Halloo!" he shouts, as he sees the fox break cover at that moment.

'"Halloo!" cries the clerk. "There he goes! Why, dammy, there's two foxes—"

'"Hush, clerk, hush! Don't let me hear that word again! Remember our calling."

'"True, sir, true. But really, good sport do carry away a man so, that he's apt to forget his high persuasion!"* And the next minute the corner of the clerk's eye shot again into the corner of the pa'son's, and the pa'son's back again to the clerk's. "Hee, hee!" said the clerk.

'"Ha, ha!" said Pa'son Toogood.

'"Ah, sir," says the clerk again, "this is better than crying Amen to your Ever-and-ever* on a winter's morning!"

'"Yes, indeed, clerk! To everything there's a season,"* says Pa'son Toogood, quite pat, for he was a learned Christian man when he liked, and had chapter and ve'se at his tongue's end, as a pa'son should.*

'At last, late in the day, the hunting came to an end by the fox running into a' old woman's cottage, under her table, and up the clock-case. The pa'son and clerk were among the first in at the death, their faces a-staring in at the old woman's winder, and the clock striking as he'd never been heard to strik' before. Then came the question of finding their way home.

'Neither the pa'son nor the clerk knowed how they were going to do this, for their beasts were wellnigh tired down to the ground. But they started back-along as well as they could, though they were so done up that they could only drag along at a' amble,* and not much of that at a time.

'"We shall never, never get there!" groaned Mr Toogood, quite bowed down.

'"Never!" groans the clerk. "'Tis a judgment upon us for our iniquities!"

'"I fear it is," murmurs the pa'son.

'Well, 'twas quite dark afore they entered the pa'sonage gate, having crept into the parish as quiet as if they'd stole a hammer, little wishing their congregation to know what they'd been up to all day long. And as they were so dog-tired, and so anxious about the horses, never once did they think of the unmarried couple. As soon as ever the horses had been stabled and fed, and the pa'son and clerk had had a bit and a sup theirselves, they went to bed.

'Next morning when Pa'son Toogood was at breakfast, thinking of the glorious sport he'd had the day before, the clerk came in a hurry to the door and asked to see him.

'"It has just come into my mind, sir, that we've forgot all about the couple that we was to have married yesterday!"

'The half-chawed victuals dropped from the pa'son's mouth as if he'd been shot. "Bless my soul," says he, "so we have! How very awkward!"

'"It is, sir; very. Perhaps we've ruined the 'ooman!"

'"Ah – to be sure – I remember! She ought to have been married before."

'"If anything has happened to her up in that there tower, and no doctor or nuss—"

('Ah – poor thing!' sighed the women.)

'" – 'twill be a quarter-sessions* matter for us, not to speak of the disgrace to the Church!"

'"Good God, clerk, don't drive me wild!" says the pa'son. "Why the hell didn't I marry 'em, drunk or sober!" (Pa'sons used to cuss in them days like plain honest men.) "Have you been to the church to see what happened to them, or inquired in the village?"

'"Not I, sir! It only came into my head a moment ago, and I always like to be second to you in church matters. You could have knocked me down with a sparrow's feather when I thought o't, sir; I assure 'ee you could!"

'Well, the pa'son jumped up from his breakfast, and together they went off to the church.

'"It is not at all likely that they are there now," says Mr Toogood, as they went; "and indeed I hope they are not. They be pretty sure to have escaped and gone home."

'However, they opened the church-hatch,* entered the churchyard, and looking up at the tower there they seed a little small white face at the belfry-winder, and a little small hand waving. 'Twas the bride.

'"God my life, clerk," says Mr Toogood. "I don't know how to face 'em!" And he sank down upon a tombstone. "How I wish I hadn't been so cussed particular!"

'"Yes – 'twas a pity we didn't finish it when we'd begun," the clerk said. "Still, since the feelings of your holy priestcraft wouldn't let ye, the couple must put up with it."

'"True, clerk, true! Does she look as if anything premature had took place?"

'"I can't see her no lower down than her armpits, sir."

'"Well – how do her face look?"

'"It do look mighty white!"

'"Well, we must know the worst! Dear me, how the small of my back do ache from that ride yesterday! ... But to more godly business!"

'They went on into the church, and unlocked the tower stairs, and immediately poor Jane and Andrey busted out like starved mice from a cupboard, Andrey limp and sober enough now, and his bride pale and cold, but otherwise as usual.

'"What," says the pa'son with a great breath of relief, "you haven't been here ever since?"

'"Yes, we have, sir!" says the bride, sinking down upon a seat in her weakness. "Not a morsel, wet or dry, have we had since! It was impossible to get out without help, and here we've stayed!"

'"But why didn't you shout, good souls?" said the pa'son.

'"She wouldn't let me," says Andrey.

'"Because we were so ashamed at what had led to it," sobs Jane. "We felt that if it were noised abroad it would cling to us all our lives! Once or twice Andrey had a good mind to toll the bell, but then he said: 'No; I'll starve first. I won't bring disgrace on my name and yours, my dear.' And so we waited and waited, and walked round and round; but never did you come till now!"

'"To my regret!" says the pa'son. "Now, then, we will soon get it over."

'"I – I should like some victuals," said Andrey. "'Twould gi'e me courage to do it, if it is only a crust o' bread and a' onion; for I am that leery* that I can feel my stomach rubbing against my backbone."*

'"I think we had better get it done," said the bride, a bit anxious in manner, "since we are all here convenient, too!"

'Andrey gave way about the victuals, and the clerk called in a second witness who wouldn't be likely to gossip about it, and soon the knot was tied,* and the bride looked smiling and calm forthwith, and Andrey limper than ever.

'"Now," said Pa'son Toogood, "you two must come to my house, and have a good lining put to your insides before you go a step further."

'They were very glad of the offer, and went out of the churchyard by one path while the pa'son and clerk went out by the other, and so did not attract notice, it being still early. They entered the rectory as if they'd just come back from their trip to Port Bredy; and then they knocked in the victuals and drink till they could hold no more.

'It was a long while before the story of what they had gone through was known, but it was talked of in time, and they themselves laugh over it now; though what Jane got for her pains was no great bargain after all. 'Tis true she saved her name.'*

'Was that the same Andrey who went to the squire's house as one of the Christmas fiddlers?' asked the seedsman.

'No, no,' replied Mr Profitt, the schoolmaster. 'It was his father did that. Ay, it was all owing to his being such a man for eating and drinking.' Finding that he had the ear of the audience, the schoolmaster continued without delay:

OLD ANDREY'S EXPERIENCE
AS A MUSICIAN

'I was one of the quire-boys at that time, and we and the players were to appear at the manor-house as usual that Christmas week, to play and sing in the hall to the Squire's people and visitors (among 'em being the archdeacon, Lord and Lady Baxby, and I don't know who); afterwards going, as we always did, to have a good supper in the servants' hall. Andrew knew this was the custom, and meeting us when we were starting to go, he said to us: "Lord, how I should like to join in that meal of beef, and turkey, and plum-pudding, and ale, that you happy ones be going to just now! One more or less will make no difference to the Squire. I am too old to pass as a singing boy, and too bearded to pass as a singing girl; can ye lend me a fiddle, neighbours, that I may come with ye as a bandsman?"

'Well, we didn't like to be hard upon him, and lent him an old one, though Andrew knew no more of music than the Giant o' Cernel;* and armed with the instrument he walked up to the Squire's house with the others of us at the time appointed, and went in boldly, his fiddle under his arm. He made himself as natural as he could in opening the music-books and moving the candles to the best points for throwing light upon the notes; and all went well till we had played and sung "While shepherds watch", and "Star, arise", and "Hark the glad sound". Then the Squire's mother, a tall gruff old lady, who was much interested in churchmusic, said quite unexpectedly to Andrew:

"My man, I see you don't play your instrument with the rest. How is that?"

'Every one of the quire was ready to sink into the earth with concern at the fix Andrew was in. We could see that he had fallen into a cold sweat, and how he would get out of it we did not know.

'"I've had a misfortune, mem,"* he says, bowing as meek as a child. "Coming along the road I fell down and broke my bow."

'"O, I am sorry to hear that," says she. "Can't it be mended?"

'"O no, mem," says Andrew. "'Twas broke all to splinters."

'"I'll see what I can do for you," says she.

'And then it seemed all over, and we played "Rejoice, ye drowsy mortals all", in D and two sharps. But no sooner had we got through it than she says to Andrew:

'"I've sent up into the attic, where we have some old musical instruments, and found a bow for you." And she hands the bow to poor wretched Andrew, who didn't even know which end to take hold of. "Now we shall have the full accompaniment," says she.

'Andrew's face looked as if it were made of rotten apple as he stood in the circle of players in front of his book; for if there was one person in the parish that everybody was afraid of, 'twas this hook-nosed old lady. However, by keeping a little behind the next man he managed to make pretence of beginning, sawing away with his bow without letting it touch the strings, so that it looked as if he were driving into the tune with heart and soul. 'Tis a question if he wouldn't have got through all right if one of the Squire's visitors (no other than the archdeacon) hadn't noticed that he held the fiddle upside down, the nut* under his chin, and the tail-piece* in his hand; and they began to crowd round him, thinking 'twas some new way of performing.

'This revealed everything; the Squire's mother had Andrew turned out of the house as a vile impostor, and there was great interruption to the harmony of the proceedings, the Squire declaring he should have notice to leave his cottage that day fortnight. However, when we got to the servants' hall there sat Andrew, who had been let in at the back door by the orders of the Squire's wife, after being turned out at the front by the orders of the Squire, and nothing more was heard about his leaving his cottage. But Andrew never performed in public as a musician after that night; and now he's dead and gone, poor man, as we all shall be!'

'I had quite forgotten the old choir, with their fiddles and bass-viols,' said the home-comer, musingly. 'Are they still going on the same as of old?'

'Bless the man!' said Christopher Twink, the master-thatcher; 'why, they've been done away with these twenty year. A young teetotaller* plays the organ in church now, and plays it very well; though 'tis not quite such good music as in old times, because the organ is one of them that go with a winch,* and the young teetotaller says he can't always throw the proper feeling into the tune without wellnigh working his arms off.'

'Why did they make the change, then?'

'Well, partly because of fashion, partly because the old musicians got into a sort of scrape. A terrible scrape 'twas, too – wasn't it, John? I shall never forget it – never! They lost their character as officers of the church as complete as if they'd never had any character at all.'

'That was very bad for them.'

'Yes.' The master-thatcher attentively regarded past times as if they lay about a mile off, and went on:

ABSENT-MINDEDNESS
IN A PARISH CHOIR

'It happened on Sunday after Christmas – the last Sunday ever they played in Longpuddle church gallery, as it turned out, though they didn't know it then. As you may know, sir, the players formed a very good band – almost as good as the Mellstock parish players that were led by the Dewys;* and that's saying a great deal. There was Nicholas Puddingcome, the leader, with the first fiddle; there was Timothy Thomas, the bass-viol man; John Biles, the tenor fiddler, Dan'l Hornhead, with the serpent; Robert Dowdle, with the clarionet; and Mr Nicks, with the oboe – all sound and powerful musicians, and strong-winded men – they that blowed. For that reason they were very much in demand Christmas week for little reels and dancing parties; for they could turn a jig or a hornpipe* out of hand* as well as ever they could turn out a psalm, and perhaps better, not to speak irreverent. In short, one half-hour they could be playing a Christmas carol in the Squire's hall to the ladies and gentlemen, and drinking tay and coffee with 'em as modest as saints; and the next, at The Tinker's Arms, blazing away like wild horses with the "Dashing White Sergeant" to nine couple of dancers and more, and swallowing rum-and-cider hot as flame.

'Well, this Christmas they'd been out to one rattling randy after another every night, and had got next to no sleep at all. Then came the Sunday after Christmas, their fatal day. 'Twas so mortal cold that year that they could hardly sit in the gallery; for though the congregation down in the body of the church had a stove to keep off the frost, the players in the gallery had nothing at all. So Nicholas said at morning service, when 'twas freezing an inch an hour, "Please the Lord I won't stand this numbing weather no longer: this afternoon we'll have something in our insides to make us warm, if it cost a king's ransom."

'So he brought a gallon of hot brandy and beer, ready mixed, to church with him in the afternoon, and by keeping the jar well wrapped up in Timothy Thomas's bass-viol bag it kept drinkably warm till they wanted it, which was just a thimbleful in the Absolution, and another after the Creed,* and the remainder at the beginning o' the sermon. When they'd had the last pull they felt quite comfortable and warm, and as the sermon went on – most unfortunately for 'em it was a long one that afternoon – they fell asleep, every man jack of 'em; and there they slept on as sound as rocks.

''Twas a very dark afternoon, and by the end of the sermon all you could see of the inside of the church were the pa'son's two candles alongside of him in the pulpit, and his spaking face behind 'em. The sermon being ended at last, the pa'son gie'd out the Evening Hymn.* But no quire set about sounding up the tune, and the people began to turn their heads to learn the reason why, and then Levi Limpet, a boy who sat in the gallery, nudged Timothy and Nicholas, and said, "Begin! begin!"

'"Hey? what?" says Nicholas, starting up; and the church being so dark and his head so muddled he thought he was at the party they had played at all the night before, and away he went, bow and fiddle, at "The Devil among the Tailors", the favourite jig of our neighbourhood at that time. The rest of the band, being in the same state of mind and nothing doubting, followed their leader with all their strength, according to custom. They poured out that there tune till the lower bass notes of "The Devil among the Tailors" made the cobwebs in the roof shiver like ghosts; then Nicholas, seeing nobody moved, shouted out as he scraped (in his usual commanding way at dances when the folk didn't know the figures), "Top couples cross hands! And when I make the fiddle squeak at the end, every man kiss his pardner under the mistletoe!"

'The boy Levi was so frightened that he bolted down the gallery stairs and out homeward like lightning. The pa'son's hair fairly stood on end when he heard the evil tune raging through the church, and thinking the quire had gone crazy he held up his hand and said: "Stop, stop, stop! Stop, stop! What's this?" But they didn't hear'n for the noise of their own playing, and the more he called the louder they played.

'Then the folks came out of their pews, wondering down to the ground, and saying: "What do they mean by such wickedness! We shall be consumed like Sodom and Gomorrah!"*

'And the Squire, too, came out of his pew lined wi' green baize, where lots of lords and ladies visiting at the house were worshipping along with him, and went and stood in front of the gallery, and shook his fist in the musicians' faces, saying, "What! In this reverent edifice! What!"

'And at last they heard'n through their playing, and stopped.

'"Never such an insulting, disgraceful thing – never!" says the Squire, who couldn't rule his passion.

'"Never!" says the pa'son, who had come down and stood beside him.

'"Not if the Angels of Heaven," says the Squire (he was a wickedish man, the Squire was, though now for once he happened to be on the Lord's side)* – "not if the Angels of Heaven come down," he says, "shall one of you villainous players ever sound a note in this church again; for the insult to me, and my family, and my visitors, and the pa'son, and God Almighty,* that you've a-perpetrated this afternoon!"

'Then the unfortunate church band came to their senses, and remembered where they were; and 'twas a sight to see Nicholas Puddingcome and Timothy Thomas and John Biles creep down the gallery stairs with their fiddles under their arms, and poor Dan'l Hornhead with his serpent, and Robert Dowdle with his clarionet, all looking as little as ninepins; and out they went. The pa'son might have forgi'ed 'em when he learned the truth o't, but the Squire would not. That very week he sent for a barrel-organ that would play two-and-twenty new psalm-tunes, so exact and particular that, however sinful inclined you was, you could play nothing but psalm-tunes whatsomever. He had a really respectable man to turn the winch, as I said, and the old players played no more.'

NOTES
_____

Under The Greenwood Tree

Title: Hardy takes his title from Shakespeare's *As You Like It* where we find the song:

> Under the Greenwood tree
> Who loves to lie with me
> And turn his merry note
> Unto the sweet bird's throat
> Come hither, come hither, come hither.
> Here shall he see
> No enemy
> But winter and rough weather.

In his 1912 Wessex edition Hardy added as a subtitle 'The Mellstock Quire'. It was an indication of the increasing importance he was seeing in that part of his story which was to do with the choir. The other sub-title, 'A Rural Painting of the Dutch School' was there from the beginning.

p. 3 Quire: Hardy deliberately uses the archaic word for 'choir'.

p. 3 west-gallery: many churches of that time had galleries at the back of the church where the choir sang and the instrumentalists played.

p. 3 ten shillings: fifty pence in modern money, but worth at least twenty or thirty times as much today.

p. 4 broad humour: many of the folk-songs of the time were bawdy.

p. 11 within living memory: the action takes place in the late 1840s or early 1850s.

p. 11 daffodowndilly: daffodil.

p. 11 With the rose ... : part of a folk-song called 'The Sheep-shearing Song'.

p. 12   **fellow-craturs:** fellow-creatures.

p. 12   **severally:** separately.

p. 13   **lath-like:** like a thin strip of wood.

p. 13   **tuens:** tunes.

p. 13   **Ewelease:** a grassy field used by sheep.

p. 13   **''Od rabbit it all':** 'Od' is a euphemism for God.

p. 13   **a sight of:** a great deal of.

p. 14   **wicket:** a small gate.

p. 14   **long low cottage:** Hardy is describing the Bockhampton cottage in which he was born and where he wrote this novel.

p. 14   **hipped roof:** sloping at the end as well as the sides.

p. 14   **dormer-windows:** small windows with a gable, projecting from a sloping roof.

p. 14   **codlin-trees:** a species of apple-tree.

p. 14   **espaliers:** trees trained on lattice-work or fences.

p. 14   **beetle:** a heavy wooden hammer.

p. 14   **scurr:** jerking noise.

p. 15   **hogshead:** a large cask.

p. 15   **horsed:** standing on a wooden frame.

p. 15   **broaching:** piercing the cask in order to prepare its contents for drinking.

p. 15   **plaits:** pleats.

p. 15   **settle:** a large, high-backed wooden seat.

p. 16   **water-cider:** cider which is the result of water added to the already wrung apples.

p. 16   **stimmilent:** stimulant.

p. 16   **Grammer:** a name for an old lady, not necessarily a grandmother.

p. 16   **fourteens:** small candles which weighed at fourteen to the pound (approximately half a kilo).

p. 16   **smock-frock:** a linen outer garment formerly worn by agricultural workers. It was usually white and often decorated with fancy stitching.

p. 17   **husbird:** rascal.

p. 17   **shillens:** shillings. In pre-decimal currency the equivalent of 10p, but worth much more at that time.

p. 17   **jimcrack:** worthless, badly made.

p. 17   **gospel:** the life of Christ as told in the four gospel books.

p. 18   **King's Arms:** a hotel still to be found in Dorchester.

p. 18   **martel:** mortal.

p. 18   **coming it very close:** taking unfair advantage of.

p. 19   **bass-viol:** a viol is a stringed musical instrument held between the legs of the player, and something like a modern cello.

p. 20   **ribstone-pippin:** a type of red apple.

p. 20   **mead:** alcoholic drink of fermented honey and water.

p. 20   **long-headed:** shrewd.

p. 20   **half-a-crown:** a coin worth $12\frac{1}{2}$ in the old currency.

p. 20   **leg-wood:** long branches cut from trees.

p. 20   **fustian:** thick cotton cloth usually of a dark colour.

p. 21   **buttery:** a room for storing and issuing food.

p. 21   **hard boy-chap:** robust, strong boy.

p. 21   **he's a good tune:** in Dorset dialect many nouns which we would normally think of as neuter and lacking a sexual identity are referred to as 'he' or 'she'.

p. 21   **linnit:** bits and pieces of lint.

p. 21   **carrel:** carol, a hymn sung at Christmas.

p. 21   **thirtingill:** obstinate, wrong-headed.

p. 21   **last:** shoemaker's wooden model for shaping a shoe.

p. 22   **bradded:** fastened with brads, small nails used in shoemaking.

p. 22   **pomace:** the pressed remains of apples left after cider-making.

p. 22   **full-butt:** with full force and accuracy.

p. 22   **husband-high:** ready for marriage.

p. 23   **bias:** tendency to turn to one side.

p. 23   **ten-and-sixpence:** ten shillings and sixpence in old currency, about 52p in today's decimal currency.

p. 23   **fantastical:** fanciful.

p. 23   **unrayed:** undressed.

p. 23   **pitch it:** dive in safely.

p. 24   **teaving:** throwing himself about.

p. 24   **Rot me:** let me rot.

p. 24   **up-sides with:** up to her standard.

p. 24   **gainsay:** deny, criticise.

p. 25   **horn-lanterns:** lanterns with pieces of translucent cow-horn instead of glass.

p. 26   **counter-boys:** altos or counter-tenors.

p. 26   **Farmer Ledlow's:** mentioned also in Hardy's poem 'Friends Beyond'.

p. 26   **metheglin:** spiced mead.

p. 26   **warmer:** saucepan.

p. 26   **church-hatch:** the north gate of the churchyard.

p. 26   **Manor:** Kingston Maurward House in Stinsford parish, the home of an aristocratic and wealthy family.

p. 27   **varmits:** rascals, objectionable things.

p. 27   **serpents:** large wind instruments with a deep bass register of notes coming from their three U-shaped turns.

p. 27   **hedger-and-ditcher's:** someone who cut the hedges and cleared the ditches.

p. 28   **Wicked One:** Satan, the devil.

p. 28   **rafting:** rousing.

p. 28   **dab:** expert.

p. 28   **dumbledores:** bumblebees.

p. 30   **thirty-nine and forty-three:** 1839 and 1843.

p. 32   **Froom:** the river Frome which flows around Dorchester, and then on to Stinsford (Mellstock) and finally into the sea near Wareham.

p. 33   **clinked off home-along:** went home making a clinking sound with his boots.

p. 33   **treble man:** the man who sings the tune.

p. 33   **scram:** silly, puny.

p. 34   **b'st:** are you.

p. 34   **snap:** a snack.

p. 34   **incumbent:** vicar.

p. 35   **gridiron:** a frame of iron bars for broiling food over a fire.

p. 36   **blacking:** black shoe polish.

p. 36   **screwed a little above concert-pitch:** the warmth in the church required this.

p. 37   **old brown music-books:** at a time when music was not available to them in printed form, the village musicians passed on the words and music from one to another and they were copied in manuscript into their music-books. Some of the Hardy family's music-books are preserved in the Dorset County Museum.

p. 37   **altar-tomb:** tomb with a top of flat rectangular stone covering it.

p. 37   **The gallery of Mellstock Church:** There is an interesting description of the arrangement of the singers and instrumentalists in the west gallery of Stinsford Church in *The Life and Work of Thomas Hardy* by Thomas Hardy (ed. M. Millgate) pp 14–15.

p. 37   **The clerk:** an official of the church who was employed to do various duties including leading the responses during the service.

p. 37   **dust-hole:** dustbin.

p. 37   studied the one which chronologically follows it: the Thanksgiving of Women after Childbirth.

p. 37   Pyramus and Thisbe: in Greek legend two separated lovers who talked to each other through a hole in the wall. The story is made fun of in Shakespeare's *A Midsummer Night's Dream*.

p. 38   churchwarden: a member of the church elected to assist the vicar and represent the parish in matters affecting the organisation of the church.

p. 39   capitals of the piers: flat protruding tops of the pillars.

p. 39   at sixes and sevens: without any kind of order.

p. 40   gentle or simple: the gentlefolk (the upper class) or the villagers.

p. 41   Shear-steel: a very high quality of steel fit for shears and cutting tools.

p. 42   turn after: take after, resemble.

p. 43   chimney-crook: a hook from which to suspend pots and kettles over a fire.

p. 43   like Cain: in the bible (Genesis 4) Adam's son, Cain, killed his brother, Abel.

p. 44   two slurs in music: a slur is an arched sign used in music to denote phrasing of notes.

p. 46   Jericho: used colloquially for a place far out of the way.

p. 46   cast off: a movement in the dance where a dancer moves down the line of dancers.

p. 47   hands-across: partners in the dance clasp hands.

p. 47   six-hands-round: a six-handed reel which Hardy is said to have named as 'The College Hornpipe'.

p. 48   pot-housey: like the kind of thing that might happen in a low-class public house (pot-house).

p. 48   stout: strong, vigorous.

p. 49   sit up on old Midsummer Eves: 'It was supposed that if an unmarried woman, fasting, laid a cloth at midnight with bread and cheese and sat down as if to eat, leaving the street-door open, the person she was to marry would come into the room and drink to her by bowing . . .' (R. Chambers, *The Book of Days*, 1866)

p. 49   **a taking**: a bewitched state.

p. 50   **by-long and by-late**: in the end.

p. 50   **miff**: quarrel.

p. 50   **go snacks with**: go shares with him, get married.

p. 50   **mid**: might.

p. 51   **village sharpener**: village schoolmistress and, therefore, sharpener of wits!

p. 51   **'Dead March'**: Handel's march from his oratorio, *Saul*, frequently played at funerals.

p. 51   **last trump**: he means the last trumpet-note of the 'Last Post', the bugle-call played at military funerals.

p. 52   **Dree Mariners**: the Three Mariners. A public house which was at one time located in the High Street, Dorchester.

p. 52   **lights**: lungs, usually of a calf.

p. 52   **chawing**: chewing.

p. 52   **common time**: four-four time, a march rhythm.

p. 53   *pro tem*: for the time being (Latin *pro tempore*).

p. 54   **Nasmyth hammer**: a steam hammer invented by James Nasmyth in 1839.

p. 54   **lime-basket**: a basket used for carrying quicklime which is particularly caustic.

p. 54   **as long-favoured as a fiddle**: as long, because of her tiredness, as a fiddle.

p. 55   **wind up the clock**: wind up the grandfather clock by drawing up the pendulum.

p. 56   **'cross-dadder'**: a children's game of touch.

p. 62   **Moroni**: Giambattista Moroni (c.1525–78) was an Italian painter. Hardy would have known his portrait of a tailor in the London National Gallery.

p. 62 gawk-hammer: a silly man.

p. 63 Old Eccl'iastes: Ecclesiastes the preacher, the pen-name of the writer of the Book of that name in the Bible,

p. 63 spouter: orator.

p. 63 Herculean: Hercules was a Greek mythological hero of great strength.

p. 63 Tory ... Whiggism: the two great political parties of those days. The Tories roughly corresponded to the Conservatives of today, the Whigs to the Liberals.

p. 64 mumbudgeting: unexpectedly, unannounced.

p. 64 pitch-halfpenny: a game played by pitching coins into a hole in the ground.

p. 65 borus-snorus: going ahead without worrying about other people's opinions.

p. 65 Titanic: colossal. The Titans were Greek mythological characters of a giant race.

p. 65 drong: a narrow passage between two walls or hedges.

p. 65 full-buff: face to face.

p. 65 strent: slit.

p. 68 spar: a wooden split stick used for fastening down thatch on to roofs.

p. 69 het: gulp down, swallow.

p. 70 arrant: errand.

p. 70 Tranter Dewy ... left: Hardy is probably alluding to the Bible (Joshua 23:6): 'Be ye therefore very courageous to keep and to do all that is written in the book of the law of Moses, that ye turn not aside therefrom to the right hand or to the left.'

p. 72 like chips in porridge: a proverbial saying for something that does neither good nor bad. Chips here means straws.

p. 72 good-now: sure enough.

p. 75   **Laodicean:** in the Bible Saint John found the church at Laodicea 'neither cold nor hot' in spirit (Revelation 3:14–16).

p. 76   **quat:** squat.

p. 78   **Michaelmas:** St Michael's day, 29 September.

p. 78   **thik gr't:** this great.

p. 79   **mischty:** mischief.

p. 79   **stud:** quandary.

p. 80   **can't onriddle her:** can't make her out, understand her.

p. 80   **twister:** someone hard to understand.

p. 80   **ink-bottle chaps:** office workers.

p. 81   **spring-cart:** a cart mounted on springs.

p. 81   **Yalbury Wood:** Hardy's name for Yellowham Wood, between Dorchester and Puddletown.

p. 81   **Casterbridge:** Hardy's name for Dorchester.

p. 82   **riser:** the vertical part of a step.

p. 82   **Noah:** in the Bible the animals in Noah's ark were all in pairs (Genesis 7).

p. 83   **dumb-waiters:** a central pole around which revolved a series of trays which carried the food and did not, therefore, require the services of a waiter.

p. 83   **warming-pans:** long-handled copper pans holding hot coals for inserting between the sheets of a bed.

p. 84   **pot-luck:** what happens to be in the pot for a meal, without special preparation.

p. 85   **kick up Bob's-a-dying:** make a great fuss.

p. 87   **raw-mil' cheese:** cheese made from raw milk and, because it has not been separated from its cream, very rich.

p. 88   **union:** workhouse for destitute persons.

p. 88   **delf:** glazed earthenware originally made at Delft in Holland.

p. 89 **poachest, jailest:** most given to poaching and most likely to end up in prison. They are words made up by Hardy.

p. 89 **charwoman:** woman paid by the hour to do the chores, i.e. the housework.

p. 90 **fire-irons:** the tongs, pokers and shovels used to control the fire.

p. 91 **pitcher:** earthenware jug.

p. 91 **muslin:** delicately woven cotton material.

p. 93 **handpost:** signpost.

p. 94 **'Od rot:** a euphemistic way of saying, 'God rot'.

p. 94 **they be all alike ... flourishes:** Hardy uses architectural images to have Reuben say that women are all basically alike and differ only in the 'flourishes', i.e. education, money, etc.

p. 94 **nation:** damnation.

p. 95 **Turk:** an exclamation with no particular meaning.

p. 96 **garden hatch:** a small garden gate.

p. 96 **White Tuesday:** the Tuesday after Whit (or White) Sunday, so called because many christenings in white robes took place on that day.

p. 96 **Mellstock Club walked:** the villages had local benefit clubs which held walks at Whitsun.

p. 96 **white-lyvered:** cowardly. The liver was at one time thought to be the seat of courage.

p. 96 **cappel-faced:** white faced with patches of red.

p. 96 **bitter weed:** cause of the trouble.

p. 98 **Budmouth Regis:** Hardy's name for Weymouth.

p. 103 **near the King's statue:** George III who by his many visits to Weymouth made it a famous and successful seaside resort or watering-place.

p. 103 **chairmen:** men who pushed the invalids and others in bath chairs.

p. 104 **burgesses:** townspeople.

p. 105 **mantle:** cloak.

p. 106 journeymen-carpenters: craftsmen who were hired by the day.

p. 107 quartering: pulling to the side of the road.

p. 107 gig: light two-wheeled, one-horse carriage.

p. 109 the Ship: the inn is still there today. It is also mentioned in Hardy's poem 'Great Things'.

p. 110 *tête-à-tête*: confidential conversation.

p. 112 dog-cart: open two-wheeled vehicle with back-to-back seats. They were originally used for carrying sporting dogs under the seats.

p. 112 crane-flies: often known as daddy-long-legs.

p. 114 stale, flat and unprofitable: from Shakespeare's *Hamlet* (1:2, 133–4).

p. 114 the fall of an apple: a humorous echo of Eve's eating the apple in Paradise.

p. 115 bird-lime: a sticky substance made from holly bark for catching small birds which were then kept in cages as pets.

p. 118 like female idlers round a bonnet-shop: note how imaginative and appropriate Hardy's images nearly always are.

p. 123 near-foot-afore: the left foreleg.

p. 124 scullery: a back-kitchen used for preparing food, washing dishes and washing clothes.

p. 126 two pecks: a peck is a measure of capacity with one peck equal to about nine litres.

p. 126 Venus: the goddess of love in Roman mythology.

p. 127 'Why are you wandering here, I pray?': said to have been one of Hardy's mother's favourite folk-songs.

p. 128 at the going down of the sun: probably an allusion to the Bible (Daniel 6:14): '. . . and he laboured till the going down of the sun to deliver him.'

p. 128 Latin crosses: an upright cross with the lowest limb longest.

p. 130 bide: wait.

p. 131   horehound: a herb with bitter aromatic juice used for coughs and colds.

p. 132   'King Arthur . . .': a well-known ballad. Hardy described it as coarsely humorous, as many of these old ballads and folk-songs were.

p. 132   broadcloth: a fine woollen black cloth.

p. 133   Hartshorn: a substance which was obtained from the antlers of deer and was formerly the chief source of ammonia.

p. 134   unrind: undress.

p. 135   I'd as lief: I'd rather.

p. 135   landed family's nursery: a landed family was one which owned land.

p. 135   keeper: game-keeper.

p. 135   irons in the fire: undertakings.

p. 136   Queen's scholars: Queen's scholarships were awarded to poor pupils to allow them to train as teachers. They began in 1846.

p. 137   Endorfield: an allusion to the witch of Endor in the Bible (1 Samuel 28:7).

p. 140   diaphanous: very thin.

p. 140   emmet: ant.

p. 140   the three creations: the creation of fowls and fishes, the beasts and man, as described in the Bible (Genesis 1).

p. 14   o'small: of light ale.

p. 141   affronted: upset by being sold bad meat.

p. 142   mother-law: i.e. stepmother.

p. 143   studding: daydreaming.

p. 143   turn chapel-member: leave the Church of England for one of the dissenting sects worshipping in chapels.

p. 143   traypse and wamble: wander to and fro aimlessly.

p. 146   'Though this has come upon us . . .': a somewhat condensed form of Psalm 44: 17–18.

p. 147 **Ham-hill stone:** from limestone quarries near Yeovil in Somerset. Hardy's father, a stonemason, used stone from there.

p. 148 **japanning:** a covering of a kind of varnish which was originally brought from Japan.

p. 151 **foot-post:** a postman who collected the letters on foot.

p. 153 **hands:** horses are measured by 'hands', each hand being about ten centimetres.

p. 153 **twenty-five want a crown:** £25 minus 5 shillings (25p), i.e. £24.75.

p. 153 **Grey's Bridge:** the stone bridge just outside Dorchester which Hardy knew well as it was on the way to and from his home at Bockhampton. Like Maybold, Michael Henchard stands on Grey's Bridge in *The Mayor of Casterbridge*.

p. 159 **'The Knot There's No Untying':** part of a poem from a song by Thomas Campbell (1777–1844) entitled 'How Delicious is the Winning!'

p. 160 **banns:** notices of intended marriage read out in church. The banns are read on three successive Sundays and provide an opportunity to object if everything is not in order.

p. 160 **called home:** when the banns were read.

p. 161 **coling:** cuddling, embracing.

p. 161 **churching:** the Churching of women, after childbirth.

p. 163 **ting:** make a ringing sound to encourage the swarming bees.

p. 163 **... for the love and the stalled ox both:** a reference to the Bible (Proverbs 15:17): 'Better is a dinner of herbs where love is, than a stalled ox and hatred therewith.' This suggests that Dick and Fancy will have both true love and material benefits in their married life.

p. 163 **was ceiled:** had a ceiling.

p. 164 **apotheosised:** glorified like a goddess.

p. 166 **march two and two . . .:** an old local custom after a wedding.

p. 166 **Bath clogs:** wooden-soled shoes made in Bath.

p. 168 **'Can a maid . . . attire?':** see the Bible (Jeremiah 2:32).

p. 168   Weatherbury stocks: Hardy's name for Puddletown. The stocks were a wooden frame with holes in which wrongdoers were locked as a punishment in public places.

p. 169   avoid ... 'thee' and 'thou': Hardy is being ironical about Fancy's snobbery. He deplored the dying of the old dialects.

p. 170   Tantrum Clangley: an imaginary place with a name suggesting a great deal of noise.

p. 170   gaffers and gammers: old men and women.

p. 171   chainey: china.

p. 172   Chanticleer's comb is a-cut: a proverbial expression meaning that when the cock's comb is cut things are less showy. Chanticleer is a traditional name for the farmyard cock who in his strutting about seems so conceited and 'cocky'.

p. 172   put the stuns upon: check, hamper.

p. 173   elder-wine: made from elderberries.

p. 174   'tis the nightingale: the nightingale is at once a symbol of happiness and a reminder of the sad Greek tale of Philomela, who was ravished and then had her tongue cut out so that she could tell no one her story. She was eventually turned into a nightingale. Fancy thinks of Philomela and of a secret she will never tell.

Our Exploits at West Poley

p. 179   title: East and West Poley are imaginary places but Hardy tells the reader that the action takes place in 'the bowels of the Mendip hills – a range of limestone rocks stretching from the shores of the Bristol Channel into the middle of Somersetshire.'

p. 179   Carlyle said of Cromwell: Thomas Carlyle (1795–1881), historian and essayist, published *Letters and Speeches of Oliver Cromwell* in 1845.

p. 181   stalactites: icicle-like pendants hanging from a cave roof.

p. 182   stalagmite: icicle-like form growing up from the floor of a cave and formed by drips from the roof or from a stalactite.

p. 183   Stygian: in Greek mythology the river Styx was one of the rivers of the underworld. The dead were ferried across on their way to Hades (hell) by Charon.

p. 184 **purling:** flowing with a murmuring sound.

p. 184 **dryshod:** without wetting the feet.

p. 185 **freehold:** i.e. he owned it without any debts to others.

p. 186 **Sabbath:** Sunday.

p. 186 **Hannah Dominy:** the miller's attempt at 'anno Domini' which means 'in the year of our Lord'.

p. 186 **loach . . . dace:** small species of fish.

p. 189 **reel:** a lively and popular dance for two or more couples.

p. 191 **indentures:** his legal contract with the miller which governed the condition of his apprenticeship.

p. 192 **white wizard:** a wizard who uses witchcraft for good purposes.

p. 192 **Jeremy Bentham:** Bentham (1748–1832) was a distinguished writer on law and politics. His fundamental principle was described as 'utilitarianism – the greatest happiness of the greatest number'.

p. 192 **Hamlet to the Ghost:** see Shakespeare's *Hamlet* I.V.

p. 193 **Yeomanry Cavalry:** a cavalry volunteer force formed during the Napoleonic War.

p. 193 *carte blanche*: permission.

p. 195 **Hi . . . horum:** Latin words learnt by the boys at school and with no meaning in this context.

p. 199 **interlocutors:** the two men involved in conversation.

p. 206 **Flaminius, the consul:** Caius Flaminius, a Roman general and politician who died in 217BC. He was defeated by Hannibal and killed at Lake Trasimeme.

p. 207 **adipose:** fatty.

p. 208 **body and soul:** an interesting insight into life for an apprentice at this time.

p. 209 **zounds:** an exclamation of anger. It is a euphemism and corruption of 'God's wounds'.

p. 219 **Romans ... Samnites:** the Romans had a number of wars with the Samnites. An entire Roman army was captured at the Caudine Forks (two passes in the mountains of Samnium) in 321BC.

p. 222 **Coleridge ... Emmerson:** Samuel Taylor Coleridge (1772–1834) was an English poet, philosopher and literary critic. Ralph Waldo Emerson (1803–82) was an American philosopher.

p. 223 **liever:** rather.

p. 224 **gentle and simple:** both those of social standing and the workfolk.

Tony Kytes, The Arch-Deceiver

p. 229 **'The Tailor's Breeches':** because tailors had particular opportunities of being with women they were the subject of very many bawdy folk-songs of which this was one of the most popular.

p. 230 **Upper Longpuddle:** probably Piddletrenthide, a village along the valley of the river Piddle several miles from Puddletown.

p. 234 **nunnywatch:** stupid situation, predicament.

p. 235 **swound:** fainting fit.

p. 235 **Lower Longpuddle:** this is probably Piddlehinton which is further down the valley of the River Piddle than Piddletrenthide.

p. 236 **if yer virtue ... risk:** if she is not in danger of finding herself pregnant. This was omitted from the first magazine publication of the story.

Andrey Satchel and the Parson and Clerk

p. 237 **other bodily circumstances:** she was pregnant.

p. 237 **Port Bredy:** Hardy's name for Bridport.

p. 238 **wambling:** unsteady.

p. 238 **keeping up:** celebrating.

p. 238 **book:** the prayer book containing the marriage service.

p. 239 **Van Amburgh's horses:** Van Amburgh was an American menagerie owner who was in England about that time.

p. 239 tole: entice.

p. 240 gentleman in pink and top-boots: the red (pink) jacket and his boots are the formal dress of a huntsman.

p. 240 tide-times: religious anniversaries and festivals.

p. 240 tops: riding top-boots.

p. 240 going to earth: hiding in their burrows.

p. 240 whipper-in: an assistant huntsman who with his whip keeps the hounds from straying.

p. 240 going to cover: taking part in the hunt.

p. 240 frantical: wildly and passionately.

p. 240 bedding: planting out in beds.

p. 240 cob: a short-legged, strong horse.

p. 240 meet: the meeting-place of the hunt.

p. 241 found: found the scent of a fox.

p. 241 threw off: were released to find and follow the scent.

p. 241 persuasion: religious beliefs.

p. 242 Amen ... Ever-and-ever: many Christian prayers end with 'for ever and ever, Amen'.

p. 242 To ... season: from the Bible (Ecclesiastes 3).

p. 242 as a pa'son should: the irony is very pointed here.

p. 242 a' amble: at an easy pace.

p. 243 quarter-sessions: a court held quarterly by justices of the peace.

p. 243 church-hatch: the door, divided into an upper and a lower half, leading into the church.

p. 244 leery: hungry.

p. 244 I can ... my backbone: Hardy endows his rustic characters with a fine turn of language when required.

p. 244 the knot was tied: Hardy is again referring to Thomas

Campbell's song, 'How Delicious is the Winning!', in which marriage is described as 'the knot there's no untying'.

p. 245 saved her name: i.e. by being married before the baby was born.

Old Andrey's Experience as a Musician

p. 245 Giant o'Cernel: a large chalk figure cut into the hill near the village of Cerne Abbas in Dorset.

p. 246 mem: madame.

p. 246 nut: the ridge at the top of the finger-board of the violin.

p. 246 tail-piece: the strip of ebony to which the strings of the violin are attached.

p. 247 teetotaller: one who doesn't touch alcoholic drinks.

p. 247 the organ ... a winch: as we read later, this is some kind of barrel-organ that plays music automatically when a winch or handle is turned.

Absent-Mindedness in a Parish Choir

p. 247 Mellstock ... Dewys: Hardy is using his *Under the Greenwood Tree* characters again.

p. 248 hornpipe: a lively dance, formerly popular among sailors.

p. 248 out of hand: straight out, extempore.

p. 248 Absolution ... Creed: the Absolution is the pardoning of sins by the parson, the Creed the statement of religious belief made by the congregation.

p. 248 Evening Hymn: Bishop Thomas Ken (1637–1711) wrote the Morning Hymn, 'Awake, My soul', and the Evening Hymn, 'Glory to Thee, My God, This Night'.

p. 249 Sodom and Gomorrah: in the Bible (Genesis 19) God destroys these two wicked cities with brimstone and fire.

p. 249 (he ... side): a great deal about the squire's character and behaviour is conveyed here very economically.

p. 249 me ... God Almighty: it is significant that God comes last!

HARDY AND HIS CRITICS

In *The Life and Work of Thomas Hardy* by Thomas Hardy (ed. Michael Millgate), we are told that *Under the Greenwood Tree* was published about the last week in May 1872 and met with a very kindly and gentle reception, being reviewed in the *Athenaeum* (15 June 1872) as a book which could induce people 'to give up valuable time to see a marriage accomplished in its pages', and in the *Pall Mall Gazette* as 'a story of much freshness and originality'. After his disappointment with some of the reviews of his first novel, *Desperate Remedies*, this must have encouraged Hardy to persevere in his plan to give up architecture and become a fulltime novelist. The *Athenaeum* review admired the novel's 'graphic pictures of rural life' and saw it as 'simply the history of a young man's courtship of a young woman', simply a simplification of a story which has far more to offer than just that. The review liked the author's humour but found fault with Hardy's tendency to 'make his characters now and then drop their personality, and speak too much like educated people'.

Hardy's friend and mentor, Horace Moule, in the *Saturday Review* (28 September 1872) began by asserting that 'This novel is the best prose idyll that we have seen for a long while past.' He particularly liked 'the power and truthfulness shown in these studies of the better class of rustics, men whose isolated lives have not impaired a shrewd common sense and insight, together with a complete independence, set off by native humour . . .' He continues:

> *Under the Greenwood Tree* is filled with touches showing the close sympathy with which the writer has watched the life, not only of his fellow-men in the country hamlets, but of woods and fields and all the outward forms of nature. But the staple of the book is made up of personal sketches, the foremost figure, as we have said, being of the 'tranter' Dewy, a man 'full of human

nature', fond of broaching his cider with his village friends about him, straightforward and out-spoken, yet inclined from good nature towards compromise, not however to the excessive degree that his duties as publican imposed upon Mr Snell in *Silas Marner*. Grouped around the tranter are several figures, all distinctive and good in their way, the chief of whom are old William Dewy, the grandfather, and the leader in all things musical, Mr Penny the bootmaker, and Thomas Leaf, who sang treble in the choir at a preternaturally late date, and whose upper 'G' could not be dispensed with, though he was otherwise 'deficient', and awkward in his movements, 'apparently on account of having grown so fast that before he had time to grow used to his height he was higher'.

It is a sign of what Hardy was up against that the *Pall Mall Gazette* (5 July 1872) found the story 'considerably marred by an episode regarding the vicar which destroys the simple character of the tale'.

In 1881 an anonymous review in the *British Quarterly Review* was full of praise for *Under the Greenwood Tree* and commented on the fact that Hardy was less well known 'than some far inferior people' because 'somewhat of his own wide sympathy with nature, and with the simpler forms of country life, is needed before he is read and understood'. Hardy is seen, like Barnes, as

> sprung of a race of labouring men in a county where the real old families are attached to the soil, and the county aristocracy, except perhaps in Purbeck, are comparatively new comers; that he is not 'too proud to care from whence he came', that, on the contrary, he regards his stock as reason for exceeding pride on two grounds – one the dignity of labour, the other that the country working-man is of nearer kin to that nature which he idealizes and personifies, till it has all the characteristics of some great supra-natural human being – that he is thus anthropomorphic, but not in a theological sense, is apparent on the face of what he writes.

J. M. Barrie in the *Contemporary Review* (July 1889) expresses the then generally accepted view that *Under the Greenwood Tree* 'is not Hardy's greatest book, but from the appearance of Dick Dewey to the nightingale scene, it is his most perfect . . .' Perhaps this view of the novel is best expressed in Annie Macdonell's book *Thomas Hardy*, published in 1894:

Under the Greenwood Tree ... is plainly in one line with the series of the principal novels; but it is, as plainly, a book that does not reach the tall level of its successors. It is, indeed, the porch through which one enters directly into the main body of Hardy's work, to see the whole length of the building stretching beyond. There is no large construction of narrative in this novel; we may regard it as a preliminary statement of the kind of material and, still more, the kind of spirit, which are to be more greatly and more elaborately used later. But it would be a strange mistake in judgment to value *Under the Greenwood Tree* only as the porch to the rest, and not for its own separate, and exquisite, sake. The rustic love of life, finely coloured by the rustic stoical acceptance of life's evils, is realised in this story with more profundity, perhaps, than might be expected from the even good-nature of it all. The characters do not do much, but they admirably live; the figures of the Mellstock quire, moving with deliberate humour through the scenes of this naive comedy, obviously come from a hand that has gained a notable plastic mastery over the human substance. And few books take their readers into closer friendship with the earth. The author's genius has nothing more to learn in the way of controlling the skill of the talent submitted to it; the powers here employed need only a deeper intellectual adventurousness in the invention of theme, to become altogether adequate to the great work soon to be required of them.

When Edmund Gosse in 1901 described *Under the Greenwood Tree* as 'an experiment carried out with complete success', he carried into the new century a view of the novel which had been almost universally accepted since its publication and was to continue to be so until a more serious critical approach to all of Hardy's novels began in the middle of the century. Until then it is true to say that *Under the Greenwood Tree* had been greatly admired but not looked at in depth. It had seemed unfair and unnecessary to submit what seemed to be such a light-hearted piece of work to the kind of criticism which *Tess* and *Jude* demanded. However, since 1950 there has been a substantial amount written about the novel, and not all of it has carried on the nineteenth-century estimate of its worth.

Albert Guerard in 1950 thought that it was 'stylized' while Dr Leavis in *Scutiny* thought that it was 'so poor a novel' that its popularity must have resulted from 'a painstaking application of rural local colour', but then Dr Leavis was peculiarly insensitive to any writer who did not qualify for his 'Great Tradition', and he was one of several critics who could not forgive Hardy for not writing the kind of book they think he ought to have written. Thus in 1974 Geoffrey Grigson accused Hardy of patronising Fancy, and in 1975 of patronising his 'peasant characters'. The same accusation could be made against many of Shakespeare's working-class people and it fails to recognise that Shakespeare and Hardy were writing for a certain kind of audience in a certain kind of context, and, as Hardy once wrote, 'had he told the truth about village life no one would have believed him'. He might have added that he would never have been published by middle-class publishers who were providing novels for middle-class readers if he had turned his novels into depictions of the poverty, hardship and cruelty of life among the agricultural workers.

However, as several critics have pointed out, there is much to admire in the rustic characters in *Under the Greenwood Tree*. There is a warmth, kindness, community spirit and an ability of the characters to enjoy themselves which adds greatly to the novel's attraction. Arnold Kettle in 1966 saw 'a contradiction between conservative and radical in the novel'. Other critics have pointed out that this was no 'contradiction'. It was the result of Hardy's ability to see the ambivalences and ambiguities in life, and it was this which was part of his greatness.

More balanced and positive criticism has come from other critics, and this has enabled us to read *Under the Greenwood Tree* with a much greater appreciation of the reasons for accepting it as a serious work of art. Norman Page in an article called 'Hardy's Dutch Painting' in the 1975 *Thomas Hardy Year Book* reveals how misleading it can be to concentrate too much on the novel's subtitle 'A Rural Painting of the Dutch School':

> Whatever the origins of the subtitle, however – and one further suggestion will be offered shortly – critics have been apt to take it at its face value and to obey Hardy's apparent directions to judge the novel by the standards of realistic art. Its earliest critics, including Hardy's close friend Horace Moule, who reviewed it in the *Saturday Review*, were able to fault it for failing to live up to the standards of realism, notably in some of the dialogue. This is to ignore, however, the main title as finally determined, with its

Shakespearian allusion and its associations with pastoral romance. In *As You Like It* the Forest of Arden is seen primarily (though not exclusively) as offering an idyllic escape from responsibility and from the corrupt world of the court. To take the hint of the main title in conjunction with that of the subtitle is to understand Hardy as offering simultaneously both romance and realism, and as demanding from his readers a correspondingly flexible approach. The point is worth stressing because he continued to make similar demands in his later novels. What can be specifically argued with respect to *Under the Greenwood Tree* is that, whilst the pictorial mode of presentation is widely used, the parallel with realistic painting put forward by the subtitle does not provide an adequate analogy to the kind of narrative and descriptive art which is in question.

He then suggests that there are relationships with schools of painting other than the Dutch. The description of Fancy Day, for example, when she is first seen 'framed as in a picture' recalls paintings of the Pre-Raphaelite school.

In an essay in his *Thomas Hardy: Art and Thought* (1977) Frank Pinion looks closely at Hardy's humour and finds it already 'full-blown' at this early stage of his career. One of his characteristics is 'the care taken to individualise his characters by visual reference to idiosyncratic movements and attitudes; in this respect Mr Spinks, once in charge of a night school, and with a reputation for learning and intelligence to maintain, makes an interesting little study wherever he seeks to say something profound and striking.' Another characteristic is the 'introduction of little *ad hoc* anecdotes such as that of Michael Mail's unfortunate friendly nod to an auctioneer'. Dr Pinion is particularly good on Hardy's ending of the novel:

The view that the story of Dick Dewy and Fancy Day is pregnant with mischief and bodes ill for the future of the married couple ... has soon become a literary cliché. The 'possibility of tragedy lies just under the surface', Hillis Miller writes. This may mean that a situation develops to which the author could easily have given a tragic turn, but all that matters is what Hardy created and intended within the limits of his novel. There can be no doubt about the ending if all factors are considered, and they are secondary to the spirit which animates the book as a whole. One could never accuse the tranter of taking his son's falling in love over-seriously (as Melbury does the question of his daughter's marriage in *The Woodlanders*), even though he says that Dick is a 'lost man'; nor is Hardy's humour 'cynical' when he adds: 'The tranter turned a quarter round and smiled a smile of miserable satire at the setting new moon, which happened to catch his eye.' This description (amusing in its context and a worthy subject for *Punch*) reflects the rustic's traditional philosophy on marriage. When Dick tells him that he repeats what 'all the common world says', the tranter avers, 'The world's a very sensible feller on things in jineral, Dick; very sensible indeed.' The 'world' is a group of grown-ups who meet in and around Mellstock; and their point of view, handed on from one generation to another, provides the groundwork of much of the humour in *Under the Greenwood Tree*. Hardy is not an idyllic sentimentalist; on the subject of marriage he is happy to present the world's view (it is largely an affection or stock response, the humour of which is plain) and laugh at it.

No one in recent years has written more informatively and perceptively about *Under the Greenwood Tree* than Simon Gatrell, and his pages on that novel in his *Hardy the Creator* (1988) are well worth reading for their description of its textual development, and the light this throws on Hardy's intentions. Here is a passage:

> What the working numeration shows is that throughout Hardy's early writing of the novel, and even during his fair-copying of it, *Under the Greenwood Tree* was a narrative which focused almost entirely on the characters making up the Mellstock choir, and on the loss of their church music-making. The story had a rather perfunctory love-plot attached to it, in which there was some uncertainty as to whether Dick Dewy the tranter's son or the innkeeper Fred Shiner would marry Fancy Day the schoolteacher. In the end we discover that Dick was successful, thanks to Fancy's stratagem of nearly starving herself to death for love.
>
> It is impossible to know whether Hardy, reviewing what he had written some time in the summer of 1871, realized himself that as it stood his story would have scant interest for the middle-class female readership who stimulated the circulating libraries into buying multiple copies of novels, or whether he showed the newly copied manuscript to someone else, who suggested to him that if

he really wanted to sell the story he would have to bring the romance to the foreground.

The dualism in the story is explored in some detail in a chapter in Marjorie Garson's *Hardy's Fables of Integrity*. She points out that the main title, *Under the Greenwood Tree*, identifies the novel as pastoral while 'A Rural Painting of the Dutch School' suggests realism:

> The world of Mellstock is a green but not a golden one: time and death are found here, along with courtship and marriage. Hardy deliberately qualifies the ideals of traditional pastoral by setting them against the real, though now extinct, world of Dorset in the 1840s ... Set against Dick's 'pastoral' romanticism is the older generation's accommodation to an imperfect world. Hardy feels affection and respect for those individuals who endure life's exigencies with generosity, compassion, and good humour, accept their fellow men unjudgmentally, and embrace the community at large with an inclusive kindliness. *Under the Greenwood Tree* is based on Hardy's memories of his own father and grandfather; it is about fathers, and about various kinds of fatherhood. The three fathers in the novel – William Dewy, Reuben Dewy, and Geoffrey Day – are alike in ways which reflect the novel's moral values. All three embody an unselfconscious, untheoretical Christianity which takes life as it comes and people as they are.

Professor Garson is particularly interesting in her observations about the part played by women in the novel:

> Every woman desires marriage, and if she sets her mind to it, almost any woman can get it – as Geoffrey Day says grimly about his second wife. 'Doom is nothing beside a elderly woman.' And getting one of their own married is something that women as a group somehow mysteriously succeed in doing. Moving towards marriage means tapping the power of the collective female will. At the opportune moment, Fancy finds herself a surrogate mother readily enough, learning from the 'witch' Elizabeth Endorfield how to exploit her father's good nature. And on her wedding day she begins to identify, apparently for the first time, with her own mother, acceding to some of the old-fashioned customs because 'Mother did'. Is the comic irony here at Fancy's expense, suggesting that as she pairs off and joins the procreative throng of couples, she loses her uniqueness and becomes assimilated to the

world of her parents? Or is it at Dick's, suggesting that when the ceremony is over the essential solidarity of all women with one another will reveal itself with a new explicitness? Certainly Fancy's determination to do things 'as Mother did' is not a promising sign for Dick, since the one thing that all three mothers in this novel share is the conviction that they have married beneath them; but then it has already been made clear that Fancy thinks she has too. In their condescension towards husbands, it seems women are united. It is significant that the only occasion on which women are shown acting as a group is the gathering of the bridesmaids and mothers on the day of the wedding – a ritual of female solidarity treated with broad and somewhat hostile irony by the narrator.

It seems a pity that such a sensitive critic should accept without question the view of a feminist, marxist critic that in using the name 'Dick', Hardy was indulging in a sexual pun. There is no evidence whatsoever that he was aware of the slang connotations of the word, and the dictionaries of slang I have consulted provide no examples of its use in this way before 1900.

SUGGESTIONS FOR FURTHER READING

Readers who wish to know more about Hardy's life and times should read Hardy's autobiography, *The Life and Work of Thomas Hardy* edited by Michael Millgate (Macmillan, 1984). The standard biography is now Michael Millgate's *Thomas Hardy: A Biography* (Oxford, 1982). A short biography is *Thomas Hardy: A Literary Life* by James Gibson (Macmillan, 1996).

Criticism

The following is a brief selection from the very many books on Hardy's writings. Most of them say something about *Under the Greenwood Tree*.

Jean Brooks, *Thomas Hardy: The Poetic Structure* (Cornell University, 1971).

Lance St John Butler (ed.), *Thomas Hardy after Fifty Years* (Macmillan, 1977).

R. G. Cox, *Thomas Hardy: The Critical Heritage* (Routledge & Kegan Paul, 1970).

R. P. Draper (ed.), *Thomas Hardy: Three Pastoral Novels* (Macmillan, 1987).

Ralph Elliott, *Thomas Hardy's English* (Blackwell, 1984).

Marjorie Garson, *Hardy's Fables of Integrity* (Oxford, 1991).

Simon Gatrell, *Hardy the Creator* (Oxford, 1988).

Ian Gregor, *The Great Web: The Form of Hardy's Major Fiction* (Faber, 1974).

Irving Howe, *Thomas Hardy* (Macmillan, 1967).

Dale Kramer (ed.), *Approaches to the Fiction of Thomas Hardy* (Macmillan, 1979).

Michael Millgate, *Thomas Hardy: His Career as a Novelist* (Macmillan, 1994).

Rosemarie Morgan, *Women and Sexuality in the Novels of Thomas Hardy* (Routledge, 1988).

Roy Morrell, *Thomas Hardy: The Will and the Way* (Oxford, 1965).

Norman Page, *Thomas Hardy* (Routledge & Kegan Paul, 1977).

F. B. Pinion, *Thomas Hardy: Art and Thought* (Macmillan, 1977).

Anne Smith (ed.), *The Novels of Thomas Hardy* (Vision, 1979).

Rosemary Sumner, *Thomas Hardy: Psychological Novelist* (Macmillan, 1981).

ACKNOWLEDGEMENTS

The editor and publishers wish to thank the following for permission to use copyright material:

Oxford University Press for material from Marjorie Garson, *Hardy's Fables of Integrity* (1991), Clarendon Press.

Every effort has been made to trace all the copyright holders but if any have been inadvertently overlooked the publishers will be pleased to make the necessary arrangement at the first opportunity.

CLASSIC NOVELS
IN EVERYMAN

The Time Machine
H. G. WELLS
*One of the books which defined
'science fiction' – a compelling
and tragic story of a brilliant
and driven scientist*
£3.99

Oliver Twist
CHARLES DICKENS
*Arguably the best-loved of
Dickens's novels. With all the
original illustrations*
£4.99

Barchester Towers
ANTHONY TROLLOPE
*The second of Trollope's
Chronicles of Barsetshire,
and one of the funniest of all
Victorian novels*
£4.99

The Heart of Darkness
JOSEPH CONRAD
*Conrad's most intense, subtle,
compressed, profound and
proleptic work*
£3.99

Tess of the d'Urbervilles
THOMAS HARDY
*The powerful, poetic classic
of wronged innocence*
£3.99

Wuthering Heights and Poems
EMILY BRONTË
*A powerful work of genius – one of
the great masterpieces of literature*
£3.99

Pride and Prejudice
JANE AUSTEN
*Proposals, rejections, infidelities,
elopements, happy marriages –
Jane Austen's most popular novel*
£2.99

North and South
ELIZABETH GASKELL
*A novel of hardship, passion
and hard-won wisdom amidst the
conflicts of the industrial revolution*
£4.99

The Newcomes
W. M. THACKERAY
*An exposé of Victorian polite
society by one of the nineteenth-
century's finest novelists*
£6.99

Adam Bede
GEORGE ELIOT
*A passionate rural drama enacted
at the turn of the eighteenth
century*
£5.99

All books are available from your local bookshop or direct from:
Littlehampton Book Services Cash Sales, 14 Eldon Way, Lineside Estate,
Littlehampton, West Sussex BN17 7HE (*prices are subject to change*)

To order any of the books, please enclose a cheque (in sterling) made payable to
Littlehampton Book Services, or phone your order through with credit card details (Access,
Visa or Mastercard) on 01903 721596 (24 hour answering service) stating card number
and expiry date. (*Please add £1.25 for package and postage to the total of your order.*)

In the USA, for further information and a complete catalogue call 1-800-526-2778

CLASSIC FICTION
IN EVERYMAN

**The Impressions of
Theophrastus Such**
GEORGE ELIOT
*An amusing collection of character
sketches, and the only paperback
edition available*
£5.99

Frankenstein
MARY SHELLEY
*A masterpiece of Gothic terror in
its original 1818 version*
£3.99

East Lynne
MRS HENRY WOOD
*A classic tale of melodrama,
murder and mystery*
£7.99

**Holiday Romance and
Other Writings for Children**
CHARLES DICKENS
*Dickens's works for children,
including 'The Life of Our Lord'
and 'A Child's History of England',
with original illustrations*
£5.99

The Ebb-Tide
R. L. STEVENSON
*A compelling study of ordinary
people in extreme circumstances*
£4.99

The Three Impostors
ARTHUR MACHEN
*The only edition available
of this cult thriller*
£4.99

Mister Johnson
JOYCE CARY
*The only edition available of this
amusing but disturbing twentieth-
century tale*
£5.99

The Jungle Book
RUDYARD KIPLING
*The classic adventures of Mowgli
and his friends*
£3.99

Glenarvon
LADY CAROLINE LAMB
*The only edition available of the
novel which throws light on the
greatest scandal of the early nineteenth century – the infatuation of
Caroline Lamb with Lord Byron*
£6.99

**Twenty Thousand Leagues
Under the Sea**
JULES VERNE
*Scientific fact combines with
fantasy in this prophetic tale
of underwater adventure*
£4.99

WOMEN'S WRITING
IN EVERYMAN

Poems and Prose
CHRISTINA ROSSETTI
A collection of her writings, poetry and prose, published to mark the centenary of her death
£5.99

Women Philosophers
edited by Mary Warnock
The great subjects of philosophy handled by women spanning four centuries, including Simone de Beauvoir and Iris Murdoch
£6.99

Glenarvon
LADY CAROLINE LAMB
A novel which throws light on the greatest scandal of the early nineteenth century – the infatuation of Caroline Lamb with Lord Byron
£6.99

Women Romantic Poets
1780 – 1830: **An Anthology**
edited by Jennifer Breen
Hidden talent from the Romantic era rediscovered
£5.99

Memoirs of the Life of Colonel Hutchinson
LUCY HUTCHINSON
One of the earliest pieces of women's biographical writing, of great historic and feminist interest
£6.99

The Secret Self 1: Short Stories by Women
edited by Hermione Lee
'A superb collection' The Guardian
£4.99

The Age of Innocence
EDITH WHARTON
A tale of the conflict between love and tradition by one of America's finest women novelists
£4.99

Frankenstein
MARY SHELLEY
A masterpiece of Gothic terror in its original 1818 version
£3.99

The Life of Charlotte Brontë
ELIZABETH GASKELL
A moving and perceptive tribute by one writer to another
£4.99

Victorian Women Poets
1830 – 1900
edited by Jennifer Breen
A superb anthology of the era's finest female poets
£5.99

Female Playwrights of the Restoration: Five Comedies
edited by Paddy Lyons
Rediscovered literary treasure in a unique selection
£5.99

All books are available from your local bookshop or direct from:
Littlehampton Book Services Cash Sales, 14 Eldon Way, Lineside Estate,
Littlehampton, West Sussex BN17 7HE (*prices are subject to change*)

To order any of the books, please enclose a cheque (in sterling) made payable to
Littlehampton Book Services, or phone your order through with credit card details (Access,
Visa or Mastercard) on 01903 721596 (24 hour answering service) stating card number
and expiry date. (*Please add £1.25 for package and postage to the total of your order.*)

In the USA, for further information and a complete catalogue call 1-800-526-2778

The Oresteia
AESCHYLUS
New translation of one of the greatest Greek dramatic trilogies which analyses the plays in performance
£5.99

Everyman and Medieval Miracle Plays
edited by A. C. Cawley
A selection of the most popular medieval plays
£4.99

Complete Plays and Poems
CHRISTOPHER MARLOWE
The complete works of this great Elizabethan in one volume
£5.99

Restoration Plays
edited by Robert Lawrence
Five comedies and two tragedies representing the best of the Restoration stage
£7.99

Female Playwrights of the Restoration: Five Comedies
edited by Paddy Lyons
Rediscovered literary treasures in a unique selection
£5.99

Plays, Prose Writings and Poems
OSCAR WILDE
The full force of Wilde's wit in one volume
£4.99

A Dolls House/The Lady from the Sea/The Wild Duck
HENRIK IBSEN
introduced by Fay Weldon
A popular selection of Ibsen's major plays
£4.99

The Beggar's Opera and Other Eighteenth-Century Plays
JOHN GAY et. al.
Including Goldsmith's She Stoops To Conquer *and Sheridan's* The School for Scandal, *this is a volume which reflects the full scope of the period's theatre*
£6.99

Female Playwrights of the Nineteenth Century
edited by Adrienne Scullion
The full range of female nineteenth-century dramatic development
£6.99

All books are available from your local bookshop or direct from:
Littlehampton Book Services Cash Sales, 14 Eldon Way, Lineside Estate,
Littlehampton, West Sussex BN17 7HE (*prices are subject to change*)

To order any of the books, please enclose a cheque (in sterling) made payable to
Littlehampton Book Services, or phone your order through with credit card details (Access,
Visa or Mastercard) on 01903 721596 (24 hour answering service) stating card number
and expiry date. (*Please add £1.25 for package and postage to the total of your order.*)

In the USA, for further information and a complete catalogue call 1-800-526-2778